THE JOHN HARVARD LIBRARY

Howard Mumford Jones
Editor-in-Chief

THE STORY OF
A COUNTRY TOWN

By

E. W. HOWE

Edited by Claude M. Simpson

THE BELKNAP PRESS OF
HARVARD UNIVERSITY PRESS
Cambridge, Massachusetts
1 9 6 1

Distributed in Great Britain by Oxford University Press, London

Library of Congress Catalog Card Number 61–13736

Printed in the United States of America

CONTENTS

THE STORY OF
A COUNTRY TOWN

CONTENTS

INTRODUCTION

For more than three-quarters of a century *The Story of a Country Town* has stood as a symbol of the anti-idealistic treatment of the village in American fiction. In the heyday of the local-color impulse, when the attention of hundreds of sketches and stories was focused on picturesque or quaint character types and folkways, Howe's novel was a signal that an anti-romantic counter-movement was possible. Only within our own century did the "revolt from the village" assume significant proportions, thanks to such documents as Masters' *Spoon River Anthology* (1915), Anderson's *Winesburg, Ohio* (1919), and Sinclair Lewis' *Main Street* (1920). But *The Story of a Country Town*, even though its cemetery was pre-Freudian, had its share of grotesques, and the village virus was at work on the mind and spirit of Twin Mounds and Gopher Prairie alike. In these respects Howe's novel of 1883 looks forward rather than backward, and though it clearly takes its place in a developing literary tradition, it is not, so far as I am aware, indebted to any American fictional models for its strategies, its tone, or even its style. The book is heavy with bitterness, but it is somehow the bitterness of a young man whose flesh burns where he touches it, though he hasn't set out to prove that the world is being consumed by fire. Howe's few theories of human nature are pragmatic and personal, but despite their strong recurrence in Howe's four novels they do not seem systematic or even susceptible to much further generalization. We may argue that Howe was not a thoroughgoing cynic or misanthrope, and I believe there is evidence that he could on occasion take a compassionate view of humanity. But he lacks the mystique of Anderson, the softness of Lewis; his subjectivity is individual without being very private, and his sense of man's fate has not been tamed by the notion of ineffectual rebellion.

INTRODUCTION

I

Howe has several times told the story of the writing of *The Story of a Country Town*, his one notable piece of fiction. The preface to the original Atchison edition of 1883 was the principal public statement until 1927, when Howe supplied a fresh foreword to a revised version of the novel issued by Dodd, Mead & Co. Chapter xxiii of his autobiography, *Plain People* (1929), repeats this latter account with a few additions. Two contemporary newspaper interviews and three hitherto unpublished letters to Mark Twain fill in details which Howe later forgot or did not remember accurately.

Howe was editor of the Atchison, Kansas, *Globe*, and as his original preface records, he wrote *The Story of a Country Town* at night in the kitchen of his home. The book was copyrighted in 1882 but was not issued until September of the following year. When a number of Eastern publishers declined the manuscript [1] he determined to issue it himself, and buying a font of minion type for the purpose ("No real book is printed in minion," he afterward wrote, "it is too small"), had it printed off in his newspaper shop, "four pages at a time, on a medium Gordon job press." [2] The edition was 1,500 copies, most of which were sold within six months, largely in the West. [3]

Although Howe had none of the book publisher's usual resources for advertising and distributing his novel, he did send copies to newspaper editors over the country, and when favorable notices began to appear, he struck off handbills to publicize

[1] These included Harper and the Boston firms of Roberts Brothers and J. R. Osgood & Co. (interview with Howe in the New York *Tribune*, Aug. 16, 1885, reprinted in *Critic*, VII [Aug. 22, 1885], 93–94); perhaps Funk & Wagnalls and Holt should be added to this list, for in his 1927 foreword, p. vi, Howe said he had been told that readers for both publishers had been discharged for returning the manuscript "without sending it higher up for further consideration."

[2] *Plain People*, p. 210.

[3] The size of the edition is vouched for in several contemporary sources, including *Critic*, V (Oct. 11, 1884), 174; the New York *Tribune* for Aug. 16, 1885, quoting Howe; and the San Antonio *Express* (an undated clipping, perhaps for Feb. 12, 1887, "Something About E. W. Howe," by "A Friend of the Author"). Howe's figures of 2,000 in 1927 (foreword, p. v) and 1,000 in 1929 (*Plain People*, p. 210) seem less reliable.

the book. One such, which shows that Brentano's was distributing the book in New York, reprints excerpts from the New York *Herald*, the Hiawatha *World*, the Topeka *Capital*, and the St. Joseph *Gazette*, together with more personal testimonials from an actor, a Methodist clergyman, and a U. S. senator.

The most important assistance came from Mark Twain and W. D. Howells, both of whom gave him as respectful a reading as he could wish. He sent Twain a copy of the book on February 2, 1884, hoping, he said, "that you will good naturedly conclude to read it, as it is a 'Missouri' story, and refers to a section with which you are familiar." [4] Although Howe supposed it would be "asking too much" to expect an opinion, Twain replied on February 13 with a long letter of appreciation and advice, the first part written for the public eye, the last pages marked private. Howe lost no time in printing extracts in the *Globe* — from both parts of the letter — and Twain's endorsement played a significant part in the further promotion of the book. [5]

"I like your book so much that I am glad of the chance to say so," wrote Twain. "Your style is so simple, sincere, direct, and at the same time so clear and so strong, that I think it must have been born to you, not made. Your pictures of that arid village life, and the insides and outsides of its people, are vivid, and what is more, true; I know, for I have seen it all, lived it all." Twain went on to point out that Howe had written a history, not a tale, and that he might have "knocked out an obstruction here and there, and then your history would have become a story, flowing with gathering speed and uninterrupted current." As one might expect, Twain disliked Biggs but was much struck

[4] This and other letters from Howe are among the Mark Twain papers in the library of the University of California, Berkeley, and are quoted with the kind permission of Mr. James P. Howe.

[5] A copy of the article, clipped from the *Globe* of Feb. 19, 1884, p. 2, is pasted into the front of the Stanford University Library copy of the first edition. The public portion of the letter appeared in the Topeka *State Journal*, Feb. 26, 1900; an excerpt was in the Kansas City *Star Magazine*, March 1, 1925. A scholarly transcript of the whole letter was published by C. E. Schorer in *American Literature*, XXVII (March 1955), 109–112. As recently as August 9, 1960, the document found its way into the *Globe* again, with a photograph of the first page and a reproduction of the complete text. In the parts of the letter presently quoted, Twain's conventional *&* has been silently expanded.

with Big Adam. He judged from Adam's minor role that Howe was unaware what a "mighty figure" he had contributed "to the procession of originals that is marching out of the ark of American literature to possess the land." George W. Cable, on hearing Twain read Big Adam scenes, "forgot himself and shouted, 'Superb, superb — he is colossal!'" This part of Twain's letter concluded: "You write as a man *talks*; and very few can reach that height of excellence. I think a man who possesses that gift is quite sure to write a readable book — and you have done that."

The private section of the letter offered shrewd criticism of matters large and small. Twain didn't like the apologetic tone of the preface and thought it should be scrapped. "Next time, I wish you'd leave out Biggs, or anybody else whose diversions interrupt the story. *Nothing* should ever be allowed to break the speed of a story." He sympathized with Mateel, "but from the beginning to the end I was pretty generally down on Joe [*sic*]; and when Mateel made her appeal to him — oh, but damnation I cut him dead, there and then, and we have never spoken since. Usually I don't care a rap what becomes of the people in a story, but I was interested in these folks." He thought the novel could be turned into a play with Big Adam the central figure.[6]

"Everybody has some small grammatical infelicity or other — yours is the continuous and accurate misplacing of your wills and shalls. But you won't do it any more." On one other technical point he offered a suggestion: "You have allowed the tears to plash on the floor once in the preface and thrice in the book. The figure is very striking — and jokes and striking figures should not be repeated. You might retort that Adam's corks should not be repeated, then; but not so — no time to explain why, but you know why. I'd rather hear Adam draw an imaginary cork than another man a real one — even at my thirstiest."

Howe's answer of February 17 is interesting for its sincere,

---

[6] In 1911 Howe wrote a dramatic version of the story. Printed copies of the play failed to interest theatrical managers in New York, but, as he noted in *Plain People*, p. 213, a stock company gave it nine performances which "brought in more money than any other play in the history of the company." Even though it was written "hurriedly and wretchedly," Howe felt that the play had "several big scenes."

straightforward response to Twain's criticism, and parts of the letter which throw light on Howe's intention are worth quoting:

I was so much impressed by the receipt of your letter that I cannot resist the temptation to address you again.

There is no doubt that the tears plashed too often, but I intended to use the figure twice; to illustrate the sullen grief of two persons, brother and sister: "Jo Erring" and "Mrs. Westlock." Perhaps this was wrong, but the other two were the result of haste.

I intended that "Jo Erring" should be an odd man, but I tried very hard in the last pages to make the people admire him, in spite of all his faults, but I failed in this, for they are all of your opinion. I do not think he is an impossible character, for I have known several men who were just like him. A well known citizen of this town came to me once, and said he was "Jo Erring" in everything except that he was too cowardly to choke his particular "Clinton Bragg."

The preface represented my exact condition of mind when it was written, though I despise it now, as I despise the entire book.

I wrote every line of it at night, after working all day as editor, proprietor and business manager of a small evening paper. (Job printing, by the way, neatly executed, which I was also compelled to find.) It bothered me so much, by interfering with my sleep, that I finally rushed it through, and published it myself, in order to be rid of it. Had I lain [sic] it aside for six months, after finishing it, and gone at it again when I was not too tired and indifferent to remark its faults, it would have been a much better book; there would have been less of "Jo" and more of "Adam" in it.

In spite of the great oaths I registered in high heaven never to attempt to write another story under such unfavorable circumstances, I am at it again, under exactly similar circumstances, but I intend to be more careful of this one.[7] I am not neglecting my business, however, which is (you will be surprised to learn, as I believe you were once familiar with the slow, measured tread of a newspaper financially) a success. During six years I have saved out of the business $15,000, which is not in "good will," but property which brings me an income. This is a very insignificant sum to you, but there is not another evening newspaper on the Missouri river with an equally good record. I write this as an apology for the defects of the book which you were kind enough to read rather than with the expectation that it will interest you.

With reference to the grammatical defects, I can only say that a school teacher is responsible for them. I employed one to revise it for

[7] *The Mystery of the Locks,* published in 1885.

grammar, and you have seen the result. My only knowledge of that important science (is it a science?) was picked out of a long primer case in my early youth. My education, like that of many another Missouri boy, was neglected.

But I hope to improve. I am only 29 now,[8] and if I ever get time I hope to write an acceptable story; I doubt if I can do it situated as I am at present, for my time is occupied in writing paid advertisements, personal mentions of unimportant people, and records of unimportant events.

I have sold about 1,100 copies [9] of "The Story"; most of them in the West, and without advertising or attention. The people of Atchison seem to be proud of it, and have taken 500 copies. You will say this is very kind of them. . . .

Howe declared that he had "read and admired every line" Twain had ever written, and the concluding paragraphs of the letter praised the humorist in characteristically generous but self-deprecatory language.

He evidently followed up this letter with a request for addresses of other influential literary men to whom he might offer his book, for on March 28 Twain sent him information concerning Howells, Aldrich, Cable, Joel C. Harris, Edmund Stedman, John Hay, and some lesser lights.[10] A gratifying response was not long in coming from Howells, who wrote him on April 16:

I wish to thank you for the copy of your Story of a Country Town which you sent me, and for the very great pleasure I have had in reading it. Consciously or unconsciously it is a very remarkable piece of realism, and, whether it makes you known now or not, it constitutes your part of the only literary movement of our time that seems to have vitality in it. I have never lived so far west as Kansas, but I have lived in your Country Town, and I know it is every word true, down to the perpetual Scriptural disputes of the inhabitants. Fairview and its people are also actualities, which even if I had never seen them — and I have — your book would persuade me of. The people in the story are excellent, all natural and sentient, except the last half of your Jo, who slops into sentimentality and driveling wickedness wholly unworthy. Biggs is delightful, and all his household. John Westlock is

[8] Howe was born in May 1853, and so was actually thirty; it was an honest mistake, however, for until many years later he thought he had been born in 1854. See *Plain People*, p. 209.

[9] Through a slip of the pen Howe actually wrote "1,100 hundred copies."

[10] Letter in possession of James P. Howe.

a grim and most pathetic tragedy; his wife moves me less, but she is alive, too. — I have no time to specify, and I don't know how to tell you of the impression of simple, naked humanness that the book gives me. It has many faults, as any fool can show you, but be sure that you have written so good a book that it will be hard for you to write a better. I am afraid that you will never write another so sincere and frank. I wish I could see you; but upon your honest piece of work, I give you my hand with my heart in it.

A postscript inquired whether he had read Zola or Turgenev.[11]

Howells also wrote a long notice of the novel, which appeared in the August 1884 *Century*,[12] and which helped to launch the book before a national audience. Beyond sketching the outlines of the story, Howells amplified his critical praise of the novel, but, as in his letter, not without a care for discriminations. Thus he said that "the great figure of the book" was the Rev. John Westlock, "and not Jo Erring, of whom the author is fond, and who finally comes near spoiling the strong, hard-headed, clear-conscienced story." It was a blemish for the narrator not to recognize "that Jo is really a culpable homicide; but on the artistic side . . . there is no fault. The art is feeblest in the direction of Agnes, who is probably true to life, but seems rather more than the rest to have come out of books. Her termagant mother, on the other hand — of whom we have scarcely more than a glimpse as she cuffs her way through a roomful of children — and her uncle, the delicious cynic Lytle Biggs, with his frank philosophy and swindling life, are unmistakably out of the soil." Although he believed that Howe had said well what he had to say, Howells added, "I do not care to praise his style, though, as far as that increasingly unimportant matter goes, it is well enough." The book, as he had earlier written Howe,

. . . has defects enough, which no one can read far without dis-

[11] This letter is transcribed from the original in the possession of Mr. James P. Howe and is published by permission of Mr. William W. Howells. Slightly variant texts have been reproduced in the Topeka *State Journal*, Feb. 26, 1900; the Kansas City *Star Magazine*, March 1, 1925; and *American Literature*, XXIX (Jan. 1958), 473–474.

[12] XXVIII, 632–633. Partially reprinted in Harper's 1917 edition of *The Story of a Country Town*, along with brief extracts from Howells' letter and Twain's missive of Feb. 13.

covering; but, except in the case of Jo Erring, they are not important — certainly not such as to spoil any one's pleasure in a fiction which is of the kind most characteristic of our time, and which no student of our time hereafter can safely ignore. . . . It does not flatter the West, nor paint its rough and rude traits as heroic; it perceives and states, and the results are perfectly imaginable American conditions, in which no trait of beauty or pathos is lost. . . . amidst the prevailing harshness and aridity there are episodes of tenderness and self-devotion that are like springs of water out of the ground.

On May 14, 1884, Howe wrote Twain again, obviously pleased to be able to tell him that Howells had liked Lytle Biggs (whom Twain had considered an impediment in the story).[13] The important news, however, was that he was about to sign a contract with Funk & Wagnalls for an illustrated edition of *The Story of a Country Town*; his only reservation seemed to be that the royalty offered was a "ruinously low" ten per cent. The letter did not indicate that any other publisher was bidding for the novel, but in the *Tribune* interview of 1885 Howe recalled that he also had propositions from J. R. Osgood & Co., Scribner, and one or two others, and that he "greedily closed" with the Osgood firm since it was "first in the field." This last detail was not strictly true, but Osgood does seem to have been the first to offer a fifteen per cent royalty contract.[14] The Boston firm gave the novel its first regular publication in September 1884 in an edition of 2,500 copies. A few weeks later Howe reported to Twain that he thought the "shalls" and "wills" were "generally all right in the Osgood edition; I paid a school teacher ten dollars to straighten them." And, acting on Twain's suggestion, he had himself elim-

[13] Howe eventually came to accept Twain's view, for in the 1927 revision Biggs' role is much reduced and Big Adam's is somewhat expanded.

[14] In a letter to Howells dated May 7, 1884 (Howells Papers, Houghton Library, Harvard; quoted in Philip H. Ropp, "Edgar Watson Howe," unpublished dissertation, University of Virginia, 1949, pp. 115–117), Howe said that he had refused a New York publisher who proposed to pay him ten per cent of receipts. If Howe's phraseology is precise, it means that royalties would have been based on the wholesale price. Since he summarily dismissed this proposal, and a week later was about to close with a Funk & Wagnalls ten per cent offer, the latter must have been on the more usual retail basis. On July 28, 1884, Howe wrote Howells (Ropp, pp. 117, 149) that after he had accepted Osgood's fifteen per cent, Scribner made an identical offer.

inated three of the four passages in which tears plashed to the floor.[15]

Aided by Howells' strong notice and a generally good reception in newspaper and magazine reviews, the novel began to make its way. By February 1885, three additional printings of a thousand copies each had been called for, and after Osgood's failure that spring, the book bore the Ticknor & Co. imprint until 1889, when Houghton, Mifflin & Co. acquired it along with almost all the Ticknor list.[16] Demand for the novel continued modest but persistent, and if we can believe a news story on Howe in the Topeka *State Journal*, it had by 1900 gone through forty printings.[17] In 1917 Harper published an edition with "An Appreciation" carved out of Howells' *Century* article of August 1884, and in 1926 Albert and Charles Boni issued an edition with a preface by Carl Van Doren; both houses used the original Osgood plates. Then it was that Howe, now almost seventy-five, re-examined the novel; he did not attempt any stylistic alteration, nor did he shift the plot in any way, but he removed about twenty thousand words in cuts large and small.[18] The new edition was published in 1927 by Dodd, Mead with illustrations by Wilfred Jones and a new historical foreword by Howe replacing the 1883 preface. Beside the regular trade edition there was a cheaper

[15] Letter of Oct. 26, 1884. Although he cited approvingly Twain's dictum that "jokes and striking figures should not be repeated," he declared his intention "to point out where you not only repeated a joke, but illustrated it a second time."

[16] One small printing of 280 copies came off the press in Jan. 1888. Meantime, the book became No. 14 of Ticknor's Paper Series, with a first printing of 3030 copies in June 1887, and a second of 1000 the following March. Howe's royalty on the 50¢ volume was 5¢. All production and royalty details are taken from the Osgood and Ticknor cost books, now deposited in Houghton Library, Harvard University.

[17] Undated clipping assignable to Feb. 1900, in possession of Mr. James P. Howe. In 1927 Howe said that over a hundred printings had been made from the Osgood plates, but according to his niece, Miss Adelaide Howe, he kept no records to substantiate this figure. More believable is the estimate of "over fifty" printings of all editions, cited in the *New York Times* obituary article on Howe, Oct. 4, 1937.

[18] Among the major cuts were the whole of chap. xxx, the temperance sermon in chap. xvii, and the reduction of Biggs' harangues in chaps. viii, xviii, xxi, and xxiii. Also omitted was the one remaining reference to plashes of tears, chap. x. The few additions were designed to enlarge Big Adam's role; in addition to more cork pulling, Adam becomes involved with Bragg by provoking a fight which leads to Bragg's arrest.

reprint issued by Blue Ribbon Books which kept the new text available for a decade or more. The revised edition has profited from blue-penciling, but the nineteenth-century text is historically of greater importance and represents Howe's immediate vision more transparently. To it we must return — *longueurs* and all — if we are to see the book as Howe conceived it and understand the original patterns of emphasis, "artless, unenhanced."

II

As Howe told Twain, *The Story of a Country Town* is a Missouri tale. The elder Howe brought his family west from Indiana in 1856, and settling in southeast Harrison County, Missouri, established Fairview church and took up farmland nearby. The geography of the novel reflected Howe's early years in the Fairview community, and the country town of Twin Mounds was modeled upon Bethany, where the family lived after Henry Howe returned from the Union army in 1863 and bought the county-seat newspaper. Young Ed worked hard on the farm, stood in eternal fear of his father, and from the age of ten got most of his education at the printer's case. The picture of Ned Westlock up to his early teens is thus highly autobiographical, at least in tone and spirit. A number of other details in the novel are drawn from life. Howe's frail, uncomplaining mother was the pattern for Mrs. Westlock, and her parents — he a shingler, she a backwoods "doctor" — were transcribed pretty literally (unless there be no warrant for their frigid behavior toward each other, chap. iii). Light-fingered Hardy Winter and his brother, E. R. Martin the wise printer, and the numerous good-humored Meeks were all actual people. The temperament of the Rev. John Westlock was closely modeled on that of his father, as some of the most chilling pages in Howe's autobiography make clear. And although there may have been no basis in fact for Westlock's melodramatic return to Twin Mounds after his wife's death, the minister's involvement with Mrs. Tremaine is somewhat paralleled by the scandal concerning the companionship of Henry Howe and his wife's widowed sister-in-law on the local evangelistic circuit. Ed Howe's uncle Nate, eight months his senior, and another uncle named Joe Irwin, seven or eight years older, were telescoped into the figure of Jo Erring; but the emotional traumas surrounding Erring's early manhood were drawn from Howe's own life, even to the one-and-only-love obsession which destroyed the possibility of a compatible marriage.[19]

When Mark Twain called *The Story of a Country Town* a history rather than a tale, he could not have known the extent to which the characters were transcriptions from life. What he noticed was that the novel was heavily dependent on non-fictional techniques. A major proportion of the book is chronicle, as distinguished from realized dramatic encounter; and beyond that, Howe devotes a number of chapters to generalized accounts of home, school, church, business life, personal morality, and so on. As plotted narrative the book scarcely comes alive until Jo Erring discovers that Clinton Bragg is his nemesis, yet the resolution of the triangle motif is perhaps the weakest and least original element in the novel. Much of the power here — the pathos, the drabness, the sense of paradox in a youth's view of the adult world — comes from the artlessness with which Ned Westlock records his observations and feelings. Through him we get both an outer and an inner story: it is his picture of Fairview and Twin Mounds, a straightforward reporting of the narrow doctrinal arguments, the spiteful rumor-mongering, the calamity-howling, mixed with his mildly sardonic moderating interpretation. Thus the townsmen are agitated by fear of disasters or prospects of boom which never come; and whisperings of libertinism, far from suggesting a seething hidden life, are debunked

[19] Ruth E. Brune ("The Early Life of Edgar Watson Howe," unpublished dissertation, University of Colorado, 1949, p. 228) quotes Howe's daughter, Mateel Howe Farnham, as saying that her mother, when newly married, confessed to a romance with a fellow student at the age of sixteen; though nothing beyond a few kisses on the cheek were involved, the knowledge of his wife's adolescent familiarities seemed to sully the marital relationship in Howe's eyes. Miss Brune shows convincingly that the tone of aphoristic paragraphs on women, love, and marriage underwent a sharp change in the Golden *Globe* upon Howe's return from his honeymoon.

Other correspondences between fact and fiction are drawn principally from *Plain People* and from the interview with Howe printed in the New York *Tribune*, Aug. 16, 1885.

as nothing more than exciting pretense — "I believe there never was a more virtuous community." But his judgment is ultimately unsparing, for he finds the people puffed up with self-importance, dedicated to small hatreds, and committed to mediocrity as an ideal. A general verdict, this, rendered with dry detachment and in the spirit of the Theophrastan character; it does not, however, seem to be in key with any action that we see. Indeed, there is very little sense of community except when groups gather at prayer meeting or revival or funeral, and at no time do they exhibit the character assigned to them. We have here a failure of technique, but there can be no doubt that the indictment was seriously intended. And though Howe may feel that the prairie dwellers are happier than they were back East, he undercuts the notion that the West can be thought of as the garden of the world. The meanness of the pioneer folk he directly attributes to a puritanical religious atmosphere they brought with them, just as he would explain the cheerless stolidity of farm families by pointing to the never-ending work that agriculture demanded. The dilapidation of Lytle Biggs' acres is probably not intended to explain rural economics, but it is clear that Big Adam alone cannot manage the farm, and Biggs' fantasies about his own rural industriousness seem as cynical as his view of others' affairs. Only the Meek family seem to stand in the sunshine of good-humored contentment.

Despite the autobiographical cast, the novel does not reveal a great deal about the narrator except during his pre-adolescent years. Even here, what Melville called the "inside" narrative is limited, for we glimpse the surfaces of his feeling but seldom his inmost thought. In Ned's boyhood the dominant figure of his father casts a pall of fear over his life, and whether it be the disapproving eye or a physical beating, his father's censure is that of an Old Testament God. Only on one occasion does the Rev. John Westlock soften, but after carrying his ill son home in his arms he cannot bring himself to compliment Ned on his overly conscientious work thereafter. Indelible in Ned's memory of these early years is his father's statement that the boy was "a positive burden and expense" until he was seven years old. Fleetingly we glimpse the companionship he enjoys with Jo

Erring, as they roam the woods on the precious Saturday afternoons or listen to Barker's strange tales of a distant world. In the spirit of a show-off Ned can regale the Shepherd family with the lore of turkey roosts and the story of killing a deer. And we are told that when called on to perform, he and Jo give an amusing imitation of camp-meeting songs and shouts. Ned's life, then, is not totally bleak, though like David Copperfield's it is filled with the terrors of loneliness and insecurity which outweigh the moments of delight.[20]

Once Ned has assumed charge of his father's newspaper, he ceases to be a primary object of interest, becoming a passive spectator of the dissolution of his direct family ties, and then a silent witness to the Jo-Mateel misfortunes dominating the second half of the book. Ned is now, in fact, a receptor, little more than a *voyeur*; here, perhaps, lies one explanation for his helpless silences, his inability to meet Jo's anguished monologues with either sympathy or healthy counter-argument. Another explanation may take us closer to the psychic center of Howe's concern: he himself is not prepared to see any point of view save that which Jo expresses. For the autobiographic drive has transferred itself from the boyhood of Ned to the young manhood of Jo, and the whole record of Jo's courtship and marriage can be read as an apologia for views which had already begun to obsess Howe, and which he continued to expound for the rest of his life. All four of his novels portray distasteful marriages from which the husband seeks an escape, and his "paragraphs" in the *Globe* and the *Monthly* are full of references to the war between men and women, almost all emphasizing that it is the man who gets the poorer bargain.

More specifically, the theme of man's right to all a woman's

[20] Since Dickens was the one novelist Howe said he had read thoroughly, it is not amiss to note that his influence was probably the strongest literary overlay upon Howe's firsthand experiences. Dickens had offered an atmospheric cue in the Murdstones; he did more in suggesting a way to give fictional shape to autobiographical record, for one can read most of Ned's history in chapter titles from *Copperfield*: "I am born," "I observe," "I have a change," "I fall into disgrace," "I begin life on my own account, and don't like it," "I am involved in mystery," "I assist at an explosion," "Agnes," and "A last retrospect." Not the least remarkable is the presence in both books of a sweet and patient Agnes who is united to the narrator only after a long platonic relationship.

love, in defense of which he cites George Eliot's dictum that the happiest women are those without a history,[21] overflows from the pages of *The Story of a Country Town* to his later paragraphing, and is the central concern of *An Ante-Mortem Statement* (1891). This semi-fictional document has as its slight plot gambit the plight of a man who on the day of a second marriage realizes his mistake and, after writing out his unhappy history, takes poison; central is the fact that his first marriage had curdled when he learned that his wife had been engaged to other men before she met him. "Every man whose wife has been in love before, hears an old story rehearsed, and knows it" (p. 46). So goes the agonized plaint, developed at such length that the book becomes a tract. Decades later Howe was still voicing the idea in the pages of the *Monthly*: "Every man is jealous of the man to whom his wife was engaged before he met her"; "A man hates to admit that anything he has is second-hand. And he probably dislikes a second-hand love a little more than anything else"; "Nothing will ever convince me that husbands do not hate old love affairs in the history of their wives." [22]

Some discontinuity between the adolescent and the adult Jo is probably inevitable. This industrious and over-ambitious youth is said to have inherited the worst qualities of both parents, including his mother's tendency toward exaggeration and his father's halting manner of speech. Howe seems to have forgotten some of these personality traits once the courtship scenes bring Jo to the center of the stage, for Jo becomes an incessant monologuist, and his tendency to exaggerate hardly prepares us for a jealousy swollen to monomania. From the conciliatory young moderator of neighborhood quarrels he becomes a blind and unreasonable antagonist, but Howe makes no effort to suggest that

[21] E. W. Howe, "Provincial Peculiarities of Western Life," *Forum*, XIV (Sept. 1892), 102.

[22] *E. W. Howe's Monthly*, II (Oct. 1912), 55; II (March 1912), 44; XII (July 1924), 4. Brune, pp. 412–413, cites these and other examples of Howe's continued preoccupation with the first-love theme. Scarcely distinguishable from them are the aphorisms in Jo's long speech in chap. xii of *The Story of a Country Town*. Further confirmations of Howe's views are found in Gene A. Howe's very personal article, "My Father Was the Most Wretchedly Unhappy Man I Ever Knew," *Saturday Evening Post*, CCXIV (Oct. 25, 1941), 45.

psychological transformations have assignable causes. As the ordinary business of life ceases to have meaning for Jo, he loses much of his humanity and becomes little more than the embodiment of an idea. Unhappily for Howe, the idea Jo embodies it not righteous indignation but overweening romantic egotism. The critics' failure to share Howe's sympathy for Jo is easy to understand, but it was not easy for Howe to accept. "Perhaps," he wrote in the 1927 foreword, "if I had it to do over, . . . I should greatly modify his life." But even at that late date the need of self-justification was apparent as he continued: "His sin is very common, and the subject an uncomfortable one to nearly every man and woman." His judgment in *Plain People* is in the same vein:

> I thought the first eleven chapters almost as good as many kind critics have said, and found pride in them, but while reading had an uneasy consciousness of trouble later on. I found it when "Jo Erring's" love affair began, but could not do much to improve it without recasting the entire book. Poor "Jo's" unreasonable jealousy does not belong in a novel from which the author hopes for permanent fame. It is natural enough, but few men, and no women, will admit it.

There follows a page-long discussion of jealousy, after which he pronounces a final reluctant acquiescence: ". . . as a literary critic, I am compelled in old age to desert poor 'Jo Erring,' as others who know about him have done. There is more of the author in 'Jo Erring' than in any other portion of 'The Story of a Country Town,' and 'Jo' did much to weaken it." [23]

In our final impression of the Rev. John Westlock we may agree with a reviewer who observed that the treatment of his "frailties and foibles" makes us more sympathetic with his weaknesses than we would be from our own personal observation of the man.[24] The towering silences, cruel as they may have been

[23] *Plain People*, pp. 216–217. With the last quoted sentence compare Howe's statement in a letter of July 7, 1889, to Hamlin Garland, quoted in Lars Åhnebrink, *The Beginnings of Naturalism in American Fiction* (1950), p. 54n: "I am the original of all the characters in the three books — at least I sometimes fear that I am. All that they say sounds like a confession to me, and I wonder that my friends do not know it. (This in confidence.)"

[24] *Critic*, V (Oct. 4, 1884), 158–159.

to his wife and children, were even more obviously signs of his inner torment, and Howe's underplayed matter-of-factness makes Westlock a powerful man more driven than driving, more victim than tyrant. For it is clear that no amount of mastery over others can bring him happiness, nor can comfort come from such a religion as he preaches.

The villainy of Clinton Bragg seems somehow synthetic, despite Howe's careful attempts to show a genetic basis for his dissoluteness. His basic flaw is that he does not subscribe to the doctrine of hard work, having been indulged by well-meaning parents. Their sending him west "to grow up with the country or get killed" is ominous, and his potentialities as civil engineer are offset by his studied shiftlessness and insolence. Howe paints him as an alien; the decoration of his rooms emphasizes an exotic, unnatural taste; the nocturnal prowling, heavily underlined with the language of diabolism, prepares us for outrages against good order. But about all that can be said against his actual conduct is that he is a lurker, and that there is suspicion in his movements — good for suspense but not explainable as the mysterious outcroppings of a rich hidden life. If the shadowy figure of Bragg hovering in the background is sinister, it is so only as another example of the author's unconscious preoccupation with voyeurism.[25]

In accounting for community attitudes on the northwest Missouri frontier Howe pays more attention to the conditioning influence of sectarian doctrinal anxieties than to the regional and sectional economic disturbances after the Civil War. Indeed, almost the only topical economic references are to the Farmers' Alliance, for which Lytle Biggs is an organizer. This important agency, through which the agrarian interests of Midwest and South expressed their opposition to Eastern concentrations of money and power, was a fundamental part of the eco-

[25] Note also that Barker stands outside the Westlock house looking in at Agnes; Jo stands outside the Shepherd dwelling watching for Mateel after their separation; Ned speaks of watching women when they are unaware of being observed. The recurrence of the motif does not seem to illuminate fictional character, but it may tell us something about Howe's mind — or it may reflect only a literary novice's lack of resourcefulness.

nomic climate in the Midwest during the 1880's and 1890's, and it would have been instructive to observe a local group at close range. Instead, Howe gives us a casual glimpse of the farmers as Biggs sees them; the emphasis is on Biggs as casuist and hypocrite, the farmers being his dupes. The distance between himself and them is unquestionable, and never greater than when he described himself and his way of life to Ned, using agrarian metaphors. The Alliance, then, is simply an opportunity which Biggs can exploit, and it is inconsequential that according to a strict time scheme the organization is an anachronism in the novel.

Biggs is a study in contradictions, for as he talks of himself the evidence before our eyes often belies his words. On the other hand, a certain ambivalence surrounds his opinions on many subjects, for upon occasion Howe evidently wishes us to take Biggs seriously. His conversations embody occasional home truths, and the interpolated chapter xxx is nothing but a series of epigrammatic paragraphs that might have been scissored from the Atchison *Globe*. There is, of course, too much of him, and his monologues are considerably abbreviated in the 1927 edition of the novel. There Howe also dropped Biggs' self-styled "philosopher" label, although it was a useful ironic symbol of Biggs' fatuousness; perhaps it seemed too stale a jest to the septuagenarian Howe, who by this time was having to defend himself from being called the "sage of Potato Hill."

III

The Story of a Country Town is historically linked with Joseph Kirkland's *Zury, The Meanest Man in Spring County* (1887) and the early fiction of Hamlin Garland. Howe was first in the field, unless we consider him to have been anticipated by Edward Eggleston's *The Hoosier Schoolmaster* (1871) and Maurice Thompson's short story collection, *Hoosier Mosaics* (1875). The mood of both Indiana works is heartier and more benign than in Howe's novel, although some pages of Eggleston pointedly defy the conventions of sentimental fiction, and his rough and uncouth details of early settlement are the equal of anything produced before the end of the century. Nevertheless, Arcadian touches are present in both Eggleston and Thompson, attributable to an optimism which became less easy to sustain in the years following.

Zury opens with a powerfully realistic treatment of pioneering in eastern Illinois. Kirkland was consciously following Hardy in his concentration on the annals of the poor "in actual contact with the soil itself"; but the novel is oddly a success story, and the later stages of the chronicle lose their distinctiveness as the ruthless dynamism of Zury Prouder is softened beyond the bounds of plausibility. The economics of homesteading, the rigors of a Midwestern winter, the young Zury's insidious genius with mortgages, the prevalent superstitions concerning folk medicine and play acting — these elements of Kirkland's study show him to be a shrewd and honest observer. He is more unflinching than Eggleston and parallels the mood of Howe in his grim early chapters, occasionally relieved by a sense of humor which Howe almost completely lacks.

Garland discovered the work of both Howe and Kirkland during his apprentice years, when through reviews and lectures he was developing his ideas on indigenous literature and local color, conscious that his own Midwest was but sparsely represented in the almost ubiquitous movement. He was critical of the abnormal and grotesque in Howe's later novels, but praised Howe for writing of his settlers "in an earnest, sincere tone *as from among them.*" He reviewed *A Moonlight Boy* and *Zury* for the Boston *Transcript* and corresponded with both authors. It was with a full awareness of their work that Garland turned to fiction in the late 1880's.[26] Like theirs, his artistry was uneven, but he documented, often tellingly, the hard role of the pioneer woman which Howe had sketched, and he emphasized the monotonous rigors of farm life in almost all the stories of *Main-Travelled Roads* (1891). Where Howe's bitterness was directed against the hypocrisy and narrowness attributable to religious orthodoxy or private eccentricity, Garland was crusading against economic

[26] See Garland, *Roadside Meetings* (1930), pp. 94–96, 106–112, and Donald Pizer, *Hamlin Garland's Early Work and Career* (1960), pp. 12, 25–27.

and political forces which Western radicalism had identified with monopolistic control over land and money. In "Up the Coolly" we are made to see not only that farm life is grim, but that it is somehow unfair; "Under the Lion's Paw" goes further to indict the whole system of interest rates and landlord-tenant relationships. To Garland man's laws were more to blame than nature's uncertainties for the troubles he saw, and during his militant days political reform seemed the answer. Howe, on the other hand, distrusting systems, addressed himself to the individual, and in his lifelong editorializing never lost his zeal for the Franklinesque maxim that reduced problem and solution alike to suspiciously simple terms. Industry was ever the key to success; the enemies were shiftlessness, dissipation, self-pity.

Mark Twain's novella, "The Man That Corrupted Hadleyburg" (1899), exploiting ideas incorporated in *The Story of a Country Town*, showed how an attack on pretense and self-importance could be devastating when effectively dramatized. Without his undercurrent of sympathy for human weakness, Twain's scorn would have suggested the nihilism of Ambrose Bierce. Even so, Hadleyburg was Twin Mounds universalized, and both Twain and Howe were conscious that they were debunking a sentimentalized view of the small town. During the vogue of Carl Van Doren's "revolt from the village" in the 1920's the chief addition to the indictment, aside from the emphasis on sexual repression, was the attack on bourgeois ideals, especially as exhibited by the business community. It is ironical, as Wilbur L. Schramm observed in summing up Howe's career,[27] that the new generation, whose way had been prepared by Howe, could easily have been quoting his own maxims in derision as they lampooned the current cult of success:

In a country so rich most men succeed, and all may, I cannot regard prosperity as vulgar.

Men hustling to do better than competitors they hate have done more for the world than the great souls who dream of universal love.

[27] "Ed Howe Versus Time," *Saturday Review of Literature,* XVII (Feb. 5, 1938), 10–11.

The surest way to make money is to be industrious, polite, temperate, and honorable.[28]

In Howe's scheme of values, the first John D. Rockefeller was the "most useful" man who ever lived, and financial success was a reliable index of merit. Toward the end of his life, Howe was regarded more and more as a village crank, but it was the times that had changed, not he. Indeed, his ideas are implicit in *The Story of a Country Town*, where his harsh judgment of his fellows actually turns on the fact that they seldom "amount to anything," hence their smugness is a fit object of scorn. We recall, too, that the Rev. John Westlock's successful operation of the county-seat newspaper draws Howe's commendation, and many paragraphs detail Jo Erring's dedication to the cardinal commercial virtues of industry and thrift. Biggs is a politician and confidence man, laying bare the schemes by which unprincipled men may live off the gullible; as both monitor and parasite he plays a role which is understandably ambiguous.

It is not easy to say why Howe's novel has continued to have an impact on readers. Its success has come in spite of the manifest faults of structure and proportion, the imperfect dramatic sense, the inexpert reduplication of motifs, the inadequate motivation of major crises. What has saved *The Story of a Country Town* is its utterly unpretentious recital of events and feelings, its refusal to improve on reality or gloss over human imperfections. The result suggests the candid familiarity of an unretouched photograph. Howe was fortunate in being so little influenced by literary tradition, for we have seen that he is often weakest where he has followed models. Most of his shortcomings represent want of sophistication, but with each generation of readers the basic honesty of his recital has outweighed the importance of ingenuity or suavity. It was so with the original reviewers, who almost never failed to point out technical weaknesses, but usually testified to the truthfulness of Howe's picture, even to the just-

[28] Samplings of Howe's aphoristic paragraphs are gathered in his *Ventures in Common Sense* (1919) and in the concluding chapter of *Plain People*, pp. 304–317.

ness of its prevailingly somber tone. This kind of response suggests that the definite article in Howe's title was not misapplied: that he did succeed in giving archetypal significance to his vision of Fairview and Twin Mounds.

Other observers, however, perceived an essentially subjective rendering which made the story seem "less an actual fact or possibility than the dream of a morbid imagination"; the effect was "very real, and yet at the same time strangely unreal." [29] Mediating between these opposed views and partaking of both is the opinion that Howe's approach to truth is personal and his view of prairie life is therefore "dull, and dreary, and unendurable." This British estimate of the book goes on to conjecture that Jo's western Missouri environment was not crucially different from that of Tom and Huck at the other end of the state. "But where Mark Twain sees things in the sunshine, and with abundant humour, Mr. Howe sees things in the shade, and with abundant melancholy." [30] Even though this contrast is oversimplified, it is useful in its assumption that each man must read life with his own eyes, and that, in Stephen Crane's words, an author "is not at all responsible for his vision — he is merely responsible for his quality of personal honesty." In his *Century* review Howells had said that what he most admired in *The Story of a Country Town* was "the apparently unconscious fearlessness with which all the facts of the case, good, bad, and indifferent, are recognized." Perhaps these statements taken together help explain why Howe's novel has the power to move us today. He rendered his personal vision honestly, and later generations, like his own, have found touchstones of truth in the brooding sadness of tone, the sense of dogged perseverance, the destructiveness of a perfectionist obsession. Whatever else one may say of the pioneering experience, Howe would have us also recognize his more unflattering view if we are fully to understand what it has meant to "grow up with the country."

March 1961   Claude M. Simpson

[29] *Literary World*, XV (Oct. 18, 1884), 352–353.
[30] *Saturday Review* (London), LVIII (Aug. 30, 1884), 284.

CHRONOLOGY OF E. W. HOWE'S LIFE

1853	Born May 3 on a farm now the site of Treaty, Wabash County, Indiana.
1856	Henry Howe and family emigrated to northwest Missouri, establishing the community of Fairview a few miles from Bethany, Harrison County; the elder Howe a farmer, Methodist preacher, and militant abolitionist.
1863	Family moved to Bethany. Edgar Howe learned the printing trade working on *The Union of States*, a weekly his father owned, 1863–1865.
1867–1873	Worked as typesetter in Gallatin and St. Joseph, Missouri; held a number of jobs as journeyman printer in Council Bluffs, Omaha, Cheyenne, Salt Lake City, and Falls City, Nebraska.
1873–1875	Conducted the weekly *Globe* in Golden, Colorado; financially disastrous.
1873	Married Clara Frank (1847–1937) of Falls City; divorced, 1901.
1875–1877	Conducted *The Little Globe* and its successors, *The Globe-Journal* and a second *Little Globe*, in Falls City.
1877–1910	Conducted the Atchison, Kansas, *Globe* with great success.
1883	Published *The Story of a Country Town*.
1885	Published *The Mystery of the Locks*. Trip to Europe, the first of several journeys abroad, including two world cruises.
1886	Published *A Moonlight Boy*.
1888	Published *A Man Story*.
1911	Transferred control of the *Globe* to his son Eugene and other employees; retired to "Potato Hill," his farmstead outside Atchison.
1911–1933	Conducted *E. W. Howe's Monthly*, a journal of "indignation and information," filled with sententious, anti-romantic commentary on economic, moral, and social topics.
1919	Published *Ventures in Common Sense*, with an introduction by H. L. Mencken; chiefly extracts from the *Monthly*.
1920	Published *The Anthology of Another Town*.
1927	Published a revised edition of *The Story of a Country Town*. Sold "Potato Hill," returned to his Atchison home.
1929	Published *Plain People*, an autobiography.
1937	Died in Atchison on October 3, three months after suffering a paralytic stroke.

A NOTE ON THE TEXT

The 1883 Atchison edition of Howe's novel is basically sound with remarkably few misprints, but it contains inconsistencies in punctuation and other incidentals which an experienced editor would have normalized. The 1884 edition published by J. R. Osgood & Co. represents a copyedited state of the Atchison text, and is substantially what any first-rank Eastern publisher would have made of Howe's manuscript. Accordingly, the 1884 text has been chosen for reproduction in the John Harvard Library.

Normalization of punctuation for the 1884 text required numberless changes, most of which simply reflect greater sensitivity toward grammatical structure than did Howe's original pointing. Beyond this, the most pervasive changes shift the informal *will* and *would* (with first person pronouns) to the more strictly correct *shall* and *should*; Mark Twain had made Howe sensitive to the misuse of these auxiliaries, and between the Atchison teacher (who got $10 for her work) and the Osgood staff the corrections were thorough enough to satisfy the most fastidious.

Other changes impose the Osgood "house style" upon the text, tucking in prepositions, completing constructions (". . . they shouted . . . because he . . . wanted them to *do so*"), and adopting such spellings as *travelled, spoilt, wilful, offence, criticise, gayly,* and *practised.* Only occasionally has an editor's blue pencil attacked wordiness.

In my aim to present an 1884 text less misprints, I have normalized *someone, anyone, everyone,* and a few other forms which appeared indifferently as one word or two. For the sake of consistency I have omitted an occasional comma found before a dash. I have run together such typographical purisms as *he 's, should n't, did n't, I 'm, you 'll.* But I have tried to observe the prevailing conventions in hyphenation (*to-night, school-house, apple-tree, over-estimate*) by silently correcting a few inconsistencies. Significant verbal alterations of the 1883 text beyond those here described are indicated in footnotes in the text.

A NOTE ON THE TEXT

I am indebted to Baker Library of Dartmouth College, its associate librarian Edward Connery Lathem, and John S. Van E. Kohn for kind courtesies in supplying copies of the novel for collation.

BIBLIOGRAPHY

Åhnebrink, Lars, *The Beginnings of Naturalism in American Fiction* (Cambridge, Mass.: Harvard University Press, 1950), pp. 50–59.

Brune, Ruth E., "The Early Life of Edgar Watson Howe," unpublished doctoral dissertation, University of Colorado, 1949.

"Four American Novels," *Saturday Review* (London), LVIII (Aug. 30, 1884), 283–284.

Herron, Ima H., *The Small Town in American Literature* (Durham: Duke University Press, 1939).

Howe, Gene A., "My Father Was the Most Wretchedly Unhappy Man I Ever Knew," *Saturday Evening Post*, CCXIV (Oct. 25, 1941), 25, 44–46, 49.

Howells, W. D., "Two Notable Novels," *Century Magazine*, XXVIII (Aug. 1884), 632–634.

Kathrens, Joseph R., "The Story of a Story," Kansas City *Star Magazine*, Feb. 22, 1925, pp. 4, 18; March 1, 1925, pp. 8–9, 17.

[Obituary], *New York Times*, Oct. 4, 1937, p. 21.

Payne, William Morton, "Recent Works of Fiction," *Dial*, V (Dec. 1884), 203–207.

"Recent Novels," *Nation*, XXXIX (Nov. 27, 1884), 463–465.

Ropp, Philip H., "Edgar Watson Howe," unpublished doctoral dissertation, University of Virginia, 1949.

Schorer, C. E., "Growing Up with the Country," *Midwest Journal*, VI (Fall 1954), 12–26.

Schramm, Wilbur L., "Ed Howe Versus Time," *Saturday Review of Literature*, XVII (Feb. 5, 1938), 10–11.

Scudder, H. E., "Recent American Fiction," *Atlantic Monthly*, LV (Jan. 1885), 121–132.

Smith, Henry Nash, *Virgin Land: The American West as Symbol and Myth* (Cambridge, Mass.: Harvard University Press, 1950), chap. xxi.

"The Story of a Country Town," *Critic*, V (Oct. 4, 1884), 158–159.

"The Story of a Country Town," *Literary World*, XV (Oct. 18, 1884), 352–353.

Stronks, James B., "William Dean Howells, Ed Howe, and *The Story of a Country Town*," *American Literature*, XXIX (Jan. 1958), 473–478.

"A Successful Novelist," New York *Tribune*, Aug. 16, 1885, p. 9.

Van Doren, Carl, "Prudence Militant: E. W. Howe, Village Sage," *Century Magazine*, CVI (May 1923), 151–156.

"A Western Novelist," *Critic*, V (Oct. 11, 1884), 174.

THE STORY OF

A COUNTRY TOWN

By

E. W. HOWE

PREFACE

SHOULD "The Story of a Country Town" find readers, it may be interesting to them to know that it was written entirely at night, after the writer had finished a hard day's work as editor and publisher of a small evening newspaper. I do not think a line of it was written while the sun was shining, but in almost every chapter there are recollections of the midnight bell.

No one can possibly find more fault with it than I have found myself. A hundred times I have been on the point of burning the manuscript, and never attempting it again; for I was always tired while working at it, and always dissatisfied after concluding an evening's work. I offer this as a general apology for its many defects, and can only hope it will meet with the charity it deserves.

I believe that when I began the story I had some sort of an idea that I might be able to write an acceptable work of fiction, but I have changed it so often, and worried about it so much, that at its conclusion I have no idea whether it is very bad, or only indifferent. I think that originally I had some hope that it might enable me to get rid of my weary newspaper work, and help me to more ease than I have ever known, but I am so tired now that I am incapable of exercising my judgment with reference to it. If it prove a success or a failure I shall not be surprised, for I have no opinion of my own on the subject.

For several years I have felt that I would like an opportunity to address a larger audience than my newspaper's circulation affords, but I find now that I am very timid about it, and worry a great deal for fear the verdict will not be favorable. A gentleman who once looked over a portion of the manuscript said his first impression was that it was the work of a tired man, and that the pen seemed to drag heavily in making the words. I fear this will be the verdict of the people, and that they will say I should

3

have given up my newspaper writing before attempting it. The reason I did not do this was that I had no confidence in my ability to become an acceptable historian of a country town, therefore I worked harder than I should during the day, and went wearily at the story at night.

Should inquiry be made as to whether any part of the story be true, I could only reply that I have never known anyone [1] who did not furnish some suggestion or idea in the construction of the book, as I have never lived in a town that did not afford some material for the description of Twin Mounds. I meet Jo Errings every day, and frequently lead them up to denounce their particular Clinton Bragg; I have known several John Westlocks, and I am afraid that Mateel Shepherds are more numerous than is desirable. I have known troops of Mrs. John Westlocks, for in the country where I was brought up all the women were pale, timid, and overworked; I hope that Agnes Deming can be duplicated in every community, and I believe that Big Adams are numerous everywhere; but I must confess that I never knew but one Little Biggs, though his wife may be seen hurrying out of the way, should you decide to look for her, in every third or fourth house.

I hope there will be general sympathy for Jo Erring. In writing the history of this creature of my fancy, I have almost come to believe that I have an uncle of that name, and that he lived and died as I have narrated. Sometimes I think of him wandering in the cave, crying, "Help! Help! I am lost!" and his voice is very pitiful and distressed. At other times he has come into my room and sat beside me as I wrote.[2] I have been with him to the cave on a stormy night, and heard the beginning of the few sweet chords of music he describes, but which were immediately broken into by the furious uproar of devils; sometimes I think I have found him in every-day life, and that he is still listening at night to the horrible noise of his skeleton. If someone should confess to me that he is Jo Erring in every particular except that when

[1] anyone: 1883 a man or woman
[2] wrote: 1883 wrote, and I could hear his tears falling in little plashes on the floor.

4

the keeper of the Twin Mounds jail gave him opportunity he ran away, I believe I should be his friend.

In our part of the country there was a strange man answering to the description of Damon Barker, and I often visited him when a boy, but he lived in a hovel on the prairie, which was dirty beyond description. He had boxes filled with strange wearing-apparel, and brass pistols without number, and he told me stories; but he ran a nursery instead of a mill, though I have heard that he had a sister. I originally intended to make these two central figures in the story, but Jo Erring wandered into my mind, and I am afraid I have made sad work of him.

E. W. H.

ATCHISON, KANSAS, Sept. 4, 1883.

I

FAIRVIEW

Ours was the prairie district out West, where we had gone to grow up with the country.

I believe that nearly every farmer for miles around moved to the neighborhood at the same time, and that my father's wagons headed the procession. I have heard that most of them gathered about him on the way, and as he preached from his wagon wherever night overtook him, and held camp-meetings on Sundays, he attracted a following of men travelling the same road who did not know themselves where they were going, although a few of the number started with him, among them my mother's father and his family. When he came to a place that suited him, he picked out the land he wanted — which any man was free to do at that time — and the others settled about him.

In the dusty tramp of civilization westward — which seems to have always been justified by a tradition that men grow up by reason of it — our section was not a favorite, and remained new and unsettled after counties and States farther west had grown old. Everyone who came there seemed favorably impressed with the steady fertility of the soil, and expressed surprise that the lands were not all occupied; but no one in the great outside world talked about it, and no one wrote about it, so that those who were looking for homes went to the west or the north, where others were going.

There were cheap lands farther on, where the people raised a crop one year, and were supported by charity the next; where towns sprang up on credit, and farms were opened with borrowed money; where the people were apparently content, for our locality did not seem to be far enough west, nor far enough north, to suit them; where no sooner was one stranger's money exhausted than another arrived to take his place; where men mortgaged their possessions at full value, and thought themselves rich, notwithstanding, so great was their faith in the country; where he who was deepest in debt was the leading citizen, and where bankruptcy caught them all at last. On these lands the dusty travellers settled, where there were churches, school-houses, and bridges — but little rain — and railroads to carry out the crops should any be raised; and when anyone stopped in our neighborhood, he was too poor and tired to follow the others.

I became early impressed with the fact that our people seemed to be miserable and discontented, and frequently wondered that they did not load their effects on wagons again, and move away from a place which made all the men surly and rough, and the women pale and fretful. Although I had never been to the country they had left, except as a baby in arms, I was unfavorably impressed with it, thinking it must have been a very poor one that such a lot of people left it and considered their condition bettered by the change, for they never talked of going back, and were therefore probably better satisfied than they had ever been before. A road ran by our house, and when I first began to think about it at all, I thought that the covered wagons travelling it carried people moving from the country from which those in our neighborhood came, and the wagons were so numerous that I was led to believe that at least half the people of the world had tried to live there, and moved away after an unfortunate experience.

On the highest and bleakest point in the county, where the winds were plenty in winter because they were not needed, and scarce in summer for an opposite reason, the meeting-house was built, in a corner of my father's field. This was called Fairview, and so the neighborhood was known. There was a graveyard around it, and cornfields next to that, but not a tree or shrub attempted its ornament, and as the building stood on the main road where the movers' wagons passed, I thought that, next to their ambition to get away from the country which had been left by those in Fairview, the movers were anxious to get away from Fairview church, and avoid the possibility of being buried in its ugly shadow, for they always seemed to drive faster after passing it.

High up in a steeple which rocked with every wind was a great bell, the gift of a missionary society, and when there was a storm this tolled with fitful and uncertain strokes, as if the ghosts from the grave lot had crawled up there, and were counting the number to be buried the coming year, keeping the people awake for miles around. Sometimes, when the wind was particularly high, there were a great number of strokes on the bell in quick succession, which the pious said was an alarm to the wicked, sounded by the devil, a warning relating to the conflagration which could never be put out, else Fairview would never have been built.

When anyone died it was the custom to toll the bell once for every year of the deceased's age, and as deaths usually occur at night, we were frequently wakened from sleep by its deep and solemn tones. When I was yet a very little boy I occasionally went with my father to toll the bell when news came that someone was dead, for we lived nearer the place than any of the others, and when the strokes ran up to forty and fifty it was very dreary work, and I sat alone in the church wondering who would ring for me, and how many strokes could be counted by those who were shivering at home in their beds.

The house was built the first year of the settlement, and the understanding was that my father contributed the little money necessary, and superintended the work, in which he was assisted by anyone who volunteered his labor. It was his original intention to build it alone, and the little help he received only irritated him, as it was not worth the boast that he had raised a temple to the Lord single-handed. All the carpenter's work, and all the plasterer's work, he performed without assistance except from members of his own household, but I believe the people turned out to the raising, and helped put up the frames.

Regularly after its completion he occupied the rough pulpit (which he built with especial reference to his own size), and every Lord's Day morning and evening preached a religion to the people which I think added to their other discomforts, for it was hard and unforgiving. There were two or three kinds of Baptists among the people of Fairview when the house was completed, and a few Presbyterians, but they all became Methodists without revolt or question when my father announced in his first preaching that Fairview would be of that denomination.

He did not solicit them to join him, though he probably intimated in a way which admitted of no discussion that the few heretics yet remaining out in the world had better save themselves before it was too late. It did not seem to occur to him that men and women who had grown up in a certain faith renounced it with difficulty; it was enough that they were wrong, and that he was forgiving enough to throw open the doors of the accepted church. If they were humiliated, he was glad of it, for that was necessary to condone their transgression; if they had arguments to excuse it, he did not care to hear them, as he had taken God into partnership, and built Fairview, and people who worshipped there would be expected to throw aside all doctrinal nonsense.

❋   ❋   ❋

As I shall have something to do with this narrative, there may be a curiosity on the part of the reader to know who I am. I state, then, that I am the only son of the Rev. John Westlock — and the only child, unless a little girl born a year before me, and whom I have heard my mother speak of tenderly as pretty and blue-eyed, is to be called up from her grave and counted; and I have the best of reason for believing (the evidence being my father's word, a man whose integrity was never doubted) that he moved to the place where my recollection begins, to do good and grow up with the country. Whether my father remarked it in my presence — he seldom said anything to me — I do not now remember, but I believe to this day, in the absence of anything to the contrary, that the circuit he rode in the country which he had left was poor, and paid him but rarely for his services, which induced him to quit preaching as a business, and resolve to evangelize in the West on his own account, at the same time putting himself in the way of growing up with the country, an idea probably new at that time, and very significant.

In the great Bible which was always lying open on a table in our house, between the Old and the New Testament, my name and the date of my birth were recorded in bold handwriting, immediately following the information that Helen Elizabeth Westlock arrived by the mercy of God on the 19th of July, and departed in like manner on the 3d of April; and I did not know, until I was old enough to read for myself, that I had been christened Abram Nedrow Westlock, as I had always been called Ned, and had often wondered if any of the prophets were of that name, for my father, and my mother, and my uncle Jo (my mother's only brother, who had lived at our house most of his life), and my grandmother, and my grandfather, were all named for some of the people I had heard referred to when the big Bible was read. But when I found Abram before the Nedrow, I knew that I had not been neglected. This discovery caused me to ask my mother so many questions that I learned in addition that the Nedrow part of the name referred to a preacher of my father's denomination, and not to a prophet, and that my father admired him and named me for him because he had once preached all day at a camp-meeting, and then spent most of the following night in prayer. I therefore concluded that it was intended that I should be pious, and early began to search the Scriptures for the name of Abram, that I might know in what manner he had distinguished himself.

The first thing I can remember, and this only indistinctly, was connected with the removal of our effects from an old house to a new one, and that the book on which I usually sat at the table was mislaid during the day, which made it necessary for me to stand during the progress of the evening meal. I began to cry when this announcement was made, whereupon my father said in a stern way that I was now too old to cry, and that I must never do it again. I remarked it that day, if I never did before, that he was a large, fierce-looking man, whom it would likely be dangerous to trifle with, and that a full set of black whiskers, and a blacker frown, completely covered his face; from that time I began to remember events, and they will appear as this narrative progresses.

Of my youth before this time I have little knowledge except that my mother said once in my presence that I was a very pretty baby, but that I had now got bravely over it, and that as a child I was known in all the country round as a great baby to cry, being possessed of a stout pair of lungs, which I used on the slightest occasion. This, coupled with an observation from my uncle Jo that when he first saw me, an hour or two after birth, I looked like a fish-worm, was all I could find out about my earlier history, and the investigation was so unsatisfactory that I gave it up.

Once I heard my father say, when he was in a good humor, that when the nurse employed for my arrival announced that I was a boy, my mother cried hysterically for half an hour, as she desired a blue-eyed girl to replace the one she had buried, and when I heard my mother tell a few weeks afterwards, in a burst of confidence, to a number of women who happened to be there, that my father stormed for an hour because I was born at all, I concluded that I had never been very welcome, and regretted that I had ever come into the world. They both wanted a girl — when the event was inevitable — to help about the house, as Jo was thought to be all the help necessary in the field, and in the earlier days of my life I remember feeling that I was out of place because I did not wear dresses, and wash dishes, thus saving the pittance paid a farmer's daughter during the busy season.

The only remarkable thing I ever did in my life — I may as well mention it here, and be rid of it — was to learn to read letters when I was five years old, and as the ability to read even print was by no means a common accomplishment in Fairview, this circumstance gave me great notoriety. I no doubt learned to read from curiosity as to what the books and papers scattered about were for, as no one took the pains to teach me, for I remember that they were all greatly surprised when I began to spell words, and pronounce them, and I am certain I was never encouraged in it.

It was the custom when my father went to the nearest post-office to bring back with him the mail of the entire neighborhood, and it was my business to deliver the letters and papers at the different houses. If I carried letters, I was requested to read them, and the surprise which I created in this direction was so pronounced that it was generally said that in time I should certainly become a great man, and be invited to teach school. If I came to a word which I did not understand I invented one to take its place, or an entire sentence, for but few of the people could read the letters themselves, and never detected the deception. This occupation gave me my first impression of the country where the people had lived before they came to Fairview, and as there was much in the letters of hard work and pinching poverty, I believed that the writers lived in a heavily timbered country, where it was necessary to dig up trees to get room for planting. Another thing I noticed was that they all seemed to be dissatisfied and anxious to get away, and when in course of time I began to write answers to the letters I was surprised to learn that the people of Fairview were satisfied, and that they were well pleased with the change.

I had never thought this before, for they all seemed as miserable as was possible, and wondered about it a great deal. This gave me fresh reason for believing that the country which our people had left was a very unfavored one, and when I saw the wagons in the road I thought that at last the writers of the letters I had been reading had arrived and would settle on some of the great tracts of prairie which could be seen in every direction, but they turned the bend in the road and went on as if a look at Fairview had frightened them, and they were going back another way.

It seems to me now that between the time I began to remember and the time I went out with my father and Jo to work, or went alone through the field to attend the school in the church, about a year elapsed, and that I was very much alone during the interval, for ours was a busy family, and none of them had time to look after me. My father and Jo went to the fields, or away with the teams, at a very early hour in the morning, and usually did not return until night, and my mother was always busy about the house, so that if I kept out of mischief no more was expected of me. I think it was during this year (it may have been two years, but certainly not a longer period) that I learned to read, for I had nothing else to do and no companions, and from looking at the pictures in the books I began to wonder what the little characters surrounding them meant.

In this I was assisted by Jo, who seemed to know everything, and by slow degrees I put the letters together to make words, and understood them. Sometimes in the middle of the day I slipped out into the field to ask him the meaning of something mysterious I had encountered, and although he would good-naturedly inform me, I noticed that he and my father worked without speaking, and that I seemed to be an annoyance, so I scampered back to my loneliness again.

During this time, too, I first noticed that my father was not like other men who came to our house, for he was always grave and quiet, and had little to say at any time. It was a relief to me to hear him ask blessings at the table, and pray morning and evening, for I seldom heard his voice at any other time. I believe I regarded his quiet manner only as an evidence that he was more pious than others of his class, for I could make nothing else out of it, but often regretted that his religion did not permit him to notice me more, or to take me with him when he went away in the wagon. Once I asked my mother why he was always so stern and silent, and if it was because we had offended him, to which she replied all in a tremble that she did not know herself, and I thought that she studied a great deal about him, too. My mother was as timid in his presence as I was, and during the day, if I came upon her suddenly, she looked frightened, thinking it was he, but when she found it was not, her composure returned again. Neither of us had reason to be afraid of him, I am certain of that, but as we never seemed able to please him (though he never said so), we were in constant dread of displeasing him more than ever, or of causing him to become more silent and dissatisfied, and to give up the short prayers in which we were graciously mentioned for a blessing.

The house where we lived, and into which we moved on the day when my recollection begins, was the largest in the settlement; a square house of two stories, painted so white that after night it looked like a ghost. It was built on lower ground than Fairview church, though the location was sightly, and not far away ran a stream fringed with thickets of brush, where I found the panting cattle and sheep on hot days, and thought they gave me more of a welcome than my father and Jo did in the field; for they were not busy, but idle like me, and I hoped it was rather a relief to them to look at me in mild-eyed wonder.

Beyond the little stream and the pasture was the great dusty road, and in my loneliness I often sat on the high fence beside it to watch for the coming of the movers' wagons, and to look curiously at those stowed away under the cover bows, tumbled together with luggage and effects of every kind. If one of the drivers asked me how far it was to the country town I supposed he had heard of my wonderful learning, and took great pains to describe the road, as I had heard my father do a hundred times in response to similar inquiries from movers. Sometimes I climbed up to the driver's seat, and drove with him out to the prairie, and I always noticed that the women and children riding behind were poorly dressed, and tired looking, and I wondered if only the unfortunate travelled our way, for only that kind of people lived in Fairview, and I had never seen any other kind in the road.

When I think of the years I lived in Fairview, I imagine that the sun was never bright there (although I am certain that it was), and I cannot relieve my mind of the impression that the cold, changing shadow of the gray church has spread during my long absence and enveloped all the houses where the people lived. When I see Fairview in my fancy now, it is always from a high place, and looking down upon it the shadow is denser around the house where I lived than anywhere else, so that I feel to this day that should I visit it, and receive permission from the new owners to walk through the rooms, I should find the walls damp and mouldy because the bright sun and the free air of Heaven had deserted them as a curse.

THE HELL QUESTION, AND THE REV. JOHN WESTLOCK

MY father's religion would have been unsatisfactory without a hell.

It was a part of his hope of the future that worldly men who scoffed at his piety would be punished, and this was as much a part of his expectation as that those who were faithful to the end would be rewarded. Everybody saved, to my father's thinking, was as bad as nobody saved, and in his well-patronized Bible not a passage for pleasurable contemplation which intimated universal salvation was marked, if such exists.

The sacrifices he made for religion were tasks, and his reward was a conviction that those who refused to make them would be punished, for he regarded it as an injustice of which the Creator was incapable to do as well by His enemies as by His friends. I believe that he would rather have gone to heaven without the members of his family than with them, unless they had earned salvation as he had earned it, and travelled as steadily as himself the hard road marked on his map as leading heavenward.

One of the best evidences to his mind of a compassionate and loving Saviour was the belief that all thought of unfortunate friends in torment was blotted from the memory of the redeemed, and the lake of fire he thought of as a remedy for the great number of disagreeable people with whom he was compelled to come in contact below, and of whom he would be happily rid above. Religion was a misery to be endured on earth, that a reward might be enjoyed after death. A man must spend the ages of his future either in a very pleasant place, with comfortable surroundings and pleasant associates, or in a very unpleasant place, with uncomfortable surroundings and all the mean people turned into devils and imps for companions. It was the inevitable law; every man of moderate sense should be able to appreciate the situation at a glance, and do that which would insure his personal safety. If there was a doubt — the thought was too absurd for his contemplation, but admitting a doubt — his future would be equal to that of the worldly man, for one cannot rot more easily than another, or be more comfortable as dust; but if there was no doubt — and all the authorities agree that there was none — then the difference would be in his favor.

It was the best thing offering under the circumstances, and should therefore be accepted without hesitation. If the conditions were hard, he could not help it; he might have suggested changes in the plan of salvation had his judgment been invited, but the plan had been formulated before his time, and there was nothing left for him but obedience. If he thought he deserved credit for all he possessed (and he was a man very likely to be seized with that suspicion), the Bible said it came from God; that settled the matter finally and forever — he gave thanks (for a punishment was provided if he did not, and a reward if he did), and pretended to have had nothing to do with accumulating his property.

Religion was a matter of thrift and self-interest as much as laying away money in youth and strength for old age and helplessness, and he called upon sinners to flee the wrath to come because he had been commanded to go out and preach to all the world, for it mattered little to him whether the people were saved or not. They had eyes, therefore let them see; ears, therefore let them hear. The danger was so plain that they ought to save themselves without solicitation.

That which he most desired seldom came to pass; that which he dreaded, frequently, but no matter; he gave thanks to the Lord because it was best to do so, and asked no questions. There were jewels for those who earned them, and as a thrifty man he desired a greater number of these than any other citizen of Fairview. He was the principal man in his neighborhood below, and desired to be a shepherd rather than a sheep above; therefore he was foremost in the church, and allowed no one to be more zealous in doing the service of the hard master he had, after careful thought and study, set out to serve, believing the reward worth the service, and determined to serve well if he served at all, as was his custom in everything else.

If I do him an injustice I do not intend it, but I have thought all my life that he regarded children as troublesome and expensive — a practical sort of punishment for sin, sent from time to time as the case seemed to require; and that he had been burdened with but two was no doubt evidence to his mind that his life had been generally blameless, if, indeed, this opinion was not confirmed by the circumstance that one of them had been taken from him in return for good service in the holy cause. Once they had arrived, however, he accepted the trust to return them to their Maker as nearly like they came as possible, for that was commanded of him.

Because he frequently referred to the road to heaven as narrow and difficult, and the highway in the other direction as broad and easy, I came to believe that but for his religion he would have been a man much given to money-getting, and ambitious for distinction, but he put such thoughts aside, and toiled away at his work as if to get out of temptation's way. When he talked of the broad and easy road it was with a relish, as though he could enjoy the pleasant places by the way-side if he dared; and in his preaching I think he described the pleasures of the world so vividly that his hearers were taken with a wish to enjoy them, though it is not probable that he knew anything about them except from hearsay, as he had always been out of temptation's way — in the backwoods during his boyhood, and on the prairie during his maturer years. But when he talked of the narrow and difficult path, his manner changed at once; a frown came upon his face; he looked determined and unforgiving, and at every point he seemed to build sign-posts marked "Duty!" It has occurred to me since that he thought of his religion as a vigorous, healthy, successful man thinks in his quiet moments of a wife sick since their marriage; although he may deserve a different fate, and desire it, he dares not complain, for the more wearisome the invalid, the louder the call of duty.

I think he disliked the necessity of being religious, and only accepted and taught religion because he believed it to be the best thing to do, for it did not afford him the peace he professed. To all appearances he was a most miserable man, although he taught that only the sinful are miserable, and the few acquaintances he had who were not equally devout (strangers passing through, or those he met at the country town, for all were pious in Fairview) lived an easy and contented life which he seemed to covet, but nobody knew it, for he reproved them with all the more vigor because of his envy.

When not engaged in reading at night, as was his custom, he sat for hours looking steadily into the fire, and was impatient if disturbed. I never knew what occupied his thoughts at these times; it may have been his preaching, or his daily work, but more likely he was seeing glimpses of forbidden pictures; caravans of coveted things passing in procession, or of hopes and ambitions dwarfed by duty. Perhaps in fancy he was out in the world mingling with people of a class more to his taste than Fairview afforded, and was thinking he could enjoy their pleasures and occupations if they were not forbidden, or wondering if, after all, his principles were not mistakes. I believe that during these hours of silent thinking he was tempted and beckoned by the invisible and mysteriously potent forces he pretended to despise, and that he was convinced that, to push them off, his religion must be made more rigorous and pitiless.

That he coveted riches could be easily seen, and but for his fear of conscience he could have easily possessed himself of everything worth owning in Fairview, for with the exception of Theodore Meek, the next best man in the neighborhood, he was about the only one among the people who read books and subscribed for newspapers. None of them was his equal in intelligence or energy, and had he desired he could have traded them out of what little they possessed, and sold it back again at a comfortable profit. But, "do unto others as you would have others do unto you," was commanded of him by his inexorable master, and he was called upon to help the weak rather than rob them; therefore he often gave them assistance which he could but poorly afford. This limited him so much that he had no other hope of becoming well-to-do than that the lands which he was constantly buying would finally become valuable by reason of the development and settlement of the country. This he regarded as honorable and fair, and to this work he applied himself with great energy.

I heard little of his father, except that he was noted where he lived as a man of large family, who provided them all with warm clothes in winter and plenty to eat all the year round. His early history was probably as unimportant and eventless as my own. He seldom mentioned his father to anyone, except in connection with a story which he occasionally told, that once, when his house was on fire, he called so loud for help that he was heard a mile. Evidently the son succeeded to this extraordinary pair of lungs, for he sang the religious songs common in that day with such excellence that no man attempted to equal him. While his singing was strong and loud, it was melodious, and he had as great a reputation for that as for piety and thrift. His was a camp-meeting voice, though he occasionally sang songs of little children, as "Moses in the Bulrushes," of which there were thirty-eight verses, and the cradle song commencing, "Hush, my dear, lie still and slumber," written by a noted hymn-writer, otherwise my father would not have patronized him. Besides a thorough familiarity with all the common, long, short, and particular metres, he had a collection of religious songs preserved in a leather-bound book, the notes being written in buckwheat characters on blue paper fast turning yellow with age, and the words on the opposite page. Feeling the necessity of a knowledge of notes once, he had learned the art in a few weeks, in his usual vigorous way, and sang at sight; and after that he preserved his old songs, and all the new ones he fancied, in the book I have mentioned. The songs to which I refer I have never seen in print, and he sang them on special occasions, as at a camp-meeting when a tiresome preacher had allowed the interest to flag. "Behold Paul a Prisoner," a complete history of the Apostle requiring almost an afternoon in its performance, or "Christ in the Garden," nearly as long, never failed to start the interest anew in an emergency, and if the case were very desperate, he called the members of his family into the pulpit, and sang a quartet called "The Glorious Eighth of April," using for the words the first hymn in the book.

This was usually sufficient to start someone to shouting, and after a short prayer he preached as vigorously and loudly as he sang, and with an equally good effect.

Of his brothers and sisters, although he had a great number, he seldom talked, and I scarcely knew the names of the States in which they lived, as they were scattered in every direction. I had heard him mention a Samuel, a Joseph, a Jacob, an Elias, a Rebecca, a Sarah, a Rachel, and an Elizabeth, from which I came to believe that my grandfather was a religious man (his own name was Amos), and I once heard that his children on Sundays carried their shoes to the brook near the meeting-house before putting them on, that they might last the longer, which confirmed the belief that there had been religion in his family as there was in ours.

Of his mother he said nothing at all, and if they had neighbors he never mentioned them. In short, he did not seem proud of his family, which caused us to wonder why he was so much like his father, which we had come to believe without exactly knowing why. We were certain he was like his father in religion; in the hard way in which he worked; in his capacity to mend his own ploughs and wagons; and in the easy manner in which he adapted himself to his surroundings, whatever they were, for in all these particulars he was unlike any other man we had ever known, and different from his neighbors, who spent half a day in asking advice in a matter which could be remedied in half an hour. The people came to our house from miles around to borrow, and to ask the best time to plant and to sow, but the Rev. John Westlock asked advice of no one, and never borrowed. If he needed an extra harrow, he made one of wood to answer until such a time as he could trade to advantage for a better one; if he broke a plough, he managed somehow to mend it until a rainy day came, when he made it as good as new. Even in cases of sickness he usually had a bottle hid away that contained relief, and in all other things was equally capable and thrifty.

If it be to the credit of a man to say that he was a slave to

21

hard work, I cheerfully add this testimony to the greatness of my father, for he went to the field at daylight only to return with the darkness, winter and summer alike; and never in my life have I seen him idle — except on the day appointed for rest — and even then he devoured the Bible like a man reading at so much per page. He worked hard when he preached, talking rapidly that he might accomplish as much as possible before the people became impatient, and he no sooner finished one song of warning, than he began another.

My father being large and positive, it followed naturally that my mother was small and weak, and thoroughly under his control. I don't think she was afraid of him, but he managed his own affairs so well that she was willing he should manage hers, as he had given her good reason to respect his judgment. She probably argued — if she argued the question at all — that as his ideas were good in everything else, he would of course know how to manage a boy, so my bringing up was left entirely to him.

She never corrected me except to say that father would not like what I was doing, and she might find it necessary to call his attention to it, but in the goodness of her heart she forgot it, and never told him unless the offence was a very grave one. While she frequently pleaded with me to be good, and cried in vexation if I would not, she never gave commands which were enforced with severe punishments, as he did; therefore I am afraid that I did not appreciate her kindness and favor, but rather enjoyed my freedom when under her care as a respite from restraint at other times. She was as quiet and thoughtful as her husband, but seemed sad rather than angry and discontented, as was the case with him, and it will be readily imagined that as a family we were not much given to happiness. While I never heard my father speak harshly to her, he was often impatient, as though he regretted he had not married a wife as ambitious and capable as himself; but if he thought of it, he gave it no other attention than to become more gloomy, and pacified himself by reading far into the night without speaking to anyone.

I could find no fault with him except that he never spoke kindly to me, and it annoyed him if I asked him questions concerning what I read in his books. When Jo and I worked with him in the field, which we both began to do very early in life, he always did that which was hardest and most disagreeable, and was not a tyrant in anything save the ungrumbling obedience he exacted to whatever he thought about the matter in hand, without reference to what others thought on the same subject. We had to be at something steadily, whether it helped him or not, because he believed idle boys grew up into idle men. Other boys in the neighborhood built the early fires, and did the early feeding, but he preferred to do these things himself — whether out of consideration for us, or because it was troublesome to drive us to it, I do not know. After starting the fire in the room in which he slept, he stepped to our door and told us to get up, to which command we mumblingly replied and slept on. After returning from the stables, he spoke to us again, but we still paid no attention. Ten minutes later he would start up the stairs with angry strides, but he never caught us, for we knew that was final and hurried on our clothes. Seeing that we were up and dressing when he reached the head of the stairs, he would say, "Well, you'd better," and go down again, where we speedily followed. This was his regular custom for years; we always expected it of him, and were never disappointed.

After the morning devotions, which consisted of reading a chapter from the Bible and a prayer always expressed in exactly the same words, he asked a blessing for the meal by this time ready (the blessing was as unvarying as the prayer), and we ate in silence. Then we were warmly clothed, if it was winter, and compelled to go out and work until we were hungry again. I suppose we helped him little enough, but his reasoning convinced him that, to work easily and naturally, work must become a habit, and should be taught from youth up, therefore we went out with him every day and came back only with the darkness.

I think he was kinder with us when at work than at any other time, and we admired him in spite of the hard and exacting tasks he gave us to do — he called them stints — for he was powerful and quick to aid us when we needed it, and tender as a child if we were sick. Sometimes on cold days we walked rather than

rode to the timber, where my father went to chop wood while Jo
and I corded it. On one of these occasions I became ill while returning home at night — a slight difficulty, it must have been,
for I was always stout and robust — and he carried me all the
way in his arms. Though I insisted I could walk, and was better,
he said I was not heavy, and trudged along like a great giant,
holding me so tenderly that I thought for the first time that perhaps he loved me. For weeks after that I tried as hard as I could
to please him, and to induce him to commend my work; but he
never did, for whether I was good or bad, he was just the same,
silent and grave, so that if I became indifferent in my tasks, I
fear he was the cause of it.

Other families had their holidays, and owned guns and dogs,
which they used in hunting the wild game then so abundant; but
there was little of this at our house, and perhaps this was the
reason why we prospered more than those around us. Usually
Jo and I were given the Saturday afternoons to ourselves, when
we roamed the country with some of the idle vagabonds who lived
in rented houses, visiting turkey roosts a great distance in the
woods, and only returning long after night-fall. I do not remember that we were ever idle in the middle of the week, unless we
were sent on errands, as buying young stock at low prices of
the less thrifty neighbors, or something else in which there was
profit; so that we had little time to learn anything except hard
work, and if we learned that well it was because we were ex-
cellently taught by a competent master. During those years work
became such a habit with me that ever since it has clung to me,
and perhaps, after all, it was an inheritance for which I have
reason to be thankful. I remember my father's saying scornfully
to me once, as if intimating that I ought to make up by unusual
industry for the years of idleness, that I was a positive burden
and expense to him until I was seven years old. So it will readily
be imagined that I was put to work early, and kept steadily at it.

III

THE HOUSE OF ERRING

THE friend and companion of my boyhood was Jo Erring, my mother's only brother, who had been in the family since before I was born. He was five years my senior, and a stout and ambitious fellow I greatly admired; but as he was regularly flogged when I was, this circumstance gave rise to his first ambition to become a man and whip my father, whom he regarded with little favor.

There was a kind of tradition that when he became of age he was to have a horse and ten dollars in money, but whether this was really the price of his work I never knew. More likely he came to our house with my mother, as he was not wanted at home, and had lived there until other disposition could be made of him. He usually had a horse picked out as the one he desired, and gave it particular attention, but as each of these in turn was disposed of at convenient opportunity, he became more than ever convinced that he was related by marriage to a very unscrupulous man.

I remember him at this period as an overgrown boy always wearing cast-off clothing either too large or too small for him, and the hero and friend of every boy on Fairview prairie. Although he was the stoutest boy in the neighborhood, and we often wondered that he did not sometimes whip all the others simply because he could, he never quarrelled, but was in every dispute a mediator, announcing his decisions in a voice good-natured and hoarse; and as he was honest and just, and very stout, there were no appeals from his decisions. In our rough amusements, which were few enough, he used his strength to secure to the smaller ones their share, and gave way himself with the same readiness that he exacted from the others; there-

25

fore he was very popular among the younger portion of the population, and there was great joy at school when it was announced — which pleasure I usually had — that Jo Erring had finished his winter's work, and was coming the next day, for all forms of oppression must cease from that date. Sometimes he came by the school on a winter evening with a rude sled, to which he had young horses attached to break them, and if the larger boys climbed on to ride home, or as far as he went, he made them all get off, and loading up with those too small to look after their own interests in the struggle, drove gayly away with me by his side.

There were few men more trusty than Jo, and he always made a round in the plough-field after my father had turned out, as if to convince him that he was mistaken in the opinion that boys were good for nothing. When there was corn to gather, he took the slowest team and the lazy hired man, and brought in more loads than my father and I, and if I found any way to aid him in this I always did it. They seemed to hate each other in secret, for the master disliked a boy who was able to equal him in anything, as if his extra years had availed him nothing; and I confess that my sympathies were always with Jo, for the grown people picked at him because of his ambition to become a man, in all other respects than age, a few years sooner than was usual. While nobody disputed that he was a capable fellow, he was always attempting something he could not carry out, and thus became a subject of ridicule in spite of his worth and ability; if he was sent to the timber for wood, he would volunteer to be back at an impossible time, and although he returned sooner than most men would have done, they laughed at him, and regarded him as a great failure.

It was said of him that he exaggerated, but I think that he was only anxious that it be known what he could do if he had an opportunity; and as everyone thought less of him than he deserved, he kept on talking of himself to correct a wrong impression, and steadily made matters worse. His activity kept him down, for another thing, for thereby he raised an opposition which would not have existed had he been content to walk

26

leisurely along in the tracks made by his elders. He accepted none of the opinions of the Fairview men, and it was said of him that he was a skeptic for no other reason than that everybody else was religious, and I am not certain but that there was some truth in this.

If the truth of a certain principle was asserted, he denied it, not by rude controversy, but by his actions; and by his ingenuity he often made a poorer one seem better, if the one proposed happened to be right, as was sometimes the case — for the Fairview people had but two ways to guess, and occasionally adopted a right method instead of a wrong one, by accident.

I believe there was nothing he could not do. He shingled hair in a superb manner for anyone who applied, and charged nothing for the service. And I helped him learn the art, for he practised on me so much that I was nearly always bald. He made everything he took a fancy for, and seemed to possess himself of the contents of a book by looking through it; for though I seldom found him reading, he was about as well-informed as the books themselves. When the folks were away at camp-meeting, he added my mother's work to his own, and got along very well with it. I never heard of anything a Fairview boy could do better than Jo Erring, and he did a great many things in which he had no competition; therefore I have often wondered that the only young man there who really amounted to anything was for some reason rather unpopular. Jo was unfortunate in the particular that he seemed to have inherited all the poorer qualities of both his father and mother instead of the good qualities of either one of them, or a commendable trait from one, and an undesirable one from the other. I have heard of men who resembled the less worthy of their parents — I believe this is the rule — but never before have I known a boy to resemble both his parents in everything they tried to hide. His tendency to exaggeration he got honestly from his mother, who was a fluent talker, but Jo was not like her in that. In this Jo was like his father, who would not say a half dozen words without becoming hopelessly entangled, and making long pauses in painful effort to extricate his meaning.

Jo was often sent to a water-mill in the woods with a grist, and while waiting for his wheat or corn to be ground, he regarded the machinery with the closest attention, and at length became impressed with the idea that after he had become a man, and whipped my father, he would like to follow milling for a business. The miller, an odd but kindly man of whom but little was known in our part of the country, admired Jo's manly way, and made friends with him by good-naturedly answering his questions, and occasionally inviting him to his house for dinner; and Jo talked so much of his ambition and his friend, that he came to be called "The Miller," and spent his spare time in making models, and trying them in the rivulets which ran through the fields after a rain.

His father's farm was skirted by Big Creek, and here he picked out a site for his mill when he should be able to build it, at a place called Erring's Ford (the location really did credit to his judgment), and having hauled a load of stones there one Saturday afternoon for a dam, the circumstance gave rise to the only pleasantry ever known in Fairview. When anyone spoke of an event not likely to happen, he said it would probably come about when the sky rained pitchforks on the roof of Jo Erring's mill; but Jo paid little attention to this banter, and hauled more stones for the dam whenever he had opportunity, in which work I assisted, in preference to idleness without him. He hoped to become apprenticed to his friend the miller to learn the business, and to complete his own enterprise by slow degrees from his small savings. And he never lost sight of this purpose, pursuing it so steadily that a few of those who at first laughed at him spoke at length encouraging words, and said they believed he would finally succeed, although it would be a long time in coming about.

I was secretly very fond of the mill enterprise, and admired Jo more than ever, that he was bold enough to attempt carrying it out. Our plan to run away was altered by this new interest, and we agreed that it would be better to wait patiently until the mill was complete, and buy our liberty from its profits; for Jo had generously agreed to ransom me as well as himself as soon as he was able.

Jo's mother, a very large woman who was the acknowledged head of the House of Erring, and doctor for half that country,

28

lived four miles from Fairview church, on Big Creek, in a house of hewn logs, the inside of which was a marvel for neatness. Of her husband the people knew nothing except that he was a shingle-maker, and that he was probably a very wicked man, for he was about the only one in the settlement who did not profess religion, and attend the gatherings at the church. The calling of shingle-making he followed winter and summer, and he never seemed to raise anything on his farm except a glassy kind of corn with a great many black grains in every ear, which he planted and cultivated with a hoe. After it was gathered, he tied most of it in bunches, and hung it up to dry on the kitchen rafters, where it was understood to be for sale as seed; although I never heard that it was good for anything except to parch, and the only use he ever made of it, that I knew anything about, was to give it to Jo and me with the air of a man conferring a great favor.

My father liked nothing about Dad Erring except his one virtue of attending to his own business, such as it was; and said of him that he selected his piece of land because it was near a spring, whereas the exercise of a little energy would have dug a well affording an equally good supply of water on vastly superior land.

Indeed, no one seemed to like him, and the dislike was mutual, for if he was familiar with anyone except Jo, my mother, and myself, I never knew of it. He seldom spoke even to my grand-mother when I was about, and I think only very rarely at any other time, for they seemed never to have recovered from some old trouble. There was this much charity for him, however — the people said no more than that he was an exceedingly odd sort of a man (a verdict true of his appearance as well as dis-position, for he was very large, very raw-boned, and clean shaven), and let him alone, which of all things he probably most desired.

The people frequently met him walking along the road swing-ing a stout stick, and taking tremendous strides (he never owned a horse, but took long journeys on foot, refusing a ride if offered him by a wagon going in the same direction), but he did not speak to them unless compelled and apparently had no other desire than to be let alone.

He never went anywhere except to the timber to make shingles, and off on excursions afoot nobody knew whither, from which he always returned in a few days in exactly the same mood as that in which he had started. I have heard that he had relatives living in a settlement south of us, but whether he went to visit them on his journeys, or spent the money he earned in shingle-making in walking about for his health, paying for his entertainment wherever night overtook him, I did not know then, nor do I know now.

Once in a long while he came to our house, always when my father was away; and, after watching my mother awhile as she went about her work, went away again, sometimes without saying a word, although she always talked kindly to him, and was glad to see him. Occasionally he would accept her invitation to refresh himself with food, but not often; and when he did he would be offended unless she took a present of money to buy something to remember him by. If she was dangerously ill — which was often the case, for she was never strong — he was never sent for. Nobody thought of him as of any use or as caring much about it; but when she had recovered, he would come over, and, after looking at her curiously, return home satisfied. I think that had she died, he would not have been invited to the funeral, but I am certain that after it was all over, he would often have visited her grave, and looked at it in quiet astonishment.

On returning from her visits to the sick, my grandmother usually stopped at our house, and sometimes I was lifted up behind to go home with her to take care of the horse she rode, for my grandfather disliked horses.

Arriving at the house of hewn logs in the edge of the woods, she dismounted and went in, and I went on to the stables. Returning after I had finished my work, I found my grandfather on one side of the fire-place, and my grandmother on the other, looking into the fire, or, if it was summer, into the cavernous recess where the backlog would have been blazing in winter. If it was evening, which was usually the case, I was soon sent out to make the fire for the evening meal, but after this was eaten, we resumed our places at the hearth. Sometimes I told them what

30

I knew was going on in the neighborhood, and caused them to ask questions, and replied to them, and tried to lure them into a conversation, but I never succeeded. If my grandmother told me that one of her patients had died, the information was really intended for her husband; and if he did not fully understand it, he directed his questions to me, and she replied in the same way. In this way they also discussed household affairs of which it was necessary for each to know, storing them up until I came, but never speaking directly to each other.

After I had sat between them for an hour or more, it would suddenly occur to my grandmother that I had been up too long already, and after divesting me of clothing, I was thrown into the centre of a great feather-bed, three of which stood in a row at the back end of the room. I was put into the middle one, as if to keep my grandparents as far apart as possible again, for I was certain that my grandmother slept in one, and my grandfather in the other. The one which I occupied was also the company bed, for my grandmother evidently desired me to know that my mother, excellent woman though she was, could not hope to learn perfectly the art of making up a feather-bed for many years yet. If I raised my head quietly, and looked out, I found the strange couple sitting by the fire as I had left them, and, in wondering whether they would remain there all night, I fell asleep.

When I awoke in the morning they were up before me, waiting for daylight, as people were early risers in those days; and I never knew certainly that they went to bed at all, but always wondered whether they did not sit beside the fire throughout the long night.

After a while my grandmother came to the bed, pulled me out and into my clothes, and sent me to the spring to wash my face for breakfast, which was soon thereafter ready. When this was over I was started for home, usually carrying a present of butter or eggs for my mother, and a box on the ears for myself.

31

IV

THE RELIGION OF FAIRVIEW

ALTHOUGH the people of Fairview frequently did not dress comfortably, and lived in the plainest manner, they never failed to attend the services at the church, to which everybody belonged, with the exception of my grandfather, and Jo, and myself. I have often wondered since that we were not made the subject of a special series of meetings, and frightened into repentance; but for some unaccountable reason we were left alone. They even discussed Jo's situation, laying it to contrariness, and saying that if all the rest of them were wicked, he would be religious; but they said nothing at all to me about the subject. I often attended the revivals, and sang the songs as loudly as the rest of them, but when I thought that I was one of those whose terrible condition the hymns described, it gave me such a turn that I left that part of the house where the excitement ran highest, and joined Jo on the back seats, who took no other interest in the novel performance than that of looker-on.

As soon as a sufficient number of children reached a suitable age to make their conversion a harvest, a revival was commenced for their benefit, and they were called upon to make a full confession with such energy, and warned to cling to the cross for safety with such earnestness, that they generally did it, and but few escaped. If there was one so stubborn that he would not yield from worldly pride, of which he had not a particle — no one ever supposed it possible that he lacked faith, though they all did — the meetings were continued from Sunday until Monday, and kept up every night of the week at the house where the owner of the obdurate heart lived, so that he finally gave in; for peace and quiet, if for nothing else.

If two or three, or four or five, would not relent within a reason-

32

able time, the people gave up every other work, and gathered at the church in great alarm, in response to the ringing of the bell, and there they prayed and shouted the livelong day for the Lord to come down among them. At these times Jo and I were usually left at home to work in the field, and if we heard the people coming home in the evening shouting and singing, we knew that the lost sheep had been recovered, and I often feared they would form a ring around us in the field, and compel a full surrender. A young woman who lived at our house to help my mother, the daughter of a neighboring farmer, once engaged their attention for nearly a week, but she gave up one hot afternoon, and came down the path which led through the cornfields from the church, shouting and going on like mad, followed by those that had been present when the Lord finally came down, who were singing and proclaiming the event as loudly as they could. This frightened me so much that I ran into the house, and hid under the bed, supposing they would soon go away, and that then I could come out; but they immediately began a prayer-meeting to give the new convert opportunity to face a frowning world by relating her experience, and thus they kept me in my uncomfortable position until I thought I must smother from the heat.

My father received little aid in the conduct of these meetings except from a very good farmer, but very bad exhorter, named Theodore Meek, whose name had been gradually shortened by neighborhood familiarity until he was known as The. Meek; and for a long time I thought he was meant when reference was made to "The Meek and lowly," supposing that Lowly was an equally good man living in some of the adjoining settlements. This remarkable man laughed his religion rather than preached, or prayed, or shouted, or sang it. His singing would be regarded at this day as a very expert rendering of a laughing song, but to us it was an impressive performance, as were his praying and occasional preaching, though I wonder we were not amused. The. Meek was, after my father, the next best man in Fairview; the next largest farmer, and the next in religion and thrift. In moving to the country I think his wagons were next to ours, which headed the procession. He sat nearest the pulpit at the meetings, was the second to arrive — my father coming first — and always took up the collections. If there was a funeral, he stood next my father, who conducted the services; at the school-meetings he was the second to speak; and if a widow needed her corn gathered, or her winter's wood chopped, my father suggested it, and The. Meek immediately said it should have been attended to before. He also lived nearer our house than any of the others, and was oftener there; and his house was built so much like ours that only experts knew it was cheaper, and not quite so large. His family, which consisted of a fat wife by a second marriage, and so many children that I never could remember all their names — there was always a new baby whenever its immediate predecessor was old enough to name — were laughers like him, and to a stranger it would have seemed that they found jokes in the Bible, for they were always reading the Bible, and always laughing.

Another assistant was Mrs. Tremaine, the miller's widowed sister, who had lived in the country before we came, a wax-faced woman who apparently had no other duty to attend to than religion; for although she lived a considerable distance from Fairview church, she was always at the meetings, and I have thought of her as being constantly occupied in coming from or going to church, finding it time to start back again as soon as she reached home. The only assistance she afforded was to pray whenever called upon in a voice so low that there was always doubt when she had finished; but this made little difference, as it gave the others opportunity to be heard in short exclamations concerning the kindness of the Lord if sinners would really renounce the world and make a full confession. Her speeches in the experience meetings were of the same order, and when she sat down the congregation invariably began a song descriptive of a noble woman always battling for the right, and sure to conquer in the end; from which grew an impression that she was a very sainted person, and that the sins of her brother, the miller, were much on her mind. It is certain that he thought little of them himself, never attending the services, or sending his regrets.

It was usually a part of my duty on Sunday to take one of the wagons, Jo taking the other, and to drive about collecting infirm and unfortunate people who would otherwise be unable to attend church; for my father believed in salvation for all who were willing to accept it, though they were poor, and unable to walk, or hear, or see, or understand; and he was kinder to the unfortunate people than to any of the others, favoring them out of his strength and abundance in a hundred ways.

There was always a suspicion in my mind, which may have been an unjust one, that they shouted and went on in response to his preaching because he was their friend, and wanted them to do so. In any event, he could throw them into the greatest excitement, and cause them to exhibit themselves in the most remarkable way, whenever he saw fit, so that they got on very well together.

One of these unfortunates was Mr. Winter, the lame shoemaker, who wheeled himself around in a low buggy. Pushing this into my wagon with the assistance of his wife, after we had first made a run-way of boards, I hauled him to Fairview, where we unloaded him in the same manner. He was a very devout man, and a shouter, and during the revivals he wheeled himself up and down the aisles in his buggy, which frequently squeaked and rattled in a very uncomfortable manner, to shake hands with the people. I suppose that at first this performance was a little odd to people, but they got used to it; for I have noticed that while strangers regarded Mr. Winter as a great curiosity, he attracted no more attention at home than a man unobjectionable in the matter of legs. There was a good deal of talk from time to time of holding special services to restore Mr. Winter's shrivelled legs by prayer, but if ever it was tried, it was in secret, for I never heard of it. There were probably half a dozen of these unfortunates altogether, and they were always given the best corner, which was near the pulpit, where their piety could be easily seen and heard.

With the addition of a blind woman who cried and lamented a great deal, and whom I also went after nearly every Sunday, those I have mentioned were the ones most conspicuous in the meetings; for while the others were very devout, they had nothing to offer for the general good except their presence and a capacity to rise to their feet and confess the Lord in a few words. My father was the leader, of course, and occupied the time himself when others could not be induced to occupy it, which was often the case after those I have mentioned had appeared in what might be called their specialties.

This, coupled with the unforgiving doctrines of Rev. John Westlock, was the religion to which I was accustomed, and which I believe added greatly to the other miseries of Fairview, for Fairview was afflicted with a melancholy that could have resulted from nothing else. There was little visiting, and there were no public gatherings except those at the church already mentioned, where the business of serving the Lord was dispatched as soon as possible to allow the people to return home and nurse their misery. The people were all overworked, and I still remember how the pale, unhappy women spoke in low and trembling tones at the experience meetings of heavy crosses to bear, and sat down crying as though their hearts were breaking. I was always touched by this pitiful proceeding, and I doubt not their petitions went further into heaven than any of the others.

V

THE SCHOOL IN THE CHURCH

WHEN there was nothing else for them to do, the children of Fairview were sent to a school kept in the church, where they studied around a big box-stove, and played at noon and recess among the mounds in the grave lot, there being no playground, as it was not intended that the children of Fairview should play.

The older boys told it in low whispers that a sunken grave meant that the person buried there had been carried away by the Devil, and it was one of our amusements to look among the graves from day to day to see if the dreadful visitor had been around during the preceding night.

These sunken graves were always carefully filled up by relatives of the persons buried, and I regarded this as evidence that they were anxious to hide the disgrace which had come upon their families from neglect of my father's religion. After a funeral — which we were all compelled to attend so that we might become practically impressed with the shortness of life, and where a hymn commencing "Hark, from the tomb, a doleful sound," was sung to such a dismal measure that the very dogs howled to hear it — I used to lie awake in speechless terror for a great many nights, fearing the Devil would call on me in my room on his way out to the grave lot to see whether the person just buried belonged to him.

The boys and girls who attended from the houses dotted about on the prairie did not differ from other children except that they were a long time in the first pages of their books, and seemed glad to come. I have heard that in some places measures are found necessary to compel attendance on the schools, but in Fairview the children regarded the teacher as their kindest and

37

most patient friend, and the school as a pleasant place of retreat, where grumbling and complaints were never heard.

The. Meek sent so many children that the teacher never pretended to know the exact number. Sometimes there were eleven, and at other times only seven or eight, for the older ones seemed to take turns about, working one day and studying the next. I think The. Meek was about the only man in our country who was as good at home as he was at church, and his family of white-headed boys were laughers like him, and always contented and happy. They never learned anything, and my recollection is that they all studied out of one book while I went to school there, reciting in a class by themselves from the same page. If the teacher came upon them suddenly in their seats, and asked them to name the first letter of the alphabet, the chances were that one of them would know the answer, whereupon they all cried "A!" in a chorus. But if one of the number was called out separately a few moments later, and asked the same question, the round, chubby face would look up into the teacher's, and after meditating awhile (moving his lips during the time as if recalling the rules governing such a difficult problem) would honestly answer that he didn't know! He was then sent back to study, with the warning that he would be called out again presently, and asked to name not only the first letter, but the second, and third, and perhaps the fourth. Going back to his seat, the white-headed brothers gathered about him, and engaged in deep contemplation of their book for awhile, but one by one their eyes wandered away from it again, and they became the prey of anyone who had it in his heart to get them into difficulty by setting them to laughing. If they all mastered the first three [1] letters that day they were content, and were so pleased with their progress that they forgot them the next.

It was always safe to go to their house and expect a warm welcome, for there seemed enough love hid away somewhere in the big house in which they lived, not only for all the white-headed boys (with a reserve stock for those yet to come), but also for the friends who came to see them. Their mother, a large,

[1] first three: 1883 three first

fresh-looking woman, who was noted for a capacity to lead in prayers and blessings when her husband was away, was good-natured, too. It was the happiest family I had ever known, for though they were all beset with difficulties, every one of them having either weak eyes or the scald-head, they seemed not to mind it, but patiently applied sulphur for one and mullein tea for the other, remedies which were kept in saucers and bottles all over the house.

I never heard The. Meek or his wife speak impatiently to any of their children, but they were obedient for all that — much more so than those of us who were beaten on the slightest prov-ocation — and were very fond of one another. While other boys were anxious to get away from home, The. Meek's children were content, and believed there was not another so pleasant place in the world as the big house, built after the architecture of a packing-box, in which they lived. I often thought of this cir-cumstance to their credit, and thought it was also to the credit of the father and the mother. There were but three rooms in the house, two down stairs, and one above as large as both of those below, in which all the boys slept; and here also were the com-pany beds, so that had I ever heard of an asylum at the time of which I write, I should certainly have thought the big room with the nine or ten beds scattered about in it was like one.

I frequently went from school to spend the night with the young Meeks, and, after we had gone to bed in the big room up stairs, I either froze their blood with ghost stories, or con-vulsed them by telling any foolish event I happened to think of, at which they laughed until I feared for their lives. If the uproar became particularly loud their father and mother came up to see what it was all about, and, on being informed of the cause, laughed themselves, and went down again.

The two sons of the crippled but devout shoemaker, Mr. Winter, were the most remarkable scholars that attended the school, for the reason that they seemed to have mastered all sorts of depravity by sheer force of native genius; for though they possessed all the accomplishments of street Arabs, and we thought they must surely be town boys, the truth was that they were seldom allowed even to go to town, and therefore could not have contracted the vices of civilization from the contagion of evil society. When one of them did go [2] he returned with a knife for nearly every boy in the school, and cloves and cinnamon bark to last for weeks, which were stolen from the stores. If one of us longed for anything in their presence, they said it would be forthcoming immediately if we got them opportunity to go to town. This was only possible by inducing someone to allow them to drive a team, as their father was poor, and did not keep horses.

The older (and I may add the worse) one was probably named Hardy, but he was always known as Hard. Winter, because of his hard character; and his brother's evil reputation was so woven into his name that we never knew what the latter really was, for he was known as Beef Hide Winter, a rebuke, I believe, for his failure to get away with a hide he had once stolen, but the boys accepted these titles with great cheerfulness, and did not mind them. They were the mildest mannered villains, I have no doubt, that ever lived, for no difference how convincing the proof was against them, they still denied it with tears in their eyes, and were always trying to convince those around them by kindness and civility that they were not so bad as represented (though they were worse), and I fear they were rather popular in spite of their weakness for things not belonging to them. In course of time their petty peculations came to be regarded in about the same light as was their father's shouting — one of the peculiarities of the neighborhood — and we paid them no other attention than to watch them. At the Fourth of July celebrations in the woods, where all sorts of persons came to set up business, the Winter boys stole a little of everything they saw on exhibition, and generously divided with their friends. If they were sent together to a house near the school after water, one went through the cellar while the other went to the well, and if he secured anything he made a division at the first opportunity.

They always had their pockets full of things to give away, and I am satisfied that they came by none of them honestly, for they were very poor, and at home but seldom had enough even to eat. A habit of theirs was to throw stones with great

[2] did go: 1883 did get to go

40

accuracy, a collection of which they carried around in their pockets, ready for use, making long journeys to the creek bottoms to select them. They always went home with Guinea-hens or geese in their possession, which they said had been "given to them," but which they had really knocked over in the road near farmers' houses. They could kill more squirrels and quails by throwing than others of a similar age could by shooting, and it will be imagined that their failings were but seldom mentioned, for they were dangerous adversaries, though usually peaceable enough.

The teacher of this school at the time of which I now write — to be more explicit, when I was eleven years old, for what I have already written is a hurried retrospect covering a period of six years — was a very young and pretty girl named Agnes Deming, certainly not over sixteen and I doubt if that, who came from a neighborhood north of Fairview, where her widowed mother lived with an eccentric brother, and although it was as poor as ours, she spoke of it in such a way — not boastingly, but tenderly and reverently — that we thought of the community of Smoky Hill as a very superior one. Her father, of whom she talked a great deal, had been captain of a sailing vessel, as I learned a little at a time, and before his death they lived in a town by the sea, where his ship loaded. Of the town, however, which was called Bradford, she had but slight recollection, for when a very little girl she was sent away to school, and came home only at long intervals to welcome her father, who was often away a year at a time.

When ten years old, and after the ship had been absent a long time, she was sent for hurriedly one day, and told on her arrival that her father's ship had gone down at sea; that all on board were lost, and that they were going West to live with her uncle, an eccentric man whom she had never seen. After a few months of preparation, during which time their effects were converted into money, they commenced their journey to the country in which they had since lived. When she was fourteen years old her uncle found her a place to teach a summer school, and, giving satisfaction in spite of her tender years, she had followed the calling since, her second engagement being in our

41

neighborhood. I remember how generally it was said on her arrival that she would not do, as she was very young, but before the summer was over she somehow convinced her patrons that she would do, very well, as she was thoughtful and intelligent, and competent in every way.

This was her brief history, and before she had lived at Fairview a year, nobody was like Agnes Deming, for she was everybody's friend and adviser, and was kinder to the people than anyone had ever been before. She was a revelation to Fairview — a woman of a kind they had never before seen; one who uttered no complaints, but who listened patiently to the complaints of others, and did what she could to help them. Whoever was in distress received her sympathy and aid, and I think the advent of this friendless little woman, with her unselfish and pretty ways, did more good for Fairview than its religion, for the people tried to become like her, and were better in every way.

From the description she gave I imagined her father to have been a bluff and manly fellow, for I had heard that such followed the sea, and when I found her crying softly to herself, I thought of course she was thinking of him, and often regretted that he was not in Fairview to be proud of his pretty daughter, instead of at the bottom of the restless and angry sea. That they had been very fond of each other I felt sure; and when the winds blew furiously around our house, as they often did, she seemed greatly distressed, as though it was just such a storm as that in which her father's ship went down. She sang to us at night sometimes, in a sad, sweet voice, but always of storms, and of shipwrecks, as if the frightful manner of her father's death was much on her mind, and as if she sorrowed always because she could not hope that some day his ship would come in, and the dreadful story of his death prove a mistake.

She said almost nothing of her mother, and in reasoning about it I thought that perhaps Mrs. Deming was so much distressed over the death of her husband as to be poor company, and anxious to be let alone; for Agnes seemed glad when vacation was over, and she was again occupying her old room in our house. Although she was originally expected to divide her time equally with every family sending children to the school, or to "board round," she was oftener at our house than anywhere else; and once when she apologized in a burst of tears for being there so much, my mother kissed her tenderly, and it was arranged immediately, to the great satisfaction of all, that in future she should be a recognized member of our family. My mother was very fond of her, and so was my father, though he seemed ashamed to be fond of anyone; and being the most influential of the school directors, he saw that her pay was good and prompt, and on bad days took her to school in a wagon.

When Jo and I were busy on the farm, Agnes taught us at night, and was so patient and encouraged us so much that we learned more than we should have done at school. While we were never at school in summer, by this means we were the head scholars in winter, though I am not certain this was much to our credit, for we had little opposition from the children of Fairview.

I have never seen a bird-of-paradise, and have no knowledge of them, except that they are very beautiful; but if their manners are as graceful as their plumage is beautiful, and it is conceded that we of Fairview were as ungainly and ugly as crows, I hope the impression made by the coming of Agnes Deming to the settlement will be understood. I am glad to be able to write it to the credit of the people that they were not envious of her, unless it be envious in one person to strive to be like another he admires, and they all loved her from the day she came until the day she went away.

Although slight in figure she was the picture of health, of which she was as careful as of her dress and manners, which were never anything but mild and gentle. As man and boy I have honestly admired a great many women who afterwards shocked my admiration by a careless habit or manner when they did not know I was about; but Agnes Deming was always the same perfect woman. My admiration for her never had a check, and every day I found in her a new quality to respect, as did everyone who came in contact with her.

Although I was a favorite with her, I believed that when she came into the fortune and position she deserved — I was always expecting some such remarkable thing as this to happen, although

43

I was not certain just what it would be — I was sure she would not speak to me, or any of those she had known at Fairview with whom she had associated temporarily, and made herself agreeable, because that was her disposition; but that she would hurry away as soon as possible, to get rid of thoughts of how uncomfortable and unhappy she had been among us. I do not think I should have blamed her, for I regarded her superiority as such that I should have been content to see her go away to enjoy proud station and rich friends, thankful that she had lived with us at all, and made us happier than we had been.

I am certain that her dress was inexpensive, and that she spent little of her money in this way,[3] for most of it was sent to her family; but her taste and skill were such that she was always neatly and becomingly attired (much more so than many I knew who spent a great deal for that[4] time to attain that end); and she was able to work over an old garment on Saturday, and appear on Sunday the best-dressed woman in the country. I have thought that she was familiar with all the fashions in woman's dress without ever having seen them, for she was always in advance of the plates in the Lady's Book taken by my mother.

With more fortunate surroundings she would have been a remarkable woman. But while there were many others less good and pretty who were better off, and while she may have had at one time bright hopes for the future, her good sense taught her that there was really no reason why she should expect anything better now; so she diligently performed her work, and gave up castle-building. And so it came to pass that she was simply mistress of the Fairview school, and mistress of all our hearts, and did what good was possible without vain regret for that which might have come to pass, but did not.

In my recollections of that time, there is nothing pleasant, except the sweet and patient face of Agnes and the memory of Jo, who were always my friends, and who protected me when I did not deserve it, and loved me in spite of all my faults.

[3] in this way: 1883 *wanting*
[4] for that: 1883 of their

VI

DAMON BARKER

Barker's Mill, visits to which had convinced Jo that he should like to be a miller, was built on Bull River, in the centre of the only woods in all that country.

It was said of its proprietor that he came to the country a great many years before with a train of wagons drawn by oxen, on which was loaded the machinery of what afterwards became the mill, together with his general effects. Nobody seemed to know where he came from, but nobody seemed to care, strangely enough, for he was trusty as a miller, and honorable as a citizen. Occasionally he came to our neighborhood dressed in an odd-fashioned cut-away coat with brass buttons, and vest and pantaloons of an equally aristocratic pattern, but I never heard of his going to the country town. If he had money to pay there, or other important business, he entrusted it to someone to transact for him, preferring to have it half done rather than to go himself. From this circumstance I came to believe that Damon Barker had been an outlaw in his time, and was anxious to avoid people, although he was very well-bred, and the only polished man I had ever known.

He came to our house originally, I believe, on some sort of business, and, becoming acquainted, happened in at long intervals afterwards, but I never knew that he went anywhere else. We all admired him, for he was a man to make himself welcome anywhere, and he sat quietly among us when he came (which was always at night, as though for private reasons he did not walk out during the day), and listened to what was being said. My father had the greatest respect for him, and was often uneasy under his steady gaze, as if he felt that Damon Barker was not a Fairview man, and had knowledge and opinions of his own.

They frequently discussed all sorts of questions (or rather my father discussed them in Barker's presence, who only made short answers indicating that he was familiar with the subject in hand), and I was forced to the belief that, had he seen fit, he could have readily torn to pieces many of the arguments advanced. His knowledge of religious topics was extensive, but he patronized the subject as he would patronize a child, dismissing it with a polite word as though it was of no consequence; and we wondered that a man who understood the subject so well could be indifferent, for it was well known that he was not religious. My father often threatened to "speak" to him about it, but he never did, either fearing that Barker might be able to defend his position, or respecting his disposition to avoid the subject.

Although he was courteous and well-bred, lifting his hat and bowing to my mother in the most courtly manner when he came and went, it was never remarked to his discredit, although a man of his manners had never been seen by us before. Had he been the least awkward in his politeness, I am sure we should have laughed at him, and regarded him as a fop, for we watched him narrowly; but his adieus and greetings were so appropriate, natural, and easy, that we received them as a matter of course, and accepted them as evidences not merely of different but of better breeding than we were accustomed to. During one of his visits to the house he invited Jo and me to the mill, asking it as a favor, and thus it came about that occasionally we went to see him on Saturday afternoons, returning the next day. Indeed, we were rather encouraged to go to Barker's, my father believing that familiarity with such a courtly gentleman would do us no harm, if no good, and he was not greatly displeased if we did not return until late Sunday evening, although he always inquired what we found so entertaining at his house, and on our replying, he found no objection to it.

The house in which Barker lived was built close to the mill, in a dense growth of trees, but as if the shadow of these was not sufficient to hide him, he had planted other trees among them, until the place was so dark that the sunlight seldom found its way in at his windows. The house was very large and strong, with doors of heavy hardwood, and I thought that if Barker should be attacked, he would make a long defence, for he always had provisions and fuel stored away in great quantities, and there was a well in the cellar which I always disliked to drink out of, fearing there might be dead men in it. There were thick wooden blinds at all the windows, which were usually closed, and heavy iron bars across the doors, and altogether the place was so mysterious and unusual that it occurred to me when I first went there that if either Jo or I should discover some of its secrets by accident, we should be cut into halves, and thrown down the well for fear we should disclose what we had seen.

In his own room, a large apartment occupying the greater part of the second story, were strange and curious things we had never seen before; and these we were free to examine and question him about. Besides brass pistols hid away in every box and drawer, there were swords and knives of odd pattern, and handsome dresses for women and men, many of them ornamented with gold lace, and all of a style we had never seen worn.

In a place for plunder which adjoined his room were kept half a dozen large chests, and in looking through them, when he gave me permission, I half expected to find bones of dead men; but I found nothing except strange instruments, scientific apparatus, maps, drawings I had no knowledge of, curiosities gathered during a long life, and the odd clothing I have mentioned. If I found something more curious than the rest, I took it to him as he sat grave and silent in his own room, and he told me its history, what use it could be put to, and where it came from. There were a great many books, the titles of which I could not pronounce with all my learning, and these gave evidence of being often used, for they were collected on a turning shelf within easy reach of the table at which he usually sat.

If we found a curious stone or leaf, he could tell its nature and kind, and if we asked of something we read in his books, he told us about it in a quiet, simple way, making it quite easy of comprehension. Knowing our ignorance, he took pains to answer the questions with which we plied him, and we often sat on either side of him until far into the night, listening to his explanations of matters we were curious about, sometimes going to sleep in our chairs.

Before he knew Jo and me he had no friends — he told me this himself early in our acquaintance — but we amused him, and he became our companion in everything we did while at the house or mill, instructing and benefiting us in a hundred ways. When I say he became our companion in everything we did, I mean no more than that he was always with us, looking on good-naturedly when we played the games at cards he taught us, accompanying us when we walked through the woods or rowed on [1] the river, and giving suggestions and help in everything. He said but little at any time, except in answer to our questions, and I think his principal enjoyment in our companionship was to listen quietly to what we had stored up to tell him on our different visits.

He was regarded as hard and exacting by those with whom he had business dealings — he dealt in nothing else — but was always kind and liberal with Jo and me, giving us money frequently, and presents when he could get them. If we were in the mill with him, the entrance of a customer would harden his features until we were afraid of him, and we went away until the customer had gone when he soon became himself again, so that we grew to be afraid of him except when we were alone.

In Barker's room was a great box-stove in which we made wonderful fires in winter, and the fire in it seemed never to go out; so that I have thought in summer that, if the ashes were stirred, live coals could be found at the bottom. Around this we always sat with him during the winter nights (and we had opportunity to visit him oftener in winter than at any other time, for during that season we had the least to do), and did whatever Barker thought would best amuse us. Sometimes he gave us suppers, prepared by his own hands from cans and bottles stored away in other chests we had not yet examined; at other times he told us the story of one of the brass pistols, or of the strange wearing-apparel we had seen, holding the article in his hand to illustrate; or if we found something belonging to a ship, he told

[1] on: 1883 in

48

us of the sea, of storms, of strange countries, and of wrecks.

In all the stories of robbers and pirates that he told us — and there were many of that kind because we preferred them — I always thought of him as one of the participants, and was pleased when the one I had picked out for Barker freed the captive maiden, flinging back his companions who would murder her, with the declaration that he would have their lives if they persisted, thereupon conducting her within sight of her home, and, having first bidden her a gallant adieu, galloped away. These recitals had much of dashing romance in them, and his robberies were committed generally from motives of daring rather than gain. It was always the mean and stingy misers who were robbed, and if a beautiful maiden was captured at sea she was always taken to her friends, unless she freely consented to marry the pirate captain, which was sometimes the case.

This kind of amusement he kept up at night until we became sleepy, and, lighting us to the room in which we were to sleep, he sat down on the bed if we desired it, and continued the story until we were asleep, when he returned to his own apartment. It seemed to me he dreaded the hour when we would go to sleep and leave him alone; and once when I awoke in the middle of the night, and crept to his door, I found him sitting over the table with his hat and coat on, as if ready to run away.

Barker's widowed sister, the Mrs. Tremaine already mentioned, whose husband had been a drunkard and a doctor, was his housekeeper (when she was at home, which was seldom the case). I believe she was originally called Betts, or Bett, but this was shortened to B., and by this name she was generally known. It was understood that Dr. Tremaine had been unkind to her before his death, and that their married life had been very miserable, though I never heard either Barker or herself say so. But such was generally thought to be the case nevertheless, for certainly the excellent woman had had trouble. It was also understood that he died in drink, probably from catching fire on the inside, and that with his last breath he referred to his wife as a snake, and to his neighbors as devils. This impression, like the other one with reference to his disposition, had no foundation

I ever heard of except that his relict worried a great deal about people who were going to ruin from drink. We supposed, of course, that she was prompted to this by the memory of her late husband, as she was prompted to insist on everybody's being religious by the wickedness of her brother, the miller. Having no other place to go after her husband's death, she determined to move West and live with her brother, and had arrived at Fairview a few years before [2] we did. Although there was not a drunkard in the county, she immediately began a war on rum, and when I first encountered the words "Delirium Tremens," in connection with drunkenness, I remember thinking I was acqainted with his widow.

Next to her desire to save everybody from drunkenness, she wanted to save everybody from sin, and spent most of her time in discussing these two questions; but she had little opposition, for everybody in that country was religious as well as temperate. When she became acquainted with the Rev. John Westlock she at once hailed him as a man raised up to do a great work, and was always with him in the meetings he held in different places, nothing being thought of it if he took her with him and brought her back again.

Together they established a lodge of Good Templars at Fairview, although the people were all sober and temperate, and once a week they met to call upon the fallen brother to shun the cup, and to redeem the country from debauchery and vice. Barker said they spent one-half the evening in "opening" and the other half in "closing." He also said once that his sister was very much offended that my father preached without pay, for she would have enjoyed making fancy work, to the neglect of her brother's house, to sell at fairs to pay the minister's salary, and that she was a brilliant woman at festivals. Barker often criticised her, half in jest and half in earnest, and once when Jo and I were at his house for dinner, and something had been lost, he remarked that if B. were as familiar with her home as she was familiar with the number of gallons of liquor consumed

[2] before: 1883 after. *The 1884 correction is in conformity with the facts about Mrs. Tremaine given in chap. iv.*

50

annually, or with the Acts of the Apostles, things would be more
comfortable. I think he disliked her because she paid so much
attention to other people's faults and so little to her own; but
he treated her courteously, although he appeared to avoid her,
and they were not much together. B. frequently left home for
days at a time, compelling her patient brother to prepare his own
meals or do without, but he never complained unless she chose
to construe half-jesting, half-earnest raillery into complaint. At
such times she had a way of replying to his light words with a
seriousness that I thought disgusted him, and made him resolve
never to mention the matter again.

That she was a miserable housekeeper I had frequent occasion
to know, and Barker's house always seemed like a bachelor's
home, as there was nothing about it to indicate that a woman
lived there. Jo used to say of Mrs. Tremaine that she talked as
the women write who furnish recipes to the newspapers; and
when she came to our house the room in which she sat seemed
damp for several days thereafter. Once after she had slept there,
and I was put into the bed she had occupied a night or two afterward, I amused my mother by asking her to change the sheets,
as they seemed like ice and would not thaw out, and the good
humor with which she did this convinced me that she did not like
B. very well herself. Her face was large and round and of a
waxen color, and though it was said by some that she was handsome I never thought so; nor did I admire her dress, which was
very rich and expensive, though exceedingly plain. Her teeth
were very white, and quite prominent, because she always wore
what was intended to be an enchanting smile, and when she
kissed me (which she usually did in the earlier days of our acquaintance, as a compliment to a child) I thought she must have
just finished washing her face, her lips were so cold and damp.
Her hair being very dark, and her face very pale, I thought she
resembled a well-dressed and affable corpse risen from the dead,
whose business it was to go among the people and warn them
that unless they repented of their sins they would very much
regret it after death.

51

VII

A NEW DISPENSATION

IN spite of the discontent which prevailed there, Fairview
progressed with the years of its history. The hard work of
the people paid, and they gradually became well-to-do, although
they seemed surprised that they were not in the poor-house, an
event they were always promising their families.

The old houses in which they had at first lived were replaced
with new ones, the new ones were furnished better than the old
ones had been, and there was a general prosperity which surprised
them, for they had not expected it so soon, if at all. New people
came to settle in spite of the fact that they were neither invited
nor expected, and many of those who came first had money ahead,
and were regarded by those who came later as of a very old and
aristocratic stock. Strangest of all, it was announced that a new
minister had been engaged, and that he would arrive with his
family, consisting of a wife and one child, in a few days. My
father made the announcement at the close of his preaching
one spring morning. He had preached to them, he said, because
they were too poor to pay a better man; the Lord had prospered
them, and he cheerfully made way for a successor who had
not only religious enthusiasm, but extensive learning as well. He
would continue to exhort his brethren whenever occasion seemed
to require, and aid in doing the work of the Master, but he
believed the good of the church demanded the arrangement
he had made.

There was unusual feeling in his words as he reviewed the
hard struggle of the settlement, and when he had finished, The.
Meek, though apparently in greater convulsions of laughter than
ever, managed to say a few kind words for their pastor, guide,
and friend, and two or three of the other men followed in a

similar strain. The women began to cry softly, as though the occasion were a funeral, and one by one the people went forward to shake him by the hand, which I thought surprised him, not being certain but that they were glad to get rid of him, while Brother Winter wheeled vigorously about, calling upon everybody to praise the Lord. It was a very unusual occasion, and those who had lounged outside to read the inscriptions on the head-boards in the grave lot came back again to see what it was all about, and heard the news with surprise and astonishment. Finally, the miller's sister prayed for everybody, but in a voice so low that nobody knew it, after which the meeting broke up, and the congregation gathered in little knots in the church and in the yard to talk of the new minister.

Great curiosity was everywhere expressed, and the curious naturally came to my father for information. He knew nothing except that the new minister had been transferred from an Eastern State at his own request; that his name was the Rev. Goode Shepherd, and that he would be there for the next service a week from that day; that a house had been secured for him in the eastern part of the settlement, and that as he was a minister, he was, of course, a good man, and without question of use to the church, else the Lord would not permit him to preach. This was all he knew, or all he cared to tell, and the people went home to wonder and to talk about it.

❋   ❋   ❋

Rev. Goode Shepherd came West, I am of the opinion, because the East was crowded with good men, and because he had heard there was a scarcity of such in our direction. Although he had some vague ideas on the subject of growing up with the country, he probably consented to come because somebody recommended it, and not because he was exactly clear himself how the move was to be of benefit.

Had someone in whose judgment he had equal confidence suggested after his arrival that he had better go back again, I have no doubt that he would have become convinced finally that the Lord had said it, instead of a friend, and quietly returned to the place from which he had come; for he was always uncertain whether his convictions were the result of inspiration, or whether they were the result of the gossip he had heard.

I had remarked of my father's religion that it was a yoke that did not fit him, and which was uncomfortable to wear; but the Rev. Goode Shepherd's religion was his vocation and pleasure, and he believed in it with all the strength of which he was capable. That he was poor was evidence to him that he was accepted of the Master who had sent him, rather than that his life had been a failure; and the work expected of him he performed cheerfully and with enthusiasm. He had no desire to do anything which was not religious; and the higher walks of his profession, and heaven finally as his reward, were all he desired or expected. There was abundant scope in theology for his ambition, and, far from craving an active business life, he rather chose his profession because it offered excuse for knowing so little about the affairs of men.

I have thought that because he took pleasure in his religion, and loved it, was one reason why it was not so hard and unforgiving as my father's, for on this question there was nothing in common between them except that both believed that there is a heaven, and that it is desirable to be saved. The Rev. Goode Shepherd believed that learning and luxury could go hand in hand with religion; my father, that luxury was an invention of the Devil to make men forget, and that learning could be trusted to only a very few, because, unless coupled with the most pronounced piety, it was very dangerous. The Rev. Goode Shepherd believed that a religious life was most easily lived, and that a merciful Providence had ordered it that way because the children of men are weak; my father, that the easy road to travel was the broad one which led to torment, and that the other was narrow and difficult, but ending very pleasantly as a recompense for travelling it, and that it was ordered that way so that only the brave and deserving should win the prize, ridding the righteous of the weak and the undeserving by burning them up. The Rev. Goode Shepherd believed that while walking the golden streets of the heavenly city he would meet many of the friends he had worried about, saved by love infinitely greater than he expected; my father, that he would miss many faces in Paradise he had half expected to see, but who had fallen exhausted by the wayside and given up the struggle.

The new dispensation did much for Fairview, and its advancement after the coming of Mr. Shepherd was certainly more rapid than it had ever been before.

I never knew, but it seems probable to me now, that Mr. Shepherd was educated for the ministry because he was quiet and religious as a boy, and had always led a blameless and exemplary life. I think his expenses at school were paid by relatives none too well off themselves, and that he went directly from college to the pulpit. I don't know what made me think it, but I always believed a widowed mother — aided, perhaps, by an older sister or two engaged in teaching — had provided for his education by the closest economy; that he had always intended to become famous to repay them for their kindness, but finding it a harder task than he had imagined, that he had, in later life, settled down to the conviction that to be good is better than to be great.

When his tall form and pale face appeared above the pulpit at Fairview for the first time, the impression was general among the people that he was older than they expected. The one child he had written he was possessed of turned out to be a pretty girl of nineteen or twenty, who attracted a great deal of attention as she came in with her mother and sat down near the pulpit. Both sat throughout the service without looking around, perhaps because they thought it was not likely they would see much if they should commit that impropriety. His first preaching impressed everyone favorably, though his side whiskers were against him, as was also the tall hat standing on the pulpit beside him. His presence, however, chilled the usual experience meeting following, for only the men talked, and it was short and dull. The. Meek's laugh was not heard at all, and Brother Winter sat quietly in his corner, as though undecided whether, under the circumstances, he would be warranted in pushing to the front. The miller's sister had nothing to say either, spending her time in watching the minister's wife and daughter, who did not recognize the impertinence, and altogether the occasion was not what was expected.

When the meeting was dismissed, my father stepped forward to welcome Mr. Shepherd to Fairview. After him came The. Meek, and so, one by one, the people advanced to be introduced, and, after awkwardly shaking him by the hand, retired again. Mr. Shepherd led my father back to where his respectable wife and pretty daughter were, and performed the ceremony of introduction, and I imagined as my father looked at them that he thought they were birds of too fine plumage for that clime, and would soon fly away again. The. Meek stood immediately behind him, and was next presented, and then came all the congregation in the order of their importance, except the younger ones, who stood near the door looking on, and who crowded out hurriedly when Mr. Shepherd came toward them, followed by his wife and daughter. Although they desired acquaintance with the new minister and his family above all other things, they were so awkward and uncertain in their politeness that they hoped the new minister would somehow gradually become acquainted with them without an introduction, and never discover that they did not know how to be comfortable in the presence of strangers. Jo Erring was among the number of the intimidated, and I thought he was anxious that the new people should not see him until he had gone home and smartened himself up, as if they were of more importance than he had expected, for he kept himself behind the others. Jo had a habit of appearing on Sunday in his every-day attire — because everybody else wore their best on that day, it was said — and this was one of the days he violated the custom of the country, probably for the reason that the occasion was an extraordinary one.

It was my father's custom to invite the ministers who came to Fairview to spend the day at our house, that they might be convenient for the evening service; and although he hesitated a long while in this case, as if afraid the accommodations he could offer were not good enough, he hurriedly consulted with my mother at the last moment, and walked out to the gate, when they were preparing to start for home. I could not hear from where I stood what was said, but I believed the invitation had been given and accepted, and when he began to look around the yard, I was so certain that I was wanted to drive them home that I put myself in his way, as the wagon road led through lanes and gates, and could not be easily described. My mother had already hurried home by the path through the field, that she might be there to meet them. When I went up to the wagon in response to my father's beckon, he lifted me into the seat beside Mr. Shepherd, his wife and daughter occupying the back one, and said I would show the way and open the gates.

As we drove off I felt that the bright eyes of the girl were devouring my plain coat, for she sat directly behind me, and I regretted I had not thought to ask Jo to trim my hair that morning. The grease on my rough boots contrasted sharply with the polish of Mr. Shepherd's patent leathers, and my great red hands were larger than his, which were very white, and shaped like a woman's. I soon saw he was a poor driver, and asked him to give me the reins, which he willingly did, with a good-natured apology for his incapacity, pleading lack of experience in that direction.

I knew they wanted to talk of Fairview and its people, but were shy of me, so I pretended to be busy in looking after the horses, but they said nothing except that there was a great number present, which was true, as the house was full. I pointed out the houses as we went along, and tried to be entertaining.

"Old Lee lives there," I said, as we passed the house of the renter on our farm. "He wasn't at church to-day; he has probably gone over to the turkey roost in Bill's Creek bottom."

I had said it to shock them, but they laughed very gayly over it, and the girl — I had heard them call her Mateel — said she presumed that wild turkeys were plentiful. I had secretly been longing to look at her, so I turned partly around, and replied that the woods were full of them. She was a very pretty girl, dressed more expensively than I had ever seen Agnes dressed, but not with so much taste. She was rather pale, too, and I could not help thinking that her health was not very good.

"There're deer here, too," I said to them, finding that the subject promised to be amusing.

Mr. Shepherd and the girl looked very much interested, but

57

the minister's wife was so stately ănd dignified that I felt sure I could never be comfortable in her presence.

"One came running through our field once when Jo and I were ploughing," I continued. "The folks were away at camp-meeting, and Jo took the gun and went after it. I heard him shoot after a long while, and then he came back, and said it was too heavy for him to carry home, but that if I would finish the land on which we were ploughing, while he rested, we would hitch to the wagon and go after it. I felt so pleased about it that I finished the work, and when I was through, he looked at the sun, and said we might as well eat supper before starting, and that I had better take the harness off the horses while they were feeding, as they would be more comfortable. At supper he asked me if under the circumstances I didn't feel it a duty to give him my pie, which I did, and after he had eaten it, he took me to one side, and said that though he was ashamed of it himself, he was compelled to confess that he had missed."

This amused them more than ever, and the girl asked who Jo was. This reminded me that I had neglected my friend, and I immediately gave a short and glowing history of him, not failing to mention that he knew of more turkey roosts than old Lee, and that we would visit one of them soon, and return by their house with a fat turkey. They thanked me, and Mr. Shepherd even said he would like to go with us, whereupon I explained the process of killing them on moonlight nights, which was by getting them between your gun and the moon, where they could be easily seen.

I should no doubt have told them other things equally ridiculous, but by this time we had reached the gates, and soon thereafter we stopped at the house, where my father came out and took them in. When Jo appeared to help me with the horses, I found that he was smartly dressed, and rightly concluded that he had hurried home to change after seeing the family at the church.

While we were at the stables he asked me a great many questions about the girl, and I pleased him by saying that I had talked so much about him on the way over that she had asked me who he was, and that I had replied he was my uncle, and the principal young man in Fairview.

"What did she say then?" he asked eagerly.

"That she desired to make your acquaintance, and that she was certain she had picked you out in church."

It was a dreadful lie, but I did not regret it, seeing how well he was pleased.

"Then what did you say?" he asked.

I was not certain what would please him most, so I replied that the conversation then became general, and that Mr. Shepherd had said he would go with us some night to the turkey roost in Bill's Creek bottom.

When we returned to the house, the three were sitting alone in the best room, looking idly at the books scattered about, and the few ornaments my mother had found time to prepare. As I sat down on the sill of the open door with a view of being handy in case I was wanted, I regretted that Agnes was not there to entertain them, for she had gone home a few weeks before, and I was certain they would have been surprised to find such a bright girl in that dull country.

"Ha!" Mr. Shepherd said, when he saw me, "The young man that drove us over. I suppose you know a great deal about horses?"

I thought he made the last remark as an apology that he had not attended to his team himself, so I replied that I knew something about them, but I was sorry he had chosen that subject, as it was not likely to interest his daughter, whom I was anxious to talk with.

"I am sorry to say I know very little about horses," he said, "but I intend to learn. I bought mine at the station where we left the railroad. What do you think of them?"

With a view of bringing Jo into the conversation again, I said I would go and ask his opinion, as he was a very good judge. I returned presently, and said Jo thought they would do very well. As if remembering Jo as a very amusing person I had been telling them about, he said: —

"Bring the young man in. I should like to talk with him."

59

I went out after Jo, but did not go far, as he had slipped up near the door, which stood open, to listen to what was being said. He was very red in the face, but followed me in.

"This is your uncle Jo, is it?" Mr. Shepherd inquired, after I had sat down again, leaving Jo standing awkwardly in the middle of the room.

"Yes, sir," I answered, having a vague notion I ought to introduce them, but not knowing how to go about it. "My uncle Jo Erring. He lives here."

Mr. Shepherd advanced toward him pleasantly, and I thought he reached him just in time to keep him from falling down with fright.

"I am very glad to know you, Mr. Erring," he said, in his easy way, taking him by the hand. "This is my wife, and this my daughter," pointing to one, and then to the other, while shaking his hand. "I have no doubt we shall become famous friends."

Jo raised his eyes to recognize the introduction, and he said to me afterwards that he was just getting ready to bolt out of the room, and run away, when somehow they made it pleasant for him to stay.

My uncle was a very intelligent fellow, and he soon became quite entertaining, giving them accounts of the country and the people which were no doubt very droll, for when I went out presently I heard them laughing merrily at what he said. At dinner Mr. Shepherd observed that since becoming acquainted with Mr. Erring he felt like an old citizen, whereupon my father looked up hurriedly and was about to ask who that was, when he suddenly remembered, and muttered, "Oh! you mean Jo."

It was sometimes the case that when there was company Jo and I were compelled to wait at dinner, but I was glad that on this day Jo was seated next Mateel, and did not suffer the humiliation. A sort of rude politeness was natural to him, and on this occasion he displayed it to such advantage that I glowed with pride. While the others were talking of graver matters he gave an account of the Fairview revivals, which amused Mateel so much that she asked to be excused for laughing. I had never seen two persons get along better together, and I felt certain that she would regard him as a very intelligent young man, which pleased me, for nobody else seemed to do him justice, and they all tried to humiliate and disgrace him whenever it was possible.

It was a very good dinner to which we sat down, and the Shepherds complimented it so gracefully that my mother was greatly pleased; indeed, they found it convenient to make themselves agreeable to all of us, so that the afternoon was passed very pleasantly, more so than any other Sunday afternoon ever passed in that house; for my father seemed to think that if Mr. Shepherd, with all his learning, could afford to throw aside his Sunday gloom, he would risk it. I had never seen him in so good a humor before, but I knew he would make up for it the next day; for whenever he was good-natured he was always particularly gloomy for a long time after it, as though he had committed an indiscretion of which he was ashamed.

Before night it had been arranged that Jo should drive the Shepherds home after the service, as it would be very dark, tying a horse behind the wagon on which to ride back; and it followed that he drove them to the church. When we arrived there the building was crowded to its utmost capacity; the new minister was a success.

VIII

THE SMOKY HILL SECRET

IT having been decided to begin the summer school a few weeks earlier than at first intended, it became necessary for me to go after the teacher; so it was arranged that I should drive over to Smoky Hill on Friday, and return anytime the following day.

My mother shared the feeling that the neighborhood where Agnes lived was superior to ours — although none of us knew why we had this impression — and after taking unusual pains with my toilet, she asked Jo to cut my hair, which he kindly did just before I drove away in the wagon, from the high seat of which my short legs barely touched the floor.

I knew nothing of the settlement except the direction, which was north, and that the uncle with whom Agnes lived was named Biggs, but they said I could easily inquire the way. The distance was twenty miles, and by repeated inquiries I found that Mr. Biggs — who was called Little Biggs by those living near him — lived in the first white house after crossing the north fork of Bull River, and when I came in sight of the place I knew it as well as if I had lived within hailing distance all my life. It was just such a place as I expected to find; an aristocratic porch on two sides of a house evidently built after the plans of an architect — the first house of such pretensions I had ever seen — with a gravel walk leading down to the gate, and a wide and neglected yard in front. A broken and dismantled wind-mill stood in the barn-yard, and around it was piled a great collection of farm machinery in an equally advanced stage of decay, all rotting away for lack of care and use. There was a general air of neglect everywhere, and I thought Mr. Biggs was an indifferent farmer, or else an invalid. Boards were off the fences, and gates off the hinges, and pigs roamed in every place where they did not belong.

A herd of them, attracted by the sound of my wheels, dashed out from under the porch, and went snorting into the vegetable garden through a broken fence. I noticed these things as I stopped at a large gate intended for wagons to drive through, and while wondering whether I had better drive in there, or tie the team and walk up to the house. While debating the question I saw that a large, boyish-looking young man was pitching hay near the barn, and, noticing that he had stopped work and was looking at me,[1] I motioned for him to come out. Impatiently throwing down his fork, he came out to the fence, and, resting his chin on the top board, he looked at me with great impudence.

"Does Mr. Biggs live here?" I civilly inquired.

"Yes, Mr. Biggs lives here," he answered, drawling the first word as if to express disgust.

"Well, then," I said, "if you will open the gate I'll come in."

He threw it open with a bang, as if to express an unfavorable opinion of me, and I drove through, and stopped down by the stables. He followed sullenly, after banging the gate again,[2] and, picking up his fork without looking at me, went on with his pitching. I began to feel uncomfortable at this cool reception, and inquired quite respectfully: —

"Is Mr. Biggs at home?"

"No," the fellow replied, "he's not at home," plunging his fork viciously into the hay as though he were wishing I was under it.

"Is Miss Agnes at home, then?"

"Yes, Miss Agnes is at home." He looked up in better humor, as though the name of Agnes was not so disagreeable as that of Biggs.

"Well, I'm told to stay here to-night, and take Agnes to her school to-morrow. If you'll show me where to stand the horses I'll put them away."

He laid down his fork at this and went to look through the stables. There seemed to be a spring somewhere near, for the stalls were oozy and wet, and unfit for use, and the fellow was debating in his mind which was the worst or the best one, I

[1] barn . . . me,: 1883 barn, and that . . . me.
[2] again: 1883 shut

could not tell which. Finally he found a place, but the feed boxes were gone; and then another, but it had no place for the hay. I was following him around by this time, and said the last one would do very well, as it was the best one there.

He helped me to unhitch the horses, and while we were about it I looked up at the house and saw Agnes at one of the windows. She went away immediately, however, and I supposed she would be down to welcome me; but she didn't come, and I began to feel very uncomfortable. I had consoled myself for the rudeness of the young man by the thought that he would be very much ashamed of his incivility when Agnes came running down to meet me; but she didn't come, and kept away from the window, and I was uncertain whether I had better return home or seek shelter for the night at another house.

I noticed in the meantime that the fellow helping me was a giant in stature, and that he had a very little head, on which was perched a hat evidently bought for one of the children. The band and shape being gone, it looked very much like an inverted V.

"I suppose you are the preacher's boy?" he said, after eying me a long while, as though that was a very good reason why he should dislike me.

On my replying that such was the case, he looked at me as if thinking I was larger or smaller than he had imagined, and continued apparently in better humor: —

"I have heard of you. I live here. I'm the hired man. My name is Big Adam; lazy Adam, *she* calls me."

I had heard that little eyes denoted cunning, and little ears great curiosity, and Big Adam's were so particularly small that I determined to be very wary of him during my stay.

"She owns the farm, though Biggs pretends to own it," Big Adam went on, "but, while they do not agree in this, they agree that Big Adam hasn't enough to do, and is very lazy, and between them I have a great deal of trouble. I do all the work that is done here, and though you may think from looking around that I am not kept very busy, I am. There are four hundred acres here, and they expect me to keep it in a high state of cultivation. You see how well I succeed; it's the worst-looking place on earth."

I began to understand him better, and said it looked very well when I drove up.

"Maybe it does — from the road, but I haven't been out there for a year to see. I am kept too busy. But if you stay here long I'll take you out into the field, and show you weeds higher than your head. Instead of spending the money to mend the stables and fences, they buy more land with it, to give Big Adam something to do; for they are always saying that I am fat from idleness. I am fat, but not from idleness. I haven't had time this spring to comb my hair. Look at it."

He took off the Λ-shaped hat, and held his head down for me to see. It reminded me of the brush heaps in which we found rabbits at home, and I wished Jo had come along; he would have been delighted to shingle it.

"But you go into the house," he said, putting on his hat again, and, taking up the fork he had laid down to hunt a stall for my horses: "you'll hear enough of lazy Adam in there. They'll tell you I'm lazy and shiftless, because I can't do the work of a dozen men; and they'll tell you I am surly, because I can't cheerfully go ahead and do all they ask me to. A fine opinion of Big Adam you'll have when you go away; but I ask you to notice while you are here if Big Adam is not always at work; and Agnes will tell you — she is the only one among them who pretends to tell the truth — that she has never seen me idle. But go on into the house; I am not allowed to talk to strangers."

Accepting this suggestion, I went through a gate which was torn off its hinges and lying flat in the path, and, walking up the steps, I knocked timidly at the front door. While waiting for someone to answer my rap, I noticed a door-plate hanging on one screw, and, careening my head around, read "Lytle Biggs." I then understood why his neighbors called him Little Biggs — it was his name.

I hadn't time to congratulate myself on this discovery, for just then the door-plate flew in, and Agnes stood before me. Although she was friendly to me as usual there was a constraint in her manner that I could not understand, and as she led the way in she looked as though she was expecting the house to blow up.

65

"My uncle is away," she said, confusedly, after we were seated in a room opening off from the hall where I had entered, "but we expect him home to-night. My mother is not well, and demands a great deal of care, or I should have come down to the gate to meet you when you drove up."

She was so ill at ease that I hurried to explain my errand, and I thought she was greatly relieved to know I had not come on a visit.

"I shall be ready in the morning at any time you are," she said; and I wondered she could leave her mother, for I had been fearing that perhaps I should have to go back without her.

There was a great romp and noise in the room above the one in which we sat, and she looked out through the door leading into the hall as if half expecting to see somebody come tumbling down the stairs.

"My uncle's children," she said, seeing I wondered at the noise. "He has eight."

I wondered she had not told of them before, and then I remembered that she seldom talked of her uncle's family or of her mother.

"How are they all?" I inquired, thinking I must say something.

There was a great crash in the room overhead and a cry of pain, and Agnes went quickly to the door to listen. Being convinced that one of them had fallen [3] over a chair, she came back, and replied to my question.

"Very noisy," she said, half laughingly. "I fear they will annoy you; it is so quiet at your house, and there is so much confusion here."

I said, "Oh! not at all," not knowing what other reply to make.

"My uncle Lytle" — I pricked up my ears at this, as her pronunciation of her uncle's name was different from that given it by his neighbors — "my uncle Lytle is trying to bring them up in town fashion here in the country, and they are seldom allowed to go out of doors, so that they can't be blamed for being rude and bad. All of them except the baby would be out at the stables with Big Adam if they were given the opportunity, but their father's

[3] had fallen: 1883 had only fallen

orders are to keep them away from the stables, and in the house. So we make the best of them."

Just then they all came tearing out into the hall above to the stair rail, and I knew they were peeping over; but someone came out hurriedly after them, and, driving them all back into the room again, shut the door with a bang.

"They are anxious to see you," Agnes said, smiling. "They have the greatest curiosity imaginable. There will be no peace until they are allowed to look at you."

Feeling that I was an intruder in the house, for some reason, I suggested that she let them come down, promising I would amuse them as best I could. She thought a moment, and then, excusing herself, went out. After a long time I heard her coming back with them. Six of them rushed into the room ahead of her, and, taking up a position behind the chairs, looked at me curiously. The other two she carried in her arms, one of them being an infant not more than four or five months old.

They seemed a queer lot to me, their clothing being of a pattern I had never seen before, and I noticed that the boys wore their hair in long curls, and that their frocks were braided. All of their faces were pale, which did not result solely from their being lately washed, and the older boys were dressed in short trousers, and wore shoes, though it was summer, a peculiarity which attracted my attention particularly, because most of the boys I had known went barefooted. Agnes placed the baby on my knee, and I soon had all the children about me, asking questions and going through my pockets. Indeed, I succeeded very well in amusing them. While they were playing around, I heard someone come down the stairs, and go down the hall to a door which I judged led into the kitchen. Presently Agnes went out too, and I supposed they were making arrangements for supper, which thought was probably suggested by the fact that it was late, and that I was very hungry. The children amused themselves with me for a considerable time, and were more noisy than ever, when unfortunately one of them fell headlong over a chair and set up a most terrible cry. Immediately a little dried-up old woman came hurrying into the room, who, picking up the screaming one, and roughly taking the

baby out of my arms, drove them all up the stairs before her, slap-
ping and banging them as they went, so that they were all screaming by the time the door up stairs closed upon them.

While she was collecting them I saw that the newcomer's hair
was twisted behind her head in a tight little knot, and that she
was very slender, and very short; that her features were small and
sharp, and dried-up like a mummy's, and that, altogether, she was
the most repulsive-looking creature I had ever seen. I half expected that she would give me a rap as she went out, she looked
so sour and ugly. I supposed she was a servant; possibly Adam's
mother, and when Agnes came in, which she did a moment after,
looking very much frightened, I had it in my mind to say that the
old woman of the sky had swept the children away with a broomstick.

"I was afraid they would annoy you," she said hurriedly, as
though it was necessary to say something before I could remark
on the queer little old woman who had driven them away.

I was about to reply that we were getting along very well until
one of them fell down, when she continued: — "My uncle has just
driven up. He is coming in."

At that moment the door opened softly, and a very small and
handsomely dressed man stepped into the room. He spoke to
Agnes pleasantly, and as he looked inquiringly at me, she explained: —

"One of my pupils from Fairview, Ned Westlock. I shall go
home with him to-morrow, as the school opens a week earlier than
was expected."

I knew now why his neighbors called him Little Biggs — because he was very short, and very thin, and very little.

"Ah! Ned Westlock."

After he had said this, he looked at me very attentively while he
removed his gloves. Placing them in his tall hat, he set both away,
and came back to me.

"I am very glad to know you," Mr. Biggs said. "I am glad to
have you a guest at our house."

This was encouraging, as nobody else had said as much, and I
felt better.

"I need not apologize," he said, "for the rough but honest ways of us farmers," looking admiringly at his thin legs, and brushing at a speck of dirt which seemed to be on one of them, "for I believe you come of an agricultural family yourself."

I was surprised at this reference to his rough ways, for he was extremely fastidious in his dress and manner. I managed to admit, however, that I came of an agricultural family.

"Those of us who live in the country, and earn our bread in the sweat of our brow," Mr. Biggs went on, seating himself beside me, "cannot be particular. Our clothing, our food, and our ways are rough, but substantial and honest. We have other matters to look after, such as following the plough, sowing the grain, and tossing the hay. We may have our ambitions like other men, but they are dwarfed and bent by holding the plough, and pitching the hay. When did you come, and how long do you stay?"

I replied that I had arrived but a few hours before, and that I would depart the next day at any hour Agnes was ready.

"I am sorry," Mr. Biggs was good enough to say, "I should be delighted to show you how we carry on a four hundred acre farm. Other great farmers have from four to a dozen hired men about them, but Big Adam and I do all the work here; and we are equal to it, though it keeps us very busy, as you will imagine. We have no time for the fine arts, you may be certain."

He ran on gayly in this way, making himself out in ignorance and muscle the equal of one of our Fairview farmers, although he was really nothing else to my mind than a fop, until Agnes came in and said we were to walk out to supper. There was no one in the supper room when we entered it, and although I expected other members of the family every moment, none came. Agnes was there most of the time, but did not sit down, and supplied the place of a servant.

"Those of us who live in the country," said Mr. Biggs, helping me to meat and bread with the greatest ceremony, "cannot be particular as to what we eat, except that it is substantial and hearty. Meat and bread and milk make muscle, and muscle is in great demand on a farm. Big Adam and I find a great deal of it necessary in tilling these four hundred acres, therefore we insist on

69

plenty of plain and substantial food. Excuse me, if I eat like a hog."

The supper was a very good one, but he talked a great deal about its being plain but hearty; and although he was dainty in his eating, and ate nothing but bread and milk, and toasted bread and tea, he kept apologizing for his ravenous appetite. He had something to say, too, about shovelling in his food with a knife, and bolting it — he did neither, but on the contrary was very delicate — and as he kept watching me, I thought that he must be apologizing for his guest, which made me very uncomfortable at my bad manners, for up to that time I had not been backward in falling to. But as he continued to denounce his unnatural craving for food, and frequently expressed the fear that the meal lacked so much of what I was accustomed to, that I could not possibly make out a comfortable supper, I finally made up my mind he did not mean me at all.

When I had finished he was waiting for me, and we adjourned to the room in which I had played with the children. Lighting a cigar (which he said was a very poor one, but which he observed in the course of the evening, as an example of his extravagance, had cost twenty cents) he took a dressing-gown from a closet, and, putting it on, sat down before me, the picture of luxurious ease.

While we sat there I heard the family of eight, accompanied by their mother and the little old woman who had frightened me, come banging down the stairs, and file [4] into the supper room, where there were a steady noise and wrangle until they had finished and gone up the stairs again. I heard Big Adam protesting to someone that it was not pleasant to be always "jawed at," and that he did all he could; but when the argument threatened to become boisterous, I heard a pleasanter voice intercede, and establish a peace, and I was sure this was Agnes's. Mr. Biggs stopped once or twice to listen to the confusion, as if trying to hear what was being said, but recollecting that if he could hear, I could as well, he began talking again to draw my attention from it. He tried to make me believe the children were making the disturbance, and said: —

[4] file: 1883 filing

"There can be no order in a house full of children, and very little comfort." He stopped to think a moment, but the uproar in the supper room was so great that he went on trying to draw my attention away from it. "I confess to thinking something of them, but every pleasure they bring is accompanied by inconvenience, expense, and annoyance. Have I told you yet that I am a philosopher?"

I had suspected that something was wrong with him, though I could not tell what it was. I replied politely, however, that he had not.

"Well, I am one," the little man said with a show of pride. "A great many men regard children as blessings. Now I have failed to discover any kind of a blessing or pleasure in being called up in the middle of the night to run for a doctor when there is croup in the house. Usually, too, in such cases the medical man lives a great many miles away, over a rough road. Whenever I go to bed early to make up lost sleep, or come home particularly tired from tossing the hay or holding the plough, either Annie, or Bennie, or Carrie, or Davie, or Effie, or Fannie, or Georgie, or Harry, is sick, and I am compelled to go for a doctor. This never fails if the night is very wet, the roads unusually heavy, or the weather particularly cold. While everybody admires little children, I am sure they would be much more popular if their teeth came more easily; and that there would be a greater demand for them if they did not take a hundred different diseases to which they are not exposed. I am that kind of philosopher."

The fire in the end of his cigar having about gone out, from holding it in his hand and waving it at me, he revived it with a great deal of puffing, and went on: —

"Understand me, Ned Westlock; I do not complain. I am like other men, except that I am not a fool; and while I accept the bitter with the sweet, I point out the bitter and refuse to call it palatable. I am at a loss to understand, for example, why the Creator is more considerate of pigs than He is of children; for I believe pigs cut their teeth before birth, and seldom die except when fat from good health, and at the hands of a butcher. Children, on the other hand" — he used his right hand to represent the pigs, and his left to represent the children — "are never well, and for every tooth there is an insolent doctor with a bill, to say nothing of measles, coughs, rashes, and fevers. I have seen it estimated that it requires three thousand eight hundred and seventy-nine dollars and thirty-five or forty cents to raise a baby to manhood or womanhood. A pig may be raised to maturity with a few hundred buckets of slop, a few bushels of corn, and a wisp of hay occasionally for a bed. What do you think of that?"

As he looked at me as though I had been stubbornly arguing the cause of the children, I replied that the pigs had the best of it, so far, decidedly.

"If you have never talked with a philosopher before, you may never have had your attention called to the fact, which possibly has escaped your own notice, that children do not appreciate good treatment, as do pigs and other animals. The very worst thing you can do for a boy is to treat him well. Where do you find the good boys?"

He made a pause as if expecting a reply, and I said, "I don't know," but I knew at once that he was impatient that I had replied, for he wanted to do all the talking himself.

"In families where boys are always hungry and abused," he resumed. "Where do you find your bad boys? In families where they are treated well, of course. A boy who has plenty to eat, and plenty to wear, and nothing to do, is always impudent and worthless; and parents who go to trouble and expense that their children may be happy and idle pay a big price for a pestilence. I do not pretend to say that in practice I am more of a philosopher than my neighbors; but it is a fact, nevertheless, that the pig that slips into the house and litters it up is beaten with a broomstick until he understands, when tempted on future occasions, that the practice is dangerous. If the pigs get on the porch, and you open the door suddenly, they run away in great haste, having been taught by harsh means that they are not expected there; and if we would teach children in the same way, we should have more comfort with them. But practically we regard the training of pigs as more important than the training of children, and suffer much discomfort in consequence. I recognize certain inexorable masters, and obey them to avoid uncomfortable consequences;

and a child must have a master, or it will become disagreeable and annoying." [5]

He stopped to listen to the noise made by his family up stairs. It was very uproarious, and I thought he was regretting that his philosophy had not been made to bear some practical fruit.

"If you were a young man," he continued, coming out of a brown study, "and had driven from Fairview to ask my advice on this question, I should advise you thus: 'Sir, if you covet the society of little children, hire them to play at your house until you are tired; for then you can send them away, and enjoy the quiet following their absence. You will find that pleasant enough, but if you have a house full of your own, that alters the case; for like the deserving poor, they then are always with you — in sickness as well as in health, and when they are disagreeable as well as when they are not.' That would be my candid advice; you may accept it, or let it alone, as you choose."

He waved the hand at me which he had previously used to represent the pigs, as though I had been asking him to counsel me on the subject, and as if he were impatient that I did not accept his advice at once. But recollecting himself, he took a delicate knife from his pocket, and after profuse apologies for his ill-manners, proceeded to pare his finger nails, looking occasionally at me as if doubting my ability to understand his philosophy, for I had scarcely said a word in reply to it.

"I understand your father is a singer," he said, after his fingers were mentally pronounced satisfactory.

I replied with a show of pride that he had the finest voice ever heard in Fairview church, and that he was famous for it.

"He ought to stop it," Mr. Biggs abruptly said. "People enjoy his singing, I have no doubt, but if he were a friend of mine — I have not even the pleasure of his acquaintance — I would say to him, 'Quit singing, Reverend John, if you would become great.' How does it come he is not in the Legislature? Because he sings. The people do not associate statesmanship with singing. When a man is honored for singing, he is honored for little else. Did you ever know a great man who sang?"

I replied that I had not, for I had never known a great man.

[5] annoying: 1883 annoying, and predestined to defeat in the battle of life.

"Well," he answered curtly, "I know them all, and none of them sing. Or play. The darkey who can sing and dance is popular with an idle crowd, but the solid people who have gardens to spade, or walls to whitewash, avoid the musical negro, for his talent is likely to be exhausted in that direction. I don't pretend to know why it is against a man that he is able to entertain people with his voice, or with the skill of his fingers; I only know it is the case. It would be a kindness for somebody to say as much to Reverend John; you may convey the information to him, with my compliments, if you wish."

I had been wishing all evening that Agnes would come in, and ask me to sing, as I thought I had talent in that direction, and even debated in my mind whether I would roar the "Hunter's Horn," or "Glorious Day of Rest" for the amusement of my host; but I was now glad she had been so considerate of my feelings, and spared me the humiliation. I was quite certain that if she should ask me to sing after what Mr. Biggs had said, I should declare I had never attempted to do such a ridiculous thing.

"Every man who tells an uncomfortable truth," Mr. Biggs began again, after lighting a fresh cigar by the remains of the old one, "is called a beast. I am called a beast in this neighborhood (which is known for taxing and voting purposes as Smoky Hill) because I tell a great many unpalatable truths; I have eyes and intelligence, therefore I cannot help noticing (and mentioning) that the people of this country pay more attention to raising thorough-bred stock than to raising thorough-bred children which you must admit is ridiculous. I hear that The. Meek, for instance, has his stable full of fine stock, and his house full of sore-eyed children. The. Meek is evidently an ass; I'm glad I do not know him. If I did, I should make myself disagreeable by mentioning the circumstance."

I may as well mention here that Mr. Biggs was not the kind of man he claimed to be. On the contrary, he made his living by indorsing the follies of other people, but he had pointed out their mistakes to himself so often that I suppose he really believed he was generally despised for telling the truth.

"We have many of the same kind of men in Smoky Hill. It

74

affords me pleasure to assure you that I am unpopular with them, and they take great comfort in the belief that I am likely to die in a year or two of consumption. But I have already had the satisfaction of attending the funerals of five men who predicted that I was not long for the world; I expect to help bury the rest of them at intervals in the future. While I get a little stronger every year, by care and common sense, they get a little weaker, by carelessness and ignorance, and finally they are buried, with L. Biggs, Esq., the consumptive, looking contentedly on. The trouble with these men is that they eat everything coming in their way, like pigs, lacking observation to teach them that a greater number of people die of over-feeding than die of over-drinking or over-working. The last Smoky Hill glutton that died was the Most Worthy Chief of a temperance society, and he was always quarrelling with his wife because she didn't have pie for breakfast. For my part, I detest pie."

I was about to say that while I agreed with him in everything else, I should be compelled to make an exception in the pie particular; but he did not give me opportunity, for he proceeded: —

"In my visits to the homes of cultured but unwise people, I am frequently tempted to do violence to my stomach by eating late at night, but recollecting the fate of the Smoky Hill men, I respectfully decline. When I am offered cake, and nightmare in other forms, I do not greedily accept and devour everything set before me, but instead I say, 'If you have cold oatmeal mush, or a bit of graham bread, I will refresh myself with that, but no cake, I thank you, although the assortment is fine, and reflects great credit on the lady of the house.' Thus I preserve my health, and prove my philosophy. But no doubt I am wearying you; I will show you to bed."

He did not ask me whether I was tired of his company, but picked up the light as though he could decide questions for boys without their assistance, and leading the way up stairs, I meekly followed. Opening a door after reaching the upper floor, he gave me the light, said good night, and went down again, as though he had not had enough of his own company, and would sit up a while longer.

There were two comfortable beds in the room to which Mr. Biggs had shown me, and Big Adam occupied one of them already, sound asleep. His clothes were piled up in a heap by the side of it, with the Λ-shaped hat on top, ready to go on the first thing in the morning. He mumbled occasionally in his sleep, and I thought he was saying he did the best he could, and that it wasn't pleasant to be "jawed at," which made me think again of the terrible old woman with the parchment face, the little head, the little body, and the little knot of hair on the back of her head. I felt like kneeling down by my bed and praying that the queer woman might not have a habit of walking through the house at night, accompanied by the kitchen butcher-knife freshly sharpened at the grindstone, for there was no lock on the door. But speedily occupying the other bed, and putting out the light, I had hardly begun thinking of the curious family before I was sound asleep.

IX

THE CHARITY OF SILENCE

WHEN I went down to breakfast the next morning, I found Agnes waiting for me, and the meal ready; and as was the case the night before, she presided at the table without sitting down. I ate alone, and in silence, as it was explained that Mr. Biggs was not yet up, though it was late, and Agnes did not seem to be in a mood for talking. The circumstance that other members of the family kept out of the room made me think that I was regarded in the house as a sort of a machine likely to explode and hurt somebody, and could be approached only by those who knew where the safety valve was which blew me off; for I supposed Mrs. Biggs and Mrs. Deming to be very aristocratic people, who could not tolerate a country-bred boy. Therefore I did not feel in very good humor myself, thinking that Agnes was ashamed to exhibit me to her friends. Going out to the stables in lazy preparation for returning home, I found Big Adam pitching hay, as I had left him the day before.

"Well, young Westlock, how are you now?" he inquired, leaning on his fork.

I returned his greeting, and said I would hitch up when he had time to help me.

"You needn't be in a hurry about it," he said, returning to his work. "If I were you I would manage to get home just at dark, for then you'll have nothing to do during the day. If you get back too early, the preacher may find something for you to do."

There was a good deal of truth in this, and I thanked him for the suggestion.

"I know something about hired help and boys on a farm. I have had a ripe experience in the service of Biggs. I thought he would talk you to death last night; it's a terrible death to die. What did he say?"

I repeated portions of the conversation, and gave particular stress to what he had said concerning his and Big Adam's doing the work of half a dozen men.

"He is always saying that," Big Adam said indignantly, "but I assure you on my honor that he never held a plough or pitched hay a day in his life. Why, he is not here a third of his time. He came home last night after an absence of four weeks; I don't know where he has been, but to some of the towns a long way off, probably. At ten or eleven o'clock he will breakfast, and then I shall hitch up and drive him over the place, during which time he will point out and suggest enough work to keep a dozen men busy for months; and after assuring me it ought all to be done before night, he will return to the house to lounge about.[1] In a day or two he will go away again, and come back when he gets ready. That's the kind of a farmer Biggs is, but I must say for him that he is quiet and peaceable. I wish I could say as much for his sister, the old pelican."

Up to this time Big Adam had been wearing his Λ-shaped hat so far back on his head that I was wondering it did not fall off; but as if there were some people so contemptible that he could not possibly mention them without showing his temper, he jerked the hat over on his low forehead when he said this, and, looking out from under it with his little eyes, viciously said, "Damn."

"And who is his sister?" I asked.

"Old Missus Deming, Agnes's mother; the little old woman they were careful you should not see."

It came to me all at once — how foolish of me not to have thought of it before — why Agnes never talked about her mother, and why she always seemed to be glad to be away from her; she was disagreeable, not only to Big Adam, but to everyone around her. I understood now that Agnes was frightened when I first came for fear I should see her mother, and not for fear her mother

[1] house to lounge about: 1883 house, where he lounges about on flowery beds of ease, figuratively speaking.

would see me, as I had imagined; and I felt so much better that I had a mind to walk in the yard in plain view of the house, that Mrs. Deming might regret not having made my acquaintance. I told Adam that I had seen her, however, and narrated the circumstance of her appearance in the room after the children.

The hired man expressed his satisfaction at this very much as I have seen young colts express it, by kicking his legs out in various directions, and snorting. After he had enjoyed himself in this manner for a while he said: —

"It's just like her, though. They might have known better than to have left her alone. It's a wonder she didn't hit you; I wish she had, for then you would despise her, as I do."

He continued to chuckle to himself as though it was a satisfaction to him that I had seen his enemy; and putting his finger in his mouth, he drew it out in such a manner that it sounded like pulling a cork; then thumping his jaws he made a sound of liquor coming out of a bottle. This pantomime I interpreted to mean that if he were better off he would celebrate the event with something expensive to drink. I found out afterward that this was a habit with him when in a good humor, and he had [2] acquired such skill by practice that if your back was turned to him the deception was perfect.

"She's the worst woman on earth," he continued, leading me behind the barn to be more confidential. "They say she never smiled in her life, and I believe it. She grumbles, and growls, and jaws from morning until night; but what can they do? Bless you, she owns the farm!"

I looked astonished, to induce him to go on.

"Yes, she owns the place, and you bet she looks after it. When she came here with Agnes, six or seven years ago, her brother had a great tract of land bought on credit, and she paid for it with the money she brought along, and built the house you slept in last night. Since then she has been so disagreeable that Biggs is seldom at home, and won't see her when he is. Did you see his wife?"

[2] good humor, and he had: 1883 festive humor, and had

I replied that I had been denied that pleasure.

"You would have seen a sight if you had; a woman who hasn't combed her hair for six years, because she has that old hen to look after, besides the care of the children. I don't believe she ever sleeps; for if I wake up in the night she is either being railed at by that she devil or is up with the children. I believe she is the only person living whose lot is worse than mine. When I am in the field I am out of my misery, but she never has that opportunity of escaping hers. When Agnes is away I often cook my own meals, and I am the only one besides Agnes that pays her any attention. Except to keep a family of children around her, I think Biggs never notices her; and when he is at home he occupies a room away from the noise and confusion. But she is patient, and never complains, although there is no hope; for the old woman will out-live us all. She lives on growling and grumbling, for she is afraid to eat for fear of poison, and hesitates to sleep for visions of stran-gling. She talks about poisoning and strangling for hours at a stretch, and accuses the Biggses of wanting to murder her, be-cause she knows it humiliates them. I hear that her late husband was a fine fellow, a sea captain. He was a very sensible man, I judge, for he drowned himself rather than live with her. I think a great deal of Captain Deming's memory; he is the only great man I know even by reputation. Here's to him."

He pulled another cork, which appeared to come with difficulty, and thumped on his jaws to represent the gurgling of liquor as it flows out of the bottle.

"Agnes is like him. It will be a great relief to her to go home with you. Does she ever talk of her mother?"

"No," I answered.

"I thought not; nor does she ever talk of the Devil. But I'll be bound she talks a great deal of her father. I think Agnes will never marry, preferring to remain an old maid rather than intro-duce a husband to her mother; and I don't blame her. She com-plains during the few weeks that the poor girl is at home because Agnes is not away earning money for her strong-box, into which goes every dollar of it. If Agnes has any money, Biggs gives it to her; for she has to account for every penny of her earnings to her mother, who says she needs that, and more, to buy something decent to wear. She talks a great deal about having nothing decent to wear, as if anything would look well on her angular old bones except a shroud."

"What does Biggs do for a living?" I asked, anxious to know as much about the family as possible.

"To be candid with you," Big Adam replied, in a confidential way, "I don't know; although he has some way of making money, for he always has it. He organizes the farmers for one thing, and is a member of the Legislature for another. Once he started a Farmers' Store here, at a place over in the hills there," pointing in the direction, "where the roads cross, and where the Smoky Hill post-office is kept. He told the people they must organize for protection, and he somehow made them agree to patronize his store if he would start one. They were honest men who made the agreement, and lived up to it a long while; but in time they found out that he was charging them a great deal more for his goods than the dangerous men he had warned them against in town. I was in the place when they came in to hang him; and one man walked up to the rope-reel, and wanted to know how much rope would be necessary. But Biggs made them a speech from a vinegar barrel, and so worked upon their feelings that they went away content with the harmless revenge of calling him a little whiffet. Biggs put me in charge, and galloped away to find a purchaser for his store. He found one by representing that an entire neighborhood of fools had signed an agreement to pay him in cash whatever price he asked for his goods. The purchaser wanted to shoot Biggs when he found out how matters really stood — for he had paid a big price — but for some reason he changed his mind. Biggs is that kind of man. Now you know as much about him as I do."

As though he had been idling away too much time already, Big Adam began to work with great energy, and refused to talk any more, so I put the horses to the wagon alone; but after I had driven through the gate and into the road he came out as if there was one word more he desired to say, and lifting himself up by putting one foot on the wheel, he whispered in my ear: —

"My father was killed by the Indians."

He looked so distressed that I expressed some sort of regret, and said it was a pity.

"Good-bye," he added, giving me his hand; "my last name is Casebolt. My mother is married the second time."

I shook his great fat hand again, and he went back to his work. Driving round to the front of the house I found Agnes waiting for me, and, lifting her little trunk into the wagon, we drove away, no one appearing at the doors or windows to bid her good-bye. My mother had told me to invite Mrs. Deming to visit her, but out of regard for Agnes I resolved to say that I had forgotten it. As we went past the stables Big Adam motioned for me to stop, and raising himself up beside me by putting his foot on the wheel again, he whispered, —

"My brothers and sisters are all dead."

He stepped down from the wheel; and putting the whip to the horses I soon left the place behind me.

I saw that Agnes had been crying, for her eyes were red and swollen; but I pretended not to notice it, and hoped her spirits would revive as we neared Fairview.

"You will excuse me, Ned," she said, after we had driven a long time in silence, "if I have neglected you, but I have not been myself for several days. Big Adam talks a great deal, and I saw you down in the yard with him a long while. You should not believe all he says. I am unhappy on my own account."

I did not know what to say in reply, for I was anxious for her to believe that I thought her mother was not at home, or something of that sort; so I jerked one of the horses roughly, and said "Whoa," as if the animal were preparing to run away. I knew she was distressed that I knew how unhappy she was at home, and was trying to lay the blame on herself, as she did in everything; therefore I watched the dangerous horse very intently for several minutes, and finally got down to walk around the wagon, to see if anything was wrong. After I had pounded the tires awhile with a stone, although they were new, I climbed back into my seat, and we drove on again.

"The people of Fairview have been very kind to me," Agnes continued, not minding that I did not care to talk on the subject, "and I have been happier there than here; although it is very ungrateful in me, and a poor return for the patient way in which they bear with me at home. I am so wicked and selfish."

The tears came into her eyes as she spoke, and I wondered whether it was wrong to tell white lies, for I was sure Agnes was fibbing in defence of her family. She thought about the matter a long time after that, and looked at me narrowly — although I pretended not to know it — and seemed to conclude at last that I had made good use of my time with Big Adam, and that she must depend upon the charity of my silence. Anyway, she said no more upon the subject, and we rode in silence for several miles.

"You have always taken a great interest in my father," she said, at last, wiping her eyes, and dismissing the unpleasant subject. "I have brought you his picture as a present."

She took it out of a little package she carried, and gave it to me. It was a handsome face, and looked very much as I had imagined, except that it was clean-shaven. I put it away carefully, and she said: —

"My life would have been very different had he lived, and I should not have been so unkind to everyone. He was always so brave and good that I should have striven to be like him, for everybody loved him. But he is dead, and I cannot be content without him. It is this that makes me fretful, and unworthy of my many good friends. Oh dear, I am going to cry."

She did cry again, apologizing for it in a way that reminded me of her uncle; and I sat there feeling like a fool while she was giving vent to her grief, and until she had regained her self-possession once more.

"I am sorry I did not see him buried, and that he did not have a quiet place to rest," Agnes continued, wiping her eyes; "for I dream at night of his storm-tossed ship, and always think of the sea as forever rolling and tossing his poor body about, refusing it rest and peace. Often in the wicked waves I see his white face turned imploringly to me, and the noises of the night I torture into

83

his cries to me for help. If I knew where he was buried, and could sometimes visit his grave, I should be more content, and less unhappy."

I had heard a song called "When the Sea gives up its Dead," and without thinking what I did I softly hummed it.

"When he came home at the time I saw him last, he carried me about in his great strong arms along the beach, and said that if some day he never came back, for me not to dislike the sea, for it had been his friend in many a storm, and had rocked him to sleep almost every night since he was born. 'It will never prove treacherous,' he said. 'My ship may, but never the sea. The "Agnes" is not like the stout girl in whose honor she was named; she is getting old, and should she founder with me in the storms, and go down, never feel unkindly toward the sea. It has been my friend so many years that should it swallow me up I desire you to think that I deserved it.' He went away soon after that, and we have never seen him since."

Although the tears came into her eyes again, she bravely wiped them away.

"I am sorry for you," I made bold to say, looking at her pretty face. "I wish I were a man, and old enough; I would marry you, and make you happy in spite of yourself. I cannot tell you how much I desire your good, or how much I love you. Your presence at our house has made us a different family. My mother is more content, and my father less gloomy; and surely Jo and I know more since you came. I love you because you are good and pretty, and I think you are prettier to-day than I have ever seen you before. If I were a little older I would fall in love with you, and worry you a great deal with my attentions."

"It wouldn't worry me, Ned," she answered, with a return of her old cheerfulness. "I should like it. But I thought you were in love with me."

"Oh, I am, of course — as a boy," I answered; "but I mean if I were a man. If you should concentrate the love you distribute in Fairview on one man, I should like to be the man. That's what I mean. You love everybody in Fairview just alike."

"I am not so certain of that," she replied. "I think I am very partial to you. Who is most gallant and thoughtful to me of all my pupils? Why, you are, of course; and I love you best of any of them. When I get to be an old woman, and you a young man, I shall show my love for you by selecting you a wife; and if I am unable to find you a very good one, you shall remain single, as I intend to do. I regard you as my best friend, and I want you to think so. When you came yesterday, I wanted to run down and kiss you, but I could not leave my mother."

"But you never have kissed me," I said, "although you say you love me."

"I will now, if you will let me," she replied, and putting her arms round me, she kissed me as innocently as if I had been a child. I was very much abashed but thanked her as for any other favor.

"You are the first girl that ever kissed me," I said.

"Well, let me be the last one, unless I should want to kiss you again. But we are in sight of Fairview, and while we are alone, I want to tell you about Big Adam. His father is an outlaw, living somewhere in the great West; and, although he occasionally comes to Smoky Hill, it is always at night. His mother is a rough woman who smokes and drinks, and his brothers and sisters are very bad people. I don't know where they all live, though I frequently hear of them, but never anything to their credit. It is said that his mother's house, which is situated in a deep hollow near the river, is a rendezvous for bad men, and frequently it is raided by the officers looking for her bold husband. Big Adam is the only honest one among them, and that is why he says they are all dead; but even he talks too much."

I knew she wanted me to believe that he had misrepresented her family, though she was certain he had not; therefore I only said that Fairview church looked very pretty from the high point over which the road led us. I had never thought so before, but the country surrounding it was much finer than the Smoky Hill district, and I began to think that if I could travel more I might grow more content with my own home.

Our house was built in a rather low place, and I noticed with surprise, what I had not had opportunity of noticing before, that a great many new fields were being opened in different directions. Fairview was quietly and rapidly settling up.

"Anything Big Adam may have said to you," Agnes said as we were nearing the house, "is to be private between you and me."

I readily promised, though I had been thinking but a moment before of adding largely to it, and astonishing Jo.

"Since we are good friends we must have our secrets, and this is our first one. You may tell Jo that I kissed you."

I blushed because she had divined that I intended to tell him about her mother, but comforted myself with the reflection that she could not know for a certainty.

My mother was waiting for us; and the place was so quiet and pleasant, and the late dinner she had prepared so good, that I began to feel like a very favored fellow. Jo and the man of the house were away somewhere, and we spent the afternoon like three happy children, suddenly free from some exacting restraint. Agnes and I made so much of my mother, that I remember her as being happier on that day than any other, and when I think of her now, so long after, I am glad that it is as she sat in her easy chair between us that afternoon, saying little, but looking content and happy.

X

JO ERRING MAKES A FULL
CONFESSION

INASMUCH as that young man continued to haul stone to Erring's
Ford for a dam, and would talk of nothing else, it became
certain, in course of time, that Jo would never make a farmer; so [1]
it was agreed, at a convention attended by my father and my
grandmother, that he should be apprenticed for two years to
Damon Barker, of the establishment on Bull River. Barker had
suggested it, I believe, as he needed someone to assist him, and
was much pleased with Jo besides, who had already learned to
help him in many ways during visits to the place. These visits
were allowed to become frequent and protracted when it was
decided that he should be sent there to learn milling as a business.
When it was announced to Jo that the arrangement had been
made — it was one Sunday afternoon — he took me out to the hayloft of the stable to talk about it.

"I am to be given a chance," he said, "and that is all I ask. I
intend to work hard, and at the end of two years I shall be in position to commence my mill in earnest. I am seventeen years old
now; I shall be nineteen then, and by the time I am twenty-one,
'Erring's Mill' will be in operation. It seems a very long time to
wait, and a big undertaking, but it is the best I can do."

He was lying on his back, looking through the holes in the roof
at the sky, and I thought more than ever that he was brave and
capable, and that he had always been treated unjustly in Fairview. I was thinking — it had not occurred to me before — that I
should be very lonesome without him; and he seemed to be thinking of it, too, for he said: —

[1] so: 1883 and

87

"But it is only for three or four years, Ned," as if we had been talking instead of thinking of the separation, "and at the end of that time I may be able to make you my assistant, or, better still, my partner. We have had a very wretched time of it in the past, but there may be a great deal of pleasure in store for us in the future. If we work as hard as we expect, I believe everything will come out right yet. They say you are old of your age. I am not old of my age; on the other hand I am very dull: but I shall be a man then, and in any event one need not be old to be useful. People here think differently, but it is because the community is slow and ignorant. Here the man who owns a piece of land and a team is supposed to have accomplished all that it is possible for a man to accomplish; but Barker told me once that there are men who make a Fairview fortune in a day. I don't want to be like the people here, for none of them are contented or happy; but I intend to be like the people who I am certain live in other countries. I cannot believe but that there is a better way to live than that accepted at Fairview, and that somewhere — I don't know where, for I have never travelled — happy homes may be found, and contented people, where parents love their children, and where people love their homes. Therefore I shall begin differently, and work harder, and to more purpose, than the people here have done, to the end that I may be a different man."

Heaven help you, Jo, in that. There never was a happy man in Fairview, and I hoped with all my heart that Jo might become one, as he deserved.

"I have always been lonely and friendless," he went on. "They never wanted me at home; your father never seemed satisfied with me here, and, excepting you, I have never had a friend in my life. I care nothing for my family; I fear it is sad depravity, but I cannot help it. They have never treated me well, and care nothing for me, and I cannot feel kindly toward them, for no one can love without a reason. You do not fall in love with the woman that wounds you, but you do fall in love with the woman that is kind to you. I think a great deal of you, but you gave me reason for it by thinking a great deal of me. I never knew until I thought of going away how much I did think of you."

He talked so pitifully of the neglect to which he had always been subject, and I knew so well it was true, that I could only reply through my tears that he was my best friend, and that I thought more of him than anyone else in the world.

"While they all occasionally have kind words for others, they never have a word of encouragement for me,[2] but I am glad that I did not deserve it. I should hate to feel that I deserve all the unkindness I have received here, and that I was as idle and unworthy as they seem to think me; but I never did, and I hope you honestly think so. You are the only one among them who was fair and just, and after I have gone away I shall only have you to remember pleasantly. I am glad that I am going to a place at last where I shall be welcome and useful."

I thought that afternoon that all of them were unjust to Jo and steadily refused to give him the credit he deserved; I think so now, a great many years after, with a maturer mind and greater experience.

"We have been very ignorant here, you and I." It was very disgraceful, but very true. "Your father is wise enough, but as he takes no pains to impart it to others, we have had little benefit of his wisdom. For the next two years I shall live with a man who is educated, and who will willingly teach me, and I intend to tax his patience with my studies. Barker is not only learned, but he is courteous, and I can learn something of polite manners. He bows like a king; only a very few men are able to make a really good bow. I asked him once where he learned it, but he only laughed, and said everyone ought to be polite without learning it anywhere. It made me ashamed, for politeness never came natural with me. Perhaps I am so awkward because I do not come of a good family."

Certainly his father and mother were not polite to each other, or to their son.

"I have made many terrible mistakes from not knowing any better, and they will humiliate me all my life. Once I went with your mother to call at the new minister's — this is in the strictest confidence, and never to be repeated — and I did a thing so dread-

[2] me: 1883 Jo

89

ful that I am blushing now in thinking of it. I wore a little cap (I have since burned it), and although I know now it was hideously ugly, I thought then that it made me very handsome. I bought it of a boy who had lived in town, and I had seen town boys wear them. So I shuffled into their parlor wearing your father's boots, with a pair of his pantaloons tucked into their tops, and the cap on my head. The Shepherds are very well-bred people, and after I had stumbled across the room, and fallen into a chair all in a heap, Mateel — how pretty she was that night, and how pretty she always is! — came over to me, and asked to lay away my cap. I thought it very amiable in me not to trouble her, so I refused to give it up. In fact, I said: —

" 'No, I THANK YOU; I AM VERY COMFORTABLE AS I AM!'

"And I sat the entire evening through with that cap on my head. Nobody had ever told me to remove my cap in the presence of ladies, and being of a poor family, I did not know it without being told. I know better now, for Barker laughed at me, and explained why it was wrong."

Under other circumstances I should have laughed, but Jo was so serious that I did not think of it.

"They asked me to sing; simply to be polite, I am now certain. Your mother did not say for me not to, so I stumbled over to the melodeon, and sang nine verses of the 'Glorious Eighth of April' in a voice so loud that the windows rattled. They were all blushing for me, but I never once suspected it. I had heard your father sing the same song a hundred times, and I supposed it was all right. 'Is that all?' they asked when I had finished. I regretted that it was, thinking they were entertained, and I came very near singing it all over again. I told Barker about it, and he gave me lessons in propriety an entire afternoon. I felt coming home that I had in some way committed an indiscretion, but I could not tell exactly what it was until Barker pointed it out. He suggested that I write an apology, and as I have it here, I will read it, if you care to listen."

He took from his pocket a neatly written note, and after I had signified an anxiety to know its contents, he read: —

MISS SHEPHERD, — I feel that my remarkable conduct at your house a few weeks ago needs an explanation, and I write this to confess candidly that it was caused by my ignorance, and should not be regarded as a lack of respect to you or your father and mother.

It is because I have lived in the backwoods all my life, and because no one ever took sufficient interest in me to say that I should have removed my cap from my head, but if I am forgiven, and allowed to visit you again, I will be careful that there is no repetition of the offence. With reference to the tiresome song I sang, I have only the same plea; I did not know any better. I know now that I cannot sing; I can only bellow. When I tell you that the noise I made is regarded as music in Fairview, you will realize more vividly than I can tell you that the community where I have grown up is not cultured. I am distressed that I acted as I did, and hope you will accept this humble apology. Please express my regrets to your father and mother, and regard this note as in confidence.

Very truly yours,   Jo Erring.

After folding the note carefully, and putting it back in the envelope from which he had taken it, he inquired: —

"What do you think of it?"

Knowing Barker had suggested it, and probably dictated the words, I said it was neat and appropriate, and the best thing that could be done under the circumstances, for I had no opinion of my own on the delicate question.

"They are the only well-bred people I have ever known, if I except Barker and Agnes," Jo said, after a long silence, "and though I should like to visit them often, I am afraid I can never get the courage to go there again. They have undoubtedly a poor opinion of me, for they can never understand how a young man of my age could be so uncouth, but other families of good manners will perhaps come to Fairview, and I intend to take lessons from Barker, and cultivate their acquaintance. I have great respect for polished people, but I never admired a quality in others that I did not lack it myself, therefore I fear I shall make but poor progress. But this is a small matter compared with learning the mill business. Perhaps I had better renounce society until I am the best miller on the river."

"It won't be long, Jo," I answered, and feeling that what I said was true.

"Barker says he can teach me all he knows in half a year. After

91

that, I will experiment for myself, and perhaps I may be able to discover something which will repay him for his kindness to me. If I am apt at anything — which I sometimes doubt — it is with machinery, and there is so little of it at Barker's that I hope I will be able to master it all in a few months. I am familiar with all of it now, and I shall work very hard until I can take it all apart, and put it together again better than it was before."

We were both quiet a long while, busy with our own thoughts, until Jo said: —

"I am going away to-morrow. When are you coming to see me?"

I had it in my mind to say, "On Tuesday," but as that would be the next day after his departure, and impossible, I said instead that I would come as soon as I could; certainly not later than that day a week.

"I shall be very busy, and lonely, too, and I hope you will come often. You haven't been out of my sight more than a day at a time since you were born, and you are the only brother I ever had. I don't intend to come here much, and as you enjoy visiting at Barker's we will arrange it in that way. They will perhaps tolerate me here once in a long while, to see if I have cut off any of my fingers in the cog-wheels, but for no other reason. I have been an intruder ever since I can remember, and lonely and homeless."

I felt that this was true, unjust and cruel as it was, and could say nothing, although Jo spoke of it in a husky voice, as though it would be a relief to cry if it were not unmanly.

"Your mother has been kinder to me than any of them, if I except Agnes, who is the friend of everyone, but her health has always been poor, and she has a great deal to do. She often comes into my room at night, if she suspects that I am not well, and asks if she can do anything for me; but I know she is always tired, and I feel more like helping her than allowing her to help me. I shall always remember her gratefully for it, and believe that were she less unhappy herself we would have been a different family."

The mention of Agnes reminded me that she had presented me with her father's picture, and taking it from my pocket I gave it to Jo, but he did not care to look at it then, and said he would take it, and give it back at some future time.

"Your father is never unkind to her," he continued, determined to talk on that subject, "but they are more like strangers than man and wife. They have not occupied the same room for years, therefore she is always striving to reconcile him, knowing that he is discontented and dissatisfied, though I cannot see that she is to blame for it, and as a true woman — and she is one, if ever one lived — this makes her very unhappy. I know less of your father every day, and I fear that something unfortunate will come of his discontent. I hope it will not turn out that religion is a bad thing for him, as Barker predicts. I never mentioned it to you before, but the night you were away your mother came softly into our room, and asked why I had gone to bed so early. I said I was unusually tired, and that I had to get up very early in the morning; nothing more than that. She remained there for two hours, as if anxious to be with me, and there was enough light in the room for me to see that tears were in her eyes, and that she was in great distress.

" 'Since six o'clock,' she said to me, 'my husband has not changed his position, or spoken. It is his habit every night. He is always thinking, and always silent and discontented. If I knew what his trouble is, perhaps I could help him, as I am anxious to do, but he will not tell me (though I do not ask him, for I am afraid). He thinks all day at his work, you have told me, and I believe he thinks all night, for I have known him to get up at midnight, and walk the floor until day. He is always considerate of me, and never speaks unkindly, but he has never been my husband except in name, and the fear that I have done something to offend him makes me very wretched, for I have always tried to be all that he desired. There is something dreadfully portentous in this; I do not know what it is, but I am certain that it will finally make us very miserable.

" 'I have never spoken of this before; I never intend to speak of it again, and I only mention it now because I feel that I can live but a few years longer, and I must speak of it to make clear a request I have to make. Ned [3] is out of the house to-night, and farther away from me than ever before since he was born. After you two have gone to sleep here in this room, I always come in to

[3] Ned: 1883 My boy

kiss him good-night. And, Jo, I frequently kiss you, too. Since he was a baby in my arms, I have never kissed him except when he was asleep, because his father seemed to dislike such exhibitions of affection. But I come to his bed every night, and kiss him after he has gone to sleep.'

"She cried softly to herself awhile, and remained so quiet that I could hear her tears fall in little plashes to the floor.

" 'The request that I have to make is that after I am dead you will tell him of this. I have made a mistake in raising him, and I know I should have cultivated his affection for me after he put on boots and mittens, and went out with his father to work, but I was afraid, for none of that is allowed in this house, as you know. I do not feel free to be kind to you, Jo, or show you any attention, for fear my husband will regard it as an interference with his discipline, which excuse he has used to separate me from my boy.

" 'I know he regards me as cold-hearted, like his father, but I am not. I love him as every mother loves her only child, but he does not understand it, and lately he avoids me whenever he can.

" 'You won't be here long; Damon Barker wants you to live at the mill, and you won't come back very often, for you have no reason to, therefore I ask you, now that I have opportunity, to tell Ned that I have always loved him as a mother should, and that I was indifferent to him because his father told me to be, and said it was for the best. He is getting to be quite a boy now, and when he comes home tired and ill-humored, I know he thinks we are unjust to make him work so hard, but tell him, Jo, that it is his father who did it, and that I always protested against it. I want you to take good care of him after I am dead, and I believe you will, for I can see you are very fond of him, as he is of you. I believe you will both become good and intelligent men some day; men who will love your wives and children, instead of treating them as they are treated in Fairview, and I want you to believe when you are grown up that I raised you as best I could. You have lived here nearly as long as I have, and this is your home, as well as Ned's, and if you have not been contented and happy, it was not because I did not love you both. I trusted too much to another's

94

judgment, and was afraid to do what I felt I should have done. When you become men you will think a great deal of this period in your lives, for it is indelibly stamped on your memory by its discomforts, but I hope you will remember that I was sick a great deal, and could not pay you the attention I wanted to. Goodnight.'"

After wiping away our tears, for the story affected us both to that extent, we resolved over and over again to be more considerate of her in the future, as we now better understood her strange disposition toward us. I do not know that we had ever been more inconsiderate than other boys, but we all seemed to be waiting at our house for an opportunity to get away, and find more pleasant companions, which made us unthoughtful of each other, and I think it was to this she referred in her talk with Jo.

When we went into the house again, my father was sitting in his accustomed place, thinking. He had not changed his position since we went out of the room, an hour or two before, and I think he regretted he could not go out into the fields and lose his thoughts in working. He looked up when we came in, and addressing himself to Jo, said: —

"Are you glad to go?"

"Yes, sir," Jo promptly responded.

This did not seem to surprise him, and he kept on thinking, as though he might have known it without asking.

"I have no doubt you think I have been a hard master," my father said. "I have been, but because I believed it was best to teach boys to work. Before you reach my age, you will know I was right, and that the course I have pursued with you was the best one. But to show you that I am anxious for your success, I offer to help you start the mill at The Ford, if you apply yourself at Barker's and give me reason to believe that you are worthy and capable. Whatever else you may think of me, you know I keep my word in everything. Bear this in mind during the next two years."

When he began thinking again, I thought it was that although he always did that which was for the best, he was blamed for it, and hated.

"I have no advice to give you, because you would take nothing

95

kindly from me, and because I seldom give it to anyone. Every man must advise himself, after he is convinced what course he had better pursue. The world is full of people giving good advice to others, but I have thought we should all be better off if we would advise ourselves more, and others less. If I could take the good advice I am capable of giving, I should have no occasion to accept it from others. The same is true in your case; advise yourself, and see that your advice is good. I believe you will succeed over there, and I earnestly hope you will. No more need be said on the subject."

When he began his thinking again, I thought it was to wonder why Jo should not feel grateful to him now instead of in the future (he was sure he would then), after he was dead, and in need of no evidence that the course he had pursued was right.

*　　*　　*

That night I resolved to remain awake to see if my mother came to me in my room. She did not disappoint me, and, coming in quietly, sat down on the foot of the bed, where she remained in deep study a long while. I could not see her face, but I was certain it was thoughtful and sad, and that she felt ill at ease, and wretched. The moon was shining outside, and she pulled aside the curtain to look at us. At last she got up, and bending over the bed kissed me tenderly. I threw my arms about her neck, and said: "Mother!"

She fell on her knees beside the bed, and sobbed in such distress that my father heard her, and came in hurriedly from the other room to inquire what was the matter. But only her sobbing answered him, and speaking to her tenderly, as if divining what had affected her, he led her away, with his arm around her.

"Your father has been thinking again," Jo said, as the door closed upon them. "I was awake, too. Ned, never keep anything from me again."

XI

WITH REFERENCE TO A MAN WHO WAS SENT WEST TO GROW UP WITH THE COUNTRY, OR GET KILLED

A FEW months after the Shepherds came to Fairview, and after they had become fairly settled in their new home (they lived beyond Erring's Ford, and on the other edge of the timber which began there), a fellow arrived who was thoroughly disliked from the moment of his appearance, because he had an insolent manner, an insolent walk, and was insolent in everything he did, to say nothing of his flashy dress and a general air of impudence. His name was Clinton Bragg, and as he appeared there in company with the Shepherds, it was soon understood that in the country from which they came their families had been intimate and friends. I think he only consented to visit Fairview church on the Sunday of his first appearance, as a geologist consents to enter a dirty pit in the earth, for the satisfaction of seeing curious specimens and formations, and he regarded the people he saw, whom he looked at with a cool stare, as a herd of peculiar beasts or a drove of something.

Mr. Shepherd had applied himself with great industry to agriculture — although it was not expected of him, as his salary was sufficient for his support — but a member of the congregation had given him the free use of a piece of land, and he devoted certain hours of each day to cultivating it. His appetite and strength (both of which had deserted him years before) had returned from this exercise, and he progressed so well that it was known that after he had remained at Fairview as long as the rules of the church allowed, he would give up preaching altogether and follow agriculture instead.

The people thought a great deal of him, as he was kind and gentle, and preached a religion less rigorous than my father's had been, and they were useful to him in so many ways that he was greatly pleased with the people and the community, for I think he had never lived in a place before where he was of so much importance. Therefore it was plain that he was annoyed by Bragg's impertinence, and I thought Mateel and her mother shared the feeling. He sat with them during the services, but went out in a rude way immediately after the preaching was over, giving the people to understand as plainly as he could that he thought them inferior. Through the open door from where I sat I could see him standing out at the gate like an evil spirit, and I could not help thinking that Fairview was progressing, for all sorts of people were coming in. I had never seen a man like this one before, for we knew by his manner that he lived without work.

When the people came out he walked ahead of them, as though fearing he would be trampled upon, and seemed anxious to get away. To this end he unhitched the minister's horses, and, after turning their heads homeward, sat holding them impatiently, until the family concluded their greetings with those who crowded around them, amusing himself by chewing bits of hay and spitting them out spitefully.

When it was announced that the family would spend the time at our house until the evening service, he was evidently displeased, as he had probably thought to pass a pleasant afternoon at the home of the Shepherds in abusing the Fairview people, but though I thought at first he would get out of the wagon, and walk back to town, he seemed to reconsider finally, as if it was worth his time to see how the animals lived.

All this I imagined while looking at him, for he said nothing, and when I rode in the seat in front of him (which I did at the invitation of Mateel) I was certain he was frowning all the way, and thinking of me as a fine specimen for a museum. His presence chilled me, as it did all the others, and I said nothing during the ride, fearing he would snap my head off. I felt, too, that, though the others disliked him, they were afraid of his tongue, should he find occasion to use it, and I drove as rapidly as I could to get rid of him.

When he was introduced to Agnes he stared at her with cold surprise, as he would look at a particular animal in a flock driven up for his inspection, should one of them prove finer than he had expected, and Agnes turned and [1] left the room. Mateel soon followed her, and I thought that she went out to apologize for her rude acquaintance. They both remained away until dinner was ready, and I found that they were good-naturedly helping my mother, who was greatly pleased. Indeed, they all deserted Bragg, leaving him alone in the best room a greater part of the time, my father and Mr. Shepherd finding it convenient to examine a lot of young trees lately planted in the orchard.

My grandmother was there that day, and finding that they were all afraid of Bragg, she went in to keep him company, and give him to understand that she was too old a bird to be frightened by such a scarecrow. After regarding him carefully over her spectacles, first wiping the glasses, as though that would help her in taking his measure, she called me in, and [2] kept up an incessant rattle of compliments for the splendid people of Fairview, frequently denouncing the ignorant upstarts who did not like them.

But Bragg paid not the slightest attention to her, and kept looking out of the window, first at the church, and then at the fields, as though he regretted he could not set them on fire by holding his eyes on them, like a sun-glass. At dinner my grandmother sat next to him, and imposed on him by crowding, and setting everything passed to her as far away as possible, which affronts he pretended not to notice. Although the others were very good-natured at the table, he remained indifferent to everything, eating whatever was offered as though he was surprised to get it in such an out-of-the-way place. I had not yet heard him speak, and began to wonder how it would sound should he finally consent to favor us with a word.

The good humor of the others was probably to show Bragg

[1] turned and: 1883 turned on her heel, and
[2] in, and: 1883 in to talk to, and

that his ill-nature was of no consequence, and that he was welcome to his mood, for I had never heard so much laughter in that house before. I was particularly proud of Agnes for the many kind things she managed to say of Fairview, though apparently without reference to Bragg. She was superior to any of them, and I could not help thinking it was to the credit of the country that she had lived there contentedly before they came. Although the dinner to which he sat down was better than he expected, and the people offering to entertain him more intelligent — he could not conceal his occasional surprise — he would not admit it, and maintained his insolent silence. When he went back into the best room, nobody followed, and he remained there undisturbed, except occasionally by my grandmother, who dashed in at intervals to turn up her nose.

I learned somehow that Bragg was the spoiled son of a well-to-do family, and that his father, after spending great amounts of money on his education, had sent him West to grow up with the country or get killed. It was evident that he was dissipated — he gave no particular evidence of it, but I supposed that must be the matter with him — and I remember thinking that the miller's sister would be glad to hear of his arrival, as it would give her opportunity to save him.

I heard Mr. Shepherd say to my father that he was a civil engineer, and would make that his business in Twin Mounds, if he concluded to do anything at all, which was not decided, as his father was rich, and would cheerfully supply him with all he needed.

"He is disagreeable to me, and to my family," he added, "but I was a boy with his father, and have known Clinton ever since he was born. He has been headstrong and wilful all his life; I sincerely hope his residence here will do him good. I don't know what his habits are, but I do know that he has always been a source of worry and trouble — at home, at school; everywhere. I think if there is anything in him, it will develop here, for I am unable to understand how any man can remain idle in a country where there is so much room for action. He intends to open an office in town, he says, and if he is competent and industrious

100

there is really no reason why he should not live to make his father proud of him. I believe his mother regards him as the most wonderful young man in the world, as he is."

My father did not reply, but I am sure he was thinking that Bragg was a very good example of his doctrine that an idle boy invariably grew up into an idle and disagreeable man.

"He is an only son," Mr. Shepherd continued, "and will one day come into possession of a considerable property; I don't know how much, for I have a poor head for such calculations, but I should say it will be sufficient to make him independent for the remainder of his life. This has been his misfortune. Had he been poor I think he would have been a better boy, but as it is he acts as his sullen temper dictates."

Barker had told Jo and me so much of rich people that I greatly admired them, but I could not believe that Bragg was a fair representative of the class, and I learned afterwards that he was hated at school and at home for his meanness, which was the only quality he cultivated.

While I was looking at him, and thinking I would get Jo to knock him down some day, Mateel and Agnes came around the house with Damon Barker, who had evidently just arrived. He had never met either of them before, but, on encountering them, introduced himself with the easy grace for which he was noted. Both had heard of him, and seemed pleased to see him, for they sat down on each side of him on a rough seat under an apple-tree. I went out to them at once, and he spoke to me in such a considerate way that I was sure it would be noticed that he was my particular friend, which I regarded as a circumstance very much in my favor. He did not treat me as a boy, as the others did, but listened kindly when I was talking, instead of waving me to silence with his hand, and altogether acted as though I was worthy of his respect and friendship.

We all inquired about Jo, who had been away several weeks, and he replied so favorably that he took another step forward in my good opinion. Jo was already the best assistant he had ever had, he said, and was certain to become a remarkable man.

"I have a few books about the house," Barker said. "Jo devours them, and keeps me up far into every night answering questions. Next to his ambition to learn all there is about the mill, he is ambitious to know all there is in the books. I think he will succeed in both particulars; I was not mistaken in my estimate of him."

We were all pleased to hear him say this, and, though not intending it, Mateel let it be known that she was greatly interested in Jo. I hoped Barker would notice it, and tell him, for it would be a pleasure for him to know it.

"A boy apprenticed on a farm has very little opportunity to learn anything — I wonder that he knows as much as he does; but he is progressive and manly, and I am very much mistaken if his advancement is not very rapid from now on. He wants to know about everything, and [3] I really believe he could run the mill very well without me now. He was familiar with every part of it before he came there to live, and I suppose he is busy to-day taking the machinery apart to look at it, since I am not there to answer his questions regarding the contents of the books."

Barker seemed to understand that Jo had never been appreciated in Fairview, and was determined that the people should know he was very favorably impressed with him. I thought it was very kind of him to come so far to defend Jo.

"A young man ready to take advantage of every opportunity is rare enough to be remarkable," Barker continued, observing Mateel very closely. "They usually have to be driven to it, and encouraged to keep at it by all sorts of stratagems, but Jo only asks opportunity, and goes at his work with an energy I greatly admire. I have known hundreds of men who knew less at middle age than Jo knows at seventeen, and who were not his equals in whatever he attempts. This seems to have been against him here, but it will be to his advantage in his new place. But I believe I have not yet asked how you liked [4] Fairview," he abruptly concluded, addressing Mateel.

She replied very much as a polite woman should — that while it was not possible that she could positively say on so short an

[3] everything, and: 1883 everything he hears, and
[4] liked: 1883 like

acquaintance, she believed she would become entirely content with it in time.

"I have lived here contentedly enough a good many years," Barker replied, "with few acquaintances and fewer friends. The country is very fair. I know little enough of the people, but no one is crowded here. There is room enough for everybody, and there are splendid opportunities to be let alone. There is a good deal in that."

In her dependent, uncertain way, Mateel looked as though it were possible to be let alone too much, although she said nothing.

"I take it that people do not come west for society, but rather because there are more acres than people in this direction," Barker said. "I have been told that it is possible to get too much of society, and that after it quiet is appreciated. To this class Fairview will prove a satisfactory place. My nearest neighbor lives two miles away; I shouldn't care if he lived ten. He is an ignorant fellow, who chops wood for a living; and he is very considerate, for he never comes to see me. I think I never spoke to my neighbor except to ask him how much was my debt. We get along very well. Who is the young man at the window?" noticing [5] Bragg, who had changed his position and was looking at the sky.

I replied that he was a friend of Mr. Shepherd's, and that he had only arrived a few days before.

"He looks as though he was in jail for murder, and meditating an escape in order to commit the same offence with greater atrocity. What is the matter with him?"

I was afraid that this might offend Mateel, but after seeing that Bragg had not heard it she laughed over it, as did the rest of us. She added, however, that he was in excellent health, and that he was more moody than sullen, and could be very agreeable when he wanted to be.

"I judge he has had too much of society, and enjoys the quiet of Fairview. He looks pleasant."

I will swear that Bragg's face was the most unpleasant and disagreeable at that moment I had ever seen.

[5] noticing: 1883 referring to

103

"He should visit the mill for quiet. We have no noise there except the roar of the water and the rumble of the wheels, and we have grown so accustomed to these that it would not be quiet without them. I hope he will like the country."

At this moment my father and Mr. Shepherd came around from the orchard, and Barker bowed low on being presented. I thought Mr. Shepherd regretted he had not known Barker was so polite, as he could have shown something in that line himself; but they got on very well together, and were soon talking like old friends. We sat there for an hour or more, listening to their easy and cultured conversation, and it occurred to me, with renewed force, that Fairview was getting out of its old ways. Mr. Shepherd promised to visit him, the invitation having been extended, and my mother and the minister's wife coming out later the party was so agreeable that I wondered we could not have more of it instead of the discontent which usually oppressed us. Hearing our peals of laughter, I hoped Bragg regretted he had not been in better humor and joined the company; but he never looked that way, and pretended to be occupied with himself.

"You have never been inside of Fairview church, Damon," my father said to him, quite familiarly, late in the afternoon; "won't you come to-night?"

"I will walk on with Ned," Barker replied, good-naturedly, and rising, "and think of it after I reach the cross-roads; I see it is almost time to start."

After taking his leave of all of them in a courteous way, I walked with him along the path leading across the field, my father excusing me from further attendance for that purpose.

We proceeded quite leisurely, as there was no hurry, and after we had walked a considerable distance my companion said: —

"A very pretty girl, and intelligent enough, but weak. She could be coaxed into anything. They say that is true of all light-haired women."

I did not know whether he meant Agnes or Mateel, so I inquired, "Who?"

"The one you call Mateel. She has a pretty face, but were I

104

inclined to criticise such a delightful girl I should say she lacks decision. The other one hardly spoke to me. What is it they call her?"

"Agnes."

"The school-teacher, I believe. She is very much of a woman, though evidently young. I admire her more than the other one. Do her people live here?"

"No; in Smoky Hill."

"Very respectable, I have no doubt. I should like to know her father, and congratulate him."

"Her father is dead," I answered.

"Oh! Dead."

He walked on in silence for a considerable distance.

"An orphan. It's a pity."

I narrated what little I could tell of the family after the promise to Agnes, though I longed to tell him of her mother; but it seemed to bore him, and he dismissed the subject after I had concluded in a rhapsody for the gentle and patient Agnes.

By this time we had reached the cross-road, leading in one direction to the church and in the other toward his home. He stopped here, and said: —

"I will not go to the church to-night, if you will be good enough to present my excuse to your father. It is a long road home, and I must walk it. You know that you are always welcome at the mill, and that Jo is anxious to see you. Good-night."

He turned abruptly on his heel, and, walking away, his form was soon lost in the rapidly approaching darkness.

When I arrived at the church I found the others all there, and was surprised to find Bragg in better humor, as if the darkness suited his disposition better. He was walking about quite contentedly, looking curiously (and impudently) at the knots of people collected in the yard, and listening to what they were saying. At times I thought he would speak to them, and his eyes, dull and heavy all day, were now as bright and active as a ferret's, and I thought he could penetrate the darkness with them, for while the services were in progress he kept walking about, closely regarding everything, as though it were broad daylight. When

105

the people came out, he met the Shepherds at the door, and went down the walk with Mateel on his arm, and when they drove away I thought I heard him talking quite good-naturedly. Had the fellow's spirits deserted him at the approach of day, and come back with the darkness?

XII

LOVE'S YOUNG DREAM

Two months had passed since Jo had gone to live at the mill, and on a Saturday afternoon it was arranged that I should visit him, and remain until Monday.

My father was at the country town a great deal of late, and the farm was being neglected in the hands of the renter and his two sons, who I often thought were shiftless men, or they would have owned a farm of their own, for land was cheap and plentiful. When he returned from these visits to Twin Mounds, he was more thoughtful than ever, and after making long rows of figures in his private book, and casting them up, he pondered over the result, as if he had added another problem to the number he was always studying over.

I did not get started until late, and as I rode away my father came out to say that, unless I hurried, night would overtake me in the woods, and as it was the first time in his life he had paid me so much attention, I thought, as I rode along, that Fairview was certainly progressing, and that the old order of things was passing away.

The road which I travelled led through the fields past Theodore Meek's, and thence through the woods, and, as I went along leisurely, when I was half way it began to grow dark. This did not alarm me, however, as I was well acquainted with the way, and there was no prospect of getting lost. As I came out upon the ridge dividing the waters of Bull River and Big Creek, where there was an opening, and the trees gave way to underbrush, I saw a man ahead of me riding on horseback, as I was. Thinking he was going my way, and would keep me company, I hurried on to come up with him, but he turned out of the road when I approached him, and rode off to the left. Although it was almost dark, I recognized the horseman as Clinton Bragg, and the direction he took indicated that he was on his way to visit the Shepherds. Coming up to the place where he had turned off, I saw that there was no road, and had a mind to halloo to him, thinking he was not familiar with the country, and might have lost his way, but before I could put that intention into execution, he urged his horse into a gallop, and passed rapidly along the deep shadow skirting the other side of the clearing. I remembered then that the fellow, like an owl, was more himself after dark than during the day, and, supposing that he had concluded to ride through the timber and darkness to save distance, I thought no more of him, except to wish that he would have trouble.

When I arrived at the mill it was long after dark, and, wishing to surprise Jo, I put the horse away alone, as I was familiar with the stables from frequent visits. Seeing no light in the house, I supposed he was at the mill, and went in there, although it was dark, and I should have thought it deserted but for the circumstance that all the machinery was in operation. Hearing someone in the basement, I sat down until he had finished and started up the stairs, when I saw it was Jo, carrying a lantern.

"And so you have come at last," he said, hanging the lantern on his arm, and taking both my hands in his. "I had almost come to believe that you had forgotten me."

"It has been impossible for me to come sooner," I replied. "We have been very busy at home since you came away, and as father spends a great deal of his time in town now, I have double work to do. I have been as anxious to come as you have been anxious to see me, for I have been very lonely since you went away."

"I am certain of that," he returned good-naturedly, using his lantern to look critically at a wheel which I am sure was all right, but he wanted me to know that he was in charge; "I am certain you came as soon as you could, my dear old friend. You, like myself, cannot always do what you please. But now that you have come, you may be quite sure that I am glad to see you, and you could not have arrived at a more favorable time. I am to stay here until midnight, at which time Barker will relieve me, and you shall stay with me and tell me the news."

108

"I think it is very much to your credit, Jo," I said, "that you are able to run alone already."

"O, it is nothing," he answered, though I could see he was proud of it. "All I have to do is to look around, and see that the belts are on and that the machinery is running smoothly. The mill runs itself, and if anything should go wrong, I have only to shut down the gate, and call Barker. But nothing is likely to go wrong. Barker is a fine miller, and he has everything so arranged that the water does the work with little assistance. But tell me how much you have missed me again, and everything that has occurred at home since I came way."

Under the first head I could have talked all night, but there was nothing new except the arrival of Bragg.

"He was here to-day," Jo said, thoughtfully, "and I don't like his looks. He came in while I was alone, and inquired if this was Barker's mill. I answered that it was, when he said he presumed my name was Jo Erring. On my confessing my name, he sat down on a pile of sacks, and watched me intently for half an hour, when he got up, and went out without saying a word. I suppose he went up to the house, and looked at Barker in the same way, for I saw him come out of the door, mount his horse, and ride away. He looks like one of the Devil's sons. Who is he?"

I told all I knew about him, and I thought Jo was much interested in the statement that he had been raised at Mateel's old home, and that they had grown up together.

"He's impudent, whoever he is; I can say that for him. I thought he wanted to buy me, he looked at me so closely. I suppose Mateel is as pretty as ever."

I answered that she wonderfully improved on acquaintance, and that, having gone down into the bottom of her trunk, she was better dressed than ever when last I saw her.

"You know that letter of apology to Mateel I read you?" Jo inquired, without paying much attention to my remark.

I said I remembered it very distinctly, but I wondered why he now regarded it so pleasantly, for he was smiling.

"Well, I received an answer to it a day or two after coming here, accompanied by an invitation to visit her, and I don't mind confessing to you that I went, as I had learned a great deal since I called there the first time with your mother, and was anxious she should know it. In fact, I have been there three times in three weeks. It's only a short distance to their house from here, and Barker gave me so many lessons in bowing and politeness that I couldn't resist the temptation to try them."

"And how did they work?"

"Oh, I forgot everything as soon as I got into the house, of course," he answered wearily, as though he were dreadfully slow in learning to be polite. "She came up to me, and stood so close that I hadn't room to bow. When her mother came in, she shook hands, and I couldn't have bowed to her without pushing over my chair. It was a total failure, though I am improving. I take off my hat now before going in at the gate. I am under contract to go there to-morrow night, and you shall accompany me. I have a new suit of clothes, too. They arrived a few days after I came here; I asked Barker who sent them, and he said he supposed it must have been God."

"Jo," I said, "you are very happy here, I can see it already."

"I confess that I am," he replied; "more contented than I ever expected to be anywhere. I am useful to Barker (so he is kind enough to say, at least), and he told me to-day that he intends to pay me wages from the time I came, instead of compelling me to work a long while for nothing. Yes, I am very happy here; you have guessed my secret."

I was heartily glad of it, and said so, and added that no one deserved it more.

"But after all there is nothing like a fairy story in it; nothing unreal, and nothing that is likely to melt away, and leave me a drudge at Fairview again. I am simply in a place where, if I work hard, I shall get something for it. Everyone ought to have that opportunity, therefore it is not too much to hope that my good fortune may continue. I should have been as comfortably situated as I am now a good many years ago (no one is so unworthy that he does not deserve pay for what work he does well), but I have learned nothing, and earned nothing, until now, though I am almost a man grown."

Jo had been a full hand on the farm for several years, but he never received anything for it, except complaints, and I understood what he meant.

"But I want to talk to you about Mateel; I think a great deal about her. It's very odd, but it is very true. At home, and at your house, the poorest corner was too good for Jo; with her the best is too poor. I should be very ungrateful did she not occupy my thoughts a great deal. Though she is a lady and I only a rough country boy, she is so considerate of me that I cannot help loving her, though it is very presuming in me, I fear. I feel as though I were visiting a queen when I go there, but she makes me so welcome that I soon forget myself, and imagine I am a king. All of my ambition is connected with her now. If I hope to become a worthy man, and well-to-do, it is that she may be proud of me, and feel that I have worked to please her; if I study Barker's books diligently by the light of this lantern at night, it is that I may become more intelligent, and worthy of the good opinion she has of me. I dream of nothing pleasant in which she does not have a part. If I fancy I am happy, she is beside me, and the cause of it; if I have grown rich and great in a night, I am only glad of it because it will please Mateel. Always and everywhere, when my better part is uppermost, she is in my thoughts, but never when I am contemptible in any way. There seems to be no doubt, in short, that I am desperately in love."

I had suspected this for some time, though I pretended to be greatly surprised.

"I have never said anything to her about it," he continued. "Maybe I never shall, but, ignorant as I am, I can see she is glad to see me when I go there, and she would not invite me back so cordially if she could not tolerate me. It is very pleasant for an ignorant fellow like me to be friends with a refined lady like Mateel. I never thought there was anything in life equal to it. She does not seem to know but that I am of a good family, but I intend to tell her honestly and truly sometime what an unfavored fellow I am."

I said she probably knew all about him already, and was satisfied.

"Do you suppose she does?" he inquired with the look of a pleasant hope in his face. "It would be comforting to know that, as it would be humiliating to tell her everything to my discredit I can think of. But if ever I become convinced that she loves me, I will tell her everything if it kills me."

He talked as though he had been a great criminal in his time, but there was really nothing more serious against him than that his father was an eccentric shingle-maker, and his mother a midwife, if I except the circumstance that everybody said he came of a shiftless family.

"There seems to be no doubt that I am madly in love," he repeated again, looking at the flame of his lantern, as though it were likely to give an opinion as to whether he was or not. "I don't know whether to regard it as a serious circumstance or a pleasant one. They say that one's first love does not amount to anything, and that one soon forgets it. It will not be that way with me, I am certain. I should be ashamed to offer my affections to another girl after having loved Mateel as madly as I do now, and I should feel that I was offering a poor return for the love I should expect of a wife. I am convinced that a man who has loved but once makes a better husband than one who is in doubt as to whether he ever loved at all. I would as soon marry a widow with children as a woman who has been engaged, and permitted the familiarities which are common under such circumstances. If there is anything in love at all, it is wrong to break an engagement. A man or woman who is so uncertain in matters of the heart as to contract a new fancy four or five times a year, is likely to be mistaken at last. I am not acquainted with many people who are happily married, but I am convinced that plenty of them may be found in looking the world over, and inquiry will no doubt reveal the fact that they were never in love but once. If I should marry, it would seriously affect my happiness to know that another man — I despise a man, anyhow — had caressed and fondled my wife as an accepted lover. I wouldn't live in the same country with him, and I should be forever unhappy for fear that she loved him the best. It would be a circumstance very much in favor of a happy married life for a man to know that his wife

112

had never seen anyone else she would marry; to know that her lips had touched only his, and that she was innocent as well as virtuous."

I did not know much about such matters, but I thought Jo expected a great deal; perhaps too much. But he had grown so serious that I knew he was deeply concerned, and though I tried to change the subject, and talk about the mill, he answered me in such a way as to indicate that he would talk of nothing but Mateel that night. He was uneasy and worried in his manner, too, although I could not understand why, unless it was regret that he had been raised so poorly, and that he was only given opportunity to learn at seventeen; for I knew that in his affair with Mateel he had every reason to feel satisfied, except that he was so young and poor as to render thoughts of his marrying her almost ridiculous. It may have been that a knowledge of the possibilities of his future made him chafe and fret that he was compelled, from no fault of his own, to begin life so late, and that he feared failure under such circumstances, although success would have been certain under circumstances more favorable.

As if the thought were disagreeable, he picked up the lantern abruptly, and went down under the mill, leaving me in the dark, and he remained so long that at last I followed. I found him leaning against a heavy timber, looking at the flame in his lantern again, as though it could enlighten him if it would on certain matters of which he was anxious to know more.

"You are becoming as great a thinker as father, Jo," I said, touching him on the shoulder, for he had been so occupied with his thoughts that he had not noticed my approach. "You used to dislike him very much for that."

Recollecting himself, he pretended that he had come down to look at something, and after seeing that it was all right, we went up again.

"If I was thinking," he said good-naturedly, "it was that I had never thought of loving until Mateel came in my way. The possibility that some day I should marry was so remote that I never considered it, and when you came down there just now, I was hoping that if ever I should marry Mateel — I don't suppose I

113

ever shall; it was only a fancy, and there is no harm in telling it —
she would confess to me that thoughts of loving and marrying
never came to her until she met me, as I intend to confess to her,
and it will be God's holy truth. I have never even divided my
poor affection among my relatives; you have had it all, but I
don't think Mateel would object to that."

Although he had only been there a short time, I thought Jo had
grown to be a man since I had seen him last. He looked larger,
and older, and acted and talked more like one than he did two
months before, when he was a boy.

"I can understand why you love me," he said, "because I have
tried to win your regard, and we have been friends all our lives,
but if Mateel cares for me, it is because there is more to me than
Fairview has ever given me credit for. If that is not the case, then
my ambition is hopeless, and if I have been thinking, it is about
that. It is pleasant for me to know that, ignorant and rough as I
am, intelligent people can admire me at all, for I am improving
very rapidly, and in time I can hope to become worthy of the
friendship of very good people. I am surprised to think how
ignorant I was a month ago; I shall be in still greater wonder
six months hence to realize how foolish I was when you first came
to see me at the mill. I have no other hope for the future than
that I can learn something every day, for if I live a long time I
can hope to know something at last. It is not a great brain that
can be exhausted at thirty, or even forty, and I expect to study
very hard from now on, that I may catch up with others of equal
capacity who began under more fortunate circumstances. I believe the day is coming when Fairview will be peopled with the
kind of men and women I am acquainted with in my fancy; and
when they arrive I am ambitious to be able to associate with
them without the restraint of stupidity and ignorance."

I was about to reply, when we heard Barker coming in, as the
hour had arrived when he was to take charge, although we had
not suspected that midnight was so near at hand, so rapidly had
the time passed. Barker greeted me pleasantly, and although I
supposed he had just crept out of bed, he was as fresh and cheer-

ful as it was possible to be. While we were walking up to the house I mentioned the circumstance to Jo.

"I have never yet found him asleep," he replied. "I think one of his eyes is always open, if not both of them, but I have given up all curiosity with reference to him. If he has a secret, and wants me to know it, I am always here, and he can easily tell me. But I am content to trust him just as he is. There can't be anything very bad about a man who is always fair, just, and honest. I have an idea that when I have earned his confidence, I shall know his secret, if he has one, and that he will tell me. In the meantime I intend to make myself as useful as possible, and not annoy him with my curiosity."

I had intended to ask Jo for a theory with reference to Barker during the visit, but after this I concluded that I would not.

XIII

THE FLOCK OF THE GOODE SHEPHERD

Jo and I agreed that we would ride over to his father's in the forenoon of the next day, and return by way of the Shepherds' in the evening. We started in the morning before Barker was stirring, as he had worked until daylight, Jo riding the horse he had received from my father together with ten dollars in money, and I a clumsy but reliable animal from the farm, which I believe had assisted in hauling our wagons to the country, and which rode about as comfortable as a wheel-barrow.

When we arrived at the Ford, and as we stopped our horses to allow them to drink, I saw that several loads of stone for the dam had arrived since my last visit there, and Jo told me he intended to haul at least one load a week until he had enough, and that there would occasionally be dull days at Barker's — as in times of high water, or ice — when he could work on his own enterprise for days at a time.

The house of hewn logs occupied by my grandfather was built on the crest of the hill above the creek, the ground on the side by which we approached it being lower, and covered with timber, and riding up to the fence surrounding it, we secured our horses, and went in. Although it was summer, Dad Erring occupied his usual corner by the fire-place, and had evidently just finished smoking a pipe, as the room was yet full of the fumes. He was very much surprised to see us, and was at once cordial and hospitable by asking us to pull up to the fire-place, which we did, although the fire had been out for several months.

"She's not at home," he said, divining that we wondered where Gran was. "She's away. But I don't know where. I never do. Both of you know that already. She has been away —" he rested one

116

hand on his knees, and counted the days on the bricks of the hearth with his walking-stick — "three days. She may be at home in an hour; she may not return in a week. Both of you are familiar with the manner in which she comes and goes."

I had frequently remarked of my grandfather that while others in Fairview said little because they were gloomy, he said little because he had little to say, and after finishing what I have quoted, he stopped as if wondering how he could find language to give his visitors to understand that they were welcome. He seemed to conclude at last that we were anxious to know next about his business (as if there was nothing in the wide world except his wife and the shingle business), and said: —

"You ask how I am getting along with my shingle-making." We had not mentioned the subject at all, by the way. "I answer, not very well. The trees cut very hard of late, and although I go to my work later, and come home earlier than formerly, I am more tired at night than usual. Shingle-making does not progress very well; I am afraid I am not as young as I was ten or twelve years ago, but we must all wear out. You two are commencing; I am finishing, but I doubt if you think of the future more pleasantly than I do. I am always tired now, and rest to me is as agreeable as hope to you. Look at my hands."

As he held them out, I saw that they were cracked and scarred, and the flesh on them dry and callous. He had been rubbing them with some kind of oil, and the fingers were so cold that it remained on them in lumps without melting.

"They hurt me a great deal." We both expressed a regret that his hands were not better. "But I am well every other way, except that I get tired so easy. If I could get the cracks out of my hands, the shingle business would get on better."

I had noticed before that he apologized for old age and weakness in this way, and tried to convince himself that he was very well, and very strong, except that his hands would crack open, and occasionally he raised them up, and looked at the sores, as though they would finally be the death of him.

"She has good success with other people, but poor luck with my hands." He always spoke of his wife as "she," as she always referred to him as "he." "They baffle her skill. I suppose they are in a bad way."

He got up at this, and began walking up and down the floor, rubbing his hands together. Remembering his great feats at walking, I thought if his hands were as sound as his legs, he would still be a stout man. Coming back to his chair presently, he sat down, and said to Jo: —

"Since we are talking of your new business, I may as well say that she has agreed that you are to have this place." I could not help wondering what boy had sat between them, and made a conversation on the subject possible. "I don't know whether it is fit for what you want it or not, but we have both decided that you may try."

I was surprised that he knew Jo had such an ambition, or that he knew Jo had gone to Barker's to live, for it was a chance that anyone had taken the pains to tell him.

"If my hands get better by the time you are ready to commence," he said, "I will help you. I was once a good hand at framing timbers, and there is enough on the place to build the mill. I have picked out a great many sticks in my trips to the woods which will be suitable."

It pleased Jo to know that he had been planning to help him, for no one else had.

"I don't want you to help me, father," he said, "though I am glad you offer to, for now I know you have confidence in me. I intend to help you, after I become a miller, instead of permitting you to help me. I am sorry I never talked to you about it before; you know more about it than any of them."

"I have thought about your mill a great deal," was his reply, "and have great hope that you will turn out a better man than your father. I have never amounted to much; both of you know that, but you have a better start. It is poor enough; you can imagine what mine was, and you know more than I did at your age. I have lived all my life in places where men were not expected to amount to much, and were satisfied if they did not. It seems to be different now."

What a dull country he must have lived in, to have thought Fairview superior to it!

"I think you ought to build your house where this one stands," he said. "I have planted a number of trees around it for you, and I hope that when you are grown up, your happy children may play under their shade. It is a pretty place here, and it is but a few rods to the best point for a mill. I have more confidence in you than anyone else. I would help you if I could."

Jo was greatly affected by this kindness, and as an excuse to get out of doors, fearing he would be weak enough to cry if he remained there, suggested that we get dinner. The idea was not a bad one, after we came to think more of it, and we soon had it under way.

My grandfather pretended not to know what we were about, but I saw him looking frequently into the kitchen, where we were, and when it was declared ready, he tried to be greatly surprised. There was a number of young chickens running around, and we had taken two of these, intending to leave word for Gran that the hawks had been about, and that the mice had been in the pickles and preserves. The dinner was Jo's best effort, and, being familiar with everything his father was fond of, he succeeding in making him very good natured.

"It is just such a dinner as I can enjoy," he said, when he sat down to it. "You seem to be able to do everything, Jo, but I hope you will get out of the way, for these Jacks are said to be able to make everything except money. I depend on you to distinguish your family; there is no one else to do it, and we come of a long line of very common folks. I enjoy your dinner, but I am sorry you can cook so well; really, I am sorry. I could cook when I was of your age, and I could cut hair, and I never amounted to anything. You should get out of the way."

His good nature continued until after the meal was concluded, and until we went away, for when we had returned to the front room again, he asked Jo and me to sing camp-meeting songs to him while he smoked, which we cheerfully did, imitating the singers in gestures, hand-shaking, shouting, and so on, which was an accomplishment we had to be very careful in exhibiting. Then we made prayers and speeches representing The. Meek, Mr. Winter, and the miller's sister, and sang the hymn through our noses, commencing, "Hark, from the tomb, a doleful sound," all of which so pleased my grandfather that he laughed, and roared, and pounded the floor with his stick, and declared that we were equal to a "show." When we said in the course of the afternoon that we must go, he replied that he sincerely regretted it, as he had never enjoyed himself so well before, and made us promise that we would come back every Sunday in the future when Gran was away, and have an equally good time. We both shook hands with him at parting — for the first time in our lives, I think — and rode away waving adieus.

❊   ❊   ❊

The Shepherds lived on the other side of Big Creek woods, on the high divide between Big Creek and Bull River, in a house originally dingy enough, but which had been wonderfully transformed by their living in it. The people said enough money had been spent in repairing it to build a house large enough for three, and it was furnished throughout in a style very unusual in that country, although it was no more than comfortable.

Mateel met us at the door, and as she ushered us into the neat parlor I thought I had never seen a handsomer woman, with the possible exception of Agnes, and I could not but inwardly congratulate Jo on his good fortune. I thought that I could see that she was very fond of him, now that it had been called to my mind, though I may only have imagined it, for she was as polite to me as to him.

"I am glad to see you," she said, taking my hat, which I was careful to remove, remembering Jo's experience. "My father did not feel well to-day, and we are all at home, as Mr. Westlock agreed to take his place at Fairview."

Mr. Shepherd came in at this moment, followed by his respectable wife (who bowed stiffly to both of us at once, as though we were not worth two separate efforts), and impressed me at once with his freedom for a Sunday evening. It was a funeral day at our house, but Mr. Shepherd laughed and talked as though we were at a party. As I looked at his pale and effeminate face, I thought that his daughter was very much like him, and that had a son been born to the family, he would have been like his mother — quiet, dignified, and capable.

"I worked in the field so late Saturday," he said, with the utmost candor and freedom, "that I felt too tired to preach to-day, so I sent word to your father that he would oblige me by preaching a sermon on future punishment. It is one of the rules of the church that this disagreeable topic be discussed from the pulpit at least once a year. I dislike it, and am glad to shirk. Your father is very fond of the subject, I am told. But no difference what he says about it, I will apologize next Sunday, and deny it. The religion of Fairview seems to make the people miserable; I shall change it if I can. I have been religious all my life, and it never caused me a sorrow. I don't believe in devils much, but I believe a great deal in angels."

As he looked at me as if he desired an expression on the subject, I said angels were certainly the most comforting to think about.

"I have been much distressed by the unhappy faces I have seen since coming here, and I hope I may be the humble instrument of brightening them. The right kind of religion will put flowers in the yard, let sunlight in at the window, and fill the house with content and happiness. I became a Christian man because I longed for heaven, rather than because I feared the dreadful abode of the wicked, and it is my intention to introduce this gospel here."

Mr. Shepherd was directing his conversation to me, as Mateel and Joe had retired to another part of the room, and were very much interested in each other. I therefore wished him success in the undertaking.

"I have always thought that the Bible is such a convincing book that it finally converts nearly all the children of men — I hope all of them — though the church to which I belong does not cheerfully accept my opinion. The Bible is only in dispute because a new set of men are coming on all the time, who have also to be convinced and saved. Its promises are so magnificent that no one can read them all his life and fail to put himself in the way of their fulfilment; therefore there is no excuse for referring to the disagreeable subject I have just mentioned. You may as well look on the bright side of religion as on the bright side of anything else, and you know we are always having maxims of this kind thrown at us. This is the religion the present pastor of Fairview believes in, and this is the religion he will teach, though I have not taught much of it to-day, for I have not mentioned the subject at all until now. But I only came in to say I was glad to see you, and will go out again," he said, rising. "I am becoming very worldly of late, for I have been thinking all day of how the potatoes and corn I ploughed last week are getting on rather than of sermons, and I am so sleepy now that you perhaps noticed me blinking. I am also forgetting a great deal of my theology in the hunger which constantly besets me, and if I raise nothing at all this year I will feel well repaid for my work by the good health I have enjoyed. When you return home express my thanks to your father for his sermon."

As he went out I thought if he was not a remarkable preacher he was certainly a good man. His respectable wife followed, and as she had not said a word I thought we should not miss her company.

"I was just saying to Miss Shepherd," Jo said, coming over to me, "that you and I have been fast friends since you were born. When I was a very little fellow and Ned only a baby he loved me, and was happier with me than with anyone else. It seems queer that anyone should live to be seventeen years old and have no other intimate friend than his sister's boy."

He addressed the remark to Mateel, but she did not seem sure whether it was queer or not; she was never certain of anything, like her father.

"I have an idea that we shall be old men together, and die greatly regretted by one another," Jo continued. "I should be content with a very few friends like Ned; a man cannot do justice to a great many as true and good as he is. If I were wealthy I should build a high wall around my house, and station a surly porter at the gate instructed to admit only a very few. It is one of the disadvantages of the trade I am learning that I shall be expected to be sociable with every kind of men. I shall never be free to tell those I dislike to forever keep off my premises, as I should like to do, but in order to live I shall be compelled to treat them well for their patronage. It has been my experience that only two men out of every ten have qualities worthy of cultivation, but it would be ruinous to introduce such a doctrine into the mill business."

I saw that Jo was in an odd humor, for he had forgotten that he should make himself agreeable, and stopped occasionally to think. Pretending not to notice it, I exchanged the gossip of the neighborhood with Mateel, until Jo said, with an effort to shake off his gloomy thoughts: —

"Miss Shepherd, I should like to hear you sing."

Mateel laughed a little at this sudden invitation, but good-naturedly opened the instrument, and, after selecting a piece, sang it. The words were of constancy, and of a lover who went mad on learning that his mistress had wedded his rival.

"It's a song about love," Jo said, after Mateel had finished it, picking up the music and looking curiously at the title-page. "Most song-writers take that for a subject. Do you believe the story it tells?"

"I sang it because I believed it," Mateel said, wincing under Jo's cold and steady gaze (he was in a very odd humor indeed). "I believe in but one love."

"There are so many people who believe in two or three, or half a dozen. I suppose you do; all good people are very honorable in matters of this kind. Sometimes very bad people believe in it — I do, for one."

I have thought of this very often since, for a great deal that was horrible might have been avoided had the conversation been candid on both sides.

"I would be afraid of getting in love's way," he said, as though we had been accusing him. "They say it never runs smooth, and I should be very unhappy were it to be interrupted. The writer speaks of the heart's silent secrets. That seems to be the general heart trouble; it is a repository of secrets, and always uncomfortable ones. The subject makes me miserable; I never thought of it in my life that I did not at once become disagreeable."

Mateel laughed merrily at this, and said people usually thought of it to be gay.

"But it is a most serious subject after all. If a man makes a mistake in any other matter it is easily remedied; a day's work, and he is as well as ever, but a mistake in love is not so easily mended. It may make life a failure, and cause a man to rest uneasily in his grave. If I should leave a wife at death, and she should marry again, my very clay would cry out in agony at the thought. Under such circumstances I should long to be an unhappy ghost, that I might be free to walk the earth and fill her nights with terror. I hope I am not naturally of an ugly disposition, but if this misfortune should happen to me, I would resign my place in heaven and join the devils, in order that I might be wicked and cruel in my revenge."

I had never seen Jo in such a serious mood before, and mentioned it. His old, cheerful smile returned for a moment as he made some good-natured response, but as he kept on thinking it was soon replaced with a frown. Mateel seemed to enjoy his mood, and encouraged it by saying that a man had a different opinion of love every year of his life.

"I never had an opinion on the subject at all until this year," was his reply, "but I will tell you what I think of it next year, and the next. If I am of the same opinion then as now, you can give me the credit that my first impressions represented me. My first impressions of the subject are that I would as soon marry a widow as a girl who had been in love before. If I were the king of a country I would punish second marriage with death, and make it unlawful for a man or woman to be engaged more than once, thus preventing the marital unhappiness which I am sure always results when either the wife or husband knows the other has been in love before."

Mateel laughed so heartily over this absurd idea that I joined her in spite of myself, though I knew Jo was very serious, and he looked at us both as though we were attending his funeral and in good spirits over the grave.

"I came here to pass a pleasant evening," I said to him, "but if you continue in this humor we shall all have the horrors presently."

"I shouldn't have begun," he said, walking over to the music rack (to look for a hornpipe, I thought), "but I have said no more than I really feel. We will settle it with that, and I will never make you uncomfortable again by referring to the subject."

Having selected a more cheerful song we tried to sing it to-gether, but it was a failure, and the evening dragged heavily after that, so much so that Jo announced his intention to go quite early.

"I was never gloomy in my life before," he said to Mateel on parting. "I don't know what caused me to be to-night, for I am usually happier here than anywhere else. It must have been the gloomy poet whose song you sang. I hope you will forgive me. When I come again we will not speak of love. I know so little of it that I can't be entertaining talking about it."

Perhaps your ignorance of love, Jo, will prove more serious than you expect. Had you more knowledge of it you would know that your lonely fancies are wrong, and that there is not such a woman in the world as you have created, and no such love as you expect. Perhaps had you mingled more with the world you would have known this and saved yourself much unhappiness.

I went out ahead of him, and he remained inside talking for a few moments. Mateel seemed to be assuring him that she was not offended, and I heard him thank her, quietly say his adieus, and close the door.

We rode a considerable distance in silence, for I was waiting for Jo to speak, as he had to my mind emerged from boyhood to manhood since coming to the mill to live, and I was not as free in his company as I had been at home.

"I have made poor progress to-night," he said, at last, "but I was not comfortable while there, for some reason, and now I am not satisfied when I am away. The next time I go there I intend to tell Mateel that I am madly in love with her. I suppose she will call her father and order me out of the house, but I can't stand this suspense. I have a notion to send you on home and go back now."

He stopped in the road to consider it, but, recollecting that it would be a ridiculous performance, rode on again.

"My love for her has taken such complete possession of me that I shall be fit for nothing else until I know what I am to expect.

If I were older, and not so poor, I would go back to-night, declare my love, and insist that she forever reject me or marry me in five minutes. But even if she accepts me — when I offer myself — it will be years before I can hope to possess her. I have always been waiting — first for release from your father, then for release from Barker, and now for Mateel. I would sell myself to the Devil to-night, to be delivered in four or five years, for a little age, a home of my own, and Mateel for my wife — NOW, not to wait a minute."

He had said NOW! so loudly that it sounded like a signal for the Devil to appear and complete the bargain of which he had spoken, and was so stern that I was afraid of him.

"I must curb this terrible passion or it will do me serious injury. There is nothing in store for me except waiting and working, and I fear that by the time I accomplish what I desire I shall be so tired and indifferent that I cannot enjoy it as I would now. But if I am as happy when I possess her as I think I shall be, I will whip the man who says this is not a happy world. If she is given to me, I shall make her a queen if it is possible. My only fear is that being of a poor family I shall not be able to accomplish all I desire. Barker says an industrious man can accomplish more than a talented one; if that is true I will make Mateel proud of me, and cause her to bless the day she came to Fairview to live. But I intend to talk less in the future, and do more."

He urged his horse into a gallop, and dashed through the dark woods like a man on fire, and I followed, expecting every moment to be thrown off and injured. I did not come entirely up with him until we had reached the mill, and after putting away the horses we went at once to bed, where Jo no doubt spent the night in waiting for daylight, that he might commence to distinguish himself.

XIV

I AM SURPRISED

Matters were going from bad to worse at Fairview. My father had been away to the country town a week, and had not yet returned.

As the attendance on the summer school was small, Agnes managed to come home very early, and go away very late, so that we were like three happy children having a holiday, for my mother remained up with us until midnight, if we did not get sleepy before that time, talking very little, but quietly enjoying our company, as though it was a pleasure usually denied her. I told them all I knew about Jo, Mateel, Barker, his strange sister, and Clinton Bragg, inventing incidents whenever the interest threatened to flag, and Agnes was always entertaining, so that we were very happy during that week.

It was the Saturday night after my return from the mill, when we were beginning to be seriously alarmed about my father's long absence, and just after we had agreed that something should be done about it, the door opened, and he walked in. I had been expecting him to return in a bad humor, but much to my surprise he was in a very good humor, and appeared to be pleased about something, as though he had accomplished all he desired, and was good enough to ask me if I had enjoyed myself at Barker's.

My mother and Agnes went out to the kitchen at once to prepare his supper, and he followed them to talk while they were about it. He had brought them presents, and, holding up the packages, asked them to guess what they were, and when they failed he laughed, and asked them to guess again. I looked on in wonder, and after he had seated himself at the table, and commenced eating without asking a blessing, he astonished us all by saying: —

127

"Well, I have bought the 'Union of States' newspaper, and a house in Twin Mounds, and we move there to live next Monday. What do you all think of it?"

We were so much surprised that we could not say what we thought of it, and he continued: —

"I have been making the trade for several weeks, but only finally closed it to-day, and I now hold the keys of the establishment in my pocket. The house in which we are to live is vacant, and I will go over with Ned on Monday, and Lee and his sons are already engaged to commence moving the next day. This may seem very sudden to you, but I have been thinking of it for months, and am already impatient at the delay. The farm will be rented to Lee, and his newly-married son will occupy this house. There is no reason I can think of why we should not move at once. In a month I shall drive over and attend the sale, which I have already advertised, and then I shall be through."

Taking from his pocket a roll of hand-bills, which were apparently fresh from the press, he handed each of us one. It began with the heading "Public Sale," and stated that the undersigned, having bought the "Union of States" newspaper in Twin Mounds, would offer at public sale, on the mentioned date, at his farm a half mile north of Fairview church, the following stock, implements, and effects. Here followed a long list of cattle, horses, ploughs, etc., with which I was very familiar, and I remember thinking they all looked exceedingly well in print.

"I am tired of Fairview," he said, pushing back from the table, and resuming his old habit of thoughtfulness. "I am tired of its work and drudgery. I don't dislike work, but, like other men, I am anxious that it pay me as much as possible. I shall continue to work as hard as ever, but I hope to more purpose. I make little enough here except in land speculations; that I can continue, and do more of. The profession I have chosen will afford me opportunity to study; that will be a part of my work, and we can live more genteelly in town than we have lived here. I feel that ten more years on a farm would make me an old man, whereas I should at that time only reach my prime. These are briefly the reasons why I made the change. I have figured it out; it will pay. I could not afford to make a mistake in this particular."

I thought of the long rows of figures which he had lately been casting up in his private book, and the hours he spent in pondering over the result.

"Three men are now necessary to do the work in publishing the 'Union of States.' In a year Ned and I will be able to do it ourselves, for we will work as hard there as here, but, as I have said, to more purpose. The time a boy spends in learning the trade of a printer is equal to so much time at school, therefore Ned will practically be at school summer and winter, and of some use besides. The boy is now reaching an age when his education should be attended to, and to all intents and purposes he will begin a term in an academy next Monday."

He got up at this and went to bed, leaving us to talk about it. From the cold and cheerless manner in which he said I would be able to do the work of a man and a half in a year, I judged there was to be little idleness for me in the new place, and besides my work he expected me to look after my education, which had certainly been neglected in the past.

Although the paper had been coming to the house for years we had paid but little attention to it, so Agnes and I took the lamp and ransacked everywhere for a copy of the "Union of States," that we might examine it in a new light. We found one at last, artistically notched, and doing duty on a pantry shelf. It was a sheet of eight columns to the page, printed in large type, and we could not help admitting (it was really the case) that it was well printed, and very fair looking. I read most of the advertisements aloud, and wondered whether we should speedily become acquainted with the parties, or whether years would be required to get into their aristocratic circles, for, in connection with statements that they carried the principal stocks of goods in their line in the West, at that distance they seemed very important and distinguished. However, as they all claimed the distinction of being the leading merchant of Twin Mounds, I thought that perhaps the advertisements were overdrawn, and that I might know them, at least by sight, within a few months.

There was almost a full page of law notices, some of them from adjoining counties, where newspapers were not published; at the foot of each one was printed, "Printer's fee, $12," and it occurred to me that most of the revenue was derived from this source. I read four or five of these, but as they were all in nearly the same language, I gave it up.

There was also a large advertisement of the paper itself, occupying two full columns, commencing with the figures of the year in which it was established, and the figures of the current year (from which I made out that the paper had been published seven years), followed by "Subscribe," "Subscribe," in large black letters. Then came a long platform of dull political principles, and a declaration that it was the duty of every good citizen to take it, because it advocated Benton County first, and the world afterward. After this came a paragraph, separated from the other part of the advertisement by dashes and o's (—o—o—), stating that job printing in all its branches, from a mammoth poster to the most delicate visiting card, would be neatly and promptly executed on the new and fast presses belonging to the establishment, and immediately above the information that all letters should be addressed to the proprietor to insure prompt attention (as though there had once been a habit of sending letters intended for the printer to the blacksmith), it was said that one copy one year would be two dollars, invariably in advance; one copy six months, one dollar, also invariably in advance; one copy three months, fifty cents, also invariably in advance; and that single copies in neat wrappers for mailing could be had on application at five cents each.

We had no idea what the business was like, and sat there until midnight discussing and wondering about it, occasionally referring to the sheet to prove or disprove a notion advanced by one of the number. My own idea was that the paper was bought in a distant market, as an article of merchandise, and that my part of the business would be to stand behind a counter and sell copies at an advance in connection with mammoth posters and delicate visiting cards, but Agnes said that while she knew nothing about the newspaper business, she was certain that idea was wrong, and so it turned out.

When I suggested that Agnes could no longer live with us — it occurred to me all of a sudden, very late in the evening, and almost took my breath away — my mother (who had evidently not thought of it before, either) got up hurriedly, and went out of the room. I expressed the fear that she had gone away to cry about it, whereupon Agnes went after her, and came leading her back presently, with her arms tenderly about her.

"I can come over every Saturday," Agnes said, "and we shall all be so busy during the week as not to notice the separation. I shall miss you more than you can possibly miss me, for I always think of this as my home, but it is not far, and we shall often be together. My school will be out in three weeks, when I will come over and stay until you are tired of me."

As though we should ever tire of Agnes! But my mother would not be comforted, and continued to cry softly to herself — thinking, I have no doubt, that she was about to separate from the only creature in all the world who had ever been kind, and considerate, and fond of her. When I went to bed, I left them together, Agnes gently stroking my mother's hair, and assuring her that she was her dear, kind, good friend, and that she would never forget how welcome she had always been made [1] in her new home.

[1] been made: 1883 made her

XV

THE COUNTRY TOWN

IT was barely daylight the following Monday morning, when I started with my father for Twin Mounds, where we were to take possession of the "Union of States" newspaper. As we were getting into the wagon, Agnes came out to hand me a letter, which she said she had written the night before because opportunity did not present itself to tell me what it contained. As my father was impatiently waiting to start, with the lines in his hands, I only had time to say that I would see her in a few weeks, and, kissing my hand to her, we drove away. She waved her handkerchief until we were out of sight, when I soon forgot her and the letter in the excitement of the visit to a strange place and the engaging in a work of which I had no knowledge.

My father's usual humor had returned, and he drove along without speaking, except occasionally to the horses. Once or twice he began to sing the songs for which he was famous, but he was evidently not in tune that day, for he soon gave it up.

I had never been to Twin Mounds, as there was a post-office and a small trading-place several miles nearer, and had no idea how it looked, and knew nothing of it, except that it had a brick court-house, a stone jail, several wooden stores, a school-house, and about six hundred very wicked people. This I had incidentally learned from listening to people talk who had been there, and I was so occupied in thinking it all over that I had no inclination to talk, and it occurred to me that after I grew up, perhaps I shall be a thinking man, like my father, for we did not exchange a word during the long drive. Several times as we drove along I caught him looking at me, and I thought he was wondering how I would get on in the new business, but as he looked away quickly when I caught him at it, I concluded he was at his old habit of mentally accusing me of being dull, which made me very wretched. I never knew what his objection to me was, but I always believed that when he looked at me, and then resumed his thinking, he was accusing me of something.

At last we came in sight of the place — we came upon it suddenly, after reaching a high place which overlooked it — and I occupied myself in wondering where the house in which we were to live, and the office in which I was to work, were located, until we stopped at a place where horses were cared for, adjoining, and evidently belonging to a hotel, in front of which a swinging sign was displayed under a bell, announcing that the Twin Mounds House was kept there. I noticed that all the business places were in a square, in the centre of which was the brick court-house, and in one corner of the yard the stone jail. In a valley north of the town ran a river, and on its banks were mills, and the site of Twin Mounds had evidently been timbered originally, for in the people's yards I saw great oak and hickory trees, and the woods adjoined the town on every side. Great numbers of impudent boys, dressed in a rakish fashion with which I was not at all familiar, abounded, and while I was thinking I should certainly have trouble with these, my father started down the street with long strides, telling me to follow.

Stopping in front of a low wooden building which had evidently been used at some time in its history as a dwelling, and on the front porch of which was a board sign reading "Printing Office," we went in, where we found three men — two with paper caps on, who were throwing their arms violently around over a high stand, and the other, a pale man seated at a desk, who was evidently the retiring proprietor. This man and one of those with a paper cap on his head spoke pleasantly to my father, and looked inquiringly at me.

"This is the son I have told you about," he explained, pointing at me as if I were a bag of corn. "He is ready to commence learning the printer's trade."

This was addressed to one of the men who wore the paper caps, and he began at once to initiate me in the mysteries of his craft. I soon learned that the high table at which he worked was covered with shallow boxes, and that each one contained a different letter; every character in the language was hid away in the nooks and corners, and my first work was to hunt them out, and remember them for future reference. This I began immediately, and became so interested in it that I did not notice for some time that a number of the rakish-looking boys I had seen when first driving into the town had collected outside the window to look at me. These were evidently the town boys of whom I had heard, and no doubt they were waiting for me to come out and fight, to see of what kind of stuff I was made. It was the understanding in the country that all town boys were knockers, and that every country boy who went there to live must fight his way to respectability. They were less ferocious than I had expected, and as I was much stronger than any of them, I should have gone out and thrown them all over the house, but for the fact that my father did not countenance fighting. They were generally delicate-looking — from high living and idleness, I thought — and while I was engaged with pleasant thoughts to myself that when Jo came over we would capture Twin Mounds, my attention was called to the circumstance, by my friend in the paper cap, that it was noon, and that my father evidently intended that I should go out with him to dinner, for he had gone himself without making any other arrangement.

I had heard them call him Martin, and he appeared to be very much of a gentleman, for before we went out he showed me through the establishment, and explained as much of it as he thought I could understand. The press was in a little room by itself — there was but one, although I remembered that in the advertisement it was said that the office was supplied with new and fast presses — and from the paper on the wall I judged that the former owner of the house had occupied that particular part of it with a bed. Back of that was a place for plunder, formerly a kitchen, and back of that still a yard and a deserted garden. There was also in the yard a large oak-tree, and to the branches of this was suspended a hammock, in which Martin said I might sometimes sleep, if I became a friend of his, as he had no doubt I should.

While we walked to the hotel he explained that he was the foreman, and that, as I was to learn the trade under him, we should be a great deal together.

"It is not much of a trade," he said, "and if you are a bright boy you will speedily acquire it. You can learn it in six months, or three years, just as you please, for I have known boys to become excellent printers in six months, while others, with thicker heads, were about it three or four years. But as your father said you were to stay with me to-night, I will tell you more about it then."

Going into the hotel, we found a large number of men seated at a long table in a long room, everyone eating hurriedly, as though oppressed with the fear that the supply in the kitchen was likely to give out before they were filled. Near the head of the table sat my father and the pale proprietor, and between them and Martin the other man who wore the paper cap, whose name seemed to be Adams, from which circumstance I thought there was no other hotel in the place. Opposite him sat Clinton Bragg, I noticed with some astonishment, forgetting for a moment that Twin Mounds was his home, and he looked as sullen and mean as ever, but he was not so well dressed as when I had seen him at Fairview. He could not help being aware of my father's presence, but they had evidently mutually agreed not to renew their acquaintance, though I noticed that Bragg stopped working his jaws when my father was speaking to his companion, and listened to what was being said, as though he wondered how it came we were both there.

Some of the other men were flashily dressed, and some of them plainly, and they talked a great deal to each other about their business, and by listening to this I learned which of them occupied shops, and stores, and offices, and which one was the driver of the stage that made two trips a week to a railroad station a long way off.

The dinner was served in large plates, distributed at convenient distances apart, and two smart girls in stiff aprons and dresses were in attendance should anyone think anything additional could be had by asking for it, and both of them seemed to be on very confidential terms with the boarders, for they talked to them familiarly, and called them tiresome, and impudent, and I don't know what all. A small man with a hump on his back, who occasionally came into the room, I took to be the proprietor, and Martin told me afterwards that I was right, and that while he was rather an agreeable man, his health was wretched. After most of the boarders had gone out, his wife came in with her family, and from her conversation I learned that she conducted a shop for making bonnets and dresses in the parlor of the house, and that business was dreadfully dull.

I spent the afternoon in studying the mystery of the boxes, and was encouraged to find all the letters of my name. My father was very busy at the desk with the pale proprietor, posting himself with reference to his future work, and was very careful and thorough in his inquiries into the details, from which I believed he would speedily become accustomed to his new position. The pale proprietor was evidently not accustomed to so much work in one afternoon, for he yawned frequently, and seemed bored, but my father kept him at it steadily.

Half the boys belonging in the town appeared at the window before night to look at me, and I noticed with alarm that they were not all pale and sickly, as the first lot had been, which evidently meant trouble ahead. Several of them wore their father's boots and coats, with leather belts around their bodies, which they buckled up from time to time as the afternoon wore away, and most of them chewed plug tobacco, which was passed around by a boy I judged belonged to a storekeeper. Occasionally they got up a game, and tried to play at it, but the interest soon flagged, and they returned to the window to look at me. Once when they became more noisy than usual, the printer named Adams dashed out, and drove them away as he would chase so many hens, but they soon came back again, and stared at me. I pretended not to notice them, as though they were of no consequence, but they made me very miserable, for they were evidently the town boys I had been warned against.

There was one who appeared late in the afternoon who looked particularly like a fighter, and the others immediately gathered around him to tell him of my arrival. He was so bow-legged that

136

I thought it would be impossible to get him off his feet when the inevitable clash came, for I was certain he was the boy picked out to do me bodily injury, and as soon as he had been told of my appearance among them, he walked straight over to the window, and, flattening his nose against the glass, looked at me with great impudence. I thought I would turn upon him suddenly, and frighten him, but he seemed rather glad that I had turned my head, that he might see my eyes and face. Indeed, instead of being abashed, he made the ugliest face at me I have ever seen, and, drawing back from the window, spit at me through a vacancy in his lower row of teeth. He remained around there for an hour or more, walking on his hands, and turning somersaults, for my benefit, and once he lay down flat in the road, and invited four of the others to hold him there. The ease with which he got up made me more uncomfortable than ever. Although they called him "Shorty," he was really a very long boy of his age, and wore a coat which hung about him in shreds, and instead of a shirt he had on a brown duster, tucked into a pair of pants as much too small as the coat was too large. To add to my discomfort, I heard Adams say to Martin that the town authorities really ought to do something with Shorty Wilkinson, for he was always fighting and hurting somebody.

When we went to supper at the hotel the same men were there, and, as I expected, Bragg was in better humor, promising by dark to be agreeable. His principal characteristic was sullen indifference, and I wondered if a bomb exploded under his chair would disturb him. They all disliked him, evidently, from which circumstance I imagined he regarded them as a herd, as he had regarded the people of Fairview. Nobody spoke to him or he to anyone, and his only tribute to the approaching darkness was a noticeable softening in his indifference, for occasionally he stopped his jaws — he munched his food like an animal, and impatiently, as though he disliked the disagreeable necessity of having a habit in common with such people — to listen to what was being said, but at dinner he was oblivious to everything. He went out before me, and when I passed through the office I saw him looking at a copy of the "Union of States," and I was glad we had not yet taken charge, for I was sure he was making fun of it.

After Martin came out we walked down to the house where we were to live, which was a considerable distance down the street from where the hotel was kept, and which was in a lonely location on the brow of a hill overlooking the valley and the mills. Directly opposite, and across the river, were the mounds which gave the town its name, a pair of little mountains where it was said the Indians built signal fires when they occupied the country, and where they buried their dead, for human bones were often found there by curious persons who dug among the rocks. The house was built of stone, in the centre of a great many lots, surrounded by heavy hardwood trees, and as we went through the rooms Martin explained that it had been occupied long before he came there by an Indian agent, and that Twin Mounds was originally an agency, where the Indians came to draw their supplies. But the agency and the Indians had been removed further west years ago, and the house sold to an eccentric bachelor, who occupied it alone until a few months before, when he died, and the place being offered for sale, it came into possession of my father. It was two stories high, built in such a manner as to contain six large rooms of about the same size, and there were iron shutters at all the windows and doors, and the roof was of slate, which Martin said was a precaution the agent had taken against the treachery of his wards. It was in good repair, but I feared we should be very lonely in it, and felt better when we were out in the street again.

Returning to the office, I sat with him until dark on the little porch in front, on top of which was the long "Printing Office" sign, and I became convinced that I should learn rapidly under him, for he took great pains to prepare me for the work, and delivered a sort of lecture with reference to printing in general which was very instructive. He said after a while that he would go out and swing in the hammock, leaving me alone, and while wondering what I should do to amuse myself, I remembered the letter Agnes had given me. I opened it eagerly, and after finding a light with some difficulty, read: —

My Dear Ned: I tried to get an opportunity to say good-bye to you on Sunday night, but it did not present itself, therefore I write you this letter.

You said to me once that I loved everyone in Fairview alike, which is very near the truth now that you are away, for I thought more of you than any of them, and express the sentiment since we are no longer to be together. I hope it will be a comfort to you to know that I esteem you as my best friend, and in your new home I desire you to think of me in the same way, for I shall never change. If I have been a blessing to you, as you have said, so you have been to me, and we have mutually enjoyed the friendship of the years we were together.

It is natural to suppose that you will rapidly improve in your new position. I sincerely hope you will, and I have so much confidence in you that I have no favor to ask except that you always remain my worthy friend. My greatest ambition for your future is that your boyhood will not fill your manhood with regrets. I have always told you that it is best to do right in everything, and while you may not suceed in this entirely, come as near it as you can. The next seven years will be the most precious of your life, and if I have a favor to ask it is that you will improve them.

I believe in you, and shall always be proud of your friendship. It has been manly, pure, and honest, and all the more acceptable because I have neither brothers nor sisters, like yourself. In one sense you have been my protégé; I undertook your education, and taught you more at home than at school, and if you succeed well in life (as I am confident you will), it will at least be evidence that I did the best I could. Probably I shall be your last teacher, for your father is a busy man, and will no doubt train you in his way; therefore I hope you will realize how necessary it is that you apply yourself, and learn whenever there is opportunity. There is nothing in the future for me but to teach other deserving boys, but everything for you. Do the best you can, and I shall be proud of you all my life.

Always your friend,

AGNES.

I had it in my mind to sit down and write a long reply at once, but much to my surprise Clinton Bragg came in at this moment and interrupted me. From what he said on entering I judged he was looking for the printer named Adams, who was a dissolute fellow, but seeing I was alone he sat down.

I had disliked Bragg from the first, but he seemed friendly enough, and, taking a bottle of liquor from his pocket, asked me to drink with him. This I refused to do; whereupon he held the bottle in his hand a long while, as if dreading to drink it. At length he went into another room and returned with a dipper of water, after which he took a drink of the liquor, but it gagged him so that he couldn't get the water to his lips to put out the fire, and he coughed and spit in such a manner as to alarm me. The tears were standing in his eyes when he finished.

"Do you like it?" I asked.

"I like GOOD liquor," he replied, wiping the tears out of his eyes. "This is horrible. I believe I will throw it away."

He made a motion as if to toss the bottle out into the street, but he didn't do it, probably reflecting that it would do very well to carry in his pocket.

I am certain that he came in to let me know that he was addicted to drink, as he was very proud of that reputation, and although liquor was revolting to him he was always trying to create the impression that he could not possibly let it alone. I inferred, also, that he was well acquainted around the establishment, by reason of his association with Adams, for he seemed quite at home.

"Martin don't drink," he said, after trying to revive the stub of his cigar, and several ineffectual attempts to light it with a match. "Martin does nothing that is not sensible. He is out there in the hammock asleep now, while I carouse around half the night. Where do you intend to sleep?"

I replied that I believed I was to sleep there, somewhere, although I had it in my mind to say it was none of his business. I showed my contempt for him so plainly that he was ill at ease, as though he felt that his attempt to convince me that he was a drinking man had failed.

"There is a cot in the plunder room; I suppose that is for you," he said. "I have a room above here. I believe I will wander up that way, and go to bed."

He skulked off like a guilty dog, going through the court-house yard, and stopped occasionally as if to wonder if something that would amuse him were not going on at some of the places lit up around the square. Being satisfied at last, apparently, that the same old loungers were probably there, with their rude jokes and uninteresting experiences, he turned the corner, and passed out of sight.

XVI

MORE OF THE VILLAGE OF TWIN MOUNDS

IN Twin Mounds the citizens spent their idle time in religious discussions, and although I lived there a great many years I do not remember that any of the questions in dispute were ever settled. They never discussed politics with any animation, and read but little, except in the Bible to find points to dispute; but of religion they never tired, and many of them could quote the sacred word by the page. No two of them ever exactly agreed in their ideas, for men who thought alike on baptism violently quarrelled when the resurrection was mentioned, and two of them who engaged a hell-redemptionist one night would in all probability fail to agree themselves the next, on the atonement. The merchants neglected their customers, when they had them, to discuss points in the Bible which I used to think were not of the slightest consequence, and in many instances the men who argued the most were those who chased deer with hounds on Sunday, and ran horse races, for they did not seem to discuss the subject so much on account of its importance as because of its fitness as a topic to quarrel about.

There was [1] always a number of famous discussions going on, as between the lawyer and the storekeeper, or the blacksmith and the druggist, or the doctor and the carpenter, and whenever I saw a crowd gathering hurriedly in the evening I knew that two of the disputants had got together again to renew their old difficulty, which they kept up until a late hour, in the presence of half the town.

There was a certain man who kept a drug store, who was al-

[1] was: 1883 were

ways in nervous excitement from something a fat blacksmith had said to him in their discussions, and who had a habit of coming in on him suddenly in the middle of the day; and whenever I went into the place of business of either one of them I heard them telling those present how they had triumphed the night before, or intended to triumph on a future occasion. Some of the greatest oaths I have ever heard were uttered by these men while discussing religion, and frequently the little and nervous drug-store keeper had to be forcibly prevented from jumping at his burly opponent and striking him. The drug store was not far away from the office where I worked, and whenever loud and boisterous talking was heard in that direction a smile went round, for we knew the blacksmith had suddenly come upon his enemy, and attacked him with something he had thought up while at his work. I never knew exactly what the trouble between them was, though I heard enough of it; but I remember that it had some reference to a literal resurrection, and a new body; and I often thought it queer that each one was able to take the Bible and establish his position so clearly. Whenever I heard the black-smith talk I was sure that the druggist was wrong, but when the druggist called upon the blacksmith to stop right there, and be-gan his argument, I became convinced that, after all, there were two sides to the question.

These two men, as well as most of the others, were members of a church known then as the Campbellite, for I do not remember that there was an infidel or unbeliever in the place. There were a great many backsliders, but none of them ever questioned religion itself, though they could never agree on doctrine. It has occurred to me since that if one of them had thought to dispute the inspiration of the Bible, and argued about that, the people would have been entirely happy, for the old discussions in time became very tiresome.

The people regarded religion as a struggle between the Camp-bellite church and the Devil, and a sensation was developed one evening when my father remarked to the druggist, in the pres-ence of the usual crowd — he happened to be in the place on an errand, as he never engaged in the amusement of the town —

that sprinkling answered every purpose of baptism. The druggist became very much excited immediately and prepared for a discussion, but my father only laughed at him and walked away. The next Sunday, however, he preached a sermon on the subject in the court-house, and attacked the town's religion with so much vigor that the excitement was very intense.

Most of the citizens of Twin Mounds came from the surrounding country, and a favorite way of increasing the population was to elect the county officers from the country, but after their terms expired a new set moved in, for it was thought they became so corrupt by a two years' residence that they could not be trusted to a re-election. The town increased in size a little in this manner, for none of these men ever went back to their farms again, though they speedily lost standing after they retired from their positions. Many others who left their farms to move to the town said in excuse that the school advantages were better, and seemed very anxious for a time that their children should be educated, but once they were established in Twin Mounds they abused the school a great deal, and said it was not satisfactory, and allowed their children to remain away if they were so inclined.

There was the usual number of merchants, professional men, mechanics, etc., who got along well enough, but I never knew how at least one half the inhabitants lived. Some of them owned teams, and farmed in the immediate vicinity; others "hauled," and others did whatever offered, but they were all poor, and were constantly changing from one house to another. These men usually had great families of boys, who grew up in the same indifferent fashion, and drifted off in time nobody knew where, coming back occasionally, after a long absence, well-dressed, and with money to rattle in their pockets. But none of them ever came back who had business of sufficient importance elsewhere to call them away again, for they usually remained until their good clothes wore out, the delusion of their respectability was broken, and they became town loafers again, or engaged in the hard pursuits of their fathers. The only resident of Twin Mounds who ever distinguished himself ran away with a circus and never came back, for although he was never heard of it was generally believed

143

that he must have become famous in some way to induce him to
forego the pleasure of returning home in good clothes, and swag-
gering up and down the street to allow the people to shake his
hand.

This class of men never paid their debts, and to get credit for
an amount was equal to earning it, to their way of thinking, and
a new merchant who came in did a great business until he found
them out. I have said they never paid; they did sometimes, but if
they paid a dollar on account they bought three or four times
that amount to go on the books.

They always seemed to me to be boys yet, surprised at being
their own masters, and only worked when they had to, as boys
do. They engaged in boys' amusements, too, for most of them
owned packs of dogs, and short-distance racehorses, and it was
one of their greatest accomplishments to drive a quarter-horse
to a wood-wagon to some out-of-the-way neighborhood, match
it against a farmer's horse threatened with speed, and come back
with all the money owned in that direction. I suppose they came
West to grow up with the country, like the rest of us, but they
were idle where they came from, and did not improve in the
West, because work was necessary, whereupon the thought no
doubt occurred to them that they could have grown rich in
that way anywhere.

A few of them were away most of the time — I never knew
where, but so far away that they seldom came home — and their
families supported themselves as best they could, but were always
expecting the husbands and fathers to return and take them away
to homes of luxury. Occasionally news came that they were
killed by Indians, and occasionally this was contradicted by the
certainty that they were locked up for disreputable transactions,
or hanged. Whenever a Twin Mounds man died away from home
otherwise than honorably, it was always said that he had been
killed by the Indians.

All of this, and much more, I learned during the first three
years of my residence there, which were generally uneventful and
without incident, save that on rare occasions I was permitted to
visit Jo and Agnes at Fairview, who made so much of me that

I dreaded to come away. I had long since displaced Adams, and Jo was out of his time at the mill, and for more than a year had been receiving wages enabling him to save considerable money, which he invested in his enterprise at the Ford with a steadfastness for which I, his best friend, did not give him credit. He was engaged now to be married to Mateel Shepherd, and he worked and studied to make himself worthy of her. Barker had been known to confess [2] that Jo was the better miller of the two — I believe he really was — and when he came to town he spent more of his time in examining the machinery in the mills on the river than in visiting me, and it was plain that the old-fashioned establishment on Bull River would not satisfy him when he began the building of his own.

Dad Erring's hands had improved somewhat during the three years, and the great piles of framed timbers lying at the ford now were his work, but Jo had paid him from his earnings as much as he would take. These were hauled from the woods, where they were fashioned by Jo himself on odd occasions, with ox teams and low wagons, assisted by the cheap labor which abounded in winter.

While the creek was low, he had laid a broad foundation for his dam, with stones so large that a great many men were necessary to handle them, which were sunk into the creek, and the succeeding layers fastened to them by a process he had invented. I think he worked there a little every week during the three years, assisted by young men he hired for almost nothing, and there was system and order in everything he did. Occasionally it happened that the water at Barker's was too high or too low to run the mill, when he worked on his own enterprise from daylight until dark, living at his father's house. Barker often gave him the half of one day, and all of the next, when trade was dull, and these opportunities he improved to the very best advantage; every time I went to Fairview I visited the mill, and it was always growing.

Jo made a good deal of money every month by running extra time, which opportunity Barker delighted to give him, and often

[2] to confess: 1883 to honestly confess

after he had worked all night or all day he would commence again and work half of his employer's time, studying his books when everything was running smoothly.

His ambition had become noised about, and partly because a mill was needed in that part of the country, and partly because the people had lately grown to admire Jo, they proposed to raise him a certain sum of money, to be returned at any time within five years after the mill should commence running. My recollection is that the amount was three or four hundred dollars, and I have always believed that Damon Barker paid Lytle Biggs out of his own pocket to solicit subscriptions to the fund, for he seemed to have something to do with it.

During this time I had mastered the mystery of the boxes so well that I wondered how it was possible I had puzzled my brain over them, they seemed so simple and easy, and if I improved the time well, I am sure it was due to the kindly encouragement and help of Martin, who was not only a very clever printer, but an intelligent man besides. It had always been a part of his work, I believe, to write the few local items of the town, and he taught me to help him; making me do it my way first, and then, after he had explained the errors, I wrote them all over again. If I employed a bad sentence, or an inappropriate word, he explained his objections at length, and I am certain that had I been less dull I should have become a much better writer than I am, for he was very competent to teach me.

My father, as an editor, was earnest and vigorous, and the subjects of which he wrote required columns for expression, so that his page of the paper was always full. I spent a quite recent rainy holiday in a dusty attic looking over an old file of the "Union of States" when he was its editor, and was surprised at the ability he displayed. The simple and honest manner in which he discussed the questions of the day became very popular, for he always advocated that which was right, and there was always more presswork to do every week, which he seemed to regard as an imposition on Martin, who had formerly had that hard part of the work to perform, and on the plea of needing exercise he early began to run the press himself, and in the history of the business at that time no man was known who could equal him in the rapid and steady manner in which he went about it.

Soon after my introduction into the office I had learned to ink the forms so acceptably with a hand roller that I was forced to keep at it, for a suitable successor could not be found, but at last we found a young man who had a passion for art (it was none other than my old enemy, Shorty Wilkinson; I fought him regularly every week during the first year of my residence in town, but we finally agreed to become friends), and after that Martin and I spent a portion of the two press days of the week in adorning our page with paragraphs of local happenings; or rather in rambling through the town hunting for them. Sometimes we invented startling things at night, and spent the time given us in wandering through the woods like idle boys, bathing and fishing in the streams in summer, and visiting the sugar-camps in early spring, where we heard many tales of adventure which afterwards appeared in print under great headings.

By reason of the fact that it was conducted by a careful and industrious man, and the great number of law advertisements which came in from that and two of the adjoining counties, the "Union of States" made a good deal of money, and certainly it was improved under my father's proprietorship. Before it came into his possession it was conducted by a man who had ideas, but not talents, beyond a country newspaper, who regarded it as a poor field in which to expect either reputation or money; but my father made it as readable as he could, and worked every day and night at something designed to improve it. The result was that its circulation rapidly extended, and the business was very profitable.

His disposition had not changed with his residence, except that he turned me over entirely to Martin, and a room had been fitted up in the building where the paper was printed for our joint occupancy, where we spent our evenings as we saw fit, but always to some purpose, for the confidence reposed in Martin was deserved.

From my mother, who was more lonely than ever in the stone house in which we lived, I learned occasionally that the Rev.

John Westlock still read and thought far into every night. Into the room in which he slept was brought every evening the dining-table, and sitting before this, spread out to its full size, he read, wrote, or thought until he went to bed, which was always at a late hour.

It occurred to me once or twice, in an indifferent sort of way, that a man who had no greater affairs than a country printing office, and a large amount of wild land constantly increasing in value, had reason to think so much as he did, but I never suspected what his trouble was until it was revealed to me, as I shall presently relate.

When I rambled through the town at night, and passed that way, if I looked in at his window, which was on the ground floor, he was oftener thinking than reading or writing, leaning back in his chair, with a scowl on his face which frightened me.[3] Whether the procession of forbidden pictures was still passing before him, and the figures accompanying them were still beckoning, will never be known until the Great Book of Men's Actions, said to be kept in Heaven, is opened, and I hope that those who are permitted to look at the writing under the head of John West-lock will be able to read, through the mercy of God: "Tempted and tried; but forgiven."

Almost every Saturday afternoon he drove away into the country without explanation, and did not return until Sunday night or early Monday morning. Where he went we never knew, but we supposed he had gone to preach in some of the country churches or school-houses, for persons who came into the office through the week spoke in a way which led us to believe that such was the case, although he was not often at Fairview, Jo told me, but he heard of him frequently in the adjoining neighborhoods.

During the latter part of the second year of our residence in Twin Mounds, my father came home one Monday morning in an unusually bad humor, and though he went away occasionally

[3] frightened me: 1883 frightened me, and looking at the light as though he expected it to become confidential presently, and tell him something he very much desired to know.

after that, it was usually late in the evening, and I came to understand somehow that he did not preach any more, the result of some sort of a misunderstanding. Even had I been anxious to know the particulars, there was no one to inform me, as no one seemed to know, and in a little while I ceased to think about it entirely, for he at once gave me more to do by teaching me the details of the business. The men who came to the office to see him after that annoyed him, and made him more irritable, therefore he taught me the routine of his affairs, that I might relieve him of them. We all usually worked together, but after this he took whatever he had to do into the room where Martin had his bed, and when the people came in I was expected to attend to them. From my going into the bedroom to ask him questions about his land business, which I did not so well understand, it came to be believed that he was failing in health, and his old friends frequently expressed the hope that he would soon be better. If I had trouble in settling with anyone, he came out impatiently, and acted as if he would like to pitch the man into the street, for his affairs were always straight and honest, and there was no occasion for trouble. Frequently he would propose to work in my place if I would go out in town, and solicit business, and when there were bills to collect, I was put about it, so that for weeks at a time he did not see anyone, and trusted almost everything to me.

When my father was away, I was expected to stay at home, and I could not help noticing that my mother was growing paler and weaker, and that the old trouble of which she had spoken to Jo was no better. The house in which we lived was built of square blocks of stone, and the walls were so thick, and the windows so small, that I used to think of her as a prisoner shut up in it. The upper part was not used, except when I went there to sleep, and it was such a dismal and lonely place that I was often awakened in the night with bad dreams, but I always had company, for I found her sleeping on a pallet by the side of my bed, as though she was glad to be near me. I never heard her come, or go away, but if I awoke in the night I was sure to find her by my side.

"There is a great change in you, Ned," she said to me one evening when I had gone to stay with her, "since coming to town."

I replied that I was glad to hear her say so, as I was very ignorant when I went into the office to work.

"The rest of us are unchanged," she said. "We are no happier here than in Fairview; just the same, I think."

It was the only reference she had ever made to the subject to me, and I did not press it, for I feared she would break down and confess the sorrow which filled her life. A great many times afterwards I could have led her up to talk about it, fully and freely, I think, but I dreaded to hear from her own lips how unhappy she really was. Had I those days to live over — how often are those words said and written, as though there is a consciousness with every man of having been unwise as well as unhappy in his youth — I would pursue a different course, but it never occurred to me then that I could be of more use to her than I was, or that I could in any way lessen her sorrow. She never regretted that I no longer slept in the house, nor that I was growing as cold toward her as my father, which must have been the case, so I never knew that she cared much about it. Indeed, I interpreted her unhappiness as indifference toward me, and it had been that way since I could remember. Had she put her arms around me, and asked me to love her because no one else did, I am sure I should have been devoted to her, but her quietness convinced me that she was so troubled in other ways that there was no time to think of me, and while I believe I was always kind and thoughtful of her, I fear I was never affectionate.

XVII

THE FELLOW

ALTHOUGH I met him almost every day, I never cared to renew my acquaintance with Clinton Bragg. The dislike was evidently mutual, for while he never came in my way, I knew he made fun of me, as he did of everyone else, and I believe he had an ill word for whatever I did or attempted.

Although it was said that he drank more than was good for him, he did not have the appearance of a drunkard, and it seemed to me that when he was drinking, he was anxious that everybody know it, and that he drank more because it was contemptible and depraved than because he had an appetite. A few of the sentimental people said that were it not for his dissipating, he could greatly distinguish himself, and that he was very talented; therefore I think he drank as an apology for his worthlessness, knowing he could never accomplish what the people said he could if he remained sober. He probably argued that if he kept his breath smelling with liquor, he would only have to answer to the public for that one fault (receiving at the same time a large amount of sympathy, which a better man would have rejected), whereas if he kept sober he would be compelled to answer to the charge of being an insolent loafer, and a worthless vagabond.

From a long experience with it, I have come to believe that the question of intemperance has never been treated with the intelligence which has distinguished this country in most other particulars. We pet drunkards too much, and a halo of sentimentality surrounds them, instead of the disgust and contempt they deserve. If a man is a noted liar, or a noted vagrant, society allows him to find his proper level, and reform himself (since no one else can do it for him), but if he drinks too much, great numbers of men and women who are perhaps temperate in nothing

151

except that they do not drink, attempt to reform him with kindness, although that method prevails in nothing else. As a reason why he should not dissipate, he is told what distinguished positions he could occupy but for the habit, and while this is well-intended, the facts generally are that the fellow is entirely worthless whether drunk or sober. The young man who practises temperance in the whiskey and other particulars because it is necessary in his ambition to be of use to himself and to those around him, is entirely neglected that the disgusting pigs who swill that which is ruinous to health, mind, and pocket may be "encouraged," and who perhaps only drink for the poor kind of attention it insures them, and from being told of it so often, they come to believe themselves that but for their dissipation they would be wonderful fellows, so it often happens that their egotism is even more detestable than their maudlin drunkenness. Many young men are thus led into the false notion that great brains feed on stimulants, and regard an appetite as intellectual.

The same mistaken people also talk too much about the allurements and pleasures of drink; of the gilded palaces where drink is sold, and of its pleasing effects, causing young men and boys who would otherwise never have thought of it to be seized with an uncontrollable desire to try the experiment for themselves, although there is nothing more certain than that all of this is untrue. They visit these places, to begin with, because they have been warned so frequently against them, and before they find out — which they are certain to, sooner or later — that whiskey is man's enemy in every particular, and his friend in nothing; that the "gilded palaces" in which it is sold are low dens kept by men whose company is not desirable; that the reputed pleasure in the cup is a myth; and that drinking is an evidence of depravity as plainly marked as idleness and viciousness — they form the habit, and become saloon loafers. I firmly believe that hundreds of young men become drunkards by misrepresentation of this sort, whereas the truth is easier told, and would prove more effective in keeping them away.

The first step in a career of dissipation is not the first glass, as is sometimes asserted, but a cultivation of saloon society. There is nothing to do in a place where drink is sold, no other amusement or excuse for being there, than to drink, gamble and gossip, and when a man learns to relish the undesirable company common to such places, the liquor habit follows as a matter of course, but not before. It is an effort for most men to drink whiskey, even after they have become accustomed to its use; it is naturally disgusting to every good quality, and every good thought; it jars every healthy nerve as it is poured down the throat; it looks hot and devilish in the bottle, and gurgles like a demon's laugh while it is being poured out, and until the young men of the country are taught that drinking is low and vicious rather than intellectual, we cannot hope for a reform in this grave matter.

I believe that familiarity with it breeds contempt, for I have noticed that very few drunkards' sons follow in the footsteps of their fathers, and the men who sell it seldom drink it. Most drunkards are such notorious liars that little can be told from their confessions, but if accurate statistics could be collected, it would no doubt turn out that most men having the habit formed it because they were particularly warned against it. To say to a man that he shall not drink creates within him a strong desire to drink to excess, and prohibitory laws generally increase rather than decrease the consumption of liquor, because of this strange peculiarity. We regulate other evils, and admit they cannot be blotted out, but with strange inconsistency we insist that liquor of every kind must be driven from the face of the earth; that to regulate such a horrible evil is a compromise with the Devil, and that efforts for its extermination only are worthy of temperate men and women.

The most convincing argument for reform in any particular is necessity. When a man says to himself, "I must quit this habit or starve," or "I can never obtain a position of trust in business, or a place of respectability in society, until I convince the people of my intelligence and manhood by reforming a habit which is the most contemptible as well as injurious of all other habits," he is on the right road, and will in time accomplish a victory over himself, and the best thing society can do for him — however heartless it may seem — is to let him alone during his reformation,

153

only visiting upon him its severe contempt when he falls, for if the fall is hard and disagreeable, he will be more careful the next time. When a man disgraces himself in any other way, we insist that he must be humiliated, as sending him to jail for petty larceny, or to public work for vagrancy; but when he becomes a disgusting, beastly drunkard, we tell him in confidence that he is not to blame, and that his enemies the saloon-keepers are responsible. The man who sells the pistol or the poison is not to blame for the suicide, nor is the man who sells the whiskey to blame for the drunkard.

It is no more remarkable that men drink too much than that men eat too much, and die, before their time, of dyspepsia. The one we regard as a glutton, and despise him that he does not use the knowledge God has given him to better advantage, but the other is fondled and pitied until he is made to feel almost comfortable in his disgrace. The result is that men are oftener cured of excessive eating than of excessive drinking. We never think of punishing the grocer for selling unhealthy but palatable food, but we are very severe on the men who sell palatable but demoralizing drink. Men have frequently been cured of kleptomania by a term in jail, and of lying and loafing by the contempt of the people among whom they live, and the same rule applied to drunkards would be equally satisfactory in its results.

Because temperance is right, too many insist that it must prevail, although the experience of ages proves that it never was, and never will become a common virtue. We might reason with equal goodness of heart that because children are pretty and healthy, they should never be stricken down with disease, and die, although our sorrowing hearts tell us that the reverse is the rule.

In everything else we profit from experience, but we seem to have learned nothing from the past in dealing with intemperance. The methods used for its suppression now are exactly the same as were used hundreds of years ago, although we know them to be ineffective. As a sensible people, as a people desiring the good of the unfortunate, we cannot afford to practise methods which we know beforehand will be of no avail. Intemperance is

154

growing too rapidly to admit of an unsatisfactory pretence that we have discharged our duty, and while the theory advanced by the writer of this may not be the best one, it is certain that the one generally adopted is wrong, for the people are disheartened and discouraged because with all their work they have accomplished nothing.

Clinton Bragg was this sort of a drunkard, and drank whiskey for no other reason than that everybody said it wasn't good for him. It was known that he always drank large quantities of water after using his bottle, as if the liquor had set fire to his throat, and the water was intended to put it out. While I never knew him to be helplessly intoxicated, he was frequently under the influence of his bottle, or pretended to be, although I have seen him sober very suddenly, and I always thought he was dissatisfied that the people did not talk more about his dissipation, as they did of Fin Wilkinson's, the town drunkard, who was often on the streets in danger of being run over by wagons.

Every two or three months he received an allowance of money from his father, which he expended selfishly but lavishly as long as it lasted, but for a few weeks before his money came, and while he was without it, he was a more decent fellow, and it occurred to me that had he been compelled to make his own way in the world, he might in time have developed into a respectable man. But as it was he had no friends, and spent the mornings of his days in sleeping, and his nights in aimless excursions over the country, riding a horse as mean and vicious as himself. A decent man would not have owned the animal, for he had a reputation for biting and kicking, but Bragg lavished upon him the greatest attention, and was delighted to hear occasionally that he had injured a stable boy. It was a pleasure to Bragg to know that his horse laid back his ears in anger at the approach of anyone, in the street or on the road, and his master teased him for hours to cultivate his devilish disposition.

Where he went on these excursions nobody ever knew, except that I knew he frequently rode by Barker's mill, as if on his way to the Shepherds', galloping back the same way at a late hour, to create the impression that he was so popular there that he only got away with difficulty, though I believe he usually rode aimlessly about to be different from other men, for while he often rode that way, it was only on rare occasions that he went to the house of the minister.

Bragg was educated, and when he talked to the town people at all it was to point out their ignorance, which he did with a bitter tongue. If he was seated in front of the usual loitering places on a summer evening, which he sometimes did because there was nothing else to do, he made everybody uncomfortable by intently watching for opportunity to insolently point out mistakes, and if he ever read or studied at all it was for this purpose. Occasionally there came to the town a traveller who was his equal in information, who beat him in argument and threatened to whip him for an insolent dog, which afforded the people much satisfaction. I remember a commercial traveller who sold the merchants nearly all their goods because he once threw a plate of soup in Bragg's face at the hotel table, and then, leading him out into the yard by the ear, gave him a sound beating; but I do not remember what the occasion of the difficulty between them was, though it was probably no more than his ordinary impudence.

He had an office and apartments over a leather store a few doors above the place where I worked, in front of which there was a porch, and he sat out upon this, when the weather was pleasant, for hours at a time, smoking cigars, and spitting spitefully into the street. The only man I ever knew who visited his rooms was the leather dealer, who called on Bragg once every three months to collect his rent. It was a part of the town gossip that this man said the rooms were splendidly furnished, but always darkened with rich and heavy curtains at the windows, and that it was full of stuffed snakes, lizards, bats, and other hideous things; that his match-safe was a human skull, and that a grinning skeleton hung against the wall, which rattled and wildly swung its arms and legs every time a draft or a visitor came in at the door. It was also related that by means of ingenious strings he made the skeleton shake or nod its head, and point with its arms, and I have imagined that when he was in his apartments he employed himself in causing the figure to nod its head in re-

156

sponse to the assertion that Clinton Bragg was a fine fellow, or shake it violently when asked if Clinton Bragg was a worthless dog, as the people said.

Occasionally people who had lines to run knocked at his door in response to the sign, "C. BRAGG, C. Engineer," but even if he was at home he would not let them in, for he had no intention of walking over the prairie in the hot sun when he put out the sign. I never knew of his doing anything in his line, although he might have been a great deal employed, and finally no one applied there for admission except the saddler for his rent, and a lame negro who swept and cleaned his apartments, although it was quite generally believed that the Devil called on him every bad night.

XVIII

THE MILL AT ERRING'S FORD

DURING the latter part of a certain week a little more than three years after we removed to the town, I was given a holiday, and determined at once to spend it in Fairview, for I had not seen Jo in a great many weeks, nor Agnes in as many months. I remember I earned it by working at night by the light of candles for a long while, and that a certain carpenter's son read the copy while I set the type, while another boy kept the night bugs away with a fan. It was a part of the contract with my father that for the extra work I was to have the use of his horses in addition to the vacation, both of which I fully earned, and Martin understood the situation so well that he said if I did not get back until Monday he would see that the work was not behind.

I started very early in the morning, and the road led over gentle hills and through light woods for a few miles, when the great prairie began which ended at Erring's Ford. It was a very pretty country, and though we frequently referred to it in the "Union of States" as the garden spot of the world, I knew it was not necessarily true, for every paper coming in exchange to the office said exactly the same thing of the different localities in which it was published. But it pleased the people who did not see the exchanges, and who no doubt regarded it as a very neat compliment.

It looked unusually attractive that morning, and in riding slowly along I admired it so much that I did not notice the approach of a horseman, who was riding very rapidly, and going in the same direction. When he came so close that the noise of the animal's hoofs attracted my attention, I turned and saw that it was Lytle Biggs, who had by this time become an old acquaintance, for he frequently wrote letters to the paper in a very bad hand, signed "Pro Bono Publico," "Tax-Payer," "Citizen," or "Farmer," and which I was usually compelled to put in type. He was a very sociable fellow, and I was pleased with the prospect of his company. I said as much, to which he replied: —

"If you have no objection, I will tie the horse behind, and ride with you, for I detest riding on a horse's back. It may do for exercise, as you swing dumb-bells on the advice of a physician, but I am surprised I did not have better sense than to attempt it with a serious intention of travelling."

I replied that I should be delighted, and when he got down I could not help wondering how he ever got on, he was such a little man, and the horse so uncommonly large. As he climbed into the buggy, and took a seat beside me, I noticed he was as faultlessly dressed as ever, and that he seemed to be growing shorter and thinner.

"You are going to Jo Erring's, of course," he said, after seeing that the horse led well. "It is a remarkable coincidence — so am I. I suppose you are not old enough to know it, but it only happens once in a lifetime that when you are walking a long road — or riding on a horse's back, which I think is worse — you overtake an easy-riding buggy going in the same direction, and containing but one person, although you meet a great many vehicles going the other way. It is on the same principle that if you go up stairs to strike a light, and take but one match, it is certain to go out, but if you take half a dozen, the first one answers every purpose."

His good spirits were rapidly returning by reason of release from the hard-trotting horse's back, and after finishing this speech he occupied himself for a while in brushing the dust from his clothing with a small wisp he took from his pocket.

"I am on my way to see Jo Erring with reference to the mill," he began at once. "I have charge of the fund being raised to help him, and I shall be able to report that the amount is subscribed. I am acting for Damon Barker, as you may, or may not, happen to know, and although our friend believes the Fairview farmers are very enthusiastic to help him, they are really very slow, and I have had some difficulty in convincing them that it was to their interest. I shall also recommend that he build the mill as soon as possible. There is no reason why it should drag through another year, and that is the promise I gave in securing these papers."

He significantly tapped a pocket-book, almost as large as himself, in an outside pocket, and which no doubt contained the obligations to pay certain sums of money at an agreed date. He always carried this book in a conspicuous way, and handled it as though it contained great sums of money, but as he looked through it for something I saw there was nothing in it except the obligations, a great many newspaper scraps, a few old letters, one or two postage stamps, and a piece of court plaster.

"I don't mind confessing to you," Mr. Biggs continued, with delightful candor, "that I flattered them into it. In case you do not become disgusted with the ignorance which renders such a thing possible, you can flatter men into anything. When I go into a new neighborhood to organize an Alliance, I get the prompt assistance of every man I meet by telling him that I can't hope to do anything without HIS aid, as HE has the popular confidence, and the people will follow wherever HE leads. 'You are a man of intelligence,' I say. 'You can readily understand what I have to offer, and will see its benefit at once. But your neighbors are slower, and I will not attempt an organization here without your assistance.' That kind of argument never fails, and as I talk to all of them in the same way, there is a great deal of enthusiasm, each one imagining that the others went into it on his recommendation. I worked up the mill subscription in that way."

I doubt if this statement was true, for the people originated the idea themselves, but to illustrate a great truth Mr. Biggs did not hesitate to tell a great lie.

"I make a great deal of money in organizing Alliances, but sometimes I think of going out of the business because I meet so many silly men that it disgusts me, and I become ashamed of my sex. But I suppose every business has that drawback, for every man I have ever talked with was of the opinion that his business developed more silly men, more contemptible men, and more mean men than any other calling, and I am forced to conclude that these qualities are so common that they are met with everywhere."

When he spoke of retiring from the business of organizing Alliances, I was about to say that publishing a newspaper collected about all the objectionable men within reach, but from what he said afterwards I judged the observation would not be well received. As if he understood that I was about to say something, which he did not allow, he continued: —

"I was about to say, however, when you interrupted me (I had not spoken at all), that the way to get rich is to go in debt, and work out, therefore I shall recommend that Jo Erring complete his mill at once. No matter if he goes in debt; he has health and can pay it. The people of the country through which we are passing believe it the [1] best to pay as you go. That party over in the field, for instance, is ploughing his corn with a single shovel plough, whereas there are dealers in town who would readily take his note for a cultivator with four shovels and a riding seat. His library no doubt consists of a book warning him against counting his chickens before they are hatched — as pointless a suggestion as I ever heard in my life, by the way (for why do we set eggs if not to bring forth chickens) — but it is regarded as fine logic here. The man will die some of these days with his single shovel plough, his slab house, his cow, his two horses, and his handful of land paid for, worth altogether from three to seven hundred dollars, but if he has a neighbor who sets a good many hens with care, AND counts the number of chickens they can reasonably be expected to hatch, he will attend the funeral in a carriage, and look at his remains through gold-rimmed spectacles."

I had regarded this pay-as-you-go principle as a very good one, but he convinced me that I was mistaken, as usual, for I could never dispute his philosophy until I had thought over it a day or two, when its sophistry seemed quite clear. I had remarked of Mr. Biggs before that he seemed to understand what was in my mind, and attack it. I was thinking that the man he was talking about — his name was McJohn, and a local curiosity because his

---

[1] the: 1883 is

voice was uncertain, and jumped from a high falsetto to a guttural bass — had the reputation of being the hardest working man in Fairview, when my companion said: —

"I never knew a man, I believe, who didn't boast occasionally that he worked harder than his neighbor; I wonder it never occurs to them that it is to their discredit, unless they are more prosperous than any of those around them, for if their neighbors work less, and succeed as well or better, it is an indication that they have more sense. I have no doubt that McJohn, as he spends his time in ploughing a field which could be done in one-fourth the time with common sense and a cultivator, thinks that no other man's lot is as hard as his, and that he is a martyr to hard work. Before I became a philosopher — when I was a fool, in short — I boasted that no man worked as hard as I did, but now I boast that no man works so little. But simply because a man says he is the hardest-working man in the country, it does not follow that it is true. Every traveller who crosses the ocean says that the captain (who had been at sea continuously for thirty years) came into the cabin during the storm, and said it was the worst he had ever experienced. I have no doubt the captains say so (there is no reason why sea captains should not lie as well as other men), but only to impress the passengers with their remarkable skill in managing the vessel under such critical circumstances. You may have noticed that every winter is the coldest ever known, and every summer the hottest; the people seem to expect picnics in December and skating in July, but the facts are that it is always cold in December and always warm in July."

I would have made oath, if necessary, that I had heard Mr. Biggs many a time complaining of the excessively hot and cold days, and declaring that there was never before anything like it.

"The people here learn nothing by experience," he proceeded. "Since I have lived in the West, every spring has been made gloomy by the lamentations of the farmers that crops were ruined, but just before the crops were burned up — as the tooth came just before the doctor killed the boy — the rains come, and the crops do very well. You will find that the men who carry the fate of the country around on their shoulders do not get on so well as the country. I have always found it safe to trust the country to take care of itself, for the country usually does very well."

We were riding on the high prairie now, with Fairview church in sight, and the little man regarded the big building with a show of the contempt I had seen him exhibit on looking at big men.

"Although the fact is as old as the world itself" — Mr. Biggs waved his hand around majestically to give me to understand that although the world was very large, and very old, he was perfectly familiar with every part of it — "it does not seem to be generally known that the weather is governed by cycles. To illustrate: It was very rainy and wet two years ago; it was rainy and wet last year, but not so rainy and wet as the year before; there has been plenty of rain this summer, but not so much as during the two previous years. Next year will be so dry as to excite comment, but still very fair for crops; the year after that, and the year following, there will probably be a partial drouth, but the seventh year, which completes the cycle, will be a general and complete drouth. The winter following will be very mild or very severe, but in any event the next summer will be extremely wet again, to be followed by the seven years of decreasing rain I have mentioned, and the drouth the seventh year. I don't know how it is in the East; it is as I have stated in the West. It would seem that everybody ought to be familiar with this fact, but they are not. Hard times and good times run in cycles the same way, and the panic and the drouth are about the same distance apart, though fortunately they never come together, for, strange as it may seem, the panics come in seasons of great crop prosperity, and times are sometimes very good when crops are very bad. It is the easiest thing in the world to get rich after you are familiar with these cycle theories. You have only to invest your money when times are hard; when everybody believes the country is down, and can never get up again. In a year or two, however, the country will get up and shake itself, and you find your investments doubled. It is the simplest thing in the world, and I am surprised there are so many poor men. We might as well all be rich if we would take advantage of the opportunities around us."

I wondered to myself why Biggs himself was so poor, since he had discovered the secret of riches, and thought some of putting the question to him, but he didn't give me opportunity, for immediately he went on to explain: —

"When I came to the country I was foolish enough to buy land because everybody else was buying, and paid too much. I warn you against this mistake — never buy anything when there is a brisk demand for it, for the price will inevitably be too high, but buy when no one else is buying, and SELL when there is a disposition on the part of everybody else to buy. I bought when I should have sold, in other words, for I was not then a philosopher. Result: The tract is worth no more to-day than what I paid for it. Since then I have never had money enough at one time to take advantage of my knowledge, and am still poor. Agnes says the principal objection to you is that you are young, but I tell her that you will outgrow it, therefore I hope you will make use of this important suggestion. Avoid the mistakes of others; let your neighbors try the doubtful experiments, and benefit by the result. A great many men are only of use to teach others by their failures, but never repeat their mistakes."

By this time we had arrived at the Ford, and, as I had hoped, Jo was at work at his mill, aided by a half dozen stout young men of the neighborhood. Since I had visited the place last Jo had completed the dam and the foundation, and the timbers were being raised. Several were already up, and held by long ropes until the others could be put in position and fastened. I noticed that Jo was helping in everything, and directing with the judgment and good sense of a man of twice his years. His father was also assisting, and it seemed important that all the frames be put up before night, for they were very busy. Jo gayly waved his hand to me from the high place to which he had climbed to pin a timber, and after he had come down again he shook hands with me in his old hearty way, and said he hoped I would understand it was not neglect if he kept at his work, for he had determined to push the mill to completion as speedily as possible, as it was necessary to prevent the building of another one further up the stream.

During the forenoon I learned from Gran Erring, from Biggs, and from Jo himself, that my father had given Jo the money promised, two or three hundred dollars; that Barker had loaned him a small amount, and that with the sum he had saved this was deemed sufficient to complete the building ready for the machinery, which was to be purchased with the money raised in the neighborhood, and a mortgage on the completed mill; that Jo had quit at Barker's, though he was there occasionally, and helped when he could; that he was to be married to Mateel the day before Christmas, and that the mill must be in operation for the fall business; that he had written for the machinery, detailing the terms on which he wanted it, and that it would be shipped at once; that a deed to the little farm had been delivered to him in consideration of certain payments in money, and promises to pay certain amounts annually during the lifetime of his father and mother, and that after the mill was completed they would move to a country below Fairview, a step they had long contemplated, as they had relatives there, leaving the house of hewn logs to be fixed over for the occupancy of Jo and Mateel; that Jo now slept at home, in the middle bed, and that he expected to be so busy the next few months that he had written Mateel a note saying that if she wished to see him during that time to stop at the little shed below the mill on her way to church on Sunday, where she would find him at work, and always glad to see her. All of this pleased me exceedingly, and caused me to watch opportunity to shake the brave fellow's hand occasionally as he hurried past me, which seemed very agreeable to him, although I doubt if he understood what it meant.

As I watched the men at their work I saw that Jo had a troubled, weary look, and I thought for the first time that his strength might not prove equal to his ambition, for I knew that there were yet several years of hard work ahead of him, but as I saw how eagerly he went at everything, as though the delay was more disagreeable than the work, I was reassured, and felt that he would accomplish all he had set out to do.

I do not remember who told me, but I learned from some source that Mateel often complained of being lonely and of having nothing to do, and I thought that this industrious man must soon overtake and pass her in learning and ability, and that she would regret in her future that she had not improved the opportunities of womanhood as he had improved the opportunities of manhood. While Mateel was a pretty and amiable woman, there was not the depth to her that Jo was acquiring, and I wondered if it ever occurred to her that Jo would finally be a man worthy to be the husband of any woman; a man self-reliant and self-taught, and expecting a return for everything he gave. I wondered if she ever thought Jo had been raised at a hard school, and would tire of simple amiability. If he was anything at all, he was an example of what well-directed effort would do, and I thought the day would come when he could not understand why Mateel was not his equal, although she was older, and had every opportunity, while he had none. I thought that as Jo had been friendless all his life he would hope for a great deal of considerate affection from his wife, and that he would be disappointed if he were compelled to continue his old habit of being thoughtful of everyone, but having to regret that no one was thoughtful of him. I wondered if Mateel knew that Jo was no longer the rough, awkward boy she had met during her first week in Fairview, and that he was now a growing, vigorous man, ahead of all his companions in ability and intelligence, and that every year he would throw away old ideas for better ones. Jo had told her in his manly love that she was a perfect woman, and that it would require his efforts for a lifetime to become her equal, and I think she was pleased with this, and believed it. I am certain she never said to Jo that he was a remarkable fellow, and that he deserved more credit than she could give him for his manly love for her — which was no more than the truth — but rather thought herself worthy of the toil he had undergone; not that she was selfish, perhaps, but because Jo had told her so, or maybe she had never thought about it at all except that Jo was very fond of her, and was anxious to please her. I would have given a great deal to know that she frequently gave Jo a word of encouragement, but if she ever did he never told me of it, and for this reason I was convinced that she never did.

In the afternoon I rode over to Fairview church, where Agnes was teaching the school, and although I half expected to find the building surrounded by young men on their knees with proposals of marriage, begging her to accept one of the number, and permit the others to drown their grief in the nearest deep water, only the smaller boys and girls were in attendance, the older ones being at home busy with the summer's work. Agnes was prettier than ever, I thought, and although I knew the style had only reached Twin Mounds the week before, she wore a dress cut in what was then known as the "Princess" pattern. She greeted me with so much genuine pleasure that I was ashamed to acknowledge that I had been in the neighborhood since morning, and felt guilty that I had not driven directly to Fairview; and leading me through the rows of benches, she seated me in a chair in front of her rude desk, which the children had adorned with wild flowers.

I sat there nearly an hour before school was dismissed, very uncomfortable from being looked at so steadily by the scholars. Two or three of The. Meek's family, who had come on since I left Fairview, were there, and I readily picked them out by their white heads and good humor. I could tell who nearly all of them were by characteristics of one kind and another, though I did not know any of them, but there was one boy — evidently the son of a renter lately arrived, for I could not imagine who he was — who made me particularly uncomfortable by mimicking me when I was not looking. He created a great deal of merriment, I remember, by pasting his hair down on his forehead as mine was (I had visited the barber's just before starting, and the barbers oiled and combed their customers' hair then as they do now, for barbers never improve), and I caught him puffing at a penholder, intimating that in the community where I lived the cigar habit was evidently common. I wore a very flashy necktie, and he made one out of the back of a blue copy-book to represent it, which he pasted on his chin, then on his neck, and then on his breast. I thought of going out into the yard to get rid of him, but I knew the impudent boy would mimic my walk, and make me ridiculous again, so I stood it in silence until the children were called up in a row for the final spelling class, in which I was invited to participate, and where I triumphed over my enemy by correctly spelling all the words he missed. Then they all read a chapter in chorus from the Bible, and were dismissed. I was afraid the renter's boy would stay around until I handed Agnes into the buggy, but he walked to the door in a manner which intimated that I was bow-legged, and disappeared with a whoop.

After they had gone Agnes sat down at a desk near the door, where she had bid the last one good-bye, and looked at me curiously.

"Are you glad to see me?" I asked, not knowing what else to say.

"Yes," she replied, with her pretty laugh, "but you don't seem to be the same boy who came to school here a few years ago. You have grown so much that you seem like a stranger instead of an ² old friend."

She laughed merrily at my look of astonishment, and pretended to be frightened when I went over and sat beside her.

"Why didn't you say when you came in," she asked, " 'This school is dismissed; I am a friend of the teacher's.' I expected you to say that, but instead you waited patiently until I should dismiss it myself. When I knew Ned Westlock he was a boy of spirit. But I am as glad to see you as I can be. This is my week at Theodore Meek's, and you may drive me there as slowly as your horses can walk."

I am sure I felt like dismissing the school when I came in, but I never thought of it. I never felt more at a loss in my life for something to say, and sat looking at her in a sort of blind astonishment, blushing like a child. I wanted to tell her how much pleasure the contemplation of this visit had afforded me, but I could not; and finally, tiring of being stared at, she got up and went to collecting the books and other articles she intended to take home. I could think of nothing else to do, so I went out and brought the buggy around to the door, and after helping her in as awkwardly as I had stared at her, we drove away.

In my desperation I could only confess that I had been think-

² an: 1883 my

168

ing for weeks how polished and agreeable I would be in my manner on meeting her, but that her pretty face and easy way had scared it all out of me; that I came to Fairview expressly to see her, and that I hoped there would never be a misunderstanding between us with reference to our friendship.

"There never will be," she said, in her innocent and earnest way, putting her arm through mine, and seeming reassured and pleased. "There could be no misunderstanding between you and me, and there never has been. Why should there be?"

She spoke as though I were still a boy, though I was now larger than she was, and nearly sixteen. I felt sure she would always treat me as a boy, no difference how old I became.

As we drove along slowly, I thought that if a stranger should see us he would think we were lovers, but Agnes evidently did not think of it, for she confessed her friendship for me in a hundred different ways, which I am sure she would not have done had she thought of me as her lover. She was in unusual spirits, and though I felt very proud to think that I was the cause of it, I thought that the arrival of a pretty baby of which she had once been fond would have made her as happy. I hinted gravely, once or twice, that we were "growing older," and that we "could not always be children," but she would only say that we were friends, and enjoyed the friendship. I think she was content with that, and did not look beyond it.

"I had almost forgotten it," she said, when we neared The. Meek's premises; "but your old friend Damon Barker comes to see me every week now, at the school. Sometimes he comes at noon, at other times in the evening, but he never fails to appear at least once a week. The first time he came the children were dismissed for the day; I was alone, and although he is a black-whiskered, fierce-looking man I was not afraid of him, and he walked part way home with me. Since then he comes frequently, and although he pretends that he only stops in while passing, I believe he comes all the way from the mill to see me."

While Barker was a little old, I was not surprised that he had fallen in love with Agnes; I only wondered that everyone did not. But after I thought more of it I became convinced that wise, good, sensible Barker only admired her sweet, pretty face, and was not in love.

"What does he say to you?" I asked.

"Nothing, except to question me about the school and make sensible suggestions with reference to its management. He never tires in listening to me, but says little himself."

I then told her what I knew about Barker, his curious home, and how much I admired him. I was glad that he had taken an interest in her, for he would see that she was never subjected to wrong nor injustice from any source, and Agnes was greatly pleased when I said that, when opportunity offered, we would visit him at the mill together.

The enthusiasm in The. Meek's family over my arrival reminded me of the feeling in a mass-meeting when a popular speaker gets up, for they were all at home, and made quite an army. The white-headed boys, who had not grown much, except in good humor, reminded me of the jack-oaks on the Twin Mounds hills, which perceptibly grew older, but not larger, and The. Meek and his wife welcomed me as though I were an old friend who had gone out into the world and greatly distinguished himself. Before I was fairly in the house it was arranged that I should remain until after supper, and return by moonlight to my grandfather's, which suited me very well, as I had not yet seen enough [3] of Agnes. I had noticed before that there was always so much to do around The. Meek's house that members of his family no sooner finished their day's work than they went to bed, and in the preparation for my entertainment they were busier than ever, so that Agnes and I were alone for an hour, which we both enjoyed, though we were not so easy as we pretended to be, for I caught her looking stealthily at me, and I am quite sure I was often admiring her.

When I started to return to the mill — which I did after a long religious service and a light supper — Agnes proposed to ride a short distance with me, and then I brought her back, and she went part way with me again, so that it was quite late when I finally got away. The country being familiar to me, I drove

[3] seen enough: 1883 seen nearly enough

through the field paths to shorten the distance, and hurried along as rapidly as I could, for I knew they would be waiting for me. As I came out into the main road, and was closing a gate, a horseman dashed by me, riding toward the mill, and I saw with some surprise that it was Clinton Bragg, on the wicked, vicious horse. I followed leisurely, preferring to avoid him, but probably knowing who it was he stopped beside the road, allowing me to pass so closely that I could have touched him with my hand had I wished. Then he would run by, as if to frighten my horses, and this performance he repeated so many times that I would have pulled him off his horse and beaten him had I the strength. When I arrived at the Ford he was there before me, allowing his vicious horse to drink below the dam, and while I stood on the hill looking at him he rode out and galloped off through the dark woods, as though he could see better by night than by day. I could not help thinking that the place where he disappeared would be a favorable one for a murder, and that if Bragg had a desperate enemy it would not be safe for him to ride through such a dark wood[4] at night.

I believe he wanted me to know he had taken the road to the Shepherds, with the hope that I would tell Jo, and annoy him; but for once he went to his trouble for nothing, for when I went into the house Jo was sound asleep in the middle bed, and resting easily and quietly.

[4] wood: 1883 woods

XIX

THE FALL OF REV. JOHN WESTLOCK

ONE Sunday morning, in the fall of the year, after I had got out of bed and dressed myself — I was still occupying a room in connection with Martin in the building where the business of printing was carried on — I found a letter on my desk addressed in my father's writing, and after Martin had gone out I sat down to read it. The first line startled me, for it read as follows: —

MY DEAR SON, — When this falls into your hands I shall be travelling the broad road I have so often warned others against; an outcast, and disgraced in the sight of God and man; for I am going away, and shall never come back.

I shall not attempt to tell you why I am going away, for I do not know myself, except that I am discontented as I am, which has been my condition since I can remember. I don't know that I believe the step I am taking will make me more contented, but I know I cannot remain as I am, for the Devil has complete possession of me, and leads me to do that which is most disgraceful and wicked.

Whether you know it or not is not important to the purposes of this letter, but for seven years I have been infatuated with the woman who is my companion in this wicked business, and she has been the temptation against which I have fought and prayed, but in spite of my efforts and prayers it has grown on me, until I am no longer a man. If you still have confidence in my truthfulness I need only say that I fought this infatuation with all my strength, but I am weaker than you know, and, after a life devoted to principle, I am adrift on an unknown sea, for as God is my witness this is my first offence.

In a package in my desk, with your name on the wrapper, will be found the deeds to all I possess, together with notes and accounts, and full instructions as to their management. The money I take with me is so small in amount that it will never be missed. If you manage well, and work well, in a few years you can almost rejoice that I went

172

away as I did, for all the property I leave you is advancing in value, and will in time make you independent, if you attend to it.

Although it may seem odd that I give you advice which I cannot accept myself, I desire that you be industrious and honest. You can be successful in no other way, and you are now the sole support and comfort of your mother, who, I can attest, was very good to you when you were helpless. That she has not been more affectionate with you since you have grown up has been partly my fault, for I do not believe in affection. Whether I was right or wrong does not matter now: as I seem to have been wrong in everything else, perhaps I was in that.

I do not know whether you partake of my discontent or not; your mother was always contented with her home, and with whatever fortune brought her, and I hope you are like her in this; but if you are not it is only a question of time when you will travel the same road I am on, for no one constituted as I am can become a good husband, a good citizen, or a good man. I wonder that I held out as long as I did, and it is the only thing I can think of to my credit that I did not take this step years ago. No one can ever know what a struggle I have had against temptation, or how humiliated I was when I found that I must give up after all, and become the subject of scandal among the small people I despise, and although I know that no man ever deserved pity more than I do now, I am certain that there is not one who will extend to me that small favor.

To tell the truth seems to have been as much a part of my nature as discontent, therefore I assure you with my last words that since I was old enough to remember I have been as unhappy as it was possible for a man to be. There has never been a favorable circumstance connected with my history. I think I never did a thing in my life that it was not distasteful, and that which I am about to do is most distasteful of all, though I cannot help it.

I am not going away with the hope of being more contented than I have been, for I do not expect it. Discontent is my disease, and this is merely a natural stage of it. I have complaint to make against no one but myself; no one has driven me away, and no one has tempted me, but I go because I cannot remain as I am. I cannot explain to you what I mean by such a strange assertion, but it is true — I am running away from myself. My health is good, my business prosperous, my family everything that a reasonable man could desire, but in spite of this I am so nervous, wretched, and unreasonable that the sight of my home, the sight of you, the greetings of people I meet, fill me with desperation and wickedness. I believe that were I compelled to remain here another week, I should murder somebody — I don't know who; anybody — and for no other reason than that I cannot control myself. I have carefully investigated my own mind, fearing I had lost my reason, but my brain is healthy and active; it is discontent, inexplicable and monstrous, and horrible beyond expression.

When I remember how discontented I have been in the past, though favorably situated, I tremble to think what it must be in the future, when I shall have my disgrace and crime to remember in addition to it, but perhaps it will serve to hasten the end, and relieve me of a life which I never desired, and which I would have rid the world of years ago, but for the reason that I was afraid.

Your father,

John Westlock.

I have a recollection of feeling faint and sick after reading the letter, and when I started up to go home, I remember that I staggered like a drunken man, and reeled along the street in such a manner that those whom I passed surely thought I was returning from a night's debauch. My first thought was that the best thing I could do was to give the office to Martin, and take my mother, and leave the country, too, before anyone knew of the disgrace, but when I remembered the advice in the letter with reference to the business, I knew it was his deliberate judgment that I should stay and live it down; and he must have thought of it a great deal. A thousand disturbing thoughts passed through my mind as I went along, and once when I went into an old and vacant house to avoid meeting a party of people who were coming toward me, the first feeling of faintness returned so strong that I was compelled to lie down on a heap of straw and rubbish.

My greatest dread in it all was to break the news to my unhappy mother, and trying to brace myself with the thought that I was now entrusted with grave responsibilities, and no longer a boy dependent on the advice of another, I passed down the street and into the house.

After considerable search I found my mother seated in a low chair in the kitchen, as I had seen her a hundred times before, but for some reason — I could not explain it then, nor can I now — I felt that she had sat there all night, and that she knew that he had gone. There was a certain timid, frightened look in her

174

eyes when I came in, an inexpressible grief in her manner, and so much sorrow in the tears which came afresh at sight of me, which convinced me that I had nothing to tell her, and I learned afterwards that he had told her what he had written me before leaving, and that he had shaken hands with her on parting, and begged her not to be distressed.

My first action was to pull down all the blinds at the windows and lock all the doors, for I was determined that no one should enter the house that day, and I hurriedly carried in a supply of wood and water, as though we were to live that way a good many days, or that we should live in the house forever, without seeing anyone.

As the day wore away, I found my determination increasing to make the best of it, and though I tried to rally my mother, she would say nothing. Finally I gently forced her to leave the low chair, and lie down, where she covered her head, and sobbed the livelong day.

Though I read the letter over a great many times (having gone to one of the upper rooms for the purpose, where I could see the people passing, and looking wonderingly at the house to see it shut up so tight), I could make nothing out of it further than that the Rev. John Westlock had run away, taking Mrs. B. Tremaine with him, and that he had been infatuated with her for seven years, a circumstance of which I had not the remotest suspicion until that day. I knew now that on his visits to the country he met this woman at some convenient place, but beyond that, and the fear once expressed by Barker that his religion would prove an unfortunate thing for him, I was puzzled to understand it, further than the letter had explained.

I knew now that the trouble which caused him to quit preaching, and to seclude himself from callers at the office, related to the woman, but I had never suspected it before, for I had never tried to explain his thoughtfulness, believing it was simply his way, and that his father had been a thinking man before him. He was a man of such excellent sense that suspicion would not attach to him, particularly suspicion of weakness in religion or morality, and I only thought of it to become more puzzled.

175

Before night I came to the conclusion, though it gave me a sad heart, that the sooner the community was made aware of the matter, the sooner would its gossiping and conjecturing cease, and when night was setting in, I hailed a boy who was passing, and sent a note to Martin requesting him to come to the house. He came soon after, when I explained everything to him, and read the letter, which he heard with great surprise. I then requested him to go wherever there was a crowd that evening, and tell it, to the end that the people might discuss it through the night, as I preferred that course to a suspense of several weeks, for we could have kept it from them that long on one pretext and another.

Martin approved of this idea, though he was too much surprised to say much else, and when he went out, I saw him stop people on the street, and talk with them, and who at once looked up at the house, and seemed greatly surprised.

No lights were lit in the house that night, and I spent the hours in wandering through the vacant rooms; in wondering what the people were saying about it; how they would feel with reference to my continuing the business, and how they explained it all. Frequently I went into the room where my mother was lying down, and she was still for such a long time that I hoped she was oblivious to her trouble in sleep, but in waiting to assure myself of it before retiring, I heard her sob in such a pitiful manner that I resumed my walk through the lonely rooms, and listened again to the echoes of my own footsteps.

* * *

I spent my evenings at home after my father's disappearance, at first from necessity, because my mother needed me there, and because I had work to do, but I gradually grew to like it, and regretted when I had to be away. My mother was much changed and broken by her desertion, and if I read far into the night — which I often did, for my education was indifferent, and I found a certain amount of knowledge indispensable in my daily work —she sat beside me, employed in knitting or mending.

If I wrote something I thought was very good — I am certain

176

now I never did — I read it to her; if I found a paragraph in a book or newspaper which I thought surprising or strange, I read that; but while she always listened attentively, she had no comments to offer. Indeed, I think there were weeks together when she did not speak to me at all, except to call me in the morning at the hour I told her I should like to get up, or to inquire after my small wants.

At first the neighbors thought it a kindness to keep the house full of callers, believing her to be lonely, but they at last discovered that it would be a greater kindness to leave her alone, which they afterwards did, so it came about that we lived a lonely life. Occasionally Martin came in the evening to sit an hour, and a few times Agnes was a visitor to the gloomy house, but these visits were so far apart that we seemed to see no one at all. Sometimes I took her out for a drive, and on these occasions she would perceptibly revive, and say that this or that place had changed since last she saw it, but of her trouble she never spoke at all. One pleasant Sunday I drove on the road to Fairview, thinking to call on Jo at the mill, but she gently touched the lines, and said "Not to Fairview," so I turned around, and drove another way.

Before my father went away he dealt a great deal in wild land, taking stock of every kind in payment, and I still kept a pair of strong and fleet horses which had belonged to him, and of which he was very proud, at first because I could not sell them for the price they were worth, and lately because I had grown to like them. They were very rapid in harness, and when we rode out my mother enjoyed more than anything else the excitement of passing other teams, speaking many kind words for "Dan" and "Dave." She took great interest, also, in seeing that they were well cared for, and though I was afterwards offered a good price for them, I kept them at considerable expense and trouble because she seemed to take an interest in nothing else.

Her condition was so lonely that I became more of a son than I had ever been before, and tried always to be careful of her wants. She reciprocated this with kindness and attention, but I cannot say with affection. When I went to my bed at night, I always left

177

her sitting in her chair, and after I had retired it was her custom to come softly up the stairs to see if I was comfortable. If it was cold, she tucked the covering about me as if I were yet a child, and I remember now — I do not believe I thought of it then — that she talked to me more at these times than at any other, as if the darkness removed a restraint. Perhaps she felt a disgrace in the presence of her son that his parents had treated him so indifferently, and only felt easy when he could not see her face. Some men remember their mothers from their good-night kisses, but I remember mine by the gentle manner in which she smoothed the covering of my bed at night, and I grew so accustomed to it that I could not have gone to sleep without it. After this was done, she lingered about the room as long as she could find excuse, frequently referring to subjects of which I had spoken in the evening, and then went slowly down the stairs.

How she passed the night I never knew, but I never found her in bed. Frequently I thought to go into her room at midnight, to see if she were awake, but in waiting for the hour, I fell asleep. If I came home late at night, whether she expected me or not, I found her up, and often when a slight complaint made me wakeful and restless, I found her by my side, offering me water, or some simple remedy. From the woman who came to the house to work through the day, but who slept at home, I learned that my mother frequently lay down in her room during the day, and probably slept; so I think that generally she did not close her eyes at night nor go to bed.

If I advised with her in reference to my father's affairs — there was really no need of it, for he left them in excellent shape, with full instructions to me, and she knew nothing about them — she listened attentively, but the details seemed to tire her. Occasionally a man would intimate that my father had not credited a payment on an account or a note, and appealing to her, she would say: "Your father was honorable in business; the man is mistaken," and so it turned out. If I told her of my own affairs, she was equally attentive, but seemed to be satisfied with my course, and had no suggestions to offer. I hoped to hear her say I was doing well, or that the business did not miss its founder, but if she thought it, she kept it to herself.

I believe that she always thought it possible that her husband would tire of his fancy, and, coming back to her poor and old, they would finish their lives together. Perhaps she never went to bed at night because she was always expecting his knock at the door, and remained up to assure him that he was welcome. She believed that a man of his sturdy, honest principles could not be content wandering aimlessly about, ashamed to own his name and his country, so the vigils through the long nights were kept up. He would not come during the day, when he would meet familiar and accusing faces at every turn, but at night, when the town was quiet, and the people were asleep, therefore there was always a light in his old room, and his deserted but forgiving wife was always waiting to hear his step in the street, and his knock on the door. The people of the town frequently came down the little street which led past the house to look at the light which was always burning, and which cast its rays out into the darkness like a kindly star; they told the story of the light to strangers in pitying whispers, and many of them believed that the patience of the lonely watcher would be rewarded at last by the return of the unhappy wanderer.

The business under my management continued to be profitable, partly because Martin and I gave it a great deal of attention, and partly because it was without opposition. Martin was really a very superior man, and together we did very well, making improvements as the money was earned, and extending the business whenever it was possible.

I was at first inclined to feel that I could never recover from the disgrace of my father's action, but after Mr. Biggs assured me that it was ignorant conceit to suppose that the people had nothing else to do than to think of my small affairs; that every family had a private history, and that ours was no worse than hundreds of others; that I now had opportunity to make a reputation for myself, having a gift of a considerable property to start with, and that so far as I was personally concerned, my father's action was really a benefit, I took a better view of it, and felt that if I conducted the business creditably, and took good care of my mother, the people would be more apt to speak of me favorably than if I moped around.

During the first few weeks a great many of my father's staunch friends came into the office, and announced that they would not believe the report; that there had been foul play, but to these I read the letter, whereupon they went away very much puzzled, and without saying a word. These men, and there was a great number of them, encouraged me in carrying on the paper in every way they could, and as they were of the class which makes public opinion, they were of great benefit to me.

It was never known where the two met, how they left the country, or what direction they took. I heard through Jo that, before the disappearance of my father, Mrs. Tremaine had been away from home several days, but as this was a common circumstance, no attention was paid to it. We learned by degrees that their names had long been connected with suspicious gossip, but they seemed to have been very discreet, for the matter was always a mystery.

XX

TWO HEARTS THAT BEAT AS ONE

T HE Rev. John Westlock went away in the latter part of September, and from that time to the day before Christmas, a period of three months, I did not visit Fairview, as I dreaded the questions of the people, for one thing, and was very busy for another, but Jo was to be married on the 24th of December, and nothing would have kept me away. With the exception that he wrote me a letter saying that he believed Barker was pleased at the disappearance of his sister, I had not even heard directly from him, much less seen his good, honest face, though I knew the mill was steadily progressing, of which fact we made appropriate mention in the columns of the "Union of States."

We had a sort of understanding that, as we should both be very busy during the summer, we would put off a meeting until his wedding, and besides this I had a great desire to come upon the completed mill in operation. Therefore, when the day came round, I was early on the road, having arranged for an absence of several days, and to call at Theodore Meek's for Agnes, who was not going home for the holidays until after Jo's marriage.

As I passed Bragg's apartments I noticed that the place was close shut up, and presumed he had already left town on the same errand as that on which I was bound; therefore I was not surprised when I came up with him a few miles out, driving his vicious horse to a light buggy. Seeing my approach, he allowed his horse to walk in the road ahead of me, undoubtedly intended as an insult, but after submitting to it a few minutes, I turned out and went by him, though he lashed his horse, and tried to prevent me. His horse was no match for mine, as he very well knew, for the team I drove trotted so briskly as to scandalize the church to which my father had belonged, but Bragg never admitted any-

181

thing without a struggle, as a dog has to be kicked out of your road every day. For several miles I could see him vigorously following, whipping his mean horse, but at last I went down into a low valley where ran a creek and lost sight of him.

During all the time I had known him, we had never spoken, except on the night of my arrival in Twin Mounds, and as I grew stronger I determined to whip him for the many insolences he had practised upon me; I had half a mind to stop where I was until he came up, and try it there, but the uncertainty of the result, and the fact that my appearance would be too much ruffled at best by the encounter to make myself presentable at a wedding, induced me to give it up, and wait for a more favorable opportunity.

When I drove up to The. Meek's, Agnes was already waiting for me, and coming out directly, we were soon on the way. Although she was always neatly dressed, and had a very decided talent in that direction, her apparel was so gorgeous that day as to cause me new surprise, but when I looked at it attentively, I was certain it was inexpensive, and that it was all the work of her own hands. I remember she was particularly gay, and had I not known differently, I might have thought of her as some favorite child of good fortune, whose paths were always pleasant. There was nothing to mar her happiness, it seemed, except the misfortune [1] of others, which she frequently mentioned, and her sympathy for my mother was so earnest and gentle that I worshipped her more than ever, though I had never admitted to myself before that I did not already love her to the greatest extent possible.

When we arrived at the Shepherds', Jo met us at the gate, and, after showing Agnes into the house, went with me out to the stables. For some reason I became convinced at once that it would be a dreary day, for Jo was not so glad to see me as I had expected, after the long separation, and he seemed dissatisfied about something, although I do not believe he really was. It was a pleasant day, though in December, and after the horses were put away we walked about, attempting to renew our old confidences and friendship, but we did not get on as we used to do. He was the same Jo

[1] misfortune: 1883 misfortunes

in most respects, but he had grown thoughtful and careworn in the last few years, and I mentioned it, to which he replied with some impatience: —

"You say that whenever we meet. You forget that we are both older, and that it has been almost four years since we were constantly together. It was always our ambition, when we were boys, to become men: we are becoming men very rapidly, and while I am satisfied, you seem to complain of it. But we never become so old that we do not have care and responsibility, and I look like a thoughtful man to you only because in the course of years I have grown to be a thoughtful man. Further than my work there is nothing to make me thoughtful but the age I have accumulated naturally, and I look older because I AM older. Let me assure you once for all, my good old friend, that I am stout as a lion; I am prosperous; I am to be married in a few hours to the woman of my choice, and that there is no reason why I should not live to a ripe old age in the greatest peace. There! Are you satisfied?"

"I enjoyed your friendship so much when you were a boy," I answered, "that perhaps it is only a fear that it will be less candid when we are men. I have had no other confidant than you, and I dread to see you grow old, for fear that a man's cares will cause you to forget our boyish friendship."

"No fear of that," he said, after he had studied awhile, as if turning it all over in his mind. "No fear of that. I shall never grow too old to confide my sorrows (if I have them) and successes to you. However poorly a man is raised, he always has a pleasant recollection of his youth. It may be only the hut in which he was born, but there is always something, and you are the one pleasant recollection of my boyhood. If I had a great trouble, I should come to you with it; not for help, perhaps, but for your honest sympathy, and for the satisfaction of talking it over freely. So long as I confess nothing to you, you may rest assured that I am very happy. I don't feel right just now, some way, and I can see that you don't; but I hope we shall get on better later in the day. I am very sorry, but for some reason the occasion does not promise to be what I expected. Probably one reason is that I have done a very mean thing to-day, and when you discover it, as you are sure to do, remember that I have confessed my humiliation, and say nothing about it."

I had no idea what it was, but as he said I should discover it, I did not press him further.

"It is very curious," Jo said, in a confidential and perplexed way, "but the nearer my marriage approaches, the less important it seems; I wonder that I am so cool over it. You remember what I said to you once about it — that I would sell myself to the Devil to be married to Mateel; THEN, not to wait a minute. I felt what I said, but the years of waiting have made a great change in me. Not that I am less fond of her, but I do not feel now about it as I did the night we rode to Barker's the first year of my apprentice-ship. It was never intended, perhaps, for anyone to be as happy as I should have been had my marriage to Mateel that night been possible. Somehow we always have to wait until the pleasure of an event is blunted by familiarity. Imperceptibly, as she became a possibility, I made the discovery that she is not an angel — she would be an angel, I have no doubt, were such a thing possible — for angels do not live in the woods, and they do not marry millers."

He tried very hard to be cheerful, but he could not, and when he spoke I thought it was an apology for his troubled face: —

"I am very tired of late, for I have worked almost night and day for four years, and I hope you will excuse me if I do not seem glad to see you, for I am; though just at present, for some un-accountable reason, I am unable to show it. I am sure I shall perceptibly revive by reason of your being here, but the mill undertaking was a big one, though I shall speedily recover, now that I have more ease. I can't just explain myself how it is, but I hope you will believe I am still Jo Erring, and still regard you as my best friend."

I made some sort of an answer, and we went into the house soon after, both of us more than ever convinced that something was wrong, though we could not tell what it was. Jo immedi-ately disappeared into another room, leaving me alone until Mr. Shepherd came in, who, although he seemed glad to see me, was in such great excitement that he had not time to express it.

184

"You will excuse me if I am not myself," he said, as he walked about, putting his hands to his head as though it pained him, a habit I had noticed before. "While I approve of this marriage, our only child leaves us to-day, and we cannot feel very gay about it. She has hardly been out of our sight since she was born, and so far from feeling gay, we are uncomfortable, although we have no objection to her husband. It distresses her poor mother more than it does me; I fear it will be like a funeral. I hope Jo will not mind if she breaks down entirely. I had been hoping we should be very happy to-day, but I have lost all hope of it."

As Mr. Shepherd walked rapidly round the room with his head down, he almost ran into a door as it opened to admit his respectable wife, followed by Agnes. Mrs. Shepherd bowed [2] to me stiffly, and, walking across the room, seated herself. I had a vague sort of notion that Mrs. Shepherd, hearing of my arrival, had come in to pay her respects, and such a long and awkward silence followed that I began to upbraid myself that, as a young man of the world, I should say something suitable. While debating between a joke and an observation on the weather, however, the door opened again, and Jo and Mateel stood before me. Jo wore the suit in which he had met me at the gate, with the addition of gloves, and Mateel was arrayed as became a bride. Both looked brave and handsome, and while admiring them, and wondering what I had better do (I was impressed with my importance there, someway, but was not certain how), Mr. Shepherd got up from his chair, and, standing before them, pronounced the simple marriage ceremony common in that day, in a low and faltering voice. Then we all knelt, and the good man earnestly and tenderly invoked the blessing of God on the union. By the time Mr. Shepherd had risen to his feet again, his wife was beside him, and, throwing her arms about Mateel, kissed her over and over again, and asked her not to cry, as she had shown evidences of doing. Somehow I thought they had agreed, as though it were brave, not to humiliate my worthy friend by creating a scene, and I wondered that they consented to the marriage at all if they did not approve of it. I had never been entirely cured of a dislike for Mrs.

[2] Agnes. Mrs. Shepherd bowed: 1883 Agnes, who bowed

Shepherd, and it came upon me with renewed force that day, for I thought she had every reason to feel gratified at the marriage, instead of sorrowful, for Jo was much the better one of the two; any unprejudiced person would have said so. She paid not the slightest attention to Jo, and I was glad when Mr. Shepherd came up and shook him by the hand, with appropriate words of congratulation, after which Agnes touched me on the arm, and we went up with our greetings. When I took Mateel by the hand Jo said for me to kiss her (which I did very awkwardly, I am afraid); then Agnes kissed Jo, and we were all very happy together. Someone brought up chairs, and Jo and Mateel sat down, and when I looked around Mr. Shepherd and his wife were gone.

After Jo and his bride had taken a long breath, and were themselves again, we four spent a very uncomfortable half hour together, for each one seemed to feel that the others were not at ease. I had thought Jo's wedding would be a merry event, but it was not, though I never knew exactly why.

I noticed while we sat there that Mateel did not regain her accustomed color, but remained very pale, from which I imagined her health was failing, for she had always been delicate. The costly finery which she wore, though in good taste, made her look ghastly, and I was compelled to admit that she had never appeared to a worse advantage. Her cheeks were sunken, and her form wasted, and she seemed entirely too old for the fresh young man by her side. I imagined that Jo thought of this, too, and regretted she was not more girlish.

When dinner was ready, I noticed that plates were laid for several guests besides Agnes and myself, as if they expected that more of Jo's friends would be present, whereupon it occurred to me to apologize that my mother was ill, and had sent her regrets.

"The regrets are accepted," Jo said, as though others had been sent. "We could not have a more cheerful company than this. So far as I am concerned, the company is satisfactory."

Mateel expressed some such sentiment, and so did we all.

"But I wonder Clinton Bragg is not here," I said. "I met him on the road, and I am certain he was dressed for a wedding."

I immediately regretted saying it, for I thought that both

186

Mateel and Jo colored at the mention of his name, but after some hesitation, Mateel said:

"He was not expected."

At this moment Mr. Shepherd excused himself to answer a knock at the door, and when he came back he said that it was Clinton Bragg, who had stopped in on a trifling errand, and who had gone away again. I was not surprised that the fellow appeared at the house on that day, for he was always where he was not wanted, but I wondered he had not accepted the invitation to dinner, which Mr. Shepherd said he had given. It would have been a splendid opportunity to make himself disagreeable.

All of them seemed to be in a worse humor after this, and they had not been merry before. Mateel got up from the table soon after, and insisted on helping her mother, which example was followed by Agnes, and finally by Mr. Shepherd, who went to do some sort of carving, leaving Jo and me alone. The dinner was an elaborate one, and the table set for at least twenty, so that we felt lost in the desert of dishes. Some of them tried to be gay at the circumstance of our being alone at the table, and they helped us very liberally, but it was a failure, and the time passed very dismally. I believe that Jo felt guilty that more of his friends were not present — or rather that he had but two to invite — and I knew that I felt very awkward in being the groom's only satellite, since he had lived in the neighborhood all his life; and, though I attempted pleasantries in great number, either they were not heard or not appreciated, so that the dinner was very much of a failure, as Jo whispered to me as we sat at one end of the long table together.

When I went into the other room, dinner being over at last, I found a letter lying on the table addressed in a neat hand to Mr. and Mrs. Goode Shepherd, and, knowing it was public, I opened and read a well-worded note of regret from my grandmother. As she could not write I knew what Jo meant when he said I would that day detect him in a mean action; he had written it himself.

❀ ❀ ❀

In order to avoid the leave-taking, and because I was uncomfortable at the Shepherds' house, I drove over to the mill with Agnes in the middle of the afternoon, where we spent several hours in putting the house in order for the coming of Jo and Mateel. I had not been in the house since it was remodelled, and was pleasantly surprised at its arrangement. The old house had but two rooms, but Jo had added two others, and furnished them neatly and comfortably and in good taste. The room in front was transformed into a pretty parlor, and opening off this was a sleeping apartment. The old kitchen remained, but I would not have known it, so great was the change, and adjoining it, and connecting with the parlor, was a dining-room, which completed the number. Agnes admired the house as much as I did, and complimented Jo so much that I regretted I had not expended my energies on one like it. I think I resolved to look about when I returned to town for an old house, and fit it up by degrees, but I have no doubt I forgot it entirely within an hour.

The mill had been completed a month before, and had been in successful operation since. I can only remember now that it was a very good one for that day, and that it was an improvement on the one belonging to Damon Barker, for its machinery was of late and improved make. Jo had never told me, but I believed he was greatly in debt, for in addition to the amount due on the machinery he had rebuilt and furnished the house where he was to live, therefore I was not surprised to find the mill in full operation in charge of his assistant, as that was a busy season. Agnes and I went through it after we had finished at the house, from the great wheels in the cellar to the small ones in the roof, and complimented Jo so much that his ears certainly tingled.

Jo and Mateel did not arrive until after dark, and we had the lights and fires burning when they came in. After laying off her wraps Mateel looked around the pleasant room, but did not say anything, seeming sick and distressed, and when she went with us through the rooms, Agnes carrying the light, she only said "Yes" when someone remarked that this or that was pretty, or "No" when it was said that something else could not be nicer. I thought that Jo was very much hurt at this, for she seemed to take everything as a matter of course, and the only words she spoke

188

were as to what should have been done rather than as referring to what had been done already, which was a great deal, for the house was better furnished and more complete in every way than the one in which she had lived. I thought at first that she was thinking the arrangements for her comfort were no more than she deserved, if as much, but I concluded later in the evening that she was not herself, and that the parting with her mother had been a great trial, although I could not understand why, for they were separated only by a few miles, and could see each other every day.

We had been sitting about the fire for an hour or more, where we seemed to get along better than at any other time during the day, when a rap came at the door, and, on its being opened by Jo, Damon Barker walked in. We were all very much delighted and surprised to see him, and after saluting Jo and his wife with a polite word of congratulation, he took the chair Agnes brought up, and sat down in the circle.

"I could not come over very well to-day," he said, speaking to Mateel, "so I came to-night. I thought I knew who would be here beside yourselves," looking at Agnes, and then at me, "and I find the company I had expected. I wish you all a merry Christmas."

We had not thought of it before, having been occupied with the events of the day, but Barker suggested it by taking a number of packages from his pockets, which he leaned against the legs of his chair. After we had returned his compliment, he said:—

"I am not fond of ceremonies of any kind, but I am fond of a fire like this on Christmas Eve, and a company like this, so I came unannounced. I hope you are glad to see me."

We all announced in a chorus that we were.

"It is very polite in you to say so," Barker replied. "I lead a lonely life over there," pointing in the direction of his mill with the hand in which he held another package from his pocket, looking very much like a long bottle wrapped in brown paper, "though probably no lonelier than I desire. Jo and I became very good friends when we were in solitude together, and I think I could not have rested to-night had I not walked over to congratulate him and his pretty bride."

189

He settled down in his chair and looked around the room as if admiring it.

"It has been a long time since I felt so much at home as I do at this moment." Having put down the package which looked like a bottle, he picked up another one and commenced unwrapping it, but soon stopped, and continued talking, leaving us to wonder what it contained. "I hope my presence will not interfere with your enjoyment. Let me sit here in the corner and look at you, without being in the way." He began unwrapping the package again, but forgot it as he became more interested. "I enjoy looking at fresh young faces, and it is not often I have the opportunity. I beg that you go on with the conversation — I warrant it was a merry one — in progress when I disturbed you by rapping. Don't mind me at all, but if you should address me occasionally, and intimate that I had added something to the occasion, I should enjoy myself very much indeed."

By this time the package was unwrapped, and it turned out to be a handsome jewel case, with a set of expensive jewelry on the inside. This he handed to Mateel with a bow, and, picking up another package, went on with his talking and unwrapping:—

"For twelve years I have been almost a hermit here in the woods, and during all that time I have not met so pleasant a company as this. I never felt more welcome in my life, whether I am or not, and I have an idea that I feel very much as the rest of you do — comfortable and happy."

By this time the other package came out, and it was so much like the first one that we could not tell them apart. This he gave to Agnes, who was greatly surprised, and she hesitated in taking it, but he did not notice her, and, diving down beside his chair, handed the bottle-looking package to me, and its mate to Jo, retaining another one of the same pattern for himself.

"These three contain liquor so old that I feel quite young in their company," he said, without noticing the surprise which his presents to Mateel and Agnes had created, for they were very valuable, "and combined and stirred with a little hot water, a little sugar, a few slices of lemon, and nutmeg, they make a punch very fit and appropriate for a party of five. If you have a bowl handy, I will stir them together."

190

As he said this, he got up from his chair, and began preparations for the punch by taking from the pockets of the coat he had laid off a bag of lemons and a corkscrew. Jo and I went out and lighted the fire for the hot water, and while we were waiting for it we heard Barker asking as a favor that nothing more be said about the presents.

Conscious that the wedding was ending better than it had commenced, Jo and I shook hands over the circumstance, and we soon had the kitchen fire roaring, and the water hot, and taking it into the front room, Barker had the bottles opened, and the lemons sliced, and, the sugar and nutmeg being brought, the punch was soon ready, which I think was composed of champagne, and a mixed liquor made for that purpose. It was certainly very good, and Jo and I drank of it very liberally.

I had never seen Barker in good spirits before, and it was not long before all of us caught the infection. We not only drank of the punch, but we went into the kitchen, and brought out something to eat, and after this the good humor of everyone increased so much that it was agreed that if Barker would give a selection from a play with which he was familiar (and which he did remarkably well), Jo and I would sing camp-meeting songs, to be followed by a duet by Mateel and Agnes.

While these arrangements were in progress, I went to the door to see how the weather was, as I had a long drive before me, and as I stood there I saw a horseman pass in the road, who I was certain was Clinton Bragg. Those on the inside were merrily laughing, and I purposely opened the door that he might hear it, and know that Mateel and Jo were happy, and surrounded by friends. I thought that he might come in with some kind of a message for Mateel, but I resolved that if he attempted it I would knock him down and beat him at the gate, for I felt the punch, and was in a humor for that kind of business. But he rode slowly past, and I am certain that he heard the gay laughter, and that no one knew of his presence except myself.

Although Barker drank as freely as Jo and I, he was evidently more accustomed to it, and did not mind it, though it had no other effect on us than to increase our good spirits. Agnes and Mateel partook but sparingly, but they were both in better humor than I

191

had ever seen them, and applauded whatever we did. Barker gave his selection from the play (it was a tragedy, and he limped in from the kitchen saying something about that being the winter of our discontent), after which Jo and I started a camp-meeting, imitating the singing, preaching, and shouting of the Fairview people, which performance was received with rounds of applause. Mateel and Agnes then sang their duet, in appreciation of which we clapped our hands until they sang another one; and thus the time passed until after midnight.

During the evening Jo found opportunity to express his pleasure that everything had turned out so well, and whenever we were alone I think both of us had a good deal to say about an "Old Boy," and the "Best friend in the world," for we lost all of the restraint which made us so uncomfortable in the morning, and fully renewed our old friendship.

When we broke up, and had said our adieus over and over, I found my team at the door, through the kindness of the assistant at the mill, and after we had closed the door for positively the last time, we opened it again for another kind word, and were very merry and gay.

There was a light fall of snow on the ground, and the night and the roads being fine, I insisted on taking Barker in the buggy and driving him home, knowing the horses would enjoy the dash along the level roads in the woods. He at first objected, but Agnes adding her entreaty, he finally consented, and after calling to Jo until he opened the door again, we waved our hands once more, crossed the creek below the mill, and dashed away.

I was proud of the speed of the team, and Barker was at first very nervous at the pace at which I drove, but finding I was a careful driver, he leaned contentedly back, and repeatedly said the drive was a pleasant ending to the agreeable evening at Jo's house. When we arrived at the mill, he invited us in, and as Agnes had never been at his house, and had often expressed a curiosity to see it, we accepted the invitation, though it was two or three o'clock in the morning. As I expected, there was still fire in the great box-stove in his room, for it seemed never to go out, and with a little stirring and fuel it was soon roaring. We walked

192

through all the rooms, Barker carrying the light, and appearing to be pleased and contented. I told Agnes of the delightful stories Barker had related to Jo and me in the big room with the heavy shutters, and even insisted that he tell another one, to give Agnes an idea of his talent in that direction, but he laughingly replied that it was late, and that they would prove very dull, now that we were older.

"I have another story to tell you, though," he said, after some reflection, "but it is not quite ready, and as it is a story for men, it is fortunate that you are almost a man. In good time I will tell it to you, and, if you choose, you may repeat it to Agnes."

While we were warming ourselves at the fire for completing the ride, I questioned him about it, but it seemed to be of no importance, for he laughed gayly, and would only say that when he was ready he would remind me of it.

After spending an hour there we started for Theodore Meek's and although I repeatedly informed Agnes that she was the best and prettiest girl in the world, and that I was very much in love with her, she was not at all serious, seeming to regard it as a part of the gayety of the night, and after reaching the house, and having a laugh all around with the family (who got up to hear about the wedding), we went to bed just as day began to appear in the east.

XXI

THE PECULIARITIES OF A
COUNTRY TOWN

THERE was one thing I noticed of Twin Mounds which is probably true of every other country town — it was constantly threatened either with great prosperity or great danger, but whether the event threatening the prosperity or the danger came to pass, the town progressed about the same. There was no perceptible effect from any of the events the people were certain would prove either very disastrous or of great benefit, from which I am led to believe that no one is familiar with the art of town-building, although I have never known a man who did not profess to know all there is worth knowing about the science. Towns seem to be the natural accretion of years, and although the people in Twin Mounds often related how desperate were their struggles with adversity, the facts probably are that the place would have been fully as large as it was three years after Jo's marriage without the great number of public meetings for public purposes, and the endless worry of individuals with reference to it.

There was a very general impression that manufactories were needed, and this was talked about so much, and so many inducements were offered, that the people became discouraged, believing that the average manufacturer had a wicked heart and a hollow head to thus wrong Twin Mounds in the face of his own interest, therefore we were very much surprised to learn once, after all hope had been abandoned, that a quiet man was building a woollen mill down the river, which he completed and afterwards operated without the help of the committees which had been appointed to aid in such matters of public weal. The trouble was that the man lived in Twin Mounds, whereas we had been expect-

194

ing a man and money to come from a distant point for that purpose, and had never thought of looking about home, but spent a great deal of money in sending committees away to make arrangements for a woollen mill. This circumstance, although humiliating, proved a good thing, for it taught the people that, if the town were to be built up at all, it must be by its own citizens, which knowledge was afterwards used to good advantage.

The people were always miserable by reason of predictions that, unless impossible amounts of money were given to certain enterprises, the town would be ruined, and although they always gave, no sooner was one fund exhausted than it became necessary to raise another. It was said during the collection of each amount that it would never be necessary again to give to this sort of charity (as the enterprise then in hand would insure the future of Twin Mounds), but there was never an end to the ridiculous business, and we were always in a state of dreariness on this account, as the men demanding the charity for insignificant enterprises loudly threatened to go to the rival towns, and permit the grass to grow in our streets. In thinking of the matter since, I have thought that Twin Mounds would have been a much better town but for the fact that it was always expecting improbable disaster, but which never came, for the people were thus prevented from exercising their energy, if they had any.

I never formed a good opinion of a man there that I was not finally told something to his discredit by another citizen, causing me to regard him with great suspicion, and if I said a good word for any of them, it was proved beyond question immediately that he was a very unscrupulous, a very ridiculous, a very weak, and a very worthless man. There were no friendships among them, and they all hated each other in secret, there being much quiet satisfaction when one of them failed. There seemed to be no regular aristocracy, either, for I heard so frequently how ignorant and awkward the prominent citizens were when they first came, that I finally found them all out. If Dr. Medicine told me what an unpromising lout the present magnificent Honorable Legal was when he first arrived, and how much difficulty he had in getting him introduced into respectable society, I was certain to meet Honorable Legal soon after, and hear him recite a similar experience with reference to Dr. Medicine. One of the stories, and I found afterwards that it was true, was that a man of ordinary worth, who seemed to be prosperous, had collected his money of a railroad company in the country he had moved from, because of an injury to his first wife, and that his second was enabled to go elegantly dressed because of the misfortune of the first. Thus it went on until I was familiar with the poor origin of all of them, and perhaps this was one reason why we did not respect one another more.

It was a popular expression that everyone favorably mentioned was the "worst overrated man in America," and the only real ability any of them ever displayed was in looking up the previous history of each other, which they carried on with great vigor, and frequently with alarming results. I began to believe in course of time that it was fortunate that the discreditable part of my history was well known, for it was the sooner forgotten, because it was not necessary to look up old records to find it out, and thus was not made worse than it really was.

Very few of the Twin Mounds men had positive opinions of their own, as they seemed to have got them second-handed from some source, and none of them was original or natural in his methods of conducting business, or in his habits. Two or three times a year most of them visited a city a good many miles away, where they spent a great deal of money they could not afford, to create an impression that they were accustomed to what they supposed was good society, and where they met men who filled their ideas of greatness. These they mimicked, each one choosing a different example; so it happened that the men of Twin Mounds were very ridiculous. There was a lawyer, I remember, who had met somewhere a distinguished member of his profession, who shook hands (Ho! ho!) with everybody, and (Ha! ha!) patronizingly wanted to know how they were getting along. It was not his natural way, and as he only adopted it because he believed it would make him popular, it became him very poorly. Perhaps it was very effective with the man the habit had been copied from, but it was very absurd with our citizen, whose pretence was that every man he shook hands with (and he shook hands cordially with everybody) was not getting along as well as he in his great compassion desired.

Another one, who carried on a business which one busy day would have exhausted, had heard of a man who achieved commercial greatness by finding fault (I am sure the man was mistaken, for no one ever made money in such a ridiculous way), and I never heard of anything that suited him. This he regarded as business shrewdness, and he finally became very sour in disposition because he was generally regarded as a fool instead of a prophet. Still another, naturally full of fool's gab, carried on a bank in awful silence because he had heard that still water runs deep, though I have seen ponds of perfectly still water which were very shallow.

As I grew older, and began to notice more, I thought that every man in Twin Mounds had reason to feel humiliated that he had not accomplished more, but most of them were as conceited as though there was nothing left in the world worthy of their attention. Their small business affairs, their quarrels over the Bible, and an occasional term in the town council, or a mention for the legislature or a county office, satisfied them, and they were as content as men who really amounted to something.

Although I believe there never was a more virtuous community, the men pretended to believe that their associates were great libertines, and many of the women were scandalized in an unjust and cruel manner. The men rather took a pride in reputations of this sort, for they never had any other, and, although pretending to deny it, they really hoped the people would continue to accuse them. I have known citizens of this description to stay out late at night, and take aimless rides into the country, to create the impression that they were having clandestine meetings with the first ladies of the town. The people watched each other so closely that there was no opportunity to be other than honest and circumspect in this particular, even if they had been differently inclined, and since the men were always looking for amours, but never found them, and believed that others were notoriously successful, they must have had a very contemptible opinion of themselves when they thought about the matter candidly.

I often heard from Jo, and frequently met him, and he always seemed to he happy and prosperous. The debt on the mill was being gradually reduced through his sturdy efforts, and in the middle of the second year of his marriage, he had built an addition to his house which made it very complete. His business was prosperous, because he gave it a great deal of intelligent attention, and he became widely known as one of the promising young men of that part of the country, for nobody worked so hard as he did, nor to so much purpose, and the business principles he had adopted were excellent. The product of his mill was called the "Erring's Ford" brand, we having agreed on the name together because it was odd, and because it celebrated a hope which had been ridiculed by the Fairview folks, and we printed large bills announcing its superiority, which were distributed so well that wherever I went I was reminded of my skill as a printer, and Jo's superiority as a miller.

At long intervals he came to our house with his pretty wife, and I always thought they were very happy, as I have no doubt they were. I do not remember that I thought much of them during the three years I am now passing rapidly over, except that Jo had made himself the equal of his wife, which was a pleasant reflection to me because he had begun so far behind her, and with the utmost friendship for Mateel, I was always pleased when Jo appeared to better advantage than she did, or when I thought that if a stranger should judge between them, the impression would be that Jo was the superior one of the two.

I had the impression that Jo was an excellent husband, for he was always thinking of what would please Mateel, and when they were together he was as gentle and gallant as he had been when they were lovers, which I have heard is very unusual. Mateel was a good wife, but I do not know that I ever heard her say a kind word for her husband, although others talked about him a great deal. She thought, no doubt, that his excellences were understood, and did not need to be mentioned. I thought of this circumstance then, because I believed it would have been no more than natural for her to say that Jo had succeeded well, or that he had bravely won her, but she never did, although she seemed pleased when I complimented her husband, as though it was an expression of a hope that if he were not so rich then as she desired, he might be in the future.

Usually when Jo and Mateel came to Twin Mounds, Agnes came with them, as it was their custom to drive over on Saturday, and back in the evening of the next day, and with so many of her old friends around her, my mother perceptibly revived, but when they had gone away, she resumed her old melancholy, and pined away in the room where she watched at night. If they offered to take her home with them, she refused, and never went out, except occasionally to ride with me, and then I thought it was more to admire the speed of "Dan" and "Dave" than because she cared to leave the house.

Although the Rev. John Westlock was never heard of, the light was always burning in his old room at night, and his deserted wife was always waiting to forgive him. I think she never for a moment gave up the hope that he would come back; for, winter and summer alike, she waited for him every night, and was weaker the next day because he did not come. The fear began to oppress me that some morning we should find her dead at her post, and I proposed to get someone to stay with her at night, but she would not hear of it, thinking, no doubt, that when he came he would much prefer to find her alone. Thus the months went by, and at the close of every one I found that her head was whiter and her step more feeble.

I saw Lytle Biggs nearly every week, and Big Adam often came there with products of the farm to sell, and he always came in to see me, usually having the information to impart that another relative had been killed by the Indians, or that his old mistress "jawed" him more than ever. If he found it necessary to stay in the town over night, which was sometimes the case, I took him home with me, and treated him with so much consideration in other ways that he soon became my greatest friend.

From him I learned that Agnes only came home during the two vacations of the year, and that her mother was about the same with respect to visions of poisoning and smothering, which humiliated them all very much except Big Adam, who said he considered it an honor for the people to believe that he would poison his mistress if he had opportunity, for they all knew she deserved it. Mrs. Biggs and the children had changed but little, except that the children had grown larger and more unruly, and their mother more shrivelled than formerly. Big Adam was quite a novelty in Twin Mounds, by reason of his great size and hoarse voice, and a crowd always gathered at the office when he was there in the evening, to hear him tell about the great farm he was expected to cultivate alone.

Although I was always hoping he would kill himself with dissipation, Clinton Bragg continued to be only about as worthless as when I had first known him, and there was no change in his manner except that he made up with every old wreck who came to town, and induced him by treats to listen to his brags about himself. Bragg came from a place somewhere in the East which was given over to the manufacture of knives and forks, and the three or four proprietors of the works comprised the aristocracy. These, lacking better company, associated occasionally with the small tradesmen and professional men of the town, which led them to talk a great deal of the excellent society in which they moved, and judging them by their representative in Twin Mounds, they became very unpopular wherever they went, by reason of this unpleasant egotism. His father, a hard-working but ignorant man, by close attention to the business of keeping a keg house, had risen to the dignity of a merchant, and was reputed to be well-to-do, although, as is usually the case, I doubt if he had half the money with which he was credited.

Bragg considered this fork-making community as the greatest the world had ever produced, and made himself very disagreeable in talking about it. Being a great liar naturally, and as no one in Twin Mounds knew differently, he used a citizen of the town where he had lived to traduce citizens of Twin Mounds, and if a lawyer lost a case, or won it, he told cheerful anecdotes of his brilliant friend Bighead, the leader of his profession in Forkston. No difference what happened in Twin Mounds, it reminded him of a friend of his in the town where knives were made, who always did whatever was in hand in a much more creditable manner.

When he was drinking, he went about inquiring who Alexander Bighead was, who Cornelius Deadhead was, who Elwyn Flathead was, who Godfrey Hardhead was, or who Isaac Jughead was. Nobody being able to inform him (none of them having ever been heard of outside of the community where they lived), Bragg would answer that Alexander Bighead was a great lawyer and a great drunkard, and that Cornelius Deadhead was as noted for his knowledge of medicine as he was noted for his intemperance; that Elwyn Flathead was a heavy trader, and a heavy drinker; that Godfrey Hardhead was frequently on the public platform, and frequently in the gutter; and that Isaac Jughead was as often on a spree as he was on the bench; which argument was intended to convey the impression that all talented men (Clinton Bragg included) drank more than was good for them.

Lytle Biggs, being a professional politician, was often in town, and as had been the case when he first met me, he was of the opinion that while I was a little delicate in asking him for the favor, I was burning with impatience to hear more of his philosophy. I had enjoyed it very much at first, and laughed a great deal at his oddities, and though it finally grew tiresome, I could not very well flatly tell him so. Hence he came in frequently when I was very busy, and when I knew he was not in a philosophical humor, but reasoning that I had grown to expect it, and had little other amusement, he consented to favor me with a few of his thoughts. Thus it came about that he walked in one evening when I was anxious to go home, and, seating himself, prepared to spend several hours with me, though I could see he regarded himself as a martyr to be compelled to instruct me in ordinary affairs which should be understood at a glance.

"Speaking of the newspaper business," he said, of which we were not speaking at all, "I make considerable money advising the farmers to patronize the 'Rural Home,' than which, in my opinion, a greater literary thug never existed, but unfortunately for an oppressed people, the publisher of the 'Home' (his name is Litch; it should be Leech) pays liberal commissions, and I must live. I have a copy in my pocket; you may examine it when there is positively nothing else to do."

He handed it to me, and although it was folded, I saw on

the first page a picture of an animal so admirably proportioned that but little was wasted in legs, being solid meat with the exception of a small head and four pins to hold it up. By examining the note at the bottom, I found it was a pig, although I should not have suspected it in the absence of the statement, and that pairs of the breed could be had by addressing the publisher, and enclosing money order or draft for fifty dollars.

"If you should do yourself the injustice at some time in the future to look it over," Mr. Biggs continued, indicating that I was not to look at it then, but to listen, "you would find it filled with all sorts of ingenious appeals for the farmer's money, and that the editor claims to be poor, but honest, and oppressed by monopolies, like the rest of them. But what are the hard, uncomfortable facts?"

I looked at him as if to say that I did not know what the facts were, but had no doubt they were bad enough.

"The facts are that while the agricultural population is cooped up in hot school-houses drinking spring water, and attending Alliance meetings, the publisher of the 'Rural' is holding ice in his mouth at an elegant club, only changing this delightful occupation to gulp down expensive champagne. He lives in a villa, does this agricultural fraud of the name of Litch, and makes a fortune every year; and, although he earnestly advises the farmers' wives and daughters to spend their spare time in churning the butter and gathering the eggs, to buy good books to improve themselves (P. S. — For which he is agent), he sends his own wife and daughters to spend their spare time in summer at cool places, where they may swim in the sea. That's the kind of an oppressed citizen of a groaning government Litch is, and I happen to know that he is the friend of the monopolists he denounces, and that he is in their pay; that he is the tool of the thieves who manufacture worthless machinery for farmers; of the confidence men who advertise eggs, pigs, and calves at a high price, and that he is the worst enemy of the farmers generally."

I pretended to be very much surprised at this, though I was not.

"If you should be caught in a lonely place on a rainy day, with no other paper in your pocket than that, you would find a column of inquiries with reference to agricultural matters addressed to the editor (who is supposed to be informed, but who really gets all his information from the agricultural departments of the metropolitan papers), each one of which closes with a good word for 'your noble,' or 'your brave,' or 'your widely circulated' paper. The scoundrel writes them himself! And there is another column from 'Aunt Sue.' He is also 'Aunt Sue.' In short, he is everything except an honest man."

Although I said nothing, I remembered that every farmer who moved to Twin Mounds found out the agricultural papers, and denounced them; in short, that everybody except the farmers knew what dreadful frauds they were.

"If I should talk as candidly and honestly to my friends of the plough as I talk to my friends of the pen," Mr. Biggs continued, "I should advise them to take the papers which other people take; the papers which censure the farmer when he deserves it, instead of pandering to his ignorance, and forever rubbing him on the back as an honest but oppressed fellow, through no fault of his own. You cannot possibly do a man more harm than to assure him that whatever he does is right, and that whatever his enemy does is wrong, but this is what Litch does, and he is well paid for doing it. The farmer follows the furrow because he can make more at that than at anything else; he is no more oppressed than other men, except as his ignorance makes it possible, for there never was an age when it was not profitable to be sensible (the world being full of unscrupulous men), therefore the pretence that a man cannot be honest except he plough or sow for a living is not warranted by the facts. Getting up very early in the morning, and going about agricultural work all day in rough clothes, does not particularly tend to clear the conscience, but because politicians who occasionally have use for them have said these things, the farmers go on accepting them, stubbornly refusing to be undeceived, because it is unpleasant to acknowledge ignorance after you have once thought yourself very cunning. In my time, I have harangued a meeting of well-to-do farmers over the wrongs they were suffering at the hands of miserable tradesmen — they call them middlemen — who did not know one day whether they would be able to open their doors the next, and received earnest applause, after which I got ten dollars for a charter for an Alliance (which cost me at the rate of two dollars a thousand) without difficulty. It would not be a greater confidence game were I to borrow ten dollars of them to pay express charges on the body of a dead brother, giving as security a bogus bond, for the time a farmer spends attending Alliance meetings should be spent at home in reading an honest work entitled, 'Thieves Exposed,' or 'The Numerous Devices Men Invent to Live Without Work,' but they rather enjoy my lectures on the beauties of combination for protection, and the cheapness of Alliance charters, for I never fail to relate how honest, how industrious, how intelligent, and how oppressed they are. If they want to pay big prices for such comforts, it is their misfortune; I must live, and if you say that I am a fraud, I reply that all men are frauds. The lawyers never go to law; the doctors never take medicine; the preachers seldom believe in religion, and I never farm. The different trades and professions are only respectable because little is known of them except by those interested in their profits, and I am no worse than the rest of them. Whoever will pay for being humbugged will find humbugs enough, and the only difference between me and other professional men is that I acknowledge that I am dishonest. My position on the reform question is briefly this (and I may add that it is the position of every man): I am against monopolies until I become a monopolist myself. I am at present engaged in the reform business that I may become a monopolist. If I should suddenly become rich, what would I do? This: Refer to Alliances as dangerous, and such demagogues as myself as suspicious loafers."

Mr. Biggs seemed to greatly enjoy this denunciation of himself, and ripped out an oath or two expressive of contempt for his victims.

"Our friend Bilderby, for example, who writes letters for your paper on finance, and who professes to know all about money, in reality knows so little about his subject that he cannot earn a living, although he seems to be constantly worried with the fear that, from a mistaken financial policy, the government will come to ruin. In fact, Bilderby only gets time to write his letters on finance, and make excuses to his creditors. The fellow owes the doctor for nearly all his children; I am certain he has not paid for the younger ones. That is Bilderby's way of being a humbug; I have a different way; you have another, and there are so many varieties, that every man is accommodated."

Mr. Biggs was warming up, and unbuttoned his collar to talk with more freedom.

"I see occasional notices in your publication to the effect that Chugg, the groceryman, or whatever the name or the business may be, has just returned from the East, which is extremely dull, and that he is extremely glad to get back to the enterprising, the pushing, the promising, the noble, and the beautiful West. That is YOUR way of being a humbug, for in reality Chugg is glad to get back to the West because he is of some importance here, and none there. The East is full of hungry and ragged men who are superior in every way to the prominent citizen of the name of Chugg, and Chugg knows it, therefore he is glad to get back where he is looked upon as a superior creature. I have no hesitancy in saying privately that the people in this direction are not warranted in the belief that all the capable and energetic men have left the East, though it would be disastrous to say as much publicly. When I am in the East it occurs to me with great force that the miles of splendid business buildings I see on every hand must be occupied by talented and energetic men, and as we have no such buildings in the West, it follows that we have no such men. When I see towering manufactories — swarming with operatives who would be ornaments to the best society out here — I think that at least a few men of energy and capacity have been left to operate them, for ordinary men could not do it. I ride down the long avenues of private palaces, each one of them worth a township in the Smoky Hill country, and I am convinced that we are mistaken in the opinion that a man must live on the frontier in order to be energetic."

I had a habit of scribbling with a pencil when idle, and as I picked up a piece of paper to amuse myself in this manner, Mr.

Biggs caught my hand, and said, "No notes!" fearing I intended to publish his opinions. He then explained, as he had often done before, that he talked candidly to me for my own good, and that he would be ruined if I quoted him either in print or privately. Being assured that I had no such intention, he went on: —

"Haven't you noticed that when a Western man gets a considerable sum of money together, he goes East to live? Well, what does it mean except that the good sense which enabled him to make money teaches him that the society there is preferable to ours? When we go away for recreation and pleasure, in what direction do we go? East, of course, because it rains oftener there than here; because the caves, the lakes, the falls, the sea, and the comforts are in that direction. If I should get rich, I would leave this country, because I know of another where I could live more comfortably. I stay here because it is to my interest; all of us do, and deserve no credit. It is rather humiliating to me than otherwise that I am compelled to live where living is cheap, because I cannot afford the luxuries. Men who are prosperous, or men who live in elegant houses, do not come West, but it is the unfortunate, the poor, the indigent, the sick — the lower classes, in short — who came here to grow up with the country, having failed to grow up with the country where they came from."

My visitor got up at this, and without ceremony took his hat, and walked out, giving me to understand that I should feel greatly favored. I followed him soon afterward, and passing along the street, I heard him gayly talking to a crowd of men in front of one of the stores, but in a different strain — in fact, he seemed to feel guilty for what he had said, and was denying it.

XXII

A SKELETON IN THE HOUSE
AT ERRING'S FORD

MORE than three years had passed since Jo and Mateel were
married, and I was alone on the last night of the year, thinking that the years were slipping away wonderfully fast of late,
it seemed so short a time since we had lived in the country; since
the Rev. John Westlock so strangely disappeared, and since I
was a boy in distress at my own and Jo's misfortunes. The good
year was dying, and would soon pass peacefully into the dim past,
after the watchers had tired of waiting, and gone to sleep. As is
the case when an old man dies, the announcement is speedily
followed by the birth of a babe, and so the race and the years
are continued. As is now said of the dying year, so it will be
said of all of us. At some time in the mysterious future — nobody
knows when — the hand that writes this will be picking uneasily
at the covering of a death-bed, and it will be whispered in the
room, and in all the house, and down the streets, "He is dying;
poor fellow, he is dead." The eye that reads this — at some time
in the future; nobody knows when — will become fixed, and it
will be gently said: "Dying; dead." The front door will be black
with crape for a few days, and the people will pass the house
reverently and silently, but after a very little while the token
of death will be removed, the house will be thrown open and
aired, and laughter will be heard on the inside. Birds will sing
merrily at the front door, and flowers appear, and happy children
play about the house, and through it, as though nothing had
happened. The dead man may have been dearly loved, but
everything and everybody encourages his friends to forget him,
and they laugh in the room where he died, and where his coffin
sat through the long nights before the burial.

The relics of departed friends, which were at first carefully laid away, are in the course of months or years resurrected, and given to their successors. The hat worn by the pretty boy who died last year, or the year before, is worn to-day by the boy who came after him, and he plays with his toys, which were at first so sacred, as though they had been brought to the house for him. The mother who put the little hat away no doubt thought she would keep it for years, and look at it to imagine that her first-born was wearing it again, but time has softened her grief; friends told her he was better off, and she hoped so, and tried to convince herself that it was all for the best.

So it will be with the dying year; it was well loved while it lasted, and brought us many good gifts, but it will be speedily forgotten, and in twelve months we shall be equally indifferent as to its successor. One dies; another is born; so go the people and the years. There will be a birth and a death to-night, but it is not an uncommon circumstance: there will be a little mourning for the death, but a great deal of rejoicing and ringing of bells for the birth.

The fire in the room where I usually worked had gone out, and I had taken my papers to an inner room, where Martin had worked late, and which was yet warm. It must have been ten o'clock, and outside the snow was falling steadily, promising great drifts in the morning, as I could see by the rays thrown out into the darkness from the single light which burned in the room. Just after I had settled down comfortably in my chair, someone opened the front door, and stood on the inside, scraping the snow from his feet, and brushing it from his coat, which startled me, for I supposed the door to be locked. Outside of the circle of the lamp it was quite dark, and as the visitor came slowly toward me, brushing the snow from his clothing, I was still in doubt as to who it was, until he stood almost beside me, when I saw with surprise that it was Jo Erring.

"Of all the men in the world," I said, getting up, and making a place for him by the fire, "you are the most welcome. I think you must be my New Year's gift, for I am lonely to-night, and was wishing you were here."

He held his hands up to the fire to warm them, but did not reply, and I noticed, when he looked at me, that his eyes were bloodshot and swollen.

"Is there anything the matter?" I asked.

Now that I was looking at him closely, I saw with alarm that tears were in his eyes.[1] He made no effort to hide this, but looked at me as though he would speak, but could not, and with a face so pitiful that I became alarmed. He still held his hands up to the fire to warm them, and I expected him every moment to burst out crying.

"Jo, my old friend," I said to him at last, laying my hand on his shoulder, "tell me the meaning of this. You distress and alarm me."

Turning his face from the light, he remained a long while in deep study, and [2] finally got up and walked to that part of the room which was the darkest, where he paced up and down a long time. I added wood to the fire, expecting him to sit down every moment and tell me his trouble, but he continued his walk, and wrapped his great-coat about him, as though he was chilled to the heart. At last he turned suddenly, and came over into the light.

"For what I am about to say," he said, sitting down, "may God forgive me, for it is a matter that concerns no one but myself, and should forever remain a secret with me. But I have thought of it so much, and am so distressed from thinking of it, that I must speak of it to you, or lose my reason. If I could show you the wickedness in my thoughts, you would run away from me in alarm, but if I could show you my heart, you would weep over the misery it contains. It is unmanly for me to tell you what I came here to tell,[3] but I am so wretched that I walked here to-night through the storm for the sympathy I am sure you will give, and which I need so much. I have not slept for weeks, except when nature asserted itself in spite of my misery, but through all the long nights I have tumbled and tossed about,

[1] eyes: 1883 eyes, and we were both so still that I heard them falling in little plashes on the floor.

[2] study, and: 1883 study, his tears still falling to the floor, and

[3] came here to tell: 1883 am about to

thinking of the matter in a different light at every turn, hoping to get some comfort out of it, but every new thought of it seems the worst of all. I came out of the house to-night to cool my hot head, and walking towards you caused me to resolve to come on, and freeze myself into forgetfulness. Mateel does not know where I am, and I must go back as I came, but I would rather walk alone in this storm than trust myself in a darkened room with my thoughts. I am sick to-night, for the first time in my life, but it is from thinking of the matter I came to tell you about, for it has taken such possession of me that even sleep is denied me."

I was so distressed and alarmed that I could not say a word, but tried to appear natural by digging at the fire. After Jo had thought awhile, he continued: —

"I need not rehearse the story of my courtship and marriage — you are familiar with that, and you know that I have been very contented and happy, except that ever since I have known Mateel, I have noticed an indifference which often humiliated me, but which I have excused for a hundred reasons, and tried to think little of. The letter which I will shortly ask you to read explains it all, and it is this which has changed me into a wicked, worthless man, without hope or ambition. The letter was written by Mateel to Clinton Bragg, when she was his promised wife, before they came to Fairview, and I received it by mail, addressed in a strange hand, six weeks ago yesterday, on an evening when I was planning for the future, and when I was in unusual good spirits. That she had been engaged to Bragg I never knew, nor did I suspect it, for although I knew they were brought up in the same neighborhood, and had been children together, the thought never occurred to me that they had been lovers, for he is more fit for a hangman's rope than for an honest woman's regard. I know now that Mateel has never loved me as the letter indicates she loved the most contemptible man I ever knew; a hundred times I have wondered if there were no better lovers in the world than Mateel, but I have found that the trouble was that she had drained her heart dry in loving my enemy, and that there was none left for me. This is what has wounded my pride, and broken my spirits, and left me a useless wreck."

He took from an inner pocket and handed me an envelope, and taking from it the letter, I began to read aloud.

"Read it to yourself," he said. "I am familiar with it."

The letter was closely written, and read as follows: —

MY BRAVE LOVER, — I write to-night to tell you for the hundredth time how much I love you. When you are away from me, I have no other pleasure than this, for it brings you to me to receive my kisses and embraces. Once you came in the middle of the day following the night I wrote you, and if you come to-morrow, and sincerely believe and never forget what I have to say, this letter will have accomplished its mission.

What I want to say is (and I write it after a great deal of serious deliberation) that if by an unlucky chance we should never be married, I should still love you as I do now, forever. I love you so much that I am anxious you should know that even though I believed you had forgotten me, and I became the wife of someone else, because all women are expected to marry, I should continue to think of you as I do now, the only man worthy of my love in all the world; and every night after my husband had gone to sleep, I would put my arms around him, and imagine that it was you, and that you would waken soon, and love me as I am sure you do this night.

I want you to believe this, for it is written with absolute sincerity, and if my hope of the future should never be realized, please read this over, and over again, and feel that I am married only in penance for being unworthy of you. Wherever I am, and whatever my condition, I beg of you to remember that I love only you; that I will never love anyone else, and that with my last breath I will tenderly speak your name.

I do not believe God will be so cruel as to separate us, but if He should, the knowledge that you knew I continued to love you would make my loss easier to bear. If I should consent to be married, it would be to someone who cared for nothing but my promise to live with him; and if I could call him up from the future now to stand beside me, I would bravely tell him that I love only Clinton Bragg, and that though my mind may change, my heart never will.

If I should be so unfortunate as to have a husband other than you, I would be dutiful and just to him, but my love I would reserve until I met you in heaven, when, realizing how perfect it is, you would accept it. Loving you always,

MATEEL.

I folded the letter, and handed it back to him, and as it touched his fingers, he shuddered, as though overtaken by a chill.

211

"The very touch of it penetrates my marrow," he said, after putting it away in his pocket as though it were red-hot; "but for all my dread of its infamous contents, I have read it a hundred times. If I am tossing about at night, unable to sleep from thinking of it, I cannot help making a light, and reading it again."

"Did you ever talk to her about it?" I asked, and I am sure I was trembling all over; for I felt that Jo Erring, with all his prospects, was now a wreck and would never be himself again.

"Not about this, directly," he answered, "but she has told me that she was engaged to Bragg. She treated it so coolly that I thought perhaps such things are common, and that I am unreasonable to feel as I do. I am not familiar with the ways of good society; it may be that love is only an amusement, to be indulged in with every agreeable person; it may be that a woman is none the less a true woman for having been caressed and fondled by different men, and that it is no fault for a young girl to spend half a night with a lover who is liable to be succeeded in a month by another, but if such is the social creed, something convinces me that society is wrong, and that my revolting manhood is right."

He rose from his chair, and walked up and down in the dark part of the room again, and I could not help thinking of what Mr. Biggs had said: That everyone has a private history.

"I do not know who broke the engagement," he said, returning to the fire at last, "but I have evidence in this letter that it was not Mateel, therefore it is fair to suppose that the insolent dog who sent this, tired of the contract, and broke it off. The girl was heart-broken, no doubt, and was brought West with the hope that she would encounter an ignorant fellow with industrious habits, but no sensibility, who could comfortably support her until old age and death came to the relief of her heart, but who could never hope to have her love, for that she had given already, although it was not wanted. Through the cruel neglect of God I became the man who is expected to labor early and late that she may be made as comfortable as possible in her affliction. I receive nothing in return for this except the knowledge that as another man did not want her love, I may have her to care for, as her family is not well-to-do, and somebody must do it.

212

"Whenever I knock at my heart's door, it is opened by a skeleton hand, and this letter handed out to me; if ambition beckons to me now, the fleshless fingers of an inexorable devil hold me back; and instead of pushing on, I sit down and cry that I have been so disgraced through no fault of my own. They thought I was a rough country boy, lacking so delicate a thing as a heart, and that I would be content with a broken flower because it had once been very beautiful; I doubt if they thought of me at all, except that I was industrious and healthy, as all the consideration was for Mateel, who had been wounded and hurt."

I listened to the wind blowing on the outside, and I thought it was more mournful than I had ever heard it before.

"I cannot tell you how much my marriage to Mateel would have done for me had this letter never been written, for I should have divined its existence though it had never fallen in my way. Before I read it I was as happy as it is possible for a man to be, though the fear often oppressed me that a dark shadow would fall across my path, for I had always been taught to believe that great sorrow followed great happiness. The shadow has come, and the devils are probably content with its black intensity. I was proud that the home I had provided for Mateel was better than any she had ever lived in before, and was kind and careful of her that she might bless the day we met; I was proud to be known as a progressing, growing man that her father might be proud of me, as he knew how hard my boyhood was, but I see now that they all regarded me as a convenience; a trusty packhorse of great endurance, and I know that my years of work for Mateel were not worthy of a man's ambition. I can never tell you, though I would willingly if I could, how great is the burden I must bear from this time forward. Hope has been killed within me, except hope to die, and my ambition has been cruelly trampled upon and killed by a man I never wronged."

He sat crouching before the fire, like a man who had been beaten without cause by superior numbers, and who felt humiliated because his oppressors had escaped, and he could not be avenged upon them.

"Until six weeks ago, Mateel was a perfect woman in my eyes, and the queen of my heart; but since that time I have begun to criticise her (to myself; she does not know it), and if I become an indifferent husband, the fault is her own. I cannot be the same as I was before, for I shall be inclined to look upon her simply as the convenience she undertook to become, instead of my wife. If she fails to be convenient — and I fear I shall be a hard critic — I cannot help observing it in my present state of mind, though I shall remark it only to myself. She has deliberately deceived me, but in spite of it I love her, and every night-wind brings me word that it is not returned. The very wheels in the mill give voice to her entreaty to Bragg to remember that she will never love me; every sound mocks me that my wife is proud of her love for another, and piteously begs that it may never be forgotten. Since reading the letter I have never kissed my wife, or put my arms about her, and I hope God may strike me dead if ever I do either again."

He stood up in great excitement, as if calling on God to witness his oath; but, as if recalling something, he meekly sat down again, and continued in a subdued tone.

"I have apologized to her for my conduct, for she seems distressed about it, and promised that perhaps I would think better of it after a while, but I never shall; it is growing worse with me, and I tremble when I think of my future. I talk with her about the old affair with Bragg over and over again, hoping it was not so bad as I think. She is very truthful and candid, and reluctantly answers every question, however searching it may be, but the more I talk of it the worse it gets. Don't imagine from what I have said that she was ever anything but a virtuous girl; but she once loved that man so madly that she denounced me before she had seen me. The fresh and innocent affection which I should have had was given to Bragg — he had the fragrance of the rose; I have the withered leaves, after he tired of its beauty, and tossed it away. You can imagine the scenes between two young people who passionately love each other, and who only delay marriage until a convenient time. If you cannot, I can; and it is this imagination which never leaves me. And to add to my wretchedness, Bragg throws himself in my way as often as possible, that I may contemplate the man who was worthy of the woman I am not.

The time may come when I would give my life to take him by the throat, and if ever it does, there will be murder done, for with my hands once upon him I would tear him into bits."

I did not know what to say in reply, for I could think of nothing that would comfort him; and though I knew he would never again need my friendship as he needed it then, this knowledge only confused me, and made me stammer when I attempted to put in a word. He seemed to have so thoroughly considered the matter that there was no defence, and stated it so candidly that I thought he only expected me to pity him.

"Jo," I said, as the thought occurred to me, "you undoubtedly received this letter from Bragg; no one else would be malicious enough to send it. Are you certain he did not write it?"

A new hope sprang into his eyes, though I noticed that his hand paused on its way to the pocket which contained the letter, as though it was of no use to look. But he unfolded the letter with trembling hands, and studied it with great care, spending so much time over it that I hoped we should have occasion to go out and find the scoundrel, and beat him, but after Jo had finished his inspection, I saw that he was satisfied that the letter was written by Mateel.

"That it might be a forgery never occurred to me before," he said, with a long sigh, "but it is genuine; there is no doubt."

"I need not tell you, my dear old friend," I said, "that I am sorry this has happened. I regret it so much that I am powerless to comfort you, if that were possible. Your tears have unmanned me."

"I want to apologize to-night for my future," he said, after a long silence, "for I no longer have ambition. I can never succeed now, and I want you to know why. If I do not advance in the future, I desire that my only friend know that I no longer care to advance; that I have no reason to wish for success, and that I am not trying. If I become a Fairview man, miserable and silent, without hope or ambition, I want you to know that I am not to blame. I have just such a business, and just such a home, as we pictured together when we were boys. I have proved to you that I did not over-estimate my strength, and if I do not progress now that I am a man, you will know that my strength has been broken. The home I built with so much care is distasteful to me; the business I own after such a struggle, I hate; and I want you to know that, while I have not tired of working, I no longer care to succeed. The one above all others who should have helped me has only brought me disgrace, and broken my heart. There was no contract between us, but when Mateel became my promised wife, I made a vow to accomplish what I have; I have succeeded, but she has succeeded in nothing except to bring me this letter and its humiliating contents. I would not be a successful man in the future if I could. Bragg will finally become a beggar, for he is a spendthrift and loafer, and I believe that she would use my means to help him. I would rather be poor than rich, for if I should die possessed of property, that scoundrel would overcome his former scruples and marry my widow. My ambition in the future will be to live long and die poor. I hope the Devil is satisfied. He has been after me a long while, and I have passed into his possession body and soul. But I must return home," he said, as if remembering the hour. "Mateel does not know where I am, though I suspect she does not care, and is soundly sleeping."

"How are you going?" I asked, as he got up, and began buttoning his great-coat around him.

"As I came — on foot."

He started to walk past me, and would have gone away had I not held him back.

"To-morrow is Saturday, and New Year," I said. "It is a holiday, and I will go with you. Wait here until I come back."

He consented without a word, and sat down, and I think did not change his position until I came back with the horses. It was an hour after midnight, and the cold was intense — a miserable night for such a ride, but I willingly undertook it, knowing it was a kindness to Jo, and that we could easily make the distance in an hour. When I told my mother that I was going to Fairview, she was not surprised, nor did she ask me any questions, and I was soon on the way, with Jo by my side.

When we drove up to the house at the mill, which we did

after a cold ride without speaking a word, I saw a curtain pulled aside in a room where there was a light, and Mateel's pale and frightened face peering out, but by the time she appeared at the door, and opened it, we had passed on to the stables, and were putting away the horses. I was chilled through with cold, but when we walked back toward the house, I am certain I shivered because I dreaded to see them meet, knowing how unhappy and how helpless both were. I opened the door, and we walked in together, Jo a little behind me, and we went direct to the fire, though I stopped and held out my hand to his frightened wife. She was very pale, and I knew she had been weeping, for her eyes were red and swollen. While she took my hat and coat, Jo took off his, and held his hands out to the fire as he had done when he came to see me in town. He had taken a hasty glance at his wife, and I thought her distress added to his own, as though now both were wretched, and nobody to blame for it.

"Jo, my husband," she said, in a piteous, hesitating tone, and almost crying, "what has happened? You look so strange. I have been walking the floor since eight o'clock waiting for you. Is there anything the matter?"

As Jo did not reply, she looked at me for an answer, and I said he had business in town which occupied him until late; and that, knowing she would be worried, I had brought him home. But this did not satisfy her, and walking over to Jo, she stood beside him.

"Why don't you speak to me? You have never treated me this way before."

As she stood trembling beside him, I thought that surely Jo's letter was a forgery, and that if she did not love her husband, a woman never did.

Looking up at her as though half ashamed, Jo said: —

"You know why I went out of the house to-night. It is nothing more than that; you say it is not serious."

Mateel walked over to a chair near me — I thought she staggered as she went — and sat down, and her face was so pale and frightened that I felt sure Jo wronged her when he said she did not care. We sat there so long in silence that I began wondering who would first speak, and what would be said, and whether it would clear up this distressing matter. When I glanced at Mateel, I saw despair and helplessness written in her face, and determined to go to bed, and leave them alone, hoping they would talk it over, and forget it. Jo saw my intention, and motioned me back.

"You say it is not serious," he said, glancing hurriedly at his wife, as if afraid that if he looked in her face, and saw its distress, his stubborn heart would relent so much so as to commit the unpardonable offence of taking her in his arms; "therefore you will not care that I have told Ned. I have talked to him more freely than to you. I went to town for that purpose."

Had my life depended upon it, I could not have told which one I pitied most.

"As I know you to be a truthful woman," he went on, after a long pause, "and you say it is not serious, I believe that you think so; but it is all the more unfortunate on that account, for it is a very grave matter to me. I can never explain to you fully why I take it so much to heart, because I should wound your feelings in doing it, but the change in me within six weeks will convince you that if I am unreasonable about it, I cannot help it, and that my pride has been humbled, and my spirit broken, by a circumstance for which you are probably not to blame, when everything is considered. It is unmanly in me to feel as I do, and I apologize to you that I have not manhood sufficient (if that is a reasonable excuse) to shake off a circumstance which will affect my future, but which you regard as trifling. I have loved you — and I do yet; it is nothing to me what those I do not care for have been — I have loved you with my whole heart, and I have never divided my affection with anyone, if I except an honest friendship for my sister's son, and who was the sole companion of my wretched boyhood; but the more I love you, the more unhappy I am. This is my unfortunate dilemma, and I only mention it because the serious truth must be known. Although it nearly killed me, I asked you never to show me affection until I felt differently; I did this because I believed you learned to be affectionate with a man I hate, and that you can never show me an

218

act of kindness you did not show him, and which your love for him taught you. No woman's lips ever touched mine — my only sister's alone excepted, and hers not frequently — until yours did; my mind was never occupied with thoughts of love until I met you, and now that I know you only consented to marry me because you could not be better suited, my simple affection is hurt. I know that you care for me in a fashion; so you do for everyone who is kind to you; but I wanted the affection you gave HIM, your first and best. I feel debased that this affair has ruined me, for it has completely, and I can no longer look an honest man in the face, for against my will I am an indifferent husband, instead of the worthy one I hoped to become. I was brought up in a community where the women were overworked, imposed upon, and unhappy; I resolved to make my wife a notable exception to this rule, but I cannot now, and I feel the disgrace keenly."

The pale, fretful women of Fairview, who talked in the church of their heavy crosses to bear, and sat down crying, passed before me in procession; and staggering behind them, with the heaviest cross of all, was Mateel.

"I was so particular to tell you how I felt about this matter before we were married," Jo went on, still looking into the fire, "though I spoke of it then only to convince you that I was a good lover, for I did not suspect that you regarded me as a victim instead of a man. I talked of it seriously that you might know I was in earnest, and much as I loved you, had I known this I would have given you up at the last moment. There might have been a remedy for it then; there is none now. As I have been during the past six weeks, so shall I be as long as I live, except that I shall grow more bitter and resentful. It is cruel that I have been mercilessly ruined, and nobody to blame for it. Were I injured in any other way, there would be someone to punish, and amends to be made, but in this no wrong has been done; indeed, I suppose I, who am so grievously injured, am more to blame than anyone else for being so absurd. I am certain everyone will regard it in this way, although that will not help the matter so far as I am concerned."

There were evidences of bitterness in his words now, rather

than of sadness and regret; and he looked around the room fiercely, as though he would do something desperate to those who had injured him. But he soon began thinking again, and went on talking: —

"I speak frankly only that we may understand each other, for it grieves me to do it. It is not a pleasure for me to command you never to touch me again. During the short time we have lived apart on account of this unfortunate matter, I have prayed every night that you would come to me, though I had locked my door so you could not. When my heart finally breaks it will be because you no longer come to me,[4] though I will not let you. One night I became so distracted thinking of your unhappiness as well as my own that I stole softly into your room intending to kiss away your tears, and ask you to forgive my unintended cruelty; but I found you quietly sleeping, and I will swear that by the light of my lamp I saw you smiling. I will swear that you spoke the name of Clinton; and I went back to my room determined to kill him, and then myself. But my cowardly heart — it was never cowardly before — failed me, and I could only become more ugly and wicked."

From the manner in which Mateel started at this I believed she had only gone to sleep when completely exhausted, and that she had only spoken the name because she was familiar with it, as she was familiar with a thousand others; but the circumstance seemed only to convince her that everything was against her, and that explanations would be useless; but, as if trying to avoid the subject, she asked, without looking up: —

"Since you have told Ned, what does he think?"

"I am not a competent judge," I answered hurriedly, sorry that she had appealed to me at all, for I could think of no comfort for either of them. "I can only say that I have so much confidence in your husband that I do not question his sorrow. It is enough for me to know that he is unhappy, though, if I should advise him, it would be to try to forget. The world is full of difficulties which have no other remedy than this, though they are seldom forgotten. I have always known that Jo was just such

4 come to me: 1883 come to me as you used to

a man as he has shown himself to be to-night; I remember distinctly how gloomy he became in talking about it the evening I first went to your house with him, and how it changed his disposition; and I remember how gayly you laughed at it as if it were of no consequence. I have always been Jo's friend; I always shall be, and am his friend in this."

She did not look up, but kept gazing at the fire, as she had done before.

"It is my most serious fault that I did not tell him of it before we were married; but I was timid, and thought of it only as one of the many little regrets with which every life is filled, and neglected it. I could not love my husband more than I do, and I only failed to tell him of it because I feared it would give him unnecessary pain. I was but sixteen then; a school-girl without serious thought or purpose, and certainly every one of my companions was as guilty as I, if it can be called guilt. It is not necessary for me to make explanations, for he has given me notice that they will not be accepted, but if there is anything I can do to make atonement — no difference what it is; even to going away from him, and dying alone and neglected — I will gladly do it, and humble myself cheerfully if that course will relieve him. I have so much confidence in my husband that I do not question the honesty of his grief, and for his sake I regret my past. In justice to my womanhood I cannot say I am ashamed of it. If I mentioned a name which was obnoxious to my husband in my sleep, it was because the name had caused me trouble. I do not remember it, for since this unhappy change in our home I have been ill and worn out. I was never strong, but I am so weak now as to be helpless."

Jo seemed to not pay [5] the slightest attention while his wife was talking, for he kept his eyes on the floor, but that he was listening intently I knew very well. Mateel looked at him timidly when she had finished, as if expecting a reply, but as he made none, she too looked at the floor. I watched her face narrowly, and there saw depicted such misery as I can never forget. She seemed to realize that she had made her husband unhappy by

[5] to not pay: 1883 to pay not

a thoughtless act, and to realize her utter inability to supply a remedy. I think a more ingenious woman could have made a more cautious statement, though not a more honest one, and won her husband back by explanations; but Mateel, as was the case with her father, gave up at once on the approach of a difficulty, and prepared for the worst. I saw in her face that she would never be able to effect a reconciliation; for, believing it to be hopeless, she would be dumb in contemplating the life they would lead in future. I knew she would be kind and attentive, and hope for the best, but in her fright and consternation she could not gather strength to test her ingenuity. I knew that she would accept her husband's increasing obstinacy as evidence that a great calamity had come upon their house, and meekly submit, instead of resolving to conquer and triumph over it. If she had put her arms around his neck then (as he wanted her to do, in spite of his commands to the contrary), and, between declarations of her love, asked him to give her a year in which to prove her devotion, and explain away the unhappy past, I believe this story would never have been written, but they misunderstood each other at the beginning, and continued it until the end. I could see, also, that Jo regarded what she had said as a sort of justification of her course, thus widening and deepening the gulf between them; and I became so uncomfortable that I walked the floor to collect myself, but I could not think of anything which, if expressed, would help them, and I became more uncomfortable still when I reflected that they would accept my embarrassment as an evidence that I thought there was nothing to be done except the worst that could be done. I sat down then determined to speak of the matter lightly, but a look at them convinced me that this would be mockery, therefore I changed my mind, and said I would go to bed. This seemed to startle them both, as though they dreaded to be left alone, and Jo asked as a favor that I stay with him.

"If you leave that chair," he said, "a Devil will occupy it, and stare at me until daylight."

I replied that I only thought of going to bed to leave them alone, because I felt like an intruder, and was not at all sleepy, and in response to his request I stirred the fire, and sat down between them. Occasionally I dozed, but on waking again, I found them sitting on either side of the fire, as far apart as possible, as my grandfather and grandmother had done before them. I felt that all had been said that could be said, and although once or twice I broke the silence by some commonplace remark, neither of them replied further than to look up as if imploring me not to go to sleep again, and leave them alone.

I thought the night would never end, but at last the room began to grow lighter, and when the sun came up over the woods, its first rays looked in upon two faces so haggard and worn that I wondered whether it did not pity them. The sun came up higher yet, but still they sat there; and the curtains being down, and the shutters closed, I thought the sunlight had deserted that house, and given it over to gloom and despair.

XXIII

THE SHADOW IN THE SMOKY HILLS

ALTHOUGH I began my career as an editor with a good deal of enthusiasm, in the course of two or three years I became so tired of the work that I longed to give away the establishment, that I might have a month's rest. I have since wondered that I did not follow the example of the founder of the "Union of States," and run off, as I came to regard myself as filling the station that my father stormed, and my mother cried, because I could not fill in my youth, not being a girl; for as a kitchen maid only cleans dishes that they may be soiled again, so it seemed that we only set up the types and inked them that we might wash and tear them down, and begin all over again.

It was peculiar to my business that the people could see at the end of every week all that had been accomplished, and it was usually so little (though I did the best I could) that I felt ashamed of it, and dreaded to see a stranger pick up the "Union of States" in my presence, for fear he would not know my connection with it and make unfavorable comment. I frequently left a public place on this account, and I never came suddenly upon a knot of men that I did not hurriedly announce my presence, so that if they were pointing out the most glaring defects of the paper, they could spare me the humiliation of listening to them.

Other trades and professions are more secret, and their contemptible transactions generously hid from the public, but all my work had to be submitted to the criticism of every idle vagrant who cared to pick up the sheet. A lawyer or a merchant might lock himself up in his office, and pretend to be engaged in grave affairs while really idling time away, but if I had attempted it, the deception would have been apparent at once.

Public attention is always called to a newspaper, for otherwise it cannot prosper, and as the people are usually disgusted when they realize how little a man can do, papers of the class I published were not popular. Other men's affairs were equally contemptible, but they were charitably hid from the public gaze, whereas mine were regarded as common property, and fault found accordingly. I did not know then, though I have since found it out, that what one complains of will please another, so that when a paper makes an enemy, it makes a friend with the same paragraph, though the enemy takes more pains to talk about it than the gentleman who is quietly delighted.

It is my opinion that to become too well known is dangerous, for under such circumstances your faults are common property, and your insignificance proverbial, and a man who writes long for a newspaper will inevitably show every weakness of which he is possessed. Each week I laid before the people every thought, every idea, and every suggestion I was possessed of, and became so tired of being criticised that I would have given ten years of my life for half a year's vacation. When Martin grew tired (he was at first a valuable assistant, but his enthusiasm, like mine, did not last long), he coolly said he was worn out; but I had no one to whom I could make that excuse, and was compelled to get along the best I could. I was subject to the beck and nod of every ridiculous man in the community, for every citizen thought it his duty to give me good advice if he did not give me patronage, and though I longed to retaliate by pointing out the offences of some of them, I found it politic to hold my peace. Occasionally I wrote a very good thing (at least, occasionally I attracted attention), but nobody gave me credit for it, and it was attributed to someone in the town who could not write an ordinary business letter without lolling out his tongue.

A man should not write for a newspaper long in one town, for he becomes so familiar with the small affairs of the people that it is a great effort to treat them with respect. In the course of a few years he will have had occasion to criticise every man of any importance in a town of the size of Twin Mounds, if he is honest and truthful, and will be generally despised in conse-

225

quence. Even if a complimentary twaddler, sowing good words to the exclusion of everything else, he will become unpopular for that, for the people will soon discover that he is a man of no discrimination or honesty, if he speaks well of everybody.

I wonder that anyone took the "Union of States," and as for its advertising I was certain the people were throwing their money away. It was the dullest paper, I have no doubt, ever published; but somehow enough people took it to make its publication profitable, though I was always expecting them to stop it, and believed that it would in the end become necessary to suspend its publication entirely. I remember that I would look over it carefully on press days, and, thinking that there was not a paragraph of news or comment which was not either old or silly, almost conclude not to print it at all, but if it was an hour late in issuing, a great many called to complain, which led me to believe that they had nothing else to do, and were anxious to get a copy and make fun of it. I am convinced now that much of this worry, if not all of it, was unnecessary, and that I need not have worked so hard, for when I went away I could not help noticing that everything got along about as usual, and that nobody missed me.

I was thinking this over one morning, and wishing I could get sick — I was always singularly strong and robust — or that the office would burn down, so that I could get a rest from my distasteful work, when the light at the open door was completely shut out, and Big Adam came in. I did not know he was in the vicinity, and was surprised to see him. He seemed in very good spirits, and, sitting down, began looking through his pockets for a note he said he carried for me. After he had found it, and given it to me, and while I was looking curiously at the envelope — it was from Agnes — wondering what was the occasion for sending it in this unusual fashion, Big Adam put his finger in his mouth, drew it out suddenly in such a manner as to make a sound like the drawing of a cork, and then, thumping his jaws slowly while he extended his lips, apparently poured out a liberal drink of liquor.

The contents of the letter were surprising enough: —

Dear Ned, — Mother died early this morning, after a short illness.
I shall esteem it as a great favor if you will attend the funeral to-
morrow morning at ten o'clock.

Your sorrowing friend,
Agnes.

Big Adam seemed to be very much offended when I looked
up from reading the note with a serious face, as he evidently expected that I would be greatly pleased, as he was, but as if to
say that if I would not drink with him over his good fortune, he
would drink alone, he pulled another [1] cork, and poured out the
liquor in very slow and distinct gurgles.

"I didn't suspect my good luck," Big Adam said, seeing my
inquiring look, "until Agnes woke me up this morning, and said
the old missus was dead, and wouldn't I please carry the note
to you. I immediately dressed up in my best and started. I think
I never enjoyed a ride more. It was equal to an excursion. I hope
there is no mistake about it."

Big Adam was about to draw another cork, when I inquired if
Mrs. Deming had been ill long.

"About a week I should say, and she kept them about her
night and day to jaw at, occasionally sending for me. Several
times she came down stairs, but no more dried up than usual, so
none of us thought anything unusual the matter. She was always
complaining about something or other, and although she was undoubtedly bad off this time, we didn't believe it. We thought she
was only pretending, to make us trouble, for she fooled us so much
that I have an idea they were all very much surprised when they
found her dead at last. It was by the merest accident that Agnes
and Biggs were at home. It will be a great day for me to-morrow.
I am to drive the remains to the graveyard."

I could not impress Big Adam with the gravity of the occasion,
and after telling him that I would go over to Smoky Hill in the
afternoon, he went out into town, but returned every little while
with packages of pickles, cloves, confectionery, crackers, etc.,
which he spread out on my table and devoured with the greatest
relish, precisely as if he were at a picnic. Usually he was followed

---

[1] another: 1883 a

by great troupes of boys, whom he hired to swear with his pickles and confectionery.

While he was out on the porch, I heard him say to one of them that he hadn't an enemy in the world, but if he had, he would like to hear the boy curse him, for up to that time he had won all the prizes with his dreadful oaths and was the raggedest and dirtiest of the lot. He was arranging for a fight between two of them, when I mildly objected to it, whereupon Big Adam laughed with hoarse good humor, and said that while he didn't know of an enemy, he might have one, and gave the wicked boy a pickle and a caramel to curse him, or her, as the case might be. The young scoundrel promptly responded with the vilest language I had ever heard, and Big Adam laughed so loudly that I thought the house would fall down, declaring that the boy was a "captain." I knew what he was about, but he seemed to be enjoying himself so much that I did not interfere again. At last he said he was certain the boy's curses had killed his enemy, and he called upon all of them to give three cheers, which they did, Big Adam joining in like a steamboat whistle.

In the afternoon I drove over to the Smoky Hill country, leaving Big Adam to follow at his leisure, as he showed a disposition to dissipate until night, and after arriving at Mr. Biggs', I put the horses away in the stable I had become familiar with on my first visit to the place, the stalls of which were still oozy and wet, and went up to the house.

Although I disliked to disturb the quiet of the place, I was compelled to ring the bell, for there was no other way of attracting attention, and after a little while Agnes came to open the door. Instead of speaking to me, she burst out crying, and, in involuntary pity for her distress, I took her in my arms, to which she made no resistance, but sobbed softly as I tried to comfort her with pitying words. I did not even think of my arms being about her, or that her head rested on my shoulder, and for the first time in several years I felt natural in her presence.

From where we stood in the hall I could see through an open door a plain coffin, supported at each end with a chair, in the room where I had sat with Biggs on my first visit to the house.

228

I was impressed that it held a friendless body, for the coffin was not ornamented in any way, and had evidently been hurriedly made by a country carpenter. The top was shut down, as though there were no friends anxious to look frequently at the face, and for the first time I felt sympathy for the dead. It was no doubt very absurd in me, but I had almost expected to find the family in good spirits on my arrival, for I had never had a kindly thought for Mrs. Deming in my life. Her brother never mentioned her at all; her only child did not, except when it was necessary, and Big Adam had told me so much of her disagreeable qualities that I was very much prejudiced against her, but when I found that no one but members of her own family were there during her sickness and death, I felt kindly toward her memory, and thought that Big Adam had certainly misrepresented her. The distress of Agnes, which continued after we were seated in the room where the coffin was, also convinced me there must have been some good in the dead woman, and as the room began to grow dark from the going down of the sun, I thought that her life had been a night, which I hoped would be followed by a glorious morning.

I heard while at the house — it may have been from her old enemy, who returned from town in the course of the night, whistling all the wild airs I had ever heard — that the family had not a single acquaintance in the neighborhood, and that no one came to the house, except a farmer occasionally to see Mr. Biggs on business; that the people all believed Mrs. Deming to be a witch, and that they kept horse-shoes and charms in their houses from dread of her. Although many of them knew and admired pretty Agnes, they believed she had been stolen by Mrs. Deming when very young, and were always expecting someone to arrive and claim her.

From an occasional noise overhead, I understood that Mr. Biggs and the family were up stairs, but none of them appearing, I volunteered to remain up during the night to watch. Agnes gratefully accepted the offer, and as I sat there trying to read after her disappearance, I could tell when each one of the eight children was put to bed. At last I heard the cradle, which had been going constantly up to that time, stop, and I knew the baby, the last one, had been disposed of. Therefore I was not surprised that soon after Mr. Biggs came softly into the room, quite elegantly dressed, in slippers and gown, though he seemed very much depressed. He bowed to me patronizingly, as much as to say that few men could look as interesting in grief as he did, and after standing before me a moment to consider the matter, took hold of my hand and shook it sideways, though I was accustomed to shake up and down. As he walked around the room with his hands clasped behind him, I wondered whether I should be compelled to take the accustomed dose of philosophy, and I soon saw that I should, for, as he walked, he meditated; this was his usual way before attacking me. Coming over to me presently in a manner indicating that he had long been waiting for opportunity to discourse on the shortness of life, and the presence of the coffin afforded it, he seated himself, and abruptly inquired: —

"What is life?"

I knew I was not expected to reply, therefore I did not give him my views on the somewhat complex question, and he soon went on: —

"Taking a man, for example, when it is first known that he is to have an existence, his mother cries, and his father says he wouldn't have had it happen for the world, or for fifty thousand dollars, although he may not have a dollar he can truthfully call his own. After a season of piling his clothes all in one place at night on the part of the coming man's father, and grief and suffering on the part of his mother, he is finally born, and the women of the neighborhood come in to see which one of his parents he resembles, although it should be known beforehand that he will be like the uglier one in face and disposition. This may ALWAYS be depended upon; it NEVER fails. When he is a month old, or on the first regular bill-day after his birth, his father quarrels with the doctor for bringing him into the world at all, and pays the price in great anger, and under protest, vowing that he will never again give the old quack opportunity to rob him. When he is three or fourth months old, his father and mother quarrel as to whether he shall be named for her people or his folks. This settled, he is attacked with colic, followed in rapid succession by the numerous

230

distressing complaints which nobody ever escaped. After this comes his boyhood, which he always remembers as being particularly disagreeable, as he never gets enough to eat, and is constantly being found fault with and whipped. At last he is started to school, where a man who is a tyrant because he is not a lawyer (or a woman who is cross because she is not married) endures him during the hours of the day when the outside is most attractive. From this he runs away, and serves an apprenticeship with the world, making so many mistakes, and doing so many foolish things, that he is crestfallen the remainder of his life. Then he marries the wrong woman, and has the experience of his father over again, meanwhile working like a slave to get something ahead. But he does not succeed, as he has a faculty of doing that which he ought not to do, although he strives very earnestly to become a great man, and make his father ashamed of himself, and after a life of misery, a boy comes out of his front door on a morning after a stormy and windy night, and hangs crape on the knob. If there is a newspaper in the town where he lives, he is given a magnificent column, to induce the relatives to buy large numbers of extra copies to send away. The next day a hearse and six gentlemen in black clothes and white cotton gloves appear at his front gate. The neighbors come straggling in to see what the mourners will do, and an hour after that a surly sexton, who is wondering who will pay him, begins to rattle clods on his coffin, whereupon the carriages on the outer edge begin to drive hurriedly away, as if too much time had been spent with him already, and in a few minutes he is an inhabitant of the silent city whose residents quietly wait to be gathered as brands for the burning. If he happened to be possessed of an extra farm, or a store, or ready money, his afflicted relatives prove that he had been crazy several years before his death, that they may divide his effects to suit themselves, and which they afterwards spend in ribald and riotous living. The principal merit of this brief sketch, as the newspaper writers say, is its entire truthfulness. Deceased" — he inclined his head towards the coffin — "had an experience like that I have mentioned, except that she was a woman. Peace to her dust."

He spoke of his sister as "Deceased" as though that had been her name, instead of Maggie, or Jennie, or whatever it really was.

"Now that she is Up There," Mr. Biggs continued, after a short silence, waving his right hand toward the ceiling, "I do not care if I mention that Deceased had an unhappy disposition. She had that tendency when a very little girl (being an angel now, she will recognize what I am saying as the truth, and commend me for it), and was usually disagreeable to those around her. Whether her complaint was poor health or disappointed hopes I do not know, but as a man who believes that it is best to tell the truth at all hazards, I confess to you she died friendless. If there is not secret joy in this house that she is dead, then my philosophy avails me nothing, and I am as a ship on an unknown sea without rudder or compass."

The expression of "a ship without rudder or compass" seemed to please him, for he repeated it quite eloquently.

"Speaking of ships reminds me of my late brother-in-law, whom I have never seen. When he promised to marry the clay which reposes in yon coffin, I was away from home — the exact facts are that I was chased away by my father, a quiet and honest worker in wood who objected to my noise and lying — but for a reason which seems to actuate all fools, I wrote home that I should never be entirely content until I had murdered the man who had bewitched my sister. I can't tell at this time what caused me to do it, unless it was knowledge of a custom that whenever a girl marries, her brothers and father make fools of themselves (and at that time I was not above custom), for Captain Deming was a very worthy young man. I think he was greatly disgusted at the absurd manner in which we carried on, and if his spirit has been released from the deep, and is hovering around this place, I desire that he hear my declaration that I am ashamed of myself."

The little man was dramatic again, and waved his hands downward to represent the deep, and upward to represent the heavens.

"None of us liked the girl," he surprised me by confessing, "and I think that there was some dissatisfaction that she did not marry, and rid my father of her keeping, but the moment there was a prospect she WOULD marry, we all began to object, though I cannot imagine why. At that time I was working in a stable in a town in the West, and I wrote to Captain Deming that only pressing business engagements prevented my coming on and snatching the girl from his relentless clutches, advising my father at the same time by letter not to scruple to burn, shoot, or stab to save the family from impending disgrace. I believe he did sharpen up his hatchet and saw with a vague idea of sawing the Deming body in two, and then cutting it to pieces. I am also informed that he said in the hearing of the Captain one evening that he would rather see the girl in her grave, and when the ceremony was finally performed, he made himself still further ridiculous by remarking to my mother in the presence of the guests that it was all her fault."

He was apparently greatly amused by the recollection of this ridiculous circumstance, and stopped to laugh to himself, although I thought it was only an expression of satisfaction that he was finally rid of Mrs. Deming. Perhaps he had been wanting to laugh all day, and was now telling me jokes as an excuse.

"I made a great spectacle of myself in the town where I lived, by going about in a dejected and wretched condition, and saying that the Princess, my sister, had married a low fellow who followed the sea, and a few months after that, when I was anxious to boast of Captain Deming, my brother-in-law, I was compelled to move to another place, as the two stories would not fit in the same town. For this reason I went further west, and finally turned up in the Smoky Hills. I believe I never told you before how I happened to come west."

Had the little old woman burst off the lid, and sat up in the coffin to protest, I could not have been more surprised than I was.

"Captain Deming turned out to be a very superior man," Mr. Biggs continued, reflectively, "and Deceased to be a very inferior woman, judging from the evidence now at hand, but for several years there was a tradition in my family that she had thrown herself away."

My companion seemed to enjoy telling the truth about himself as much as I had already noticed he delighted in telling it of others, and while wondering what family confidence he would next let me into, he said: —

"Although in my youth I had a great deal to say about the

233

surprising respectability of my family, they were really a very unpromising crowd. While none of them ever walked between the minister and the sheriff to a hanging, or was ever locked up for theft, none of them amounted to anything, and I am glad that they are all in ignorance as to where I am, for I never want to see any of them again. I am bad enough, but they are worse. My favorite uncle, the Duke, was a barber in the town where I was raised; his sister, the Duchess, was a disagreeable old maid who existed entirely on her respectability, for she spent her time in visiting those of her relatives who had houses, and in boasting of it (she was the laziest woman I ever knew in my life, by the way); my grandfather, the Count, was a market gardener, and there was an Earl on my mother's side who was a fireman; and the heir to all his possessions rode horses at races because he was old and little. The others I have forgotten, and I am sincerely grateful to my memory for the favor."

It was very late, and as I did not relish the thought of remaining alone in the room with the coffin, I was sincerely obliged to my companion for his company, and was pleased when I saw that he had more to say: —

"Naturally I am a great liar." I tried to look astonished, as he intended I should, but I am afraid I did not. "I did not know until a few years ago that honesty was the best policy, and as a boy and young man I never told the truth, even when it would do as well as a falsehood, but of late years I deal in nothing but facts, truths, and principles. I go even farther than that: I rake up the past to find truths that might be kept secret, for I now enjoy honesty as I formerly enjoyed dishonesty. The world is full of men like me in the particular that they tell the truth for no other reason than that experience has taught them it is best to do it. I know hundreds of men naturally thieves who are scrupulously honest for the same reason, and there is a great deal in the saying that honesty is the best policy. It cost me several years of disagreeable experience to make the discovery, but you may depend upon it that honesty is the best policy."

I had never heard anyone accuse Mr. Biggs of having reformed except Mr. Biggs himself, for it was generally understood that he was thoroughly unscrupulous in everything, and the people would no more trust him for money than they would take his word.

"If I lived on a lonely island, without a neighbor, I would do right in everything, for the reason that even under such circumstances honesty would be the best policy. It pays better to be honest to yourself, in fact, than to your neighbor. It's a pity these facts are not more generally known and accepted, for we should then have a very different world; I am ashamed of it as it is."

He walked out of the room soon after, and left me alone, where I remained in great terror until an hour or two after midnight, when fortunately I went to sleep in my chair, and did not awaken until Agnes came down in the morning.

The funeral was without incident, except that, very much to the surprise of everybody, Damon Barker appeared soon after the procession started, and walked reverently behind the wagon in which Mr. Biggs, Agnes, and myself rode, Big Adam driving ahead with the coffin. Mrs. Biggs and the children remained at the house for some reason, and I did not see any of them during my visit. A few neighbors appeared at the grave, and threw in the dirt after the body had been lowered, as I believe they had thrown it out, but none of them came to the house. There was no funeral service, but as soon as we arrived at the place selected for the burial, the coffin was put down and covered up, after which we returned to the house, and threw open the shutters. Although Barker was invited to return with us, he politely refused, and went directly home from the church, which was located within a few rods of the place where Biggs had opened the store, and where the post-office was still kept.

In the course of the afternoon it was arranged that Agnes should return home with me, and live there in future, as my mother had long been anxious to have her do, and during the drive to Twin Mounds, little was said, for neither was in the mood for talking. I can only remember of that afternoon that when we arrived at home my mother was waiting, and that for the first time someone seemed considerate of Agnes; for my mother caressed her tenderly, and led her, weeping, into the house.

XXIV

A LETTER FROM JO

My Dear Old Friend, — I am much alarmed when I realize that I am becoming a thinking man, like your father, and that my trouble will sometime become so great that I shall disgrace myself and everyone connected with me. Since you were here last I have done little else than think, and I have been very lonely, for I have no companion now. I have not spoken to Mateel since you went away, except when it was necessary, and that has not been a frequent circumstance. This adds to my wretchedness, for I feel contemptible that I am not able to be to all appearance what I always was. I have tried to be, but to no purpose, so I have given it up. I cannot say that I wish I could forget, for then I should feel that I was the man she described in the letter. I am a shrinking, dejected coward, which I never was before, and I think it is because I am not treating Mateel as I should, though I solemnly assert that I cannot do differently.

A man who mistreats a woman becomes a coward as I am, and I accept the ignominy as my punishment. I was bold as a lion when we were happy together, and could look any man in the face; but I cannot now, for I think that everyone who looks at me is an accuser that I am worrying and fretting a helpless woman, which I believe to be the meanest crime of which a man can be guilty. I cannot but acknowledge the accusation, though it is not intentional. I am low and despicable in spite of all I can do, and I can think of no remedy for it.

I continue to make new discoveries which add to my wretchedness. A long while before we were married, Mateel gave me a book full of pretty love stories, and I valued it highly, because many of the passages were underscored, with notes on the margin indors-

236

ing the sentiment. The stories were very pretty, and I read them a great deal, but I have discovered that the book was originally given to Bragg; that it was returned when he tired of her, and that the pretty passages were marked for him. It was given to me, no doubt, because it happened to be convenient, and no one else wanted it. Mateel, with the candor which I have come to dread, admitted it, though reluctantly, on being questioned.

One of the romances to which I refer tells of a lady who had quarrelled with her lover, and in a pique married a cold, heartless man, who had no other good quality than that he was kind, and successful, and the story is her reverie. After seven or eight years she accidentally meets her old lover, and confesses that she loves him yet, and has loved him all the while, though she is kind enough to refer to her husband as a dear, good soul. This was particularly full of pencil marks, as though it aptly stated her case, and I think that after she knew a separation with Bragg was imminent, she was anxious to let him know that her future would be something like that.

Another one tells of an eccentric bachelor who meets a pale but strikingly beautiful girl on the street on a cold winter's night. He once loved a face like that, and interested himself in the girl. In course of time it developed that the bachelor had been engaged to the girl's mother, and that they were separated by some sort of an unfortunate mistake, and she married a man who was willing to support her in her grief, but who unfortunately died, and could no longer feed her while she mourned. Humiliated and broken, she refused to return to her old friends, but lived with her only daughter in poverty, talking a great deal of her lover, but not a word of the poor fellow who had been her husband. When she finds death approaching she writes a letter to her lover, consigning the girl to his care, and the letter of course falls into his hands, which affects him so much that he surprised his friends by marrying the daughter. I suppose the inference is that Mateel, acknowledging her own weakness, desired Bragg to understand that she would only consent to marry another man with the hope of rearing a daughter good enough for him.

There have been a few sweet chords of music in my life (a very,

very few, and simple in construction), but while never complete in my boyhood, I have listened to them in my lonely hours with a great deal of pleasure. They were the whisperings of hope; of happiness which I had never known, but now the familiar air scarcely begins until it is lost in the yells of demons and the harsh laughter of devils. I do not know whether I read it, or dreamed it, but there was once a deep cave said to be haunted. The people who went there without lights, and did not speak for a long while, heard the beginning of the most delicious symphony, as sweet and perfect as the music of the choirs in heaven, but suddenly it was all lost in coarse uproar and laughter, as if the Devil and his imps were flushed with wine at a banquet, and were telling each other of the follies of men, to laugh at them. This dreadful tumult continued until the music was quite forgotten, and no one could remember the strain, although they all said it was very tender and beautiful. Sometimes the people who went there would hear neither the music nor the tumult which always broke into it, but this always happened when the night was fine, and the visitors noisy and in good spirits. But every dark and threatening night, when the wind came hurrying down from the north to be present at the destruction threatened, those who went into the cave always heard the music, and it was notably tender and touching on such occasions, but the devils broke into it more quickly, and were hoarser and louder in their laughing and jeering.

Everything conspires against me now; even Mateel's religion torments me. I can think of nothing that cannot in some way be construed into misery. Mateel's hope of heaven is a hope of torment for me. She knows my unbelief, and must be convinced that, if she is right, the years of her happiness in the future can only be measured by the years of my suffering, but she has no other comfort to offer than the hope that I shall be "saved." How natural it is to disguise fear with hope! I would not regard it as a kindness in a man who saw me drowning to stand peacefully on the bank, and hope I would take hold of a straw, and save myself, but I should admire him if he jumped in, and pulled me out. Hope is often nothing more than an excuse for incapacity and for mistakes, as we hope, in case of an accident caused by carelessness, that nothing serious will result, or as we hope, when we do not do our duty, that everything will turn out fortunately anyway.

If my love for Mateel had never been interrupted, and I had her faith, and she my doubts, I should go mad from thinking of her future. I would make my interest in her impending fate so great that she would become alarmed, and be rescued; or, failing in that, I would be lost with her. I would not own a faith which would not save one I loved, and whom I knew to be honest and pure-minded. I have no particular fears for myself, but, knowing Mateel's belief as I do, I am hurt at her indifference. I am always thinking — really, I cannot help it, much as I try — that she offers up her prayers for Bragg, and that to be reunited with him I must be burned up, for I am certain that I could not exist with him comfortably anywhere.

I take a kind of delight in finding out how unfortunate I am, and once I wrung a confession from her that she thought it extremely probable that I would be lost, but that all knowledge of it would be blotted out of her memory, and forget in her happiness that I had ever lived. If Mateel's religion turns out to be true, I think it will be a part of my punishment to be permitted to look into heaven, and see her happy, without a care or thought of me. I don't think it would be possible to save such a man, but it may become necessary to properly punish my wickedness to place Bragg by her side, in Paradise, that I may contemplate them walking lovingly together.

The skeleton which has found its way into my closet is very noisy now. I think someone, out of consideration for me, has been trying to chain him up, but he has broken loose, and drags his fetters about in the most dismal manner. Either that, or he has company, and I am honored with two skeletons. If other people have but one, I think I shall eventually have two, if I have not now, and be compelled to enlarge my closet. I have occasionally courageously unlocked my skeleton, and tried to look him out of countenance, but he is so indifferent, and I am so unhappy, that I have never succeeded. He is the most impudent skeleton that ever took up an abode in a man's house against his will, and its grinning, malicious face I cannot lock up, for it follows me about the mill at my work, and walks before me into the dark cellar, and into the lonely loft. Once I thought I saw his tracks in the flour dust, but I found it was only where my unmanly tears had fallen. After I have attacked him, he is more noisy than ever at night, and rattles about so much that I acknowledge his power by thinking my disgrace all over, and admitting that there is no hope.

The affairs of men are so small that I wonder they can be serious about them. I wonder about this every time I meet a grave and thoughtful man, and then I remember that I am grave and thoughtful. I have no doubt that, if I were told of a case similar to my own, I should say the man ought to dismiss it without a curse, and never think of it again, but somehow I cannot do it, though I have tried earnestly and honestly. I had so little peace and content as a boy, and expected so much from my marriage, that I cannot resign myself to a life without hope and without happiness. I suppose the people would laugh at my troubles if they knew them, and I call their affairs trivial, so that altogether we have a very contemptuous opinion of each other. Many of those who come to the mill look at me curiously already, and I suppose it is being said that I am queer, or that I am subject to fits of despondency, which is the first symptom of a crazy man. Next to the original difficulty, I dread most to be called queer, for I never heard it said of a man I respected. But this will probably be added to my other troubles, for when once a man becomes involved in trouble's web, everything goes against him.

I am only unhappy because I expected the home I built with so much care to be pleasant, but it is not. I expected no more than this, and I would have been a willing slave to insure that result, but there is not the slightest prospect of it now.

Jo Erring.

XXV

THE SEA GIVES UP ITS DEAD

My mother was never strong, and her health seemed to be rapidly failing, but she was perceptibly revived by the presence of Agnes. When I told her that Agnes would now live there all the time, and never go away again, she expressed great pleasure, and for days was not content to be out of her company, but followed her slowly around the house as she went about her work. We were like three children again, suddenly released from restraint, but when we spoke in the evening of the happy years we should spend together, my mother became thoughtful at once, and would say no more that night.

Her step was slower than it had ever been; and she walked more feebly, but she still kept up the lonely vigils in her own room at night, and the light was always burning, casting its rays across the deserted street like a pitying star. If I became restless in my bed from thinking of her pale face, and went softly down the stairs to her door, I found her quietly seated in the low chair, as if waiting for a step in the street and a hand on the door. She no longer came to my room at night, as she had done when we were alone, but she apologized for it once because of growing weakness, and believing that she dreaded to be alone, I sometimes lay down on her bed and slept there, but if I awoke in the night, I found her in the old corner, with her head bowed low, and wrapped in deep meditation.

The coming of Agnes brightened the lonely house, which had always been cold and cheerless, as if it were very old, and were inhabited only by very old people, and I was more content than I had been, until I remembered that my mother was slowly dying of a broken heart. This thought came to me whenever we were spending the evening pleasantly together, and often I went away to hide my tears. When I talked to Agnes about it, which I often did before and after she came there to live, I saw by her troubled face that she shared my fears, and that she, too, had marked the faltering steps and whitening hairs. Though we resolved over and over again to do more for her comfort and happiness, and be more watchful of her, she was always just the same — silent and sorrowful, with a look in her white face of worry and sorrow. Whenever she opened a door, or looked into a box or drawer, she seemed to find something to remind her of her husband — an article of wearing apparel, a scrap of paper on which he had written — and this she kept in her hand, and carried about, holding it until she took her place in the low chair for the night, where it remained the subject of her thoughts. We both called her mother, and though we were anxious that she should commend [1] us, she seemed shy, as if she were in the way, and Agnes told me that once when she put her hand lovingly on her head, and said we were good children, she did it timidly, fearful of giving offence. She still slept a little during the day — or, at least, she would darken her room when no one was around, and lie down — but we never found her asleep at night, and believed that she never left her chair.

It may have been two months after Agnes came there to live, when we were sitting together one evening, and Agnes was telling us again of her father, of which she never tired, and I recollect that I made more inquiries about him than I had ever done, because my mother was much interested in my statement that men sometimes came back after an absence of a great many years, and told strange stories of adventure. I had no idea this was true of Captain Deming, of whose death there had never been any question, but my mother was listening closely, and I recalled several instances of the return of those given up for dead.

"What evidence have you," I asked, "that your father is dead, other than that he never came back?"

Evidently Agnes had no thought of a possibility that he was alive, for though she immediately became grave and thoughtful, there was no expression of hope in her earnest face. After thinking about it a long while, she confessed that there was no evidence of

[1] commend: 1883 command

his death except that he had never been heard from, which was the brief story of hundreds who had been drowned at sea.

There was one part of the story which I had never before heard, though probably it was not important. The crew which her father had shipped at Bradford was discharged on reaching the first port, the captain claiming there were evidences of mutiny among them, though when they returned they declared that never were men more faithful and honest. Since that time neither the ship nor its captain had ever been heard of, and the returning sailors believed it had gone down because of the shipping of an incompetent crew. Agnes did not know, nor could the sailors who came back to Bradford tell her, what port the vessel loaded for when they were discharged, and this seemed so strange to me that I determined to insert an advertisement in a paper published in a sea town, and solicit information from the captains of that day. This would require a long time, so I resolved to say nothing of my intention, though I had little hope anything would come of it. I found that Agnes knew little about the matter, as she was very young when her father sailed away never to return, but her mother, she said, had made investigations which left no doubt of the shipwreck and death.

My mother and Agnes were sitting together at the other end of the room, while I was facing the door which led into the hall, and into the street. I remember these details distinctly because the ghostly turn the talk had taken led me to think that if the sea should give up its dead, and the captain of the "Agnes" walk in dripping with wet, I should be nearest the door by which he would enter. Agnes was sitting with my mother, who was quietly stroking her hair, and as I looked at them, I wondered if there were two wanderers out in the world wearily travelling toward them, or whether those for whom they mourned were dead, and would never be heard from. It was the merest fancy, for I have since tried to remember whether I believed that night that Captain Deming was alive, or that my father would ever return, and I have decided that I had no real belief in such a possibility.

They were both deeply interested in what I was saying, though incredulous, and I must have been amusing myself in seeing how much I could move them, though I had no intention of being cruel. Perhaps I thought hope was pleasant, even if it had no foundation, for I kept on in such a way that both became very much excited. The wind was rising outside, and when it rattled at the doors and windows I thought it sounded as if someone was demanding admittance.

"It wouldn't surprise me," I said gravely, after a long silence, as if I had been debating the question for several years, though I had never thought of it before, "if your father should come to this house some night — I think it would be a dark and stormy night, for they say those long absent only return at such times — and, sitting among us, tell strange stories of his wanderings, and of his search for you. The two travellers we seem to be always expecting here may meet on the road as they near the town, and come on together. Perhaps it is not likely, but it is possible."

They were both looking strangely at each other, and then at me, and then timidly at the door leading into the hall, and out into the street.

"If they should return to-night, they could easily step into the hall, and listen to what we are saying, for the front door is wide open. Maybe they are there; go and look into the hall."

This was addressed to Agnes, and there was so much distress in her face when she looked up at me that I regretted having said so much, for I might as well have asked her to look into the hall, and expect to find her mother, who I knew was securely in her grave.

While thinking how to get out of the dilemma into which I had unconsciously talked myself, I thought I heard a noise of feet in the hall, and from where I sat I could look squarely at the door leading into it, though neither Agnes nor my mother could. I supposed it was Martin, who occasionally came to the house in the evening, though I wondered why he should be so quiet, and while deliberating whether to go out and invite him in, or await his knock, the door opened a little, and I was surprised to see Damon Barker standing on the outside. Supposing he had heard all that had been said, I again bantered Agnes to look into the hall.

"I think I heard someone in there," I said. "Whoever it is he is welcome."

244

The visitor did not seem to appreciate my humor, but was very grave, and did not look at me, keeping his eyes on Agnes. He trembled as he came softly into the room, as I have seen men in great excitement since, and was breathing quickly and heavily. At this moment Agnes turned around in such a manner that she saw the face, and with a startled cry she sprang to her feet, and throwing her hands to her head, looked curiously at Barker, and then at me, as if she thought we were in a plot to frighten her.

The silence that followed was of such duration that I would have broken it — as I felt that I was the cause of the awkward situation — but for the fact that as Barker walked in he acted in a manner so odd that I could not speak. Once I thought he would burst out crying, and again he turned as if he would run away. As he advanced toward the middle of the room Agnes shrank further into the shadow, though her eyes were riveted on his face. Two or three times he attempted to speak, and at last he said: —

"Agnes, don't you know me now?"

His voice trembled so much that the last word was a sob, and the next moment Agnes was in his arms. I was in the greatest wonder, and had not the remotest idea what it all meant, but my mother was shrewder than I, and when she began crying softly I knew she understood it and was satisfied. They remained locked in each other's arms, both sobbing convulsively, for such a length of time that I began counting the seconds as they were told off by the clock, and when I had got up to sixty Barker held Agnes off at arm's length to look at her, but he could not see through his tears, and sobbed again like a man who had been holding up for a long time. Even then I did not realize what it all meant, and my jealous heart brought the suggestion to my mind that Barker's frequent visits to the school meant something after all, and that they had quarrelled, and were making it up.

Just when the thought came to me that Damon Barker was the missing commander of the "Agnes" I cannot now remember, but it almost took my breath away, and a great lump rose in my throat.

Agnes kissed her father over and over, and, wiping away his tears, placed his arms about her again, and hid her face on his breast. He was such a large man, and Agnes such a little girl, that his great arms almost hid her from sight.

"It is so strange as to need an explanation," Barker said, with an effort, looking at my mother, who was still softly crying, and then at me, who could no nothing but look on in wonder; "but I will never explain to Agnes further than that she has been the object of my thoughts and prayers ever since I so strangely deserted her. However much I may have sinned in other ways I have always loved the child; there is nothing between us. I have been an honest man except in the particular which must be in all your minds, and which it is best never to mention. My secret shall be buried in the grave which we filled up out yonder;" he pointed his hand in the direction of the Smoky Hills, and I thought his old look of hate came into his eyes; "though I have the story written, and Ned shall read it and judge me. I ask him now to read what I have written from my heart during these two months, and then tell you two whether I was justified in the course I took; whether I have been worse than other men who have erred, and suffered. But if I have sinned I have wiped it all out by waiting in the solitude of the woods for the day when I could claim Agnes; in the dreadful fear for her safety, and the prickings of conscience; but if this is not enough I will do penance the remainder of my life that I may be father to my child again. Will you accept me, Agnes, with no other explanation?"

The strange house at the mill, and its strange occupant, were now clear to me, for I knew that when I had seen him in the middle of the night ready to run away, when I had seen him always quickly looking about like a hunted man, he was fearful the little old woman who had frightened me at the house of Lytle Biggs would burst in upon him like a phantom, with her snarling voice, and ugly face, and scold him as she scolded Big Adam.

"Yes, father, yes," Agnes said, as she looked into his face, "if there is anything to forgive, I forgive it without asking to know what it is. We will be father and child again, and the old house at the mill shall be our home. I ask nothing further than that you love me, and that you have come back to me, never to go away again. You were always so good, and I love you so much, that I believe whatever you did was for the best; I don't want to know what it is. Ned and his mother can bear testimony to how tenderly

I have always cherished your memory, and how much I missed you, though I believed you were dead. The hope that you were alive was never in my mind for a moment, or I should have known you when you were so kind to me in Fairview, after Ned and his mother had moved away, and when I was lonely and friendless. I wondered then why I was not afraid of you, for you were stern and fierce, but I know now; I could not be afraid of my father, though I did not know him. I am content that we commence our lives anew, never to refer to events beyond this night. I am more than content; I am happy, much happier than I have ever been before, or ever expected to be."

They were walking up and down the room now, locked in each other's arms, and I thought with Agnes that I would freely accept his explanation without hearing it; I was so certain he was a good and honest man. As my mother looked at them timidly, I thought she was wondering if her wanderer would ever return, and if she would ever be as happy as Agnes. As if convinced that it would never come to pass, she went softly from the room, still hiding her eyes, and we heard her sobbing in the next room. Barker was very much affected, and when Agnes went out to speak to her, he kept saying, "It's too bad," until she returned. As for me, I could only stare at him, and look out of the window into the darkness.

"We will agree then," Barker said, when Agnes was again seated beside him, "that the book of the past, with all its unhappy secrets, shall be closed forever, and we will only open the new leaves, which I hope we can contemplate with pleasure. But before dismissing the past forever, never to recall it again, I want to say that I have watched over you constantly for the past eight years, when I first learned you were living in Fairview. Let me say this to excuse my other neglect, and that you may know how honest my affection for you has always been. You may recollect that you once gave Ned my picture in appreciation of his friendship, and he sent it to me by Jo. He showed it to me one night when I had almost resolved to look for you at Bradford, no difference what the consequence might be, and though I recognized it at once, I tossed it to one side with a glance, though I was so much agitated that soon after I left the room to hide it. When I returned, and inquired as carelessly as I could whom the picture represented, Jo replied that it was the father of the little school-teacher, Agnes Deming, and that he had been drowned at sea. By degrees I learned when you came, how you looked, and where you lived; and how often I have made them tell the story without suspecting; how often I have set them to talking of pretty Agnes, and when they told how much she mourned her father, I went away and walked in the woods until I was calm again. Since then I have been near you a hundred times when you did not know it, and a hundred times when you did. Very often I have stolen up to your window in the night, and seeing you were safe and well, crept back through the woods to my desolate home, waiting for this night to come. Once when I looked into your window — it was at Ned's father's house, in the country — I saw you kneel, and I heard you ask blessings on my head, though you supposed I was in heaven. It has been a long time to wait,[2] and I have suffered a great deal, but I am satisfied; I believe I shall be happier that it came about as it did."

I noticed that they at once put into execution their resolve to bury the past in the lonely grave out in Smoky Hill, around which we had all stood two months before, for during the remainder of the night nothing was talked of but the happy future; the to-morrow of their lives, instead of the yesterday.

When I had sufficiently recovered myself to congratulate them, we laughed merrily over my attempt to frighten Agnes, and Barker started to explain how he happened to come when he did, but recollecting his resolve to speak no more of that, he waived it off, and told instead how the house at the mill should be remodelled and refurnished, and the heavy shutters taken down; how the people who passed that way would wonder at the change, and how they should be told that the owner had been blessed through the mercy of God.

"I shall remain plain Damon Barker," he said. "It is a good name, and has never been disgraced, and I shall keep it. It is as good as any other, and it would be confusing to change."

I remained with them until long after midnight, and when I

[2] long time to wait: 1883 long wait

went softly up the stairs to my room, I could hear them talking in low tones. During the night, as I restlessly tossed about, I heard the hum of their voices, and when I came down early in the morning after a disturbed rest, I found Agnes quietly sleeping, with her head on her father's knee, but Damon Barker's eyes were wide open, and there was a smile on his face, and I thought he had grown younger during the night.

I can never forget the loneliness which came over me when they drove away in the morning, waving their adieus, nor the coldness which came into the house, and would not be driven out. I am certain we lighted fires that night, though they had not been necessary before, and when Martin came down to sit with us, he shivered as he entered the room, and rubbed his hands to warm them.

XXVI

BARKER'S STORY

$\mathbf{M}$Y first recollection is of being on board a sailing ship at sea, and by degrees I learned that my mother was dead; that the rough commander who was dreaded and feared by everyone else as well as myself was my father, and that I was kept with him on the ship because I was less troublesome there than anywhere else, and because he desired to look after my education in person, which began when I was five years old.

I heard somewhere that my father, the rough commander, had been very fond of my mother, who died the day I was born, and that his disposition had been different since he gave her an ocean burial, on which occasion he read the service himself in a choking voice, and, locking himself in his cabin directly after it was over, did not come out again for three days and four nights. There was but one other woman on the ship, the stewardess, and I was put in her care, but before I was old enough to remember, she went away, so that I have not the slightest recollection of her.

The mate, who had been in my father's employ a long while, told me that when my mother was alive she accompanied the ship on all its voyages, and that the commander was not then so hard with the men, but frequently gave them holidays, when it was possible, and was amused with their sports. Indeed, he spent much of his time in her company, trusting the management of the vessel to the first officer while at sea, and was altogether very gallant and attentive, which he had not been to anyone since. The mate's recollection of my mother was that she was pretty, and fair-haired, and very young and girlish, and evidently well-bred, for her hands were small and white, and she was graceful and accomplished. He believed she had run away to marry my father, for she never left the ship after coming to it as a bride until she was buried in mid-ocean, and neither of them seemed to have friends on shore they were anxious to see, but were entirely content with each other. When the ship was at anchor in the little American port where it was owned, all hands went away for a time except my father and his young bride, and the mate said they seemed to be sorry when the noisy, rough men came back again, as if they had greatly enjoyed being alone.

My father kept her picture in an expensive case in his room, and although I frequently saw him looking at it himself — indeed, when he was not busy with the maps and charts, he had the picture on the table in front of him — I was only permitted to see the face on rare occasions, as on holidays, or after I had learned my lessons particularly well, when he held it before me for a few moments, but never allowing me to take it in my own hands. When I was still a very little boy, I excused much of his neglect of me because of the grief he felt over my mother's death, and I think my first thoughts were that he in some way laid it all to me, for when I caught him looking at me his face was covered with a frown, and I almost expected him to grasp my throat and inquire why I had been so wicked and so inconsiderate of his feelings. For a great many years I believed her death was due to some blunder of mine, and I suppose this was one reason why I avoided my father as much as possible, that he might not accuse me of it.

I lived on the sea, never being away from it a day, until I was fourteen years old, and, occupying a little room connected with my father's cabin, was compelled to study a certain number of hours each day, and recite to him at night. If I did not learn as much during the day as he thought I ought to learn, he sent for a sailor, and ordered me whipped, but the sailors were my friends, and, begging me to apply myself more in the future, beat the masts instead of my legs. But usually I learned my lessons to amuse myself, for he would not allow me to talk with the sailors, and did not talk to me himself, so that I was very lonely, and studied my books from necessity. Although I never attended school, in this way I became something of a scholar, for I did little else than study under my father's hard tutelage for eight years — from the day I was five years old until I was thirteen, when he began to grow tired of teaching me. Being an educated man himself, he taught me everything it was necessary for one in my position to know, and selected my studies with so much good judgment, and instructed me with so much vigor and clearness, that I could not have learned more during a like number of years at school.

After I was nine years old he gave me permission to mingle with the sailors to learn their languages, for nearly every country under sunlight was represented in the forecastle mess, and after that I spent all my idle time among them, telling them the story of the stars in return for their strange words, or explaining the mysteries of the winds and currents. I have said that before this he did not allow me to talk to the men, but perhaps I had better write that it was generally understood that I should not mingle with them freely, so that we were all conspirators in getting together. The most pleasant recollection of my youth is of taking an occasional dinner with the sailors, or of spending an hour with them when they were off watch, when there was always a lookout to give notice should the captain approach. Although we were always changing crews, they were all my friends, and the companions of my boyhood were gray and grizzled men, who adapted themselves to my condition, and did whatever pleased me most.

Ours was a merchant ship, though we carried a few passengers, and, as the voyages were long, I became well acquainted with them, for I sat beside my father at the cabin table, and was a great deal in their company, when not engaged with the books. What I know of manners and of polite society I learned from them, and although I thought I liked every new set the best, I believe I cried equally hard when any of them went away. There were many brides among them, going with their husbands to homes in distant countries, and after hearing of my strange childhood, they were all very kind to me. Frequently they asked my father to allow me to visit them at their homes, until his ship touched again at the port where they left us, but always to my inexpressible sorrow he refused, saying he was liable to put the vessel into another trade at any time. I do not remember that we ever had children for passengers, except very small ones, so that I grew up entirely in the company of my elders, and do not now feel that I ever had any childhood at all.

When fifteen years old I was permitted to go on an excursion into the interior with a party of the men, while the ship was lying at a Spanish town, and by an accident I was separated from the rest, and did not find my way back for two days. When the men returned, my father supposed I had run away, and sailed without me, leaving my effects at a shipping office in case I should call for them, together with a sum of money, which was to be forwarded to him unless claimed in a given number of weeks. I really felt relief when I found that I was free, I had lived so wretchedly with my father, and by representing my dilemma to other captains whose ships were in, I had no difficulty in securing a situation, which I desired more than a passage to my own country, and engaged with a captain who was going in an entirely opposite direction. Having studied navigation with my father, I was able to make myself useful to the captain who employed me, and I remained in his service a number of years, at first as his secretary, and finally as confidential adviser and third officer, during which time I learned accidentally that my father was dead, and that his estate did not pay his debts. This induced me to hoard my earnings, which were considerable, and when I was twenty I was part owner and third officer of a ship sailing between a small American port and the Indies. After I had been at this a year or two, my vessel was put in the docks for repairs, and having nothing else to do I fell in love, which is the part of my history upon which I shall dwell.

The girl with whom I became acquainted — I cannot say infatuated, for I never was; I suppose it was a kind of curiosity — and who afterwards became my wife, was the only one I had ever known since reaching manhood, and I persisted in calling at her house mainly because she had told me that her father and mother objected to it, though I cannot see why they should, as my station in life was better than theirs, and I had excellent prospects. I do not offer it as an excuse for my later conduct, but it is really the case that I never asked her to become my wife. She took it for granted that I desired to marry her, and said one evening that since it was well understood that we were to be married sometime — nothing of the kind was well understood — we might as well agree on a date, and in my weakness I said the

sooner the better, or something to that effect, which she understood as a proposal, and accepted in due form. There was never
any love between us, but she always gave me to understand that
I was distressing her by being there against her father's will, and
never having known a woman before, I supposed the kind of regard she had for me was all that women generally gave, and to
vindicate her, and to show her father that he was mistaken in his
judgment of me, I allowed the matter to go on until we were married, although I assure you that there was never a moment that I
was not trying to devise some means to get out of it, being convinced that it would never do. I am too old a man — and I hope
too honorable — to misrepresent any particular in the story I am
telling, therefore I have been careful to write only the exact truth,
the benefit of a doubt always being given to the dead.

I soon saw that I had made a mistake, but hoped for the best,
and, after making extensive arrangements for her comfort, sailed
on a voyage which occupied me a year and a half. On returning I
found that a daughter had been born to me; but in spite of this
I formed such a dislike for my wife that it was with the greatest
difficulty I treated her civilly. During the few months I was at
home the child became very dear to me, but as my love for it
grew, my repugnance for the mother increased so much that I
sailed earlier than at first intended (I was captain of the ship by
this time) to be out of her company. I had not been at sea a week
until I began to dread to return, and often I seriously contemplated drowning, to be rid of it all. But when I thought of the
pretty child, I tried to banish the thought for her sake, though I
could not do it, and as we neared home on the return trip I
dreaded my native town as I dreaded sunken reefs and rocks. The
crew counted the days until they could expect to see their wives
and sweethearts waving welcome from the shore, but the thought
of a meeting with my wife was horrible beyond my ability to
relate. I thought of it in a hundred different ways, trying to devise
some way to rob the meeting of its terror, but I could never
arrange it satisfactorily, and suffered as the damned are said to
suffer. On coming home I dreaded most to kiss her, as I was expected to do, and next to that, the first meeting. I cannot ex-

plain to you this aversion fully, but it was so strong that I was constantly in the most horrible misery, and the more I thought of it, the more I loathed her.

I am crowding the results of several years into a few lines, during which time I came and went, the aversion all the time growing upon me. Sometimes I was at home only a week; at other times a month or more, and the length of the voyages varied in the same manner. I will not worry you with the details; it is enough to say that she was petulant, an invalid, uninviting in person, without charms of any kind, and utterly lacking in what is now known as common sense. It will be said (you will remark it, no doubt) that I should have made these discoveries before I married her, which is true; I should have, but I did not, as others have failed to make vitally important discoveries until it was too late to take advantage of them; hence this candid avowal of my disgraceful history. I wish to say again that I make these statements with all respect to the charity which should be shown the memory of the dead, yet in justification of myself it is necessary to tell the truth, which may be spoken with propriety at any time.

Other men's wives were intellectual if not beautiful, or beautiful if not intellectual, but mine was neither. It is my candid judgment, and I write it with sorrow and pity, that she had not a single good quality. (I have thought it all over, before proceeding, and assert it again: Not one.) I think she never went to bed in her life that she did not drink some sort of tea for some sort of complaint, and it was her only boast that in all the world a woman could not be found who "bore up" as well as she did. She took pride in nothing else; she had no other ambition than to demonstrate that such was the case, and had no other delight than to cite evidences of it. I beg you will remember that these are cold, calculated assertions of fact, and not illustrative in any degree. I have spent several weeks in writing this letter, in a manner that cannot be misconstrued; every word has been weighed, and put down after its effect and the impression it would convey had been carefully considered.

She took not the slightest interest in me nor my affairs; indeed, she took interest in nothing except her family, which worried her so much that frequently she awakened in the night, and cried for hours like a silly child for fear her mother, or her father, or her brothers, or her sisters, were not well, although there would not be the slightest reason to suppose they were not enjoying their usual health. This circumstance is particularly worthy of note when it is known that she did not get along with her family, for they were always quarrelling when together, and although they were the most ordinary people, she talked of them, and wondered what would they say to this or that, so much that I gently remonstrated with her. This she construed into an attack, and while I lived with her she regularly vindicated "her family" whenever I came into her presence, in a manner indicating that they were of royal blood. They moved away from there after we had been married a few years, and this gave her occasion to bewail her separation from them, which she never lost opportunity to do. Her father was a perfect type of a common man; the mother was a little better, perhaps, but the brothers and sisters did not average with the young people in the poor town where they were brought up, so that this great admiration was unwarranted, and ridiculous. But if it were disagreeable when "her family" were in the same town with us, it was unbearable when they were away. For every month of their separation she added a hall, park or castle to her father's possessions — which consisted in reality of battered household goods that a really vigorous man could have carried away on his back. Finally I began to think seriously of running away.

Inasmuch as this is a hurried sketch of my life, I will mention as a single example of how we lived, and which might be multiplied by any figure below a thousand, that if I complained that we seldom had fish on the table, we had fish regularly thereafter until I complained that we had nothing else, whereupon she said I was a grumbler, and hard to please, and from that time fish was banished from the house. No matter how much I longed for fish after that, I was afraid to ask for it, for we would then get nothing else.

I think I never sat down at the table with her that she did not bring out a depraved private dish for herself which I abhorred and despised. Tripe boiled in vinegar was one of these; roasted cheese was another, and the fumes from either made me so sick that I was compelled to get up and go out. She persisted in bringing these dishes to the table to "show her spirit," although many times she did not want them, I am thoroughly convinced.

In addition to the disagreeable qualities I have hastily mentioned, she was always complaining; if not of me, of her health; if not of her health, of the trouble the child was, or of the house in which we lived, which I am certain was the best she had ever seen; but she never complained of my long voyages, and I think she enjoyed my absence as much as I did hers. In short, although by this time I realized the fitness of a suitable marriage, I knew mine was the most unsuitable in the world; that we had nothing in common; that we should grow gradually worse instead of better, and that I should surely become, by reason of it, a dissatisfied, incapable and worthless man. Therefore, I began to weigh the consequences of running away.

This brought to mind the love I bore the child, which had grown steadily during the eight years since she was born, and I came to the conclusion that if I remained as I was I should become a man so gross and selfish as to shrink under her increasing intelligence and refinement, for she was as pure and good as an angel, and I concluded it would be better for her to think of me as a good man dead than as a bad man alive, therefore after I had lived in the manner I have described for nearly nine years, making my voyages as long as possible, I went away, and determined never to return.

The more I thought of it, once I was away, the stronger my determination became never to enter the presence of my wife again, and after thinking of it night and day for several weeks, I accepted the disgrace. Public opinion is always against a man in matters of this kind, no difference what his wrongs may be, and men who are contemplating running away from family difficulties themselves regard the offence the greatest of which someone else can be guilty, but I accepted the consequences, and felt relief when I knew I was finally rid of her.

I had accumulated a good deal of property during my career as a shipmaster, and I left it all, except the ship, and in such condition that she could use it. The ship I determined to keep as my share, as it was no more than half. My first idea was to locate somewhere — I had no idea where, but a long way off — and after Agnes had reached a reasoning age, to secretly write her the story I have written to you, and ask her to decide between us, in the hope that she would come to me. This hope supported me, and without it I could never have put into execution my plan of escape.

On reaching the first port after sailing from home, I pretended to find evidences of mutiny among the crew, which caused me a great deal of pain, for many of the men had been with me for years, and were as true and honest as men become, but it was necessary to carry out my plan, and I discharged them all. After they had left the place by taking positions on other ships, I engaged another crew, and went into another trade, which carried me thousands of miles further away from my own country. Again I discharged the crew, and after allowing the ship to be idle in the docks for several weeks, I rebuilt and repainted it in such a manner that its old acquaintances would not have known it had they encountered it on the high seas. I also changed the name. After another voyage, I sold the ship at a sacrifice, and took passage for my native land as Damon Barker, where I arrived after an absence of two years, and by mingling with seafaring men, I heard that the "Agnes" had been lost, which impression was generally accepted.

I then determined to locate in the West, and for this purpose bought the machinery which you have often seen in operation on Bull River, as I believed milling would be a profitable business. I worked for a time as a laborer in a mill, to become familiar with its workings, and I bribed the head man to teach me at night. How I came to locate within twenty miles of my wife and child, God only knows, for they arrived here before I did, although I did not know it until four years afterward, as I have already related. What has occurred since, you know.

One more paragraph, and I dismiss this part of my life forever. I have given an inference that I am an only child, which is true so far as my mother is concerned, but Mrs. Tremaine, whose disappearance with your father will give you an interest in the subject, was the child of my father's first marriage. I believe, although I do not know exactly why, that his first marriage was something like mine, and a few months after securing a divorce he was married secretly to my mother, who was but seventeen, and a member of an excellent family. While I knew where Mrs. Tremaine lived, and knew of her relation to me, I had never seen her but once or twice, which was long before I was married at all, and in my desperation when I first came to this country, I sent her a sum of money, accompanied by a letter of explanation, and entreated her to visit Bradford, and learn how the child prospered. It happened that she was widowed about that time, and instead of doing as I directed, she came out to live with me. I confess to you that I always disliked her, and was glad when she went away. Her husband was a quiet, good man, and I think he must have died of neglect, for she neglected everybody except sinners and drunkards. He was neither, and I think he died from indigestion, induced by living on food prepared by himself. That she was a failure as a woman, you and I know very well, and I have no doubt your unfortunate father admits it by this time.

I have told you, in brevity and in truth, my life, and I only ask that you destroy this immediately after you have finished the reading. If you treat me in the future as you have in the past, I shall believe that you think I was justified in my course; if your manner toward me changes, I will understand that I am censured, but do not refer to this matter in any manner in your future intercourse with me. I dismiss it forever.

Your friend,

DAMON BARKER.

XXVII

THE LIGHT GOES OUT FOREVER

During the fall following the summer when Agnes went to live with her new-found father at the mill, I was so occupied with my work, and with my mother, whose health was failing more rapidly than ever, that I met my old friends in Fairview only occasionally. Several times Jo came to Twin Mounds, but it was usually at night, as if he desired to meet as few of the people as possible, dreading the glances of wonder which his changed appearance attracted. Often I transacted business for him because of his dislike to come to town during the day, and went to great trouble on his account, but I was glad to do it, as I felt that I could never repay his acts of kindness to me.

He said to me often that nothing was so distasteful to him as wrangles over business affairs, as if nothing in the world was so important as the possession of money, and that he allowed himself to be robbed rather than dispute and quarrel, which knowledge I am afraid his customers often used to their own advantage. His business remained profitable, I also heard him say, because he had to keep busy to avoid self-destruction, and that motive seemed to succeed quite as well as the nobler one of ambition.

If he came to the house, and met my mother, her painful condition had a bad effect upon him, so that he finally avoided her, usually coming to the office in the evenings when he knew I should be there. I think she never knew he was in trouble, for I never told her, and she seldom talked to anyone else, though she must have wondered at the remarkable change in his manner, for he had grown nervous to a painful degree, and looked anxiously about like a hunted man. Usually when he came to Twin Mounds he had no other errand than to be with me for a few hours; at these times he would go over his painful story in detail, and, in explaining his wretchedness, try to justify himself, talking of it in such a pitiful way that I became nervous myself in trying to devise some way out of the difficulty. He talked a great deal of how the people would blame him if they knew the story; how they would say his brain was softening, or that he ought to be sent to an asylum, and then he would put the case to me again, and ask me to judge if his trouble was not justified. I always believed that it was, more because I knew that my friend, a man of promise, was in distress, than because I had impartially judged it, and so I always told him, but this gave him little satisfaction, for he said that in my friendship for him perhaps I did not do Mateel the justice she deserved.

When the weather was fine, I drove him home at night, and I think we always met Bragg driving toward the town. Except that he was more of a dog than ever, there was little change in the fellow, and he moped about in his usual listless fashion, doing nothing but mischief, and occasionally becoming maudlin from drinking out of his bottle. He probably watched Jo's coming that he might meet him on the road as an annoyance, and I always trembled when I saw them meet, for Jo's hatred for him was intense, and he would have been delighted with the slightest excuse to beat him.

Once when he gave so little of the road that his wheels locked in ours, Jo sprang out, and, pulling him from his buggy with one hand, hit him such a blow with the other that he reeled and fell in the underbrush beside the road. I could not leave the team, or I should have sprung between them, but Jo realized his superior strength, and did not strike him the second time, but stood over him with every muscle quivering in restraint. The vicious horse was awed by his master's misfortune, and stood trembling in the road, as if afraid to move. When we drove on I saw Bragg pick himself up, and after wiping the blood from his face with leaves, climb into the buggy, and hurry away, and although night was coming on, I could see him on the next hill, an ugly speck on the horizon, still wiping away the blood, as though there had been a profuse flow. For several days after that when I met him I could see a livid mark on the left side of his face, and there was a cut on his lip which did not entirely heal for weeks.

I never knew, but I think it is probable that Mateel believed that I accused her more than I did, or that I rather encouraged Jo in his ugly moods, which was not the case, though I confess that I did little to effect a reconciliation, being impressed from the first that it was impossible. His humiliation was so intense that I could not bring myself to speak lightly of it, as though he were a weak man harboring a caprice, and I still believe that in this I was right. Anyway, she barely recognized my presence when I went there at night with her husband, and never spoke to me about the trouble between them. I was more impressed on each visit that she was helpless, and had not the strength to attempt to reclaim him from his depression, or else she had tried everything at the beginning and given up in despair. Had she attempted to win him back to her he would have told me, but as he only spoke of the ease with which she accepted his request to never show him the slightest attention, I am sure she never did.

Although I cannot now remember whether he told me directly, or whether I learned it from all that was said, I knew that he was always waiting for her to ask him to modify or withdraw his request, and that in the stillness of the night he prayed that she would at least come to him and regret his unhappiness, but if she was not indifferent to it all she was an admirable actress. I knew he would have gone to her but for this indifference, but she seemed to care so little about it that he was ashamed to go. Once in my presence — and often when I was not there — he apologized for his cruelty, but her manner indicated that the apology was unnecessary, and that there was no occasion to mention it. I felt that Jo was mortified at this, and that they were now further apart than ever.

Perhaps I worried so much about Jo at this time that I never tried to form an opinion as to whether she loved her husband as much as I knew he loved her, or whether her dejected manner was due to mortification or regret. I was witness to incidents which confirmed me in both these opinions, so that I think I must have concluded that one caused her as much trouble as the other.

I often thought to speak to her and say she misjudged me; that I would gladly serve her if I could, and that in my friendship for Jo I had no unkind thought of her, but the favorable opportunity never came, and I neglected it.

Although at long intervals Agnes came to visit my mother, she usually went away again before I had seen her, and only once during this time did I find opportunity to visit her at the mill. It was in the winter, when my mother seemed much better, and I was greatly impressed by the change at the mill. The heavy wooden shutters formerly at the windows were taken down entirely, or left wide open; the thick growth of trees had been cleared out, and in every way the house seemed more cheerful than it had been. I could no longer, as I had done before, think of the house as the home of a desperate man who had retired with his ill-gotten gains and who was always expecting occasion to defend himself; and I thought I had never seen Agnes look so contented and happy as she did in her own home, although she had always been that. A great lump rose in my throat as I remembered that all of them seemed to be getting on better than myself, for as I looked around the pleasant place, the cheerless rooms at home, where my mother sat the day out and in again, appeared before me; I thought of the unhappiness at Jo's, where I intended to stop on my return, of my father wandering about, a homeless and disgraced man, and of my tiresome work, which seemed never to end, but I could not help feeling keen pleasure that patient Agnes had reason to be happy at last, as I knew she was, for every action showed it, and the house and everything in it seemed to be repeating it.

When I first went there as a boy to visit Barker the room which Agnes afterwards made into a parlor was used for storing sacks, and I never looked in at the door that I did not see venerable rats hurrying away to their holes, evidently as much alarmed at my presence as I was at theirs, and even the damp room where B. used to sit and collect moisture had dried out from having the sun often let into it. The great room above, where we had [1] the suppers and the stories, was not much changed, except that it was cleaner

[1] had: 1883 had had

and lighter, and the magic of a woman's touch was everywhere apparent. The box-stove in which we had made the famous fires, the table at which Barker sat, and the revolving shelf where he kept his books, were just the same, and but for the presence of Agnes I should have imagined that the master had stepped into the next room to look through the mysterious boxes for relics to amuse the two barefoot boys who came over from Fairview occasionally to visit him. But I found that the boxes were no longer in the next room; they had been sent to the mill loft, for nothing was left to remind them that they had ever been separated, or that there had been a shadow across their path. The room where Jo and I had slept when visiting Barker was now occupied by Agnes herself, and I sat down by the window and told her how her father came in and stood beside the bed after we had retired, as if dreading to be left alone, where he remained until we were sound asleep; how I had wakened once in the middle of the night, and, creeping to his door, found him sitting at the table with his hat and coat on, as if ready to run away; how generous and considerate he had always been with us, and how we esteemed him as a noble man, and how glad I was that she had found in my old friend one greater than a friend. To this Agnes would only reply that there was nothing now to interfere with their peace and content except the knowledge that some of their old friends were in trouble.

Although I knew that Big Adam had followed Agnes to the mill, and become the assistant, I was made further aware of it by hearing him talking about his work while we were yet in the house, which sounded like distant thunder, for his voice seemed to have grown hoarser with age. When I went down to call on him he hugged me like a bear, and only released me when the miller himself appeared to greet me.

Big Adam seemed to be pleased with his new position, and he frequently came around to remark secretly to me that every family had its deaths by Indians, which I understood was a reference to the mysterious manner in which Agnes had found her father, and he was a sworn friend of Barker's because he seemed to hate his old enemy. When not engaged in this manner, Big

Adam was rubbing against me, that I might get flour dust on my clothes, and understand that he was a miller, but after noticing it, he brushed me down with great ceremony and many apologies. As I walked about the mill with the proprietor, I heard the assistant draw a great many corks, and pour out liquor which seemed to be very old and rich, and which came out of the bottle in hoarse gurgles.

I could not help remarking of Barker that time had suddenly ceased to tell on him, and that he seemed to be growing younger; for all the distressed lines of care had disappeared from his face, and his eyes were brighter, and smiles were no longer strangers to him. His old habit of casting quick glances in every direction, as if always expecting the sudden arrival of a dreaded visitor, was no longer a characteristic; it had disappeared entirely, and instead he was quiet in his manner, and apparently quite at his ease. When I had known him in my boyhood, there were times when I feared him; when I expected him to break out in a violent temper, and, declaring that he was tired of a lawful existence, murder Jo and me with a volley from all his brass pistols at once, and set out to join his old companions, but now there was a serenity on his face which betokened peace and quiet content. He had no ambition beyond the happiness of his child and a quiet life at the mill, and as he had means in abundance, he had little to disturb and annoy him.

I did not have long to talk with him, as my visit was hurried, but he told me during the time that he was worried about Jo, and that if at any time I concluded that he needed his aid — I was with him more, and apt to know should that emergency arise — I had only to command him, no difference what the service was. I think he imagined the trouble was in some way connected with money, for he said repeatedly that he was now easy in that particular, and ready to assist his friends. When I told him it was not that, he was very much concerned, although he did not inquire further, and afterwards became grave and thoughtful in thinking about it.

In returning from this visit to Barker's — it was in mid-winter, a short time after the holidays — I was very much surprised to meet Jo Erring walking toward me in the road, apparently on his way to the mill. He stopped before I came up with him, as if considering whether he should go on, or back with me, and, settling it as I drove up, he stepped into the buggy and sat down beside me.

Although the day was cold, he said as we drove along that he had been walking through the woods to amuse himself, and was not going anywhere. I remember him particularly on this afternoon because he declared that he would not mention his trouble to me again, as even I must have concluded that he was in the wrong. I replied in such a way as to confirm him in this belief — through hesitancy in framing my answer, it must have been, for I did not mean to — and this hurt him so much that he looked away to hide his tears. I assured him that I never questioned his manliness in the matter, and only thought of it to pity him, but he would only say that he was about convinced himself that he was wrong, although he could not help it; he could not keep his thoughts off his humiliating marriage, and there was nothing left him but disgrace and ruin.

As I looked at him I became more than ever aware of his haggard, desperate appearance; of his nervous twitching, and the quick and excited way in which he did everything. He had formerly been very neat in his dress, but he was now careless in this regard, and instead of sitting upright beside me, he wobbled about, and seemed to be unjointed as well as uncomfortable. No position was easy for him, and at times he acted like a drunken man. He started several times to say something in justification of himself, but before he had fairly begun the sentence, he gave it up, and leaned back in his seat again, convinced that it was a waste of time to talk further about it, or remembering that he had resolved to say less in future. Perhaps he had thought so much over his trouble that his brain was tired, and it was painful to speak. Although he had previously been a robust man, he had grown pale and thin, and there were indications of fever in his face, though when I put the question to him, he said he was as well as usual.

When we came in sight of his house — we were on the other

side of the creek, opposite the mill — I was surprised to find
Clinton Bragg's buggy hitched at the gate. At that time Jo was
looking down at his feet, so that he did not see it, and I thought
to turn around, and drive another way, but my unusual action attracted his notice, and he quickly raised his head. I shall never
forget the look of indignation and horror which appeared on his
face when he looked up, and, taking a second glance, he sprang
out of the buggy, and ran toward the dam. I knew his intention
was to cross it, and though it was a dangerous undertaking, he
jumped the gaps in it like a desperate animal after prey.

The ford was a short distance below, but before I reached it,
I saw him climbing the abrupt bluff on the other side, helping
himself by grasping the underbrush, and slipping and falling on
the frozen ground. I turned the corner of the mill at this moment,
and drove into the ford, and when I came up to the house, Jo
had disappeared on the inside. Hurriedly hitching the team, I
almost ran into the house, fearing there would be murder done,
but when I opened the door, and stepped in, I found them all
in the front room — Clinton Bragg, pale and trembling, near the
door; Jo, on the opposite side of the room, in a great state of
excitement, and Mateel between them. I had never seen her
assert herself before, and it awed her angry husband into sub-
mission. There was a look of dignity in her face, and her eyes
flashed as I had never seen them. I could see she had been
talking excitedly, and she continued after looking up as I came
in: —

"You have insulted my womanhood by this action, and cast
suspicion on my honor," she said, trembling violently. "The gentleman drove up but a moment ago on a trifling errand from my
mother, and I could do nothing else than admit him. He sat
down by the fire to warm, when you came bounding in like a
jealous demon whose worst suspicions had been confirmed, and
would have killed him had I not thrown myself in the way. You
have given him reason to believe that you doubted my honor;
everyone who hears of this disgraceful proceeding will have the
same opinion. You have wronged me in the most cruel manner,
and I can no longer remain silent. In justice to myself as your

wife I protest, and demand that you save me from disgrace by allowing him to depart in peace."

She was magnificent in her indignation, and Jo cowered before her, though there was so much hatred in his face that he looked like an animal.

"I shall ask him in your presence to take me back to my mother," Mateel went on to say, watching her husband narrowly, as if fearing that he would spring at Clinton Bragg at the suggestion, "to remain there until you come to me, and acknowledge that you were wrong." I felt sick and faint when she said it, for I believed that if she went away with Bragg she would never come back. "When you come to yourself you will respect me for it. I have allowed you so much liberty in the past that I feel that I must do this to vindicate your wife; to redeem her from the stain your disordered fancy has put upon her."

She swept past me and up the stairs to her room to prepare for the journey, and like a cowardly dog Bragg crept out behind her, and on out to the front gate, where he shivered and waited in the cold.

Her determination so impressed me as a mistaken one that I would have followed her up the stairs, and begged her to think again before taking the step, but Jo made a mute appeal to me to remain where I was, which I reluctantly did. Falling into a chair which stood near him, he raised his head occasionally to listen as his wife went about the room above where we sat, collecting a few articles into a package; when she stopped a moment he listened more eagerly than before, hoping, I have no doubt, that she was debating in her own mind whether her determination was not rash and hasty; he followed her footsteps as they came part way down the stairs; he followed them back into the room again, where she went as if something had been forgotten, and down the stairs until she paused timidly at the door, and as she pushed it open and came in he shuddered to see that she was dressed for the ride. I think he never doubted that she would come back, and say she had given it up, but when he saw that her determination continued he buried his face in his hands, and leaned his head on the back of the chair on which he sat.

I could see that Mateel had been weeping while out of the room, and that it was with great effort she maintained her composure. She stood near the door, buttoning her gloves, and spoke to me as much as to Jo: —

"I hope that what I am about to do is for the best; if it were not I am sure that God would not permit me to go away. Surely in His wisdom He would guide me differently if my action threatens to make us more unhappy than we have been."

She had finished putting on her gloves, and there was no further excuse for her to stay, but she remained, and trembled and hesitated.

"He has imagined so much," she was talking to me now, "that if I allow this to go unrebuked he will be confirmed in his unjust suspicions. I feel that if I do this it will be better for my husband, better for myself, and for all of us. I have heretofore said nothing, submitting to a great many indignities which his changed disposition implied; but he has grown unhappier every day. It cannot be wrong if I ask that he respect my womanhood as I have always respected his manhood. I have felt that I have pursued [2] a wrong course from the first; at this late day I attempt reparation, though it almost kills me to do it."

She had advanced a step or two toward her husband, and as he made no reply to what she said, she seemed anxious to justify her course still further, and continued, this time talking to both of us: —

"If I have failed to be an acceptable wife, it was because my husband's unhappiness distressed me so much that I was unable to accomplish all that my heart suggested. I have thought of this so much that my health has become impaired, and I have lost the power to act. I was a weak and puny girl; I fear I am a weaker woman, and if I seem to have been helpless in the sorrow which has come upon our house, it was because I was dumb at the enormity of it. I tried in my weak way to explain it and effect a reconciliation, but he told me that everything I said made it worse. I could do nothing then but bear the burden bravely. He asked me as a favor to let him alone; as an obedient

[2] I have pursued: 1883 I pursued

269

wife I did the best I could, hoping all the time that he would re-call his cruel request. I have not dared to express my regret at his unhappiness, fearing he would not like it, and God is my wit-ness that it is not my fault that we have lived as strangers so long."

As I paid respectful attention, and her husband none at all — his face was turned from her — she addressed herself to me again: —

"I hope it will be always understood that I am taking this step not in anger, but because I feel that I must do something. I can-not live as I have been living, and self-preservation suggests action of some kind. Perhaps what I am doing is not wise, but I can think of nothing else. I have always felt that I should have been more independent, and asserted myself more. I hope he will understand, and respect my determination."

Although I felt that I ought to interfere, I knew it was useless and idle, and perhaps would offend them both, so I held my peace.

"If he will ask me to remain," she was losing her dignity and composure very rapidly, and when I realized how pale and weak she was I wondered she had held up so long, "I will reconsider; or I will ask you to take me home, instead of Clinton Bragg, if he desires it. I will do anything he wishes."

Not a word, Jo? Will you refuse your trembling wife advice when she asks it, and then hold her responsible if she adopts the wrong course?

When Jo did not reply, Mateel seemed to think that there was nothing left for her to do but to go, and never come back; and walking over to him, she said in a voice which has since remained a sob in my memory: —

"Won't you bid me good-bye?"

He remained still and motionless, as before.[3]

Falling on her knees before him, and holding her hands out to him imploringly, she repeated the request, but he did not move or speak, and after waiting a moment, Mateel rose to her feet in a dazed sort of way, and, staggering toward the door,

[3] before: 1883 before, though I could hear his tears falling in little plashes on the floor.

270

went out into the hall and down the steps, without once looking back. When he heard the door close upon her, Jo ran to the window, and as he looked out his breathing was short and quick. Standing beside him, I saw that a snow-storm was commencing, and that the day was far advanced. Bragg helped Mateel into the buggy with an insolent sort of politeness, and, seating himself beside her, drove away.

After they had passed down the hill which led to the ford, Jo sprang nimbly up to the sill of the window, and eagerly watched them. As soon as they passed out of sight from that position, he jumped down, and ran up the stairs, and when I followed, I found him standing in the window in Mateel's room, peering after his rapidly departing wife. As they drove out of the ford, and into the edge of the woods, they were for a moment in full view, but, turning directly away, were soon lost in the gathering twilight. Hoping that a turn in the road, or an opening in the timber, would reveal them again, he remained watching for several minutes, jumping down, and running hurriedly from window to window. When he was at last certain that they had finally gone, he got down slowly from his perch, and, throwing himself on the bed, wept and sobbed aloud.

Knowing that I could not leave him, and that I was expected at home, I went down to the mill, and asked the assistant to drive to town and inform my mother that Jo was ill, and that I should not return till morning. This he readily agreed to do and was soon on the way.

Returning to the house, I soon had the lamps lighted, and the fires burning, and went up stairs to where Jo still lay motionless on the bed. He had not changed his position, although he was no longer sobbing except at long intervals, like a child recovering from a protracted period of weeping. I now noticed for the first time that he was much like my mother in his sullen grief, for a hundred times I had sat beside her bed for hours when she was depressed, asking her to speak to me, but while she seemed to appreciate my thoughtfulness in remaining with her, she would never answer, but tossed about from side to side, always avoiding my eyes. I repeatedly asked him if there was anything I

271

could do, but he would not reply, and at last covered his head, as if he would hide his sorrow from me. Out of consideration for him, I removed the light to another room, and, returning, sat down in the darkness by his side.

An hour passed, and then another, and still another, and nothing could be heard but the ticking of the clock, and the occasional sighs of the unhappy man on the bed, which became so painful to me that I began to watch for and dread them, and wonder whether the most pitiful thing in the world was not a strong man weeping. I have since heard my own children sob in their sleep as Jo Erring did that night, and felt again how wretched I was as I sat there waiting for him to speak.

When it was time for the man to return from town, I began to listen for the first noise of his approach, until at last, becoming nervous that he delayed so long, I went down to the front door, and out to the gate to look down the road, when I found that the snow was falling in earnest, threatening a great storm. Another hour passed, and at last I heard the sound of wheels. Hurrying down to the gate, I received from the hands of the assistant a note, and when I went back to the light, I was alarmed to find that it was from a neighbor of ours, and to the effect that my mother was dangerously ill, and that my coming should not be delayed. I went into Jo's room, and told him of it, hoping he would propose to go to town with me, but as he paid no attention, I left the note on the table beside him, and hurried away.

The horses were jaded from the long day's work, but I urged them along the rough roads at a rapid pace. Every bush had grown into a white-robed phantom, and I imagined that one of them was my father, pleading to be taken up, and hurried to the end of his long journey; that another was my mother come out to meet me, distressed at my long delay; in still another I could see a resemblance to Jo as I left him lying on the bed, except that the drapery of white covered everything. I saw Mateel kneeling at a tomb in which I thought must be buried her hope, and so many mounds took the shape of graves that I mercilessly lashed the horses, and it was but an hour after midnight when the lights of Twin Mounds began to appear. When I came into the town, the houses seemed to be great monuments of white, as though the people had said their prayers and died when the snow came, and down the street I could see the light which was always shining for one who never came.

When I hurried into the house I saw that my mother's room was full of pitying faces, and that the people made way for me as I approached the pale form on the bed. I was so frightened that I could do nothing but kneel down, and burst into tears, and while I knelt thus I knew that my mother's hand was placed lovingly on my head. When I recovered sufficient composure to look at her, I saw that she was lying precisely as I had left Jo; her arms thrown out carelessly on either side, and there were tears in her eyes, and a look of inexpressible grief on her face. Occasionally she took a long breath, and sobbed, as her brother had done, and she turned her head away from me, as he had done, but not until I saw that there was blood on her lips, when it was softly explained in answer to my look of alarm that she had had a hæmorrhage. I tried to make myself believe that it was but an attack which would soon be over, but the people who were gathered about were so serious that my tears came afresh, and I could do nothing but hope.

She had turned her face away from me, and remained in that position so long that it was suggested that perhaps she was asleep. Someone went softly around to that side of the room to see her face, and looking at the others in quick alarm, they came crowding around the bed: the patient watcher was dead.

Let the bleak winds take up the cry of the unhappy son, and carry it across rivers and fields to the wanderer, that he need not return; that the light in the window has gone out, and that the watcher who waited so long to forgive him is dead. Let them look for him in all the places where hunted men hide, and deliver the message that a pitying angel came, and, taking the light which offered forgiveness and peace so long, planted it in the heavens, where it will remain forever, a pitying star, offering mercy to all men who are weary and in distress.

XXVIII

TOO LATE

THE fall of snow continued through the night, and during the following day, and there was grave doubt whether those who had been sent for could arrive in time for the funeral, for great drifts had collected in the roads, and it was very cold. The people who came in talked more of the weather than of the dead, and it was whispered among them that such a storm had never been known before in the history of the country. A man who had been out to dig the grave came in and whispered to his wife that the ground was frozen to a wonderful depth, and that those who were helping him could only work a few minutes at a time, and that the grave filled up with drifting snow almost as fast as they could throw it out.

This was on the afternoon of the next day, and as the evening wore on, lights were brought into the room where I sat. One by one the people who were at the house went away, leaving only those who were to watch through the night, and as each one went out, they remarked the severity of the weather, and shuddered and shivered before stepping out into the drifting snow. I believe I felt a relief when they were gone, for I desired to be alone. I hoped [1] I was not ungrateful for their kindness, but the attentions the people showed me were almost annoying, and frequently during the day I left them, and repaired to one of the lonely upper rooms, where I tried to sleep, but I could only think of my mother lying cold and dead; of Jo in his lonely home, and of the mountain of snow which seemed to be covering up all hope of happiness for any of us.

My mother lay in the front room, which was almost as cold and cheerless as the outside, for when the watchers went in to

[1] hoped: 1883 hope

see that all was right, which they did by turns, they wore heavy coverings, and shuddered, and came out again as soon as they could. A wide hall ran between that room and the one in which I sat, and straight down the hall was that part of the house where the watchers dozed by turns, and talked in low voices, which only came to me when the doors were opened.

As the night wore away the storm increased with every hour, and feeling that my mother was in a cheerless and lonely place, I got up and opened the door leading into the hall, and that which led into the room where the plain black coffin stood. As I went back I noticed that heavy blankets had been thrown at the foot of the front door, to keep out the drifting snow and keen winds, but in spite of them the snow had crept in, and was lying about in little drifts, which impressed me more than ever with the severity of the storm on the outside. Going into the room where the watchers were, I found them all asleep, though they wakened with an apology as I opened the door.

Knowing that they were all tired and worn out, I told them to sleep if they could, and that I would watch until midnight, when I would call them if I tired of the undertaking. Going back to my own room — the one in which my mother had sat, and where the light was always kept burning — I stirred the fire and sat down again. I glanced up at the clock to see what the hour was, but the pendulum was still, and then I remembered that it had been stopped when my mother died, for the first time within my recollection.

I must have fallen into a light sleep, and slept for some time, for, when I started up, the fire was low, although I had left it burning brightly. Something, I could not tell what, had disturbed me, and I hastened into the other room to see that all was well. Everything remained as I had left it, and coming back I sat down to listen for the noise again. After listening for a time, without really expecting to hear anything, I was startled by a timid rapping at the front door. It frightened me so that I thought of calling the watchers, but finally determined to open the door myself, thinking it might be some of those who had been sent for. Going out and opening the door a little way, I saw that a strange man, wrapped up in mufflers and furs, was standing at the gate, as if he had despaired of an answer to his knock and was going away. After a moment of hesitation, he walked towards me, and I was almost tempted to shut and lock the door in his face, for I did not know him. He seemed to recognize me, however, for he walked into the house, and, passing me, sat down at the fire I had left, where he shivered and trembled so much that I thought he must be a belated traveller attracted by the friendly light, which was perhaps the only one in the town.

As I stepped behind him to stir the fire, and looked at him curiously, I became aware that it was my father. His beard was gray, and his face wrapped for walking in the storm, but I knew him. The wanderer had returned at last, but too late! He continued to shiver and tremble, the result of agitation and the extreme cold through which he had come, and sat for a long time trying to warm himself, while I walked up and down the room in nervous agitation.

After stirring the fire, I closed the door leading into the hall, and stood by his side, and when he removed the wrappings from his neck and face, and looked curiously about, I saw that he was poorly clad, and that he was old and broken. He was timid in his manner, and looked at me as though he expected I would denounce him, and drive him out of the house, and when he moved, it was with difficulty, from which I thought he had walked a long distance. His shoes were wrapped in coarse bagging, which was tied to his feet with cords, and when he held out his hands to warm them, I saw that they were bruised and cracked, and I was sure he had been working as a laborer during his long absence.

"It is after midnight," he said at length, in a hesitating voice, as though he were afraid to speak. "Why are you here alone?"

Then he did not know! He had come back, as my mother always thought he would, at night, repentant and old, to ask forgiveness, but the one who could forgive him was dead. I did not know what to say or do, and walked up and down the room thinking how to answer. He followed my movements curiously for a time, and then suddenly cowered down into his chair again, as if to meditate over one of the old problems. While I was wondering how to break the news to him, he turned toward me, and said: —

"I saw the lights in the front room as I came up, but hoped it was a sign of welcome rather than of death; but I know now why you are alone. You need not explain."

The tears came into his eyes, but he tried to brush them away with his rough sleeve, as though he were a child and had been warned not to cry. I think he realized in a moment, while wondering why I was so much agitated, that she was dead, though he had cheerfully imagined, when approaching the house, that the lower rooms were lit up on purpose to receive him.

"She died this morning just after midnight," I said to him, coming over to his side, and placing my hand on his shoulder, "but I know she always believed you would come back. She sat in this room every night waiting, and her last words were a blessing on your name."

He did not look up, but I thought this assurance cheered him, though he remained motionless so long that I think he must have reviewed his entire life, from his boyhood in the backwoods to his manhood on the prairie, where the forbidden processions were always passing, and from his career in Twin Mounds through all his hard wanderings as an outcast; a long record of discontent, sorrow, and disgrace, with nothing to excuse it save the natural unrest with which his life had been beset like a hell. Inexplicable and monstrous as it was, I knew it was real, and that a devil had possession of him for whose acts he was unjustly held accountable. A hundred times since then I have thought of John Westlock as a worthy man driven by a fiend with whip and lash, always sullenly protesting, but never able to resist the evil which was bred into his nature, and against which he had struggled all his life.

I tried to decide in my own mind, as he was thinking, whether I knew him any better, and whether I was less afraid of him now than the day he went away, but I could not help concluding that he was the same mysterious man he had always been.

"If you will let me, I should like to look at her," he said, when he looked up again, in the voice of a suppliant asking a favor of a hard master, and so unlike him that I shuddered to think of the sorrow necessary to make such a change in a man of his disposition.

I was very anxious that the watchers should not see him; I don't know why, because his arrival and presence would certainly be known in all the town in the early morning, but I knew they would only look upon him with inward reproaches. From this I was anxious to shield him, and, carefully going to their door, I found they slept. I then went into the room where the coffin was, to remove the lid, which had been shut down, from the face. I was thankful that the face wore a pleasanter smile than I had ever seen it wear in life, and, placing the light where it fell directly upon it, I returned to where he sat, and motioned him to follow. He got up from his chair with difficulty, and, staggering after me, hesitated before entering the room, but at last he followed me in timidly, and after looking at the face for a moment, fell on his knees before the coffin, and sobbed aloud. His grief was so great that I feared the watchers would hear him, and waken, but, determined that he should be left alone with the dead, I stood at the door to keep them back should they attempt to come out. But they slept on, and when I went into the room again, he was still on his knees, his hands covering his face as it rested on the coffin, and I thought he was praying. I had often bitterly denounced him in my own mind for the unhappiness he had brought upon our house, and for the misfortunes he had founded, but I forgave him from my heart as I saw his gray head bowed in repentance over the dead body of the principal sufferer; nor did I regard it as a kindness to him, but as an act of justice to an unfortunate man. I accepted his misery as his excuse, and forgave him, as I hope that I shall be forgiven.

When he was aroused by my touch on his shoulder, I led him gently away, and we returned to the room we had left. Here he hugged the fire again, as if he were still cold, and sat without speaking so long that I thought he was trying to solve the hardest problem of his life.

"It was I who made the mistake," he said finally, without changing his position, and as though we had been saying that

278

someone had made a mistake. "She was always patient, but I was dissatisfied and restless. I thought that if I were married to a flashy, ambitious woman, nothing would be impossible; but I know now that her quiet patience and content were rare jewels which I spurned and neglected. I confess to you now that I was wrong, and that she was right."

He seemed never to have confessed this to himself before, and repeated it, so there could be no mistake.

"I thought I was more a man than I really was, and that there was nothing I could not do, but I have found" — he looked at his rough clothes as if I could judge by them that he had had a hard struggle in finding it out — "I have found that I could not rid my mind of unrest for committing a wrong. During all the years I have been away I have carried a heavy cross, and worn a crown of thorns on my forehead, in repentance, but since she is dead, and I cannot ask her to forgive me, I must continue to travel the long road, and carry my burden. She could have lightened it, but she is dead, and I must carry it on and on until I fall exhausted into my dishonored grave."

I could not help thinking he would not be long compelled to carry his heavy cross, for now that the hope of finding his wife alive had left him, he was weak and trembling.

"Had I found her alive and well to-night," he continued, "and waiting to forgive me, I might have consented to remain here, and hide away where no one except my injured wife and son could see me, but as it is now, I will go out into the world again, before it is known that I returned at all, so that the charitable may think of me as dead."

I realized in a moment, without having had a thought of it before, that he would go away again, and hide from his accusers in Twin Mounds, but before I could protest he went on speaking, as if in a hurry to finish: —

"Of my history since I went away it is only necessary for you to know that I lived alone after the first three months, and worked hard that I might forget, but I could not, and within the last few years I have been travelling this way a little distance every month, and I only completed my long journey to-night. Of my companion — she is no longer my companion, nor has she been for years — I will only say she is as unhappy as I am. We separated within three months, and the first oath that ever passed my lips was a curse for her. We hated each other within a week, each blaming the other for the mistake, and I know no more of her now than she knows of me."

A suggestion of his old spirit returned while he was talking of B., and there was the old scowl upon his face, but it disappeared when he mentioned my mother again.

"Before I go I want to say that I was wrong; that I am repentant, and that my last breath will be spent in supplicating mercy for my crime against your mother. I was always a man of few words, and my heart was always stubborn, and I cannot make more of a confession than this. She was a good woman, and I was a bad man, and while she was brave and noble, and always true, I was everything I should not have been."

I could make no reply,[2] though he looked at me as if expecting one.

"It may be of profit to you, who are young, to know that I have been punished for my offence. If I have had a moment's peace since I went away; if I have had an hour's sound and refreshing sleep; if I have not been in hell all the while, may God strike me dead! Day and night, night and day, always, everywhere, my crime has taken the shape of a demon, and taunted me; I have not looked into a book that I did not find accusing words staring at me; I have not heard a sound which did not mock me, and wherever I have gone I have heard the people telling what should be done with a man who ran away from his wife. If I avoided them they hunted me up, and told of a patient wife who was mourning for her runaway husband; God, the world seems to be full of such cases! However secretly I moved from place to place I met people who seemed to say: 'There he goes; there he goes; a man who has run away from his wife. Hate him; beat him; he is a coward; he is dangerous.' If I went into a church, the minister seemed to point at me and say: 'Put that man out; he has disgraced us. Put him out, I say, and hurry him from this honorable neighborhood. He is the man who has brought reproach on the

[2] make no reply: 1883 say nothing in reply

church; put him out; put him out.' If I slept out in the fields to avoid them, the wind always blew from the direction of Twin Mounds, and there were moans in it which came from this house. The very cattle ran away from me, as if to say: 'He has been unjust to a woman; he will probably kill us; get up there, all of you, and run for your lives.' This is the life I have led, and which I have deserved. It is the price of discontent; if you have a trace of it in your nature, root it out! Be contented, though it kills you!"

He said this in great excitement, and, getting up, began slowly to wrap the comforter about his neck, and knowing his determined nature I felt that it would be impossible for me to persuade him to stay. Never in my life had I offered him a suggestion, and even in his present broken condition I was afraid of him.

"You probably remember," he said, pausing in the process of wrapping himself up, "that every year since I have been away a stranger has sent you money for your paper; first from one place and then from another. That stranger was your father, so that I know what a good son you have been, and how hard you have worked to support your mother, who was so cruelly neglected by me. I am satisfied that you have conducted my affairs with good judgment, and that I have been missed but little."

He got up at this and began to button his great-coat about him, and to wrap his scarf around his neck and head.

"Whether it is your judgment that I should or should not, I am going away again, and will never come back. I am not wanted here, though I see you would insist on my staying, but it is useless. I have made up my mind."

I had stepped before him, but he pushed me aside, and walked toward the door.

"Listen to me a moment," I said, taking hold of him. "You are poor and old; I am young, and have ready money. If you will not remain here, as Heaven knows I desire you should, take it with you. I have no one to care for now, and you need it. I will ask it on my knees if it will move you. It is all yours, and I shall feel guilty all my life if you refuse this request, fearing you are poor and in need of it."

"Rather than that," he answered, "I would live again in this

281

town, where every man is my enemy and accuser. No, I will take none of the money; my needs are few and easily satisfied. But if you will grant me your forgiveness" — there was more tenderness in his voice as he said it than I had ever heard before — "I will take that."

I answered that he had suffered enough, and that I had already forgiven him; that we all had, and that we had long been sure that he had repented of his one fault.

"There are but few of us who have to answer for but one fault," I said. "I know nothing to your discredit except this one mistake."

He stood by this time near the door, with his hand on the latch, and, simply saying good-bye, he opened it, and went out into the storm.

Determined to make one more effort to induce him to remain at home, I ran bareheaded into the street after him, floundering in the snow almost waist deep as I went, but he was already a considerable distance ahead of me, walking with long strides, and looking straight ahead. The louder I called to him the faster he walked, and after following him almost to where the stores and the square began, he turned the corner, and disappeared forever.

XXIX

THE SKELETON AGAIN

ALTHOUGH Jo came to Twin Mounds the day after my mother's burial, and a few times during the winter, I did not visit him for several months, for I dreaded to go into his house and find him alone in it. I hoped that Mateel would come back, and that their separation would cause them to be happier than they had been, but as Jo ceased his visits to town because I did not return them, at last I could do nothing else.

Another sorrow had been lately added to his life; the messenger who had been sent into the lower country to inform Gran Erring of her daughter's death returned a few days later with the information that my grandmother and grandfather were both dead. We had been so taken up with our own affairs of late that we had scarcely thought of them, as often we did not hear for a year at a time how they fared; and Jo felt that he had neglected them, although he knew they were never in need, for regularly every quarter he sent them an amount of money amply sufficient for their small necessities, which was partly in payment for the mill site, and according to agreement, though he had long since paid more than the place was worth. My grandfather had a relative in the lower country — whether it was a brother, a sister, or an uncle, I never knew, nor do I know yet, our family relations were always so miserable — and this relative, having probably heard of our other distresses, never notified us of his death, or that of his wife, which occurred a few months later. It was very disgraceful, and I felt almost as much humiliation over it as Jo.

The house and mill looked so gray when I came in sight of them that they reminded me of ghosts, although it was more from neglect than age, for neither of them was old, and there was a general air of decay everywhere which said plainly enough that

283

something was wrong. The traveller who passed that way would have remarked it; he could not have known what it was, but he would have felt certain that a disappointed man lived in the house and carried on business in the mill. I have thought that the trees shading the mill pond drooped their heads in mortification at the history of the place, and certainly the water was quiet and subdued, like the master, except when it dashed into the race and after a furious onslaught on its old enemy, the wheel, fell exhausted into the peaceful river below.

I came upon the place late in the afternoon, at least half a year after Mateel went away, and seeing customers about the mill I went down there to find the proprietor, but the assistant was working alone, and said that Jo was probably up at the house. Going in there and failing to find him in the lower rooms, I went up the stairs, where I found him asleep in his room, but the noise of my footsteps awakened him. As he shook hands with me I could not help thinking of the skeleton that kept him awake at night, making it necessary for him to sleep during the day, for he was pale and haggard, and I am not certain but that I looked around for the closet in which it was kept.

The house was a very large one, and while he bathed his face after his long sleep, I walked through the rooms, which seemed so empty that the noise of my feet made echoes as though a troop were following me. When I went into Mateel's room, where I had left Jo sobbing on the bed on the dreadful night when his wife went away, I found it ready for her reception, as though she were expected to arrive at any time. The woman who kept the house, and who lived so near that she went home every night, had thrown all her woman's ingenuity into making the room tasteful and pretty, as a compliment to her wretched employer, and it was aired and dusted as regularly as though it had been regularly occupied. All the articles of ornament and comfort prepared by Mateel while she had lived there were in their accustomed places, and her picture, which had been taken shortly after her marriage, had been made gay by the kind-hearted housekeeper in a pretty frame for the pleasure of the master, should he ever come in to look at it. There were seven or eight rooms besides this one, and I thought that a man in the best of spirits would have been lonely to stay there without companions.

When Jo joined me in the hall we went down stairs to supper, and after seeing that everything was at hand, the housekeeper left for home to prepare her husband's supper, leaving us alone. On looking about I saw that Jo had been adding articles of furniture during his wife's absence, as if to surprise and please her when she should finally return; and I have no doubt he was always expecting she would come back to-morrow, that fateful day which never arrives, though all of us expect so much of it. I think he believed every time he went to sleep that when he awakened she would be standing by his side, and from the miller and the housekeeper I learned that he turned quickly at every noise, expecting that it was the step of his returning wife. He never told me, but I believe that had she come back and said that she could not live without him they would have been much happier than they were before, and perhaps finished their lives in peace together. His life alone in the great house must have been a greater sorrow than his letter and the skeleton, and I think he would have consented to forget a great deal to avoid it.

He only mentioned his horror of the empty house at night in general terms, but I have always been convinced that his greatest trial was his loneliness, and that he would have closed the place and left it but for the hope that Mateel would surely come to-morrow; not as a humble suppliant, but as his wife, with a request that she be allowed to occupy her old place in the house, if not in his heart. Had Mateel opened the right door to his heart she would have found such a wealth of love and consideration there that she would never have ceased trying to reclaim it, for his love for her was so great that he could not have resisted the smallest effort. I do not remember that I thought this until I went to his house a half year after the separation, but I firmly believed it then, and I believe it yet. Perhaps I shall be better understood if I explain that while Jo was frequently at fault before the separation, six months of loneliness had wrought a great change in him, and he was willing to admit that his estimate of women was too high; that they were weak like himself, and that he was to blame for having made a serious matter of love. In the early days of his acquaintance with Mateel he had worshipped her as an angel rather than admired her as a woman, but he was now ready to give up his idol, and forgive her faults as she forgave his. He had regarded his marriage as a piece of unusual good fortune, whereby he secured a perfect being who would bring him only happiness in her train, but the experience of a few years had taught him that it was only a ceremony pledging two persons to charity for the failings of each other.

Many times after that I got up from my bed at night, after thinking about it, determined to go to Mateel, and tell her of my conviction, but upon consideration would conclude that she must know it, and that she did not desire a reconciliation. Although there was always an unspoken hope that such was not the case, Jo probably took this view of it — that she preferred to live without him. Perhaps I had better say that he did not ask her to come back for fear of the humiliating reply that she did not care to come, for he was always in doubt with reference to her.

When there was occasion Jo ran the mill at night, preferring to be there at work than alone in the house, and he was seldom in the mill at any other time, trusting his business almost entirely to his assistant, who, fortunately, was capable of managing it with Jo's advice. He told me after we had finished an early supper that he was to take charge at seven o'clock, and when that hour arrived we went down there and were soon alone. There was little to do, except to see that everything was running smoothly, and by the time Jo had made a general inspection it was dark, and we were seated in the largest room without a light, with nothing to disturb us except the subdued hum of the machinery, and the gentle fall of the water.

"It is out of the friendliest curiosity that I ask, Jo," I said to him in the course of the evening, "but have you heard nothing from Mateel since she went away?"

"Not a word," he replied with a long sigh. "I have not even seen anyone who has spoken to her, unless it is Bragg, who passes here regularly every day, going to the Shepherds', and returning noisily at night. During the six months she has been away, I have not even seen her father, who formerly came to the mill quite frequently. I have about concluded that she is glad of the opportunity to be rid of me. I have always thought that she married me as a penance, and that she was determined to be an excellent wife in every way except that she could not love me. I think that sometimes she pitied my friendless condition, and was kind to me for that reason, for she was always that."

"But why do you not go to her," I asked, "and settle these doubts?"

"She went away," he replied, after thinking awhile, "without cause, and if she cared to prevent a separation, she would come back. It was an insult to me to allow that fellow to come into my house, and I only expected that she would tell him so. I did not doubt her womanly integrity, as she said; I only felt she wronged me in permitting him to annoy me. It would have been an easy thing for her to have said to him that his presence there was presumptuous and annoying to me, but instead she invited him in, and I suppose treated him civilly. I know she did this entirely out of considerations of politeness, but I regret that she did not have more consideration for me. I did wrong to run into the house with the intention of murdering him; I know I should have greeted him pleasantly, and made him believe that I cared nothing for him, but he had pursued me so long, and with so little reason, that his impudence caused me to lose all control. When she went away with him I took an oath that I would never think of her again; that should she come back to me on her knees, I would curse her, but I am so lonely that I should almost welcome her if she came to taunt me. I have not closed my eyes in natural sleep since she went away, and with the darkness come troops of faces to peer at me through the night. However bright I make the house, there are always dark corners, and the phantoms hide in them to attack me when the light is out. If I wonder whether she be gay or sad, I always conclude — I can't tell why — that she is quite content, and in the roar of the water I can hear her gay laughter; not as I ever heard her, but as Bragg heard her laugh when she was his young and pretty lover. In the rumbling of the wheels down below, when I sit here alone at night, I can distinguish the voices of them all; even Bragg is good humored, and Mrs. Shepherd, her husband, and Mateel seem to be mocking me with their merriment. Of course it is all fancy, but it is so real to me that I listen to it breathlessly, and sometimes it annoys me so much that I stop the wheels."

He had formerly talked of the matter in a resentful tone, but it was sorrowful now, as if he were convinced that he gave himself a credit he did not deserve when he thought she worried because he was unhappy.

"Frequently when there is nothing to occupy my attention all night," Jo said later in the evening, "I walk through the woods, and steal up to her father's house, and remain under her window until the approach of day warns me to depart. I cannot say that I expect it, but I always hope that she will divine my presence, and speak to me, but the house is always dark, though I have heard them walking on the inside."

His habit of being startled at every noise, and nervously looking about, was growing upon him, for when someone appeared at the door, he went hastily into another part of the mill, to avoid him. It was only the miller come after something he had forgotten during the day, but Jo would not come back until after he had gone, not caring to see even him. In contrasting his present condition with his former manliness, I thought his sufferings must have been great to work such a change.

"The people who come here," he said, in explanation of his going away, "look at me as though I were a curiosity, and I avoid them. Although no one has told me what they say, I know what it is, and I do not care to meet them. At first I thought not to mind it, but among them all I did not find a single pitying face; they were all against me, and I determined to run from them and get out of their way. I see no one now except you, and there is nothing I dread so much as a pair of curious eyes, and a head containing a brain which I know must be conjecturing and wondering with reference to me."

I tried to laugh away this notion, although I knew it was well founded, but he paid little attention, and resumed what he was saying when interrupted by the entrance of the miller.

"When I light my lamp at night there are insects which seem to have a fatal fascination for the flame, and hover around it until they are wounded or killed. I am a good deal like them; I cannot give up Mateel, who is the cause of all my unhappiness, although I have every reason to believe that she does not even care for me. I hover about her as the insects hover about my lamp, and sooner or later I shall fall into the flame. I cannot help thinking now that she never kissed me voluntarily in her life. She has kissed me, of course, but it was only because she had heard that good wives — one of which she desired to be — showed that mark of affection for their husbands, but it was mechanical, as was every other kindness she ever showed me. I was not a hard critic when we were first married, as I am now, and I noticed it then, and my honest affection was frequently wounded because it was necessary for me to do all the loving. I am not certain that you understand what I mean; she was a good wife in every way except that it was an effort for her to love me; there was nothing natural about it, and I was never satisfied."

I had noticed this peculiarity in his wife many times myself, and wondered at it; for he was a handsome man, and sensible and considerate, and I was surprised that Mateel was not very fond of him, as I was. If I ever explained the matter to my own mind at all it was on the theory of Mr. Biggs, that the two people in a community the least suited to each other always got together and married.

"When we were first married," he continued, "I was greatly in debt, and very uncomfortable in consequence. I could not sleep at night for worrying about it, and once I told Mateel. She seemed very much concerned for a few moments, but soon forgot it entirely, and for weeks afterwards wondered why I was moody and silent. I owed everybody, and invented hundreds of ways to avoid the bills when they were due. I remember once I wrote in a disguised hand to a man who wanted his pay, that Mr. Erring was at present away collecting money, but that he would no doubt soon return, and make satisfactory settlement. I also said I knew

Mr. Erring very well, and that although at present a little pushed, he was an honest man, and would soon be all right. I signed 'Jo Erring' to the letter, with an L below it, intimating that a party named Leepson, Lawson, or Liar was one of his numerous clerks. At that time I made every mistake it was possible for a man to make; I knew absolutely nothing, and paid the highest tuition in the school of experience. At night, although she knew I was distressed from some cause, Mateel would lie down beside me, and after inquiring what was the matter, go to sleep before I had framed my answer. It was very absurd in me, but I frequently flounced around to waken her, that she might know I was still unable to sleep."

This was so ridiculous, and so like Jo, that I was really amused, though apparently he could not see why I should be, for he looked up in surprise at my merriment.

"I have never doubted that Mateel was constantly trying to do that which was right, but her nature was such that, although I recognized that she was a good woman, I was never contented. Perhaps this was wicked in me, but I always did the best I could, though in my weakness I was very often wrong. I despair of being able to explain to anyone exactly what I mean, and probably I shall always seem to have been a ridiculous and unreasonable man, though I can fully justify myself in protesting against a life without hope. I only regret that Mateel is not as much concerned as I am, for then there would be a possibility of bridging the difficulty. When I think how careful you are of my wishes, and how easily you please me, I cannot help remembering how innocently Mateel did that which was distasteful, though all the time I realized that she was upright and honest, and a better woman than I was a man. I can only say in excuse of my conduct that the more contemptible I became in all other eyes than yours and my own — I believe you would love me even though I should commit murder — the more I hoped Mateel would realize the necessity of hunting out a remedy, and applying it, for I thought I would rather die than live as wretchedly as I did, but matters have grown steadily worse, and instead of understanding that whatever I did was prompted by love for her, she seems to believe that I am depraved and wicked. She had great sympathy for everybody and everything except me, and I have frequently found her weeping over a newspaper scrap when I was so much in need of her sympathy that I almost asked it on my knees. She was always thinking of the unfortunate birds, the unfortunate people, or worrying over distress of some kind, but upon my honor she never in her life, of her own motion, had any sympathy for my affairs. I was always robust, but occasionally I regretted that she was not anxious about my health. I never worked too hard, but I regretted she did not think so, and remonstrate with me in such a way as to prove that she had an interest in me. Before we were married, and when I was building the mill, I worked harder than any man had ever before worked in Fairview, and really became quite pale and wan, but she never mentioned it. Although I was glad to do what I did for her, it would have pleased me had she said I was a worthy man for it, and encouraged me a little. I suppose she thought everything came to me naturally and easily, but it did not. Or she may have thought that much that I did for her was the work of the Lord. What makes me most miserable of all, however, is the certainty that she possesses all the womanly tenderness I feel the lack of, but I was not the man to bring it out. It was the misfortune of both of us."

I thought of what he had said about becoming a hard critic, but he was criticising himself rather than his wife, for he always gave me the impression that the trouble was his own failure to inspire her love and enthusiasm. I regarded this as an admission from his bleeding heart that, had she married Clinton Bragg, there would have been no cause for complaint.

"I often set about to make Mateel happy, and I always accomplished it," my moody companion said at another time. "I could tell it in her face, and in her pleasant surprises, but although she has always said that she had no other ambition in life than to make me contented, she never succeeded in a single instance. I should have continued this devotion to her happiness all my life had she been able to give me anything in return, but I grew tired of always being considerate of others, while no one was considerate of me. I hope I may say this without causing a suspicion in your mind that I was contemptible, for I should have been perfectly content had she anticipated my wishes as you do, or as Agnes did for both of us when we were boys. If I was enthusiastic over my small successes, she did not share it with me, and made me feel silly that I was so easily moved; everything she did (although it was not intended, I am certain of that) was an accusation that she was the right woman, though I was the wrong man. I make these statements more in explanation of my own conduct, which seems inexplicable, than to accuse her, for everyone must be saying that I am wrong.

"And while I have lacked the sympathy of my wife, I have also lacked the sympathy of the people. They say I am too prosperous, although I have simply had an ambition to be an honest and worthy man; others might have been equally prosperous had they denied themselves and worked as hard as I have done. Many of the Fairview men are suspicious of those who use punctuation marks in their letters and spell their words correctly. They go a long way around me to patronize my rival up the river, but somehow he does not get along, for he is extravagant, while I save and work hard that I may live in a house like a man, instead of in a shed, like the cattle. The vagrants who idle in the shadow of my buildings say that I am 'lucky,' but they are incapable of understanding the work I do."

When the work we had set out to do was completed, it was near midnight, but after shutting down, Jo showed no disposition to return to the house, for I think he hated it, and was seldom there at night. There were boats on the mill pond, and I proposed a row. With his strong arms at the oars, we were soon far up the stream, and although I tried to rally him, he had little to say, except to answer my questions.

Two miles above the mill there was a bend in the river, and for a considerable distance I knew the road leading to the Shepherds' skirted the stream, and before we reached it I was certain we should find Clinton Bragg travelling it. I became so impressed with the idea that I suggested that we turn back, but with the strange fascination which always pursued him, Jo said he needed exercise, and continued to pull at the oars.

As I feared, when we came to the point where the road ran close to the river, Clinton Bragg appeared on horseback, riding leisurely toward town. It was rather a dark night, but we were so close to him that I could see that while we had tried to avoid noticing his presence, he stared insolently at us, and even slackened the speed of his horse.

Jo pretended not to see him, continuing to work at the oars, but I could hear his hot, heavy breathing, and knew that he was in great excitement. He had not been disposed to talk before, but I could get nothing out of him after this, and, changing places with him, I pulled the boat back to the mill in silence.

The next day was Sunday, and it happened that we saw Bragg pass, going toward the Shepherds' in the morning, and return at night, and Jo told me that it was always so; a day never passed of late that he did not come upon him going or coming, and from his fierce manner when he spoke of it I thought that if Bragg knew the danger he was in, he would travel the other road, for there was another one, which was several miles shorter.

XXX

A LETTER FROM MR. BIGGS

MY DEAR SIR, — Occasionally a gem occurs to me which I am unable to favor you with because of late we are not much together. Appreciating the keen delight with which you have been kind enough to receive my philosophy, I take the liberty of sending herewith a number of ideas which may please and benefit you, and which I have divided into paragraphs with headings.

HAPPINESS.

I have observed that happiness and brains seldom go together. The pin-headed woman who regards her thin-witted husband as the greatest man in the world, is happy, and much good may it do her. In such cases ignorance is a positive blessing, for good sense would cause the woman to realize her distressed condition. A man who can think he is as "good as anybody" is happy. The fact may be notorious that the man is not so "good as anybody" until he is as industrious, as educated, and as refined as anybody, but he has not brains enough to know this, and, content with conceit, is happy. A man with a brain large enough to understand mankind is always wretched and ashamed of himself.

REPUTATION.

Reputation is not always desirable. The only thing I have ever heard said in Twin Mounds concerning Smoky Hill is that good hired girls may be had there.

WOMEN.

1. Most women seem to love for no other reason than that it is expected of them.

2. I know too much about women to honor them more than

294

they deserve; in fact, I know all about them. I visited a place once where doctors are made, and saw them cut up one.

3. A woman loses her power when she allows a man to find out all there is to her; I mean by this that familiarity breeds contempt. I knew a young man once who worked beside a woman in an office, and he never married.

4. If men would only tell what they actually know about women, instead of what they believe or hear, they would receive more credit for chastity than is now the case, for they deserve more.

LACK OF SELF-CONFIDENCE.

As a people we lack self-confidence. The country is full of men that will readily talk you to death privately, who [1] would run away in alarm if asked to preside at a public meeting. In my Alliance movement I often have trouble in getting out a crowd, every farmer in the neighborhood feeling of so much importance as to fear that if he attends he will be called upon to say something.

IN DISPUTE.

In some communities where I have lived the women were mean to their husbands; in others, the husbands were mean to their wives. It is usually the case that the friends of a wife believe her husband to be a brute, and the friends of the husband believe the wife to possess no other talent than to make him miserable. You can't tell how it is; the evidence is divided.

MAN.

There is only one grade of men; they are all contemptible. The judge may seem to be a superior creature so long as he keeps at a distance, for I have never known one who was not constantly trying to look wise and grave; but when you know him, you find there is nothing remarkable about him except a plug hat, a respectable coat, and a great deal of vanity, induced by the servility of those who expect favors.

[1] who: 1883 but who

OPPORTUNITY.

You hear a great many persons regretting lack of opportunity. If every man had opportunity for his desires, this would be a nation of murderers and disgraced women.

EXPECTATION.

Always be ready for that which you do not expect. Nothing that you expect ever happens. You have perhaps observed that when you are waiting for a visitor at the front door, he comes in at the back, and surprises you.

WOMAN'S WORK.

A woman's work is never done, as the almanacs state, for the reason that she does not go about it in time to finish it.

THE GREATEST OF THESE IS CHARITY.

If you cannot resist the low impulse to talk about people, say only what you actually know, instead of what you have heard. And, while you are about it, stop and consider whether you are not in need of charity yourself.

NEIGHBORS.

Every man over-estimates his neighbors, because he does not know them so well as he knows himself. A sensible man despises himself because he knows what a contemptible creature he is. I despise Lytle Biggs, but I happen to know that his neighbors are just as bad.

VIRTUE.

Men are virtuous because the women are; women are virtuous from necessity.

ASHAMED OF THE TRUTH.

I believe I never knew anyone who was not ashamed of the truth. Did you ever notice that a railroad company numbers its cars from 1,000, instead of from 1?

A LETTER FROM MR. BIGGS

KNOWING ONLY ONE OF THEM.

We are sometimes unable to understand why a pretty little woman marries a fellow we know to be worthless; but the fellow, who knows the woman better than we do, considers that he has thrown himself away. We know the fellow, but we do not know the woman.

AN APOLOGY.

I detest an apology. The world is full of people who are always making trouble and apologizing for it. If a man respects me, he will not give himself occasion for apology. An offence cannot be wiped out in that way. If it could, we would substitute apologies for hangings. I hope you will never apologize to me; I should regard it as evidence that you had wronged me.

OLDEST INHABITANTS.

The people of Smoky Hill are only fit for oldest inhabitants. In thirty or forty years from now, there will be a great demand for reminiscences of the pioneer days. I recommend that they pre-serve extensive data for the only period in their lives when they can hope to attract attention.

Be good enough, sir, to regard me, as of old, your friend,

L. BIGGS.

To NED WESTLOCK, *Twin Mounds.*

XXXI

KILLED AT THE FORD

Jo ERRING and his wife had been separated a year and a half, during which time I saw Jo frequently, but never his wife, for I had grown to accept her husband's opinion that she was glad to be rid of him. I was often at the mill, and he often came to town, when I saw that he was growing gradually more desperate and wretched, and uneasy in his manner, but I was not prepared for the announcement which Damon Barker made to me by letter one day that he had secured a divorce from his wife, and that the case was more serious than I supposed. On investigating the matter I found that the divorce had been granted a few months before, on the ground of desertion, and so quietly was it done that but few knew of it. Jo had probably attended to the details on his visits to the town, and as it was a clear case the application was quietly granted by the judge in chambers, who happened to be familiar with all the circumstances.

I shall always believe that the unhappy man made the application in desperation, hoping it would bring his affairs to a crisis, but as Mateel never appeared to answer, he concluded she was satisfied with his course, which made him more sullen and resentful.

The Shepherds were seldom seen since the difficulty, and it was thought that they were proud and haughty, so that but few went to their house, and these Mateel always avoided. Occasionally the minister was seen working about his place, but he never left it, and it was believed by a great many that he received financial help from Clinton Bragg.

Within a year Clinton Bragg had greatly improved. He no longer patronized his bottle, and he dressed better than before, and his temper was visibly better. Although I knew this, I did not

298

particularly remark it or his visits to the Shepherds', for he had been a frequent visitor there from the time he came to the country, which I had always regarded simply as an annoyance to Jo; therefore my surprise may be imagined when I received a note from Barker one morning, at the hands of Big Adam, stating that Bragg and Mateel were to be married that evening. I had not seen Jo since learning of the divorce, and at once resolved to go to the mill. Knowing Bragg's malicious nature, I was certain that he would drive by the ford on his return to Twin Mounds with Mateel, and I hoped that in some way I should be able to prevent Jo's seeing them. I cannot remember now whether I thought a sight of them would cause him a burst of grief or anger, but I was sure I could be of use to him in some way, and at once determined to leave for Fairview and spend the night at the mill.

The pity and friendliness I had formerly entertained for Mateel vanished with the messenger who brought me the letter announcing her contemplated marriage to Clinton Bragg, though my first feeling was of horror and indignation at a step which seemed so indelicate and cruel. I think that during that day I hated her more than I had ever hated Bragg, for I could make nothing out of it further than that she desired the ruin and disgrace of Jo. I even brought to mind incidents familiar to me to prove that she was malicious, cunning, and deceitful, and upbraided myself that I had not warned Jo of it long ago.

I intended to drive over early in the afternoon, but customers came in to detain me, and it was late before I left the office to get ready. I had walked about like a man in an uncomfortable dream all day and could do nothing, for the more closely I applied myself to whatever I was about, the less I accomplished. Tiresome men I did not care to see, but whom I could not very well avoid, came in one after another, and I became so nervous at their appearance as to be almost helpless. When at last I started for the house, a thousand voices seemed to be urging me to hurry, and I ran like a madman to complete my simple preparations for the trip. Once on the road, I lashed the horses into a run, but in spite of this I seemed to make only slow progress, like a man in a troubled dream pursued by devils. It became so dark when I was half way that in the creek valleys I was compelled to get out and lead the horses, and when I was yet a long way from Fairview, the dull tolling of the great bell in the steeple of the church startled me.

It was a wild night in April,[1] with a storm threatening, and the hawks and owls flew almost in my face in their hurry to find shelter. A single black cloud, which was gathering in the south when I started, had overspread the heavens, resulting in almost inky darkness, and gusts of wind come dashing upon me with such sudden fury, following a dead calm, that the horses tried to take the bits in their teeth and run away from it.

The bell continued to toll at intervals, not distinctly, but only as you remember noises after a stormy night, and once I thought I heard a great number of strokes in quick succession, as though an alarm were being sounded. By this time I was travelling on a high divide where I knew the road to be safe, and urging the horses again into quicker speed, they ran as if they, too, had heard the alarm from the bell. If I was frightened at the fearful speed I was travelling, I thought of the howling winds behind me, which seemed to be always overtaking and passing me to make mischief beyond; as I passed the occasional houses I saw the people, attracted by the noise of my wheels, run to the windows, and, flattening their faces against the panes, peer out into the night. I wondered why they did not come out and follow me, and, half convinced that they would, I determined to beat them to the mill and lashed the horses into greater speed.

When at last I arrived at the mill everything seemed so quiet and safe that I was ashamed of my alarm, and after hitching the horses at the gate I walked up to the house, trying to recover my composure. The house dog, which I had known all his life, dashed at me in the greatest fury when I came up to the door, and his old companion, the house cat, screamed out on seeing me, and dashed away as if pursued. Everything was wrong, and there were wild cries and alarms in the wind, which was now blowing furiously.

A light burned in the front room, and a fire in the grate, but going in I found the room empty. Even the fire dashed at me with puffs of smoke, and the lamp burned low without cause. I found

[1] April: 1883 June

300

the room in the greatest confusion, and Jo's bed, which had been brought down from the upper part of the house, was in disorder, as though it had been lately used. I went into all the other rooms, calling the name of Jo, but I found them dark and silent. I walked out into the yard and called him, but the dog dashed at me again as though I were a robber, and would not recognize my voice. The water pouring over the dam, which had lulled me to sleep a hundred times, roared to-night, and I will swear that the wind was sobbing at every door and window when I returned to the house. Ill at ease I went to the door and called again, but the wind took up the sound of my voice and hurried off with it into the darkness of the woods.

Hoping that Jo would soon return I sat down by the open fire, but I saw such faces in it that they made me shudder, and I tried to listen for his approaching footsteps, but the wind had turned into a fierce cry of agony or vengeance, I could not tell which, and I could hear nothing else. Impatiently taking up a book I thought to read, but the first lines were of murder and of blood, and I threw it down, cursing the dog, the book, and the storm. Occasionally the rain came dashing down on the roof, preceded by great drops which seemed to me like tears shed by a pitying heaven, and then the rain ceased again, as if the elements were not yet ready for a bad night.

While trying to decide whether to go out and hunt for Jo, or wait quietly for his return, the door suddenly burst open, and my uncle came in, carrying Mateel in his arms, as easily as though she were a child. Going straight to the bed, without looking to the right or to the left, and apparently without seeing me, he gently laid her down, and, falling on his knees, passionately kissed the pale face. As he kneeled over her, he sobbed and cried aloud, as he had done on the night she went away, but, recollecting himself, he roughly wiped away his tears, and tenderly contemplated the insensible woman before him, for she seemed to be in a faint. I thought that could the devils he told about as haunting the cave fully realize his abject wretchedness, they would have been awed into respectful silence, and allowed the tender symphony to find its way to his bleeding heart.

He was in such excitement that I was almost afraid to speak to him, for his eyes were wild and fierce, his hair dishevelled like a madman's, and his clothing in such disorder that I thought he had been long out in the storm. As he turned and saw me, he cried out fiercely: —

"She belongs to me, and I have protected her honor! The dog whose ambition it was to disgrace me through her weakness is dead!"

He was a giant in physical stature, and every muscle quivered with excitement. I thought that had he been called upon to rescue his wife from a dozen men in his present state, he would have undertaken and accomplished it, and I shuddered to think what had befallen the one man against him. I had never noticed it there before, but the tolling of the great bell at Fairview could be distinctly heard.

When I stood up and looked at Mateel, I drew back in horror at the change in her appearance. Her form was wasted and thin, and her face so pale that I feared she was dead. Instead of wearing a bridal dress, her apparel was of black material, which made her look more ghastly.

"Oh! Jo," I said, "what have you done?"

"This," he answered, looking first at Mateel's motionless form on the bed, and then coming toward me. "This: I picked up Clinton Bragg from his seat beside Mateel as they came through the woods by the ford, and strangled him as I would strangle a dog. I held him out at arm's length until he was limp and dead, and threw his carcass into the brush. Then, taking Mateel in my arms, I lashed the devilish horse until he ran away through the timber, when I waded the creek, and came here!"

It was a short but terrible story, and his tragic telling of it so impressed me that I almost cheered him, knowing the wrong he had suffered.

Mateel still lay quietly on the bed, occasionally moaning, and Jo went to her again, and lovingly caressed her, as he might have done had she been his lawful wife in temporary distress, and I thought his manner was softened by contemplating her misery, for when he spoke again it was half in apology.

"I have always feared this, and although I have done an awful

302

thing, I could not do less." He walked toward me and stood by my side. "Bragg pursued me with relentless hate, and he is as much to blame as I am. They might have known I would not submit to this cruelty; it was more than I could bear, and I could not help doing what I did."

I had been oppressed for a long time with a vague fear, though I was never clear as to what it was, that something dreadful would come of the separation, and as I sat there, looking from the helpless woman lying on the bed to the wretched man walking the floor, I almost concluded that the murder of Clinton Bragg was the result I had expected.

"There is so much wickedness in my heart to-night that I am proud of what I have done," Jo said, stopping in his walk, as though he had been thinking it over and had come to that conclusion. "I cannot regret it; the murder of that man has given me the only relief I have known in three years, and I feel like calling at the houses of honest people, and crying, 'A man who deserved death is dead!' Even the wind was crying fiercely for revenge when he was seated beside my wife intent on his unnatural and fiendish purpose, but it is quiet now, and sobbing in pity for me. I never insulted my manhood nor mankind by trying to curb my fierce passion when I heard he intended to pass my house with Mateel. I resolved to murder him, and all honest men will say I could have done nothing less!"

He began pacing up and down the room again, at one moment a fierce demon, and at another a man softened by tears, and I saw by his manner that he realized that Mateel must not remain there, for he went over to her side, and fondly kissed her, as if for the last time. Perhaps he thought when he took her in his arms in the woods that his troubles would end after crossing the stream and entering his own door, and that they would live in peace thereafter, but he realized now that his action had only tightened the coils of misfortune about him.

"She would despise me for this deed if she knew it," he said. "I have killed her husband, and she does not belong here. Take her to her mother before she wakens and reproaches me, and then come back to me."

303

Realizing the force of the suggestion, I answered that my team was hitched in front of the house, and without further words he picked Mateel up, and carried her out. Although able to sit up, she did not seem to be conscious of what had happened, but sat moaning and crying beside me when I drove away, leaving Jo standing at the gate.

The night was very dark, but the wind had gone down, and I was only able to find my way by the frequent flashes of livid lightning. After I passed the ford, and entered the woods, in spite of myself I began to watch the road-side for the body of the dead man, hoping that he was only stunned, and had crawled away. I had stopped for the lightning to flash again to show me the road through the trees, and when it came I saw Bragg prostrate beside me, so close to the road that I feared the horses had trampled upon him. In the instant I saw that he was lying on his back; his arms thrown out on either side, and that his face was white in death. In looking at him I had neglected to observe the road, and sat there waiting for another flash. With it came the rain, and seeing my way I started the impatient horses at a brisk trot.

When I stopped in front of Mr. Shepherd's house, I saw that a light still burned within, and, hurriedly securing the horses, I took Mateel in my arms, and rapped at the door. Mr. Shepherd came in answer to it, bearing a light in his hand, and, seeing me with my strange burden, staggered back in alarm.

"There has been an accident," I said, "but your daughter is not hurt; only frightened, and in a faint."

He took his child tenderly in his arms, and with the assistance of his wife tried to revive her.

"I must hurry away," I said, dreading to tell them all. "You will hear further news to-morrow."

Neither of them said a word, but I believed they knew what the accident was, for they acted as though they had been waiting for it, and were not surprised that their unhappy child had been returned to them alone.

The lightning by this time came in such rapidly following flashes that I had no difficulty in driving at a smart gait, and when I approached the ford my eyes were again drawn against my will

304

to the prostrate form under the trees. It had not been disturbed, and I hurried past it, and into the house, where Jo was sitting by the fire with his hat on, ready to go out. He looked up when I came in, but made no inquiries, and, buttoning his coat, said he was ready to go. In response to my curious look he replied: —

"There is but one thing to do; to notify the officers, and finish this night's work in jail. I have thoroughly considered the matter while you were away, and that is my decision. When I heard that this marriage was to take place, I resolved to do what I have done to-night, and arranged my business for it by leasing the mill. The man who is to operate it is my present assistant, and all the necessary arrangements have been made; I only hope now that I shall be disposed of as soon as possible. I do not regret what I have done, now that it is done, and the most pleasant moment of my life was when I clutched the throat of the man who has been relentlessly pursuing me for five years. He could not be induced to give up his design, and I could do nothing else than murder him. I have only lived for the past few months to guard Mateel against him, and now that she is no longer in danger, I am ready for the worst. When I looked into her face to-night, it startled me to see how she has failed since we separated. I shall always feel grateful to her that she was not dressed as a bride, but in mournful black. Always delicate, she is but a shadow now, and the marriage of Bragg to a woman who is but a puny invalid convinces me that he, at least, brought it about to revenge himself on me. He brought on the quarrel; I hope he is satisfied. I am sure only Mateel's weakness is to blame for her part in the affair, for marriage in her condition was mockery."

He appeared more contented and easy than he had been since the separation, like a man who had accomplished an object that had been his ambition for a long time, and sat down again, quite at ease, when he saw I was not yet ready to go, but was trying to dry my wet garments at the fire. I even thought he felt in good spirits, for he straightened himself in such a manner as to be comfortable in his chair, and beat a merry tattoo with the fingers of his hand which rested on the table.

When at last I was ready to start to town with him — I had

never thought of opposing him, he seemed so satisfied with the course he had marked out — he collected a few articles which he said might be of use to him during his imprisonment, and, making them into a bundle, extinguished the light, and followed me, after locking the door and handing me the key.

"I shall never see the place again, of course, nor do I want to see it," he said. "I have had a hard time of it here, from first to last, and for all my work I get nothing but a ride to jail to be locked up for murder. A splendid fellow, I, that could work to no better purpose. I thought once I was something of a genius, and rather a remarkable fellow, but like all other fools I am found out. There is one satisfaction in it all; I was not all my life finding out my mistake. I am now but twenty-six; I have known greater fools than I am, at seventy. I am glad there is a storm; I like to be out in it."

On the way he kept talking in a half-boisterous manner, though I could detect a mournful strain through it all. Once he wondered if there was a possibility that Bragg had only been stunned, and, stopping the horses, wanted to go back to see. But after thinking about it awhile, he said: —

"No danger of that. He fell out of my grasp as limp as a rag. I held him at arm's length to represent a gibbet, and my fingers were the rope, for the brute deserved hanging. I was determined that he should die a dishonorable death as well as I. When he is found, there will be marks about his throat as though he had been hanged; his tongue will protrude from his mouth, and his eyes start from their sockets, as they say men look who have been hanged. My only regret is that there was not a crowd present to witness his dog's death. But the crowd will gather around him to-morrow, and be horrified at his appearance."

Several times he described with pleasure the horrible tragedy in the woods near the ford, hoarsely laughing as he told how Bragg had writhed and struggled in his grasp, and once he asked me to feel the bunch of muscle on the strong arm which had righted his wrong. He told how he had skulked under the trees waiting for their approach, dodging from one to another when he saw them in the road; how he had hidden behind a tree until they were be-

306

side him; how Bragg had trembled in fear when he felt his fingers
about his throat; how fast and furious the vicious horse ran crash-
ing through the underbrush when he lashed him with a keen
hickory withe cut for the purpose, and how he almost shouted in
exultation when he had Mateel in his arms. He recited all the
sickening particulars with so much pleasure that I feared he was
out of his head, and occupied myself in mentally making notes of
what he said to prove that he was not responsible for his act. At
another time he cried out impatiently: —

"Why don't you applaud what I have done? You have not said
a word all evening, though you usually cry, 'Brave Jo!' when I
have accomplished a purpose, but you seem ashamed of me
now."

"Oh, Jo," I replied, "you have done an awful thing, and while
I know you were wronged by Bragg, I shudder to think of the
consequences. I cannot approve of this act, Jo, the first one you
ever did at which I could not cry, 'Brave Jo!' "

"Can you, my only friend, wish that Bragg were alive again?"
he answered, "and asleep in the arms of Mateel, with me alone in
my unhappy home? Surely it is better as it is; I should have killed
myself if I had not killed Bragg, and you must say — you cannot
help it — that he deserved death as much as I. He deserved it
more, for he is the cause of it all; but we shall both give up our
lives in the tragedy. I took no more from him than the law will
take from me, and although he is to blame he makes no greater
sacrifice than I do. I would not be unjust to a dog; I have not been
unjust to him. If there can be pity in such a business, I am more
deserving of it than he."

I did not dare to express my real sentiments for fear of encouraging him, as I felt he had fairly expressed it when he said he
could do nothing else than murder Clinton Bragg. He had pursued him for years in the face of repeated warnings, and knowing
Jo's desperation, his action in inducing Mateel to take the step at a
time when she was weak and sick could have been nothing else
than wickedness and villainy. But I said as little as possible
during the drive, and occupied myself in devising plans for his
escape. I believed that Bragg's unpopularity would be of benefit

in the trial, as well as all the circumstances of the case, and felt certain that the people would generally be in sympathy with Jo.

When we arrived in the town it was as still as the country we had just left, and rattling loudly at the sheriff's door, whose residence was in the upper part of the jail, the officer soon appeared, and hearing with surprise our mission, he locked me up with Jo at my own request, as I desired to spend the night with him. A few moments later his establishment was astir, and in half an hour we heard a posse start off in a wagon, which rattled and jolted in a frightful manner, to bring in the body. The news seemed to spread rapidly, for by climbing up at the grated window I saw lights in several directions where there were none before, and two or three curious people had already appeared in the yard.

XXXII

THE TWIN MOUNDS JAIL

THERE had never been a murder in Fairview before, or the sight of a man who had died a violent death, and when I looked out of the grated windows a few hours after midday — for we both slept long and soundly once we were in the hard and cheerless prison beds — I saw that the news had spread rapidly, for the town was already full of people, curious to look at the body and talk of the tragedy. A misty rain was falling, a continuation of the storm of the night before, and a fog spread over the town, and a crowd of people was collected in front of the jail, looking curiously up at the windows, as though they were likely to catch a glimpse of the culprit. When one of the number went up to the court-house, his place in the mud and mire in front of the jail was immediately taken by someone who came from the court-house, and I supposed that the dead man was on exhibition there. I scanned the upturned faces eagerly for looks of sympathy for Jo, for from my perch I could look into them without being seen, but I could only make out that the people were no more than curious. Occasionally a knot of men gathered about one of their number while he expressed an opinion, and though I could not hear all that was said, I distinguished enough to convince me that there was no regret that Clinton Bragg was dead.

Late in the afternoon I left the jail by the entrance used by the sheriff's family, without attracting attention, and went into the court-house, where the body was on exhibition. The crowd then present did not know my relation to Jo, with which circumstance I was pleased, and I looked at the sight as any other idler would. He was lying in the middle of the assembly room, on a wide plank, and I judged the coroner's jury had not yet assembled, for it was still in the condition in which it was found.

309

The clothing was wet from lying out in the rain, and I was certain the face retained the expression it wore when I had passed it in the woods, for it was horrible to look at. A livid mark ran round the neck, showing the prints of fingers; the tongue protruded from the mouth, and the eyes started from their sockets, precisely as would have been the case had Clinton Bragg been hanged, and altogether the sight was so horrible that I wondered the people did not leave it in terror, as I did, and hurry away, for the sight made me sick and faint. But the people continued to arrive by every road, and hurry to the court-house, and then to the jail, to look up curiously at the windows, and I was so anxious to avoid them and their questions that, after a few minutes with Martin, I hurried back to the jail, and was again admitted, where I found Jo still lying about in his night-clothes, apparently very comfortable and unconcerned. He had been asleep most of the day, lounging about in an easy way precisely as I have since known men to do who spent a rainy Sunday in their rooms. The fierce manner which had distinguished him the night before was gone, and in its place was a sort of contentment that was very surprising under the circumstances. He had but little to say, making no inquiries, when I returned, as to where I had been, and, a short time after the lamps were brought in for the night, he excused himself, and lying down on his cot went to sleep, after pleasantly wishing me good-night.

The main road leading toward the Fairview country ran past the outer wall of the jail, a part of it being built on the street line, and for hours I heard the wagons rattling past, filled with crowds of men returning home, who were sitting close together and talking in low tones. I turned down the light, and, climbing up to the single window which looked that way, watched them, and tried to conjecture what the verdict would be, but their curiosity was satisfied, and they were now only intent on getting home and repeating the story to others, who would in turn repeat it, and spread the news through the woods, over the prairies, and into the valleys, where it would be talked of and wondered at, and be voted the greatest wonder, and the greatest horror, that ever had happened.

310

The coroner and a jury examined the body the next day, and when it was learned that the only witness of the affray was very ill, it was agreed to adjourn the inquest until a time when she was better, and Clinton Bragg was buried in a grave which was at first thought to be temporary, but it proved his final resting place, as the remains were never disturbed.

At Jo's earnest request — it was the rule anyway, I believe — the jailer allowed none of the curious to see him, and after he was locked up I slept there every night. Fortunately there were only a few petty offenders in the jail, which gave us an entire room to ourselves, and bringing in furniture and beds from the house, I made the place as comfortable as possible. I covered the walls with pictures, and scarcely a day passed that something was not left with me for the prisoner. The sheriff being a kindly man, and an old friend of ours, he trusted me fully, so that had I been disposed I could have easily released Jo, or furnished him means of escape.

I have thought that the sheriff often looked at me in surprise that I did not take advantage of the liberty given me, and get him away, and he often went into the cell himself to talk cheerfully and hopefully. In many of the packages sent me were fire-arms, drills, files, and chisels, as well as little articles of comfort, and in almost every one notes written in heavy hands saying that no harm should come to Jo, but we handed these over to the officer in return for his kindness, who good-naturedly guessed with us who sent them.

Jo seemed to be more contented than since the night he came to me with the fatal letter, and spent his days in reading, and lounging about. I thought of him as a man taking a long-contemplated rest from weary work, and as one who thoroughly enjoyed his ease. Although there was always something of sadness in his manner, he was more like himself than since we were boys, and we spent our evenings so pleasantly together that I often regretted that we could not have been as contented as we were without the commission of so great a crime.

Before he went to prison he was unable to sleep at night, but now he retired to his bed early, and slept soundly. Indeed, frequently he did not waken until the middle of the day, as if he were making up for lost time, and often spoke thankfully of the circumstance that he could enjoy his rest again, as he did when a boy. His manner was so gentle that I thought of him as one who had been purified by great suffering, and if I had loved him before, in his misfortune and danger I loved him a thousand times more. After he had gone to sleep at night, it was my custom to toss about for a long while, thinking how we could avoid the consequences of his crime, and, after a troubled night, get up early in the morning to talk over and over again with those I had employed to advise me, for Jo would not see them. They had the greatest hope, and took unusual interest in the case, and I understood their policy would be to delay a trial as long as possible, when opportunities for his release would be plentiful enough. When they were finally forced to trial, they could at least secure a jury that would fail to agree, and as no one had seen the murder, they hoped to be able to establish that Bragg had fallen out of his buggy in fright when Jo appeared before him, thus permitting the wheels to run across his neck.

Damon Barker came to town on the second afternoon following the murder, accompanied by Big Adam, who carried an immense club of green hickory with a knot on the end, as though he expected a few friends would attack the jail and release the prisoner, and during the grave interview between his master and myself, he kept critically examining the club, squinting along it to see if it were properly proportioned, or hefting it from the little end. With a piece of chalk he marked out a rude figure of a man on the wall, and after writing "Officer" over it in great capital letters, he stood off, and measured the distance he would have to stand from it in order to do effective service with his club. After this point was settled, he calculated by experiment where a man of the size of the figure could be injured most by striking, and having decided that the head was the place, he made an X with the chalk at the point selected, and practised until he could hit that spot every time. He did this with so much seriousness, and we were all so serious that day, that we paid little attention to him. When Barker inquired what time he could see Jo, and I answered "To-night,"

Big Adam said, in a voice hoarser than usual, "The earlier the better, and let those who stand in the way look out for their heads!" at the same time ominously shaking his stick of hickory. When informed that there was to be no rescue, he was very much disappointed and was silent the remainder of the day.

Barker was never a man of words, and he expressed no opinion about the matter, although he frequently said that at any time I needed him, I had only to say the word, no matter what the service might be. If he was at a loss to understand the difference between Jo's case and his own, he did not mention it, and held his peace. When he went to the prison to see Jo in the evening, I thought his word of greeting was almost a sob, as I remember him on the night he came to claim Agnes, but he soon recovered himself, and we spent the evening quite pleasantly. Big Adam, who accompanied us, spent his time in critically examining the bars at the windows, and in testing their strength, and he apparently became convinced that there was little hope in that direction, and that the only thing to do was to storm it from the outside. During the evening he wrote a note and asked me to deliver it to the sheriff, and after he went away I looked at it. It began, "My opinion of the officer," followed by the largest number of blasphemous words I have ever seen collected, though they had no reference to each other, every one being complete in itself, as an expression of hate. There were also a great many vile words mixed in with the blasphemous ones, and at the bottom he signed his name in full, whereby I came into possession of the fact that his full name was John Adam Casebolt.

At this time I cannot remember how long it was before Bragg's father came, but within an hour after his arrival he walked quietly into the office, and, after waiting my pleasure, asked me to tell the story of his son's death. He was a distressed sort of a man, as though he had had a great deal of trouble in his life, and I honestly tried to tell the circumstances of the death without prejudice. Of Bragg's systematic persecution of Jo; of his aimless excursions past his house; of his insolence and overbearance, I spoke at considerable length, and detailed numerous instances when I knew he had passed the mill at midnight,

313

though he had not been at the Shepherds'. I told him of his son's renewed attentions after the separation, though he had been the cause of it, and I expressed the opinion that he had brought about the marriage, not for love of Mateel, but for revenge on a man who had never harmed him, for she was such a hopeless invalid that marriage with anyone was the merest farce.

He made no replies to anything I said, but occasionally asked a question to make a point clearer, and when I had finished, he thanked me for my trouble, and went out, walking past the jail on his way back to the hotel, and I thought he peered curiously up at the windows, as if he were anxious to see Jo.

I saw him a great deal after that, and knew that he was in consultation with an attorney, but he talked to no one else. After remaining two or three weeks, he quietly disappeared, and it was learned that he had returned home, leaving his case in the hands of the public prosecutor.

When I told Jo of my strange visitor, he was much interested, and referred to him as a "poor fellow," saying it was too bad that he had travelled so far on such a sad journey. He inquired carefully after his personal appearance, his manners, etc., and I almost expected that he would ask that he be invited to see him.

It was my custom to leave the prison at an early hour in the morning and not return again until night, except to call cheerfully to Jo as I passed that way, but I always spent my evenings with him, and greatly enjoyed them, because we were never disturbed.

When I came round to be admitted, Jo was always waiting for me, and one evening, when he had been unusually thoughtful, he said to me: —

"You remember I told you once of the haunted cave where the people went, and heard the sweetest strains of music, but which was soon broken into by a hideous tumult. I often visit the place now in my dreams, or in my fancy, and it has a new attraction: Someone is lost there, and there is no hope of a rescue. This is such a lonely place that sometimes when I lie here through the day waiting for you, I visit the place when I am awake. I am very familiar with the rugged path which leads through the dark

314

ravine to its mouth, and when the day is bad I never fail to go. Although it is horrible, there is a certain fascination about it I am unable to resist.

"When last I visited it, I did not hear the music at all, but instead someone crying, which was drowned by the usual tumult. When this had subsided, I heard the same voice distinctly crying, 'Help! help! I am lost,' which so excited me that I awoke. Since then, every time I fall asleep I visit the cave, and after sitting a long while in silence, suddenly I hear the same agonizing cry, 'Help! help! I am lost.' Then come such pitiful sobs that I awake again. I have come to regard the man lost in the cave as myself, and while waiting to hear him call I have tried to invent a plan for his rescue, and wondered if you and Barker would not help me. Perhaps this is a premonition of my future; it may be that after I am dead, it will be my punishment to wander in a dark and gloomy place, unable to die, but forever calling, 'Help! help! I am lost.'

"I have thought, too, that it is possible, when I am sick and tired from wandering about and calling for help, always expecting that rescue is near at hand, that suddenly a light so great as to dazzle my poor eyes will appear; that I shall be permitted to see a beautiful place, with running streams and shady paths under the trees, and that I shall realize that it is the eternal city.

"As I look, Mateel and Bragg, attired in raiment befitting their new condition, will appear, happy in their perfected love. My imprisonment in that awful place will have unmanned me so much that I shall cry to them, 'Help! help! I am lost!' but they will not be permitted to hear, and when I stagger toward the blessed light, the figures will disappear, and I shall fall on my face in the darkness."

He always talked of the cave and the vision in such a mournful, hopeless way, that it greatly affected me, but he would soon rally, and become cheerful again, as though I had a right to expect that of him in return for my attention. He talked in this strain a great deal, and seemed to take more interest [1] in it than in anything else, or it may have been a fascination which he

[1] interest: 1883 pleasure

315

could not avoid. Every evening when I came in he had a new experience with the cave or the vision to relate, and I shudder yet when I remember his descriptions of the man who was always wandering in the dark and awful place his fancy had created, and who was always calling for help which never came.

Although he was as much a mystery to me as ever, I never looked at him that I could not see his love for me. I did no more for him than anyone would have done under the same circumstances, but he talked about it a great deal, and expressed his gratitude that he had one friend in the world, in spite of his disgrace and crime.

Very often I assured him of the pleasure it gave me to be of service to him, and the keen regrets I felt that I could not do more, and at these times he turned his head away, and I believed that tears were in his eyes.[2] I can never explain the sympathy and affection I felt for him while he was in prison, for, knowing him as I did, I could not help feeling that he was justified, and when I saw that he took no interest in the plans I proposed for his escaping the consequences, hope died within me, and I felt that when the time came, he would acknowledge his guilt, and ask me as his last request to attend him on the scaffold. Further than his remark that he would give his own life for the one he had taken, he but barely mentioned the tragedy in any way, and seemed only to be waiting to keep his oath.

Inasmuch as the coroner's jury had not yet assembled to listen to evidence in the case, the only witness being too ill to attend, I could not conjecture what course he would adopt when called upon to express himself, and I was afraid to ask him. He would not see the attorneys I had selected to advise me, saying in excuse that he was not ready, or that whatever I did represented him, so that I seemed to be the culprit rather than Jo, for I worried more about it, and was oftener in despair.

Only once during his confinement did he refer to the causes leading to the tragedy in the woods. I had been reading to him until far into the night, with the light between us as we lay on

---

[2] I believed . . . eyes: 1883 I could hear his tears falling on the floor.

the rough prison cots, when he interrupted me by inquiring: —

"Are you quite sure that you fully forgive me for my desperate crime?"

"Yes, Jo."

"I might have been a credit to you instead of a disgrace had I acted differently," he said, turning on his side to look at me. "When you were reading just now I thought of the afternoon in Fairview when we went out to the hayloft to talk of our future, after it was announced that I was to go to Damon Barker's to live, and I thought that while we have turned out very much as we hoped we should, you were brave and patient in your sorrow, while I was utterly cast down by mine and ruined. Do you forgive me for that?"

"Yes, Jo; everything. I love you so much that I cannot think of your faults."

He turned on his back again, and remained quiet so long that I, too, thought of the Sunday afternoon in Fairview, and of what he had said. Jo was evidently thinking of the same thing, for at last he continued: —

"I remember of your mother saying to me once that she believed you and I would grow up into brave and honorable men; men who would love their wives and children instead of treating them as they were treated in Fairview, and I feel very guilty now that I realize that she was mistaken in her opinion of me. It would have been genuine bravery had I conquered my horror of the letter, my hate for Clinton Bragg, and made Mateel love me in spite of everything; but I did not know what the word meant then, though I do now, and your mother probably meant something like that. My boyhood was so wretched that I expected relief from wretchedness when I was married, but perhaps I should have known that unhappiness attends every condition in life, and that bravery and nobility consists in forgiving and forgetting, together with gentleness and capacity. My life has been one long mistake; I should think you would find it hard to forgive that, after expecting so much of me."

"No, Jo; not at all hard. If you are entitled to charity from me,

I gave it without knowing it, for I only think of you to regret that a man so worthy has been so unfortunate. I never reproached you in my life."

"Although I believe you forgive me fully," he continued, "I cannot forgive myself, though I confess my weakness, and say that I always did the best I could. I conquered everything except shame over the contents of the letter and hate at the sight of Bragg. These dragged me down as discontent dragged John Westlock down; perhaps any man could be ruined if attacked at the right place."

Wiser men than you, Jo, are of that opinion, and I regarded it as the most eloquent defence he had ever made. Those who believe in their own strength have great charity for themselves and none at all for others, but those of us who are more candid, and learned in the world's affairs, acknowledge our own weakness in admitting the weakness of others.

"I am satisfied now that I made a mistake in thinking of love as it should be, not as it really is, and I unwisely built on that foundation, but I blame no one for it; a man who is ignorant should submit to the penalties without complaint. But I shall always think that I should have been very contented had it turned out as I expected; I shall always justify myself with the belief that had Mateel brought as much enthusiasm into our marriage contract as I did, we should have been of great use to each other. I hope you will not think hard of me if I say that she had the experience which I should have had, while I had the innocence and faith in marriage which a wife should possess."

He had little to say after that, and tossed about uneasily in his bed after I put out the light, which was unusual, for I had frequently remarked with surprise that he slept well in the jail, and seemed greatly refreshed by it. Perhaps he had never permitted himself to think of his wife until that evening since he had struggled with Bragg in the woods, and the indiscretion had brought on his old trouble, for if I dozed off, and wakened again, I found him pacing up and down the floor, as he had done so many nights in the house at the mill when he lived alone in it. As I watched him I tried to compute the number of weary miles

318

he had travelled in this manner since the separation; up and down, from the right to the left, carrying his aching and troubled head, which refused him peace night and day; thinking, thinking, thinking; up and down from the right to the left; so the long road was travelled, growing more painful and difficult every day. I followed the road he had been travelling to where it ended and encountered a jail, in which Jo Erring's hope and ambition, the pride and comfort of my boyhood, were locked up, with my old friend, changed but little, pacing wearily up and down to see that there was no escape. Oh, Jo, my dearest friend, is there nothing I can do to lighten your sorrow? Must I watch you travelling a road which grows more suggestive of the damp of graves with every day's journey without putting out a hand to help you? Will you continue to put me off with no other reply than tears when I offer to help you until we enter the churchyard together, and I come out alone?

Getting up from my bed, I joined him in the walk, putting my arm through his, and as we [3] paced up and down, encountering a cruel stone wall at every turn, I bitterly accused myself that I had not been with him more during his trouble, but when I mentioned it I knew that he believed I had done all I could, though he did not speak a word, and I could not see his face; I knew it, though I did not know why. Up and down, from the right to the left; I thought half the night had passed before he returned to his bed, and even then I was convinced that he ceased walking more out of consideration for me than because he was tired. When the first rays of morning light came straggling into the dismal place I wakened again, but Jo was not in bed; he had climbed up to the grated window, and was looking out in the direction of Fairview, motionless as a statue. What was in his mind will never be known, but I have always believed that it was a longing to see his wife and the house at the mill. I fell into a light sleep again, and when it was broad daylight, he was still looking longingly toward Fairview, the little world in which his simple life had been passed; where he had created and destroyed, and where he hoped to find rest at last in the shadow of the old church.

[3] we: 1883 I

XXXIII

REAPING THE WHIRLWIND

AFRAID to trust my own judgment with reference to Jo, whom I always thought of now as standing in the shadow of a scaffold, about four weeks after he went to jail, I resolved to visit the mill on Bull River and solicit Damon Barker's advice, which I knew would be friendly and sensible. He was a man of excellent judgment, and though he had been to Twin Mounds but once since the trouble, I knew he was ready at any time to aid Jo, as he had said, no difference what necessity might require, and that he was only waiting a summons, trusting to me to bring it. I felt sure that Jo's intention was to admit his guilt when called upon, and suffer the penalty, and I was not satisfied that I had done enough to dissuade him from the intention. Barker had great influence with him, and for this reason I sought his counsel and advice.

I intended to start in the middle of the afternoon, hoping to reach the mill by nightfall, and return early the next day, and an hour before my departure I went into the jail to announce to Jo that I would be away during the night. It was the first night I had been out of his company since his confinement in the prison, and I was therefore surprised that he seemed rather pleased with the prospect, though he apologized for it by saying that I had been there so long that I would enjoy a night out. He seemed to know that I was going to Barker's to talk about him, for he asked me to thank him and Agnes for any good they might find it in their hearts to say of him; and he said over and over again how kind we all were, and how much trouble we had been to on his account.

"You must not go away feeling down at heart, or ill at ease, but cheerful," he said, when I confessed that I was going to

Barker's in his behalf. "I will tell you something that will please you. I have studied over this matter a great deal during the past few weeks, and have come to a conclusion that will relieve us all. I will only say now that it will end all confusion and worry, and that it is the very best thing that can be done. I know that you have confidence in my judgment, and will be content to wait until you return, when you shall know all. It is not a plan that will cause you more trouble, but one that will be a relief to you, therefore be as happy as you can while away, and carry my kindest wishes to Agnes and her father. Tell them that I am well, and that in a little while we shall be through worrying over this matter, for I have hit upon a plan to relieve us of it. It is sure to work, tell them, and that they need not fear as to that. I may say it is the only thing that can be done, which you will be glad to hear, for it is sometimes hard to hit upon the right plan, but after a great deal of thought I have it. You feel better now, do you not?"

I answered him that I did, which was the case, for I believed that while I was away during the day he was thinking, and hoped that he had hit upon something that would meet with the approval of all his friends. Probably it was an escape, and a life in some distant country, where I would join him in course of time, or perhaps a plea of self-defence, backed by circumstances of which I knew nothing, but at any rate I was sure the plan was a good one, for Jo did not often make mistakes in such matters, and I felt a relief of which I was greatly in need. I determined at once to bring Barker back with me to hear the plan, and aid in its execution.

"You look happier to-day," he said, taking both my hands in his own, "than I have seen you in a long while. I am very glad of that, and I hope I, too, look pleasant, for I am sure the plan is a good one. Do I not look much as I did when we were happy boys together; when I was your good friend, and loved you more than anyone else in the world? Look at me and answer."

I did as he requested, and saw that there was the old cheerfulness in his smile, as there had been the old tenderness in his voice.

"A little older, and a little paler," I replied, "but certainly you look more natural to me this moment than you have for four years. And you look more like my old friend, too; for when we were boys, and you told me of your friendship, you were so earnest and feeling that tears came into your eyes.[1] There are tears in your eyes now."[2]

He did not brush them[3] away, as I expected he would, but let them roll down his cheeks[4] and fall to the floor.

"I did not know there were tears in my eyes until you spoke," he said. "But they are only tears of gratitude that I am permitted to have one friend like you."

He still held both my hands, and looked at me in such a way that I thought he was thinking he had a bold piece of work to demand of me to effect his release — a part of his plan — and that I would undertake it without hesitating, no matter what the risk, as I would have done.

"It is as much as a man ought to expect during his life to realize a friendship as pure and unselfish as yours has always been for me, and I want to say while I am looking in your eyes — please do not say it is nothing, for it is a great deal — that you have been the one solace of a very unhappy man. I may not have deserved it, but it has been given to me, and I love you as a bad man ought to love a good wife who has been faithful to him through all his misdeeds. I am very wicked, and have a wicked heart, but you can have it to say that you had all the love there was in one man's life. All the tenderness in my rough nature has been given to you, and no one else has ever found welcome in my heart. No one, not even my father or mother, divided my affection for you. It is not much, but it is all I have."

I assured him it was a great deal, and that it had been a comfort to me from the day I began to remember.

"You are the only one who was ever thoughtful or kind to me, though I have always coveted such attention," he added. "I suppose I deserved all the neglect I have received — I hope not,

[1] eyes: 1883 eyes, as they are now.
[2] There . . . now: 1883 *wanting*
[3] them: 1883 his tears
[4] cheeks: 1883 cheek

but I cannot think anything else — and you brought the only ray of genuine sunshine that ever found its way into my desolate heart; without you I should have been friendless all my life. I hope I could have made myself worthy of friends had they come in my way, but they never came, and I have had no other object in life than to deserve your good opinion. I am afraid I can never repay you, but I am very thankful."

He was very earnest, but not sad, and I believed he was telling me this because when I came back there would be active work to do, and a long separation, and when I turned again to call the keeper to release me, Jo said for me to remember that it was all for the best.

"All for the best, I am certain," I replied.

"And do I look cheerful again, as though I felt that what I say is true?"

"I have not seen a pleasant smile on your face before in a long while," I said, "and I feel greatly encouraged. I hope my recollection of you will always be as you appear now." There was a mingled look of bravery and tenderness in his face which made me very fond of him. "I am sure the plan is a good one, for it has made us both happier already."

"I am glad to hear you say that," he said, putting his hand through the little wicket to bid me good-bye, when I was finally in the corridor, "and so it will turn out. But even if it did not meet your approval at first, you would not upbraid me, or think less of me than you do now?"

"No, Jo," I answered, for I thought that if ever a man was justified in breaking jail and hiding away in a place where he could make amends for his mistakes, he was. "I could not think less of you than I do, for even if my judgment should not accord with yours, I should believe it to be my own fault, and that I should finally discover that you were right. I have so much confidence in you that I am sure that the plan is a good one."

"I am glad to hear you say that," he repeated, "and so it will turn out. Good-bye."

How his hand trembled in mine! I thought it was joy over the prospect of once more being free, and I had so much confidence in the friendship of the sheriff, who stood beside me, that I had a mind to tell him that Jo had at last consented to take advantage of the opportunities he delighted to give him, and escape; I was so pleased with it all that I thought I must talk to someone, but, thinking better of it, I waved my hand gayly to the prisoner, and, passing out at the front door, was soon on my way to Fairview.

As I drove rapidly along the familiar road, I had a hundred pleasant conjectures of the morrow, when Jo would reveal to me the plan by which he was to be free. The one I fixed upon and took most pleasure in was an escape to some distant country, where I would follow him in a few months, and where we should live happily together the remainder of our lives. There was a rough rugged country beyond ours where hunted men went, and where no questions were asked, and I thought of our living together in a cabin on a mountain side, companions in toil and peace. I thought this plan might make it necessary for me to give up Agnes for a while, but her patience I knew was great, and she would think of me all the more kindly for the sacrifice I had made for love of Jo.

He had said there was nothing else to do; that surely meant a rapid flight to the mountains, for that was the speedy and the certain way out of the difficulty, and I almost rejoiced in it, for I determined to go with him at once, and leave my affairs to be settled up by Barker, who alone should know of my whereabouts. I even regarded it as a prospect of a happy relief from my weary work, and thought that while Jo would say it was best I should remain, and settle our joint affairs in person, I stoutly decided to go with him, and even planned how to get ready money for the purpose.

These thoughts so occupied my mind that I was surprised when I came in the vicinity of the mill, and also by the circumstance that it was growing dark, for I had taken no note of time. As was usually the case at that season of the year, the mill was in operation when I arrived a half hour after dark, and, hoping to find Agnes alone in the house, I dismounted at the side gate and went in. The evening being pleasant, the front door was wide open, and, stepping on the inside, I was debating whether they were not all down at the mill, when Agnes came out suddenly from the room, and stood beside me. It may have been surprise at her sudden appearance, but without thinking what I did, I put my arms about her, and kissed her.

"I have been in so much trouble of late," I said, still holding her in my arms, "and felt your absence so keenly, that I could not resist the temptation. I hope you will forgive me; I came on an important errand, but my distress has made me brave, and I cannot help showing how much I love you."

She was perfectly still, looking into my eyes, and I thought that, though it was the same sweet face, it was different from what it had ever been before; no longer the face of my patient friend, but the face of my sweetheart — a picture of a woman's perfect love.

"It has been so often necessary for you to forgive me — I always made so many mistakes, while you were so womanly — that you will forgive me once more for declaring, though I came on an errand in poor Jo's behalf, that I have loved you as man and boy for eight years; that you have been so necessary to me that I could not have lived but for the hope your friendship gave me. I have never been able to show you how dear you have been to me, I was always so awkward, but I show you my heart now, and declare what I may not have acted, that I have never had any other wish to live than that I might win you."

She attempted to speak, but I would not permit it, for I had not yet finished.

"When I was a boy, it was my hope of the future to become a worthy man, and prepare a home for homeless Agnes, who was always my friend, no matter how undeserving I was. In all my hard life, which has seemed like a night, you have been the kindly star which was always shining and bidding me hope. When your father came back to you, I feared that your happiness was so great that I could never again add to it, but even if this is so, I can no longer keep my secret. It has been crying out at its confinement for years, and I must tell you that I love you."

She remained silent and motionless so long that I began to fear that what I had said without believing was really true; that she was so happy with her father that she would never leave him, and that she was framing an answer that would not offend me.

"I have always known," she said at last, "that you loved me, and have always believed that sometime you would come to me and declare it, just as you have to-night. It was my only wish ungratified, for nothing was lacking besides that to complete my happiness."

I pressed her closer to me, and for the first time in a great many months the tears came into my eyes until I could not see her. During all the trouble at Jo's my concern found no relief, but her love for me made me realize how wretched I had been, and in spite of all I could do the tears came into my eyes. I tried to apologize for the weakness, but she wiped the tears away so tenderly that I thought certainly there was never such a loving touch as hers, and blessed her for the hundredth time. I led her into the adjoining room, and when we sat down by the window, and opened the shutters, I saw by the moonlight which came streaming in that she was dressed in white, and that she so much resembled a pretty bride that I could not help holding her off from me, and admiring her.

"You remember I used to tell you," Agnes said, "that some day my ship would come in after a stormy voyage, and bring me many rich gifts. I think you always thought I referred to my father."

I acknowledged that I did.

"But really I referred to your coming to me, and telling me (as I believed you would) that you loved me. I never had a hope that my father was alive, and as I told you about my ship sailing toward me when you were but a boy — I was but a girl when I first came to Fairview — I must have referred to you, as I certainly did."

She was sitting near an open piano, and lightly touching the keys, I recognized the air of an old love song she had taught me the first year of our acquaintance, "In flattering dreams I dreamed thee mine."

"We were both so wretched during the first years of our acquaintance," Agnes said, "that I sometimes feared we must always remain apart, but I never for a moment thought you did not love me. I always knew it, and was constantly trying to deserve it. If I heard of you in a creditable connection, I was pleased, and strived harder than ever, and there never was a doubt but that you would come to me — sometime; I did not know when — and tell me what you have told me to-night. I have nothing to wish for now except that I may be long spared to show you how much I love you for it."

We must have been very happy during the hour or more we sat by the window, for during that time I did not once think of Jo, nor should I have thought of him for a much longer time had not Barker's step on the walk aroused me.

We both went out to meet him — he had finished his work, and was coming to the house for the night — and, frightened at my neglect, I hurriedly ran over what I came to say. He looked at me in grave surprise, and, leading me back to the room, asked me to repeat what I had said.

I then told them both substantially what Jo had said to me on my leaving, and that I had come for him to go back with me, for I was sure that in this important emergency his cool judgment would be valuable. Agnes was very much pleased, but Barker was as grave as usual, and only said that he would return with me at once if I thought it necessary.

It was agreed that before we started we should refresh ourselves with food, and while Agnes was preparing it (how gay she was; I think even her father must have noticed it) he again inquired very particularly as to what Jo had said, and when I had finished, he went out and sat on the porch alone until Agnes called him. I believed he was thinking that, no matter what the plan was, he would not falter in his part in it, and I was so much encouraged that I went out to tell Agnes that within a week our dear friend Jo would be free.

During the drive back to town Barker was very grave, saying but little, and in consequence I drove rapidly. As we passed the jail I saw that all the lights were out, and supposing that Jo was asleep, we went on to the house to spend the night, and in a very little while I was fast asleep.

327

XXXIV

THE GRAVE BY THE PATH

I HAVE heard that dreams go by contraries; whether they do or not Jo was in my mind a great deal that night, and he was once more free to go where he pleased, without the restraint of cruel stone walls and iron doors. I thought of him as I had seen him during the first year of his apprenticeship at Damon Barker's, when he was full of hope for the future, and tender as a child because of his love for Mateel, and we were happy together again, without knowledge of the unhappiness in both our lives.

I slept until rather a late hour, and was awakened by the sheriff from the jail, who came up to my bed in great excitement, holding a letter in his hand. I did not know how he got into the room, but supposed Barker was up before me, and had admitted him.

The letter was addressed to me, and, hurriedly opening it while yet in bed, I read: —

My Dear Old Friend, — When this shall fall into your hands, the plan I spoke to you about will have been carried into effect, and I shall be dead.

After several months of careful consideration — for I thought about it long before Bragg was killed — I determined to do myself a kindness by taking my own life, and I write this an hour before I carry that resolution into effect.

To a friend who has been as true as you have been, it is only necessary for me to say that I have fully justified myself in this course. Next to the horror I have of escaping from this jail, I have a horror of a public execution, which would certainly befall me, for I am guilty, and take so much pleasure in my guilt that I cannot deny it.

Since the first thought of taking my own life came into my mind, it has never been a horrible one, and when I first knew that Bragg was to marry Mateel, I resolved to kill him, and then myself. The first part of the resolve I carried out as I intended; the second will have been accomplished when this falls into your hands.

As I wrote just now I laid down my pen to consider whether I had any regrets in leaving the world. I found there was one; your sorrow when you read this, but beyond that, nothing. There is no reason why I should care to live, and there are a great many why I wish to die, the principal one being oblivion of my disgrace and crime. Whether the religion we were taught is true or not, I shall probably peacefully sleep a long time before I am judged, and I am almost willing to submit to a future of torture for a period of forgetfulness, for my trouble comes to me in my sleep of late, and I have no rest. My head is such a trouble to me now that I have feared that it will not die with my body, but that after I am buried it will still ache and toss about.

If I have a hope of the future at all — I don't know that I have — it is that when the Creator is collecting the dead for the judgment, He will shed a tear on my grave, and, knowing my unhappy life, permit me to sleep on. If this cannot be, my fate cannot be much worse elsewhere than it is here, and for the chance of oblivion I am willing to take the risk. In any event, my judge will be a just one, and I am willing to appear before Him.

I once told you that I hoped none of my friends would be permitted to look upon my dead face, therefore I request that you do not look at me when you visit the jail to arrange for my burial. I prefer that you remember my face as you saw it last night, when you went away, for you said it looked natural again. I am sure that when last you looked into my face I was smiling, and I want your recollection to be that of me. If you should see me dead, the horror would so fasten on your mind that you would always think of my eyes as set and staring, and of my face as pale and ghastly. Therefore I ask that you do not look at me, or permit anyone else who has ever been my friend to do so.

You will find me ready for burial, as I shall dress for that purpose before taking the draught which will end my life. When I feel death approaching, I intend to fix in a position I have seen dead bodies lie in, so that I shall have to be disturbed as little as possible. It may please you to know that I died without pain; that I went to sleep, and never wakened. Among the books I had access to at Barker's was one on chemistry, and on pretence of illness I procured a drug which first put me into a pleasant sleep, and then killed me.

I want you to bury me in Fairview churchyard, near the path that leads toward our old home. Theodore Meek has three children buried near it, and there was so much sorrow when they died, and there was always so much love and kindness in that family, that I should like to be in their company. You and I always chose that path on our way to and from the church, and I shall think of two pairs of little feet forever travelling up and down it, spirits of the past, keeping vigil over my grave.

I am sure that you and Agnes will frequently visit it, and talk tenderly of me, and I hope that grim and honest Damon Barker will stop there when he passes the church, and go away in deep reflection. I have never imagined that Mateel will visit it, but if she should — if it should ever appear that I was in any way mistaken in this unhappy business — I hope you will come upon her while she is there, and say that Jo Erring loved her so much that he laid down his life for her sake.

Only say to the people with reference to me that I took life in a wicked moment, and gave my own to avenge it, and that I died in the full possession of all my faculties. They may be unable to understand why my life has been such a tragedy, but they can understand that I have made all the reparation possible for a crime which I could not help committing.

I have only to say now that if you could realize how unhappy I am, you would freely forgive my action, and feel that it was for the best, as I made you say before you went away. For your numberless acts of kindness to me I can only thank you, which is a small return, but I have nothing else.

It is now eleven o'clock; in half an hour I shall be dead, and I find that I am stronger in my purpose than ever before. There is but one sad duty yet before me; that is to write good-bye.

JO ERRING.

Barker and the sheriff were sitting beside me when I had finished reading the letter aloud, and while I was hurriedly dressing, I heard the sheriff say to Barker that after I left the jail the evening before, Jo fell in a heap on the floor, where he remained a long while, but at length recovered his composure, and stood looking out of the window in the direction I had taken until long after the night had come on. Later in the evening he pitied his lonely condition so much that he went in to sit awhile with him, but he had little to say, and showed a disposition to retire early. In the morning he remembered his strange agitation of the night before, and, opening the cell door soon after, he saw him lying on his bed, covered with a white sheet. Going in he found him dead, and dressed for burial, lying on his back, with his hands, in which was clutched the letter addressed to me, folded across his breast. He had not even told his wife of the discovery, so that in the minds of the people Jo Erring was still alive.

We went to the jail together, and, admitting ourselves to the room where [1] the body lay, decided what to do. It was agreed that a coroner's jury should be summoned from among Jo's friends, who would hold an inquest immediately, after which we would take the body to Fairview for burial. Fortunately we found a number of his friends in town, among them Theodore Meek and Lytle Biggs, and, summoning them to the jail, they first heard of the death there. After we were all inside, I read the letter to them, and as none of them wished to look at the face after listening to what Jo had written, it was agreed that the coroner, who was a physician, should examine the body alone, and that the verdict should be in accordance with his discoveries. The verdict was death from poison, administered by his own hands, and we all signed it.

By the middle of the afternoon the sheriff and his assistant had the body arranged in a neat burial case which Barker and I had procured, and, a messenger having been sent ahead to dig the grave and notify Agnes, at three o'clock the little procession left the jail yard for Fairview. Barker and I led the way with a light wagon, in which was the coffin, and a half dozen other vehicles followed, carrying a few people from town, and those of the Fairview men who had been on the jury. There was a great crowd present when we drove away, and as we passed down the street, a great many women and children came out of the different doors with offerings of flowers, which they either tossed to me or laid on the casket.

Owing to the slow pace at which we travelled, we did not come in sight of Fairview church until near dark, and just as the steeple appeared, there was a single stroke of the great bell. This continued at intervals until twenty-six strokes had been tolled, when it ceased entirely, which was quite right, as the deceased would not have been twenty-seven years old for several months.

We had halted in front of the gate by this time, and I saw

[1] to the room where: 1883 to where

331

that a great many people were present; that some of them carried lanterns, and that they respectfully uncovered their heads as they gathered about the wagon in which the coffin lay. Six stout young men appearing, they carried the casket to the grave by the path, where all the people followed, and it was put down on two sticks laid across it. If ever I felt an unfriendliness for the people there, it vanished as I stood sobbing by the grave of my only relative and best friend. Many of the women were softly crying, as I remembered them when they told of their heavy crosses and burdens at the experience meetings, and when some one of the number began singing a hymn full of hope and forgiveness, I thought I never could thank them enough for the kindness. I had expected that only a few idlers would attend; but all the neighborhood was there, and they showed that they loved Jo, and respected him, in spite of his crime. I had not shed a tear until I saw the open grave — my grief was so great that I could not find even that poor relief — but I could not control myself then, and wept as I never had before. I shuddered when I remembered that I had often sung in mockery the hymn the people were singing — how I hoped Jo had not! — but I am sure it was not intended for mockery, and that we did not think what we were doing.

There was a slight pause just before the straps were put under the coffin to lower it into the grave, and greatly to the surprise of everyone, Rev. Goode Shepherd came pushing his way through the crowd. I saw in one glance that he was poorly dressed, and pale, and distressed, and, taking a place at the head of the grave, he delivered an address which I have never heard surpassed in tenderness, and paid a tribute to the dead which started the tears of the tired, sorrowing women afresh. When he had finished he raised his trembling hands to heaven, and prayed fervently for the peace and rest of all weary men beyond the grave. He then stepped aside to make room for the young men who were to lower the coffin, and though we looked for him afterward, he could not be found.

When the grave was filled up, I remember sitting down upon the mound, and sobbing afresh, and that the women who had known my mother — some of them had heard my first cry when I came into the world — put their hands tenderly on my head, and tried to comfort me. I could not thank them, or speak, and one by one they went away, until I was alone with my dead. But there was a figure which came to me then whose touch I could not mistake; oh, Agnes, how welcome to-night.

XXXV

THE HISTORY OF A MISTAKE

WHETHER Jo left a message with me for Mateel I do not now remember, it seems so long ago, but it must have been an unimportant one if he did, for, from the time of their separation to his death, he talked of her only as one who had deliberately meditated and agreed to his disgrace. Although he always loved her, he believed that his memory must have passed entirely out of her mind during the time they lived apart, and was ashamed to confess it, even to me, in the face of her contemplated marriage to Clinton Bragg, which she must have known was the greatest humiliation to which she could subject him, and if he left any word at all, it was only a regret that their lives had been mutually so unhappy. I had not seen her, or talked with anyone who had, since the dreadful night when I carried her moaning into her father's house, and I knew nothing of her except occasional rumors which came to me from people who passed that way that she was very ill, and that but few went to the Shepherds', and that none of those who did ever saw Mateel.

But the appearance of her father at Jo's grave, and his tender tribute to the memory of my dead friend, affected me so much that I felt it my duty to call at their house before I slept. I cannot explain this determination further than that I was anxious to appear among them; it may have been that I wanted to tell them how good and brave Jo had always been, and how much he loved his wife to the last, or it might have been that I was convinced there was some terrible mistake on our part, for the appearance of Mr. Shepherd as we stood around the grave implied that he had one friend among them, although we had always imagined that they were all against him. However it was, I could not resist the impulse to call at their house that night, and when

334

we arrived at the mill after the burial, I informed Barker and Agnes of my determination. They offered no objection, if they said anything at all, and I still remember that both bade me good-night tenderly when I drove away into the darkness, leaving them standing at their door.

There was a road from Barker's to the home of the Shepherds which followed the river a distance, and then led up on to the divide where their house was built, and I was very familiar with it, having travelled it many times. It was the road which Jo had used on his visits to Mateel when he was an apprentice at Bar-ker's, and part of it the road which Clinton Bragg had travelled on his fatal journey the night he was married to Mateel, and if I saw one spectre in the darkness around me, I saw a thousand. The story I have written was produced in white lines etched on the darkness of the night — Jo returning from the minister's house, young and hopeful; Jo going to his own home, with Mateel by his side, a little older, and looking careworn, but still hopeful; Jo coming toward Barker's after the separation from Mateel, with a frown upon his face so fierce and distressed that I could not tell whether his enemy should pity or fear him; Jo skulking behind the trees, and watching up the road; Jo carrying Mateel in his arms, and clambering up the hill which led from the mill to his house; Jo in jail, with the white shroud about him, under which none of us was to look, and wherever I turned my eyes, upward or downward, to the right or to the left, ahead or behind, was his grave, which I had just left at Fairview. Clinton Bragg was lying under every tree, first as I had seen him dead in the woods, and then as he lay surrounded by the crowd in the town, and walking wearily in front of me was my father, bending low under a heavy burden which he carried. If I whipped up the horses, and hurried on, the spectre disappeared for a moment, but after I had slowed up again, and had almost forgotten it in feeling my way through the trees, it appeared ahead of me as before, only that the load he carried was heavier, and that he pursued his journey with more difficulty. This fancy took such hold upon my im-agination that I thought of the distant light which finally ap-peared as the lamp which always burned in my mother's room, toward which the bending figure was always travelling, and when it turned out to be a light in Mr. Shepherd's window, I looked about for the man with the load on his back, but he had disappeared, with Jo, and Bragg, and the rest of them.

My timid knock at the door was answered by Mr. Shepherd himself, who carried a light in his hand, as he did on the night when I had seen him last, and he seemed as much surprised as when I had stood on the same steps a few months before, bearing his moaning child in my arms, for he started back, and, throwing his unoccupied hand to his head, looked first at me and then around the room, as though he ought to recollect, but somehow could not. When he recovered himself, which he did apparently on discovering that I carried no insensible form in my arms, he set down the light he carried to the door, and asked me to be seated, which I did, feeling uncertain whether, after all, I had not better have remained away, not knowing what to say my errand was should he ask the question.

He put his hand to his head again, as if he always felt a pain there now, and could only forget it in moments of excitement, and then, resting his arm on the table at which he had seated himself, looked at the floor in the piteous, helpless way which was common to him. I thought if he had spoken it would have been that he was very sorry, but really he could not help it. He brushed the tears out of his eyes with his sleeve, as my father did when I had seen him last, and as though he had been warned not to cry, and for the first time in my life I thought the two were much alike; perhaps all men are alike when they are old, and poor, and broken. I knew now for the first time that he was distressed as much on Jo's account as on Mateel's; that there was equal pity in his heart for them both, for his manner indicated it as much as if he had made the declaration.

"My poor children," he said, as if they both stood before him, "how you both have suffered! And neither to blame. Both of them were always doing what they thought to be for the best, but always wrong. My poor children!"

I had never thought of this before; neither to blame, and always wrong, but I felt now that it was true. In my own mind I had accused Mateel, but her good old father called them both his unhappy children, and said neither was to blame, and in my heart I could not think less.

"When Mateel came home after the unfortunate separation," Mr. Shepherd continued, timidly looking about the room, as if to assure himself that no ghosts were present to accuse him, "although I thought it was but a temporary affair, I regretted it no more on account of the one than the other, and through it all — during the long months which have brought nothing to this house but bruised and broken hearts — I have had this sentiment, and no one has spoken ill of him here any more than they have spoken ill of Mateel. This is as true as that I have spoken it, for with the graves filling up around me so rapidly, I could not give reason for a wrong inference, even if I were anxious to excuse a mistaken action. Jo has always had justice done him here the same as Mateel."

I was surprised to hear this, for I had felt that Mrs. Shepherd and Bragg had upbraided Jo to Mateel, to induce her to take the step she did, and that her father held his peace, if he did not approve of it. We never talked about it, but this was the understanding Jo and I had, and I think we accepted it so thoroughly that we blamed Mateel that she permitted it. We thought she had little regard for her husband that she allowed her mother and Clinton Bragg to counsel her against him, and I began to realize that in this we had been cruel and unjust.

"I allowed them to do what they pleased," he went on again slowly and painfully, "hoping and praying it would all turn out for the best, but I always thought of Jo as one of my children, and have been tempted to call on him in his lonely home and tell him how sorry I was it had happened. I knew how unhappy a man of his fine ability must have been under such unfortunate circumstances, but my pride kept me from it. I see now that there has been too much pride all around in this affair; I have known it all the time, but —" I knew what he was going to say — "but I could not help it; really, I could not; I have done the best I could, but it has gone wrong in spite of me."

He was always saying that; everything went wrong in spite of him, which has been the experience of so many thousands before him, but I felt with a keen pang of conscience that he had done more than I, for while I was secretly blaming Mateel, he did not blame Jo; that while I had never thought of aiding a reconciliation, unless Mateel should ask it, that had been his one prayer and hope.

"I see now, after it is too late — somehow I never see anything in time to be of use to others or to myself — that this is all a dreadful mistake. You have not said it, but your coming here tells me that what I think is true; that he was always waiting for Mateel to come to him, and I know so well that she was always praying that he would come to her; not to ask forgiveness, but to say he missed her, and loved her, and that his home and heart were lonely. She was waiting for him to write her just a line — what a little thing to have prevented all this — that she must see him or die, as she will die now without it. He was expecting a simple request from his wife to come to her, and had it been sent, my brave Jo would have come though a thousand Braggs blocked the way."

He got up from his chair, and walked up and down the room, wringing his hands helplessly, and repeating: "My poor children; my poor children! How they have suffered!

"We thought in our pride — how unjust it was I now see, though you have not said a word — that he was determined to live without her, and that he had steeled his heart against a reconciliation, and you believed that we were determined she should not go back to him except upon promises and conditions, but I swear to you my belief that she would have crawled on her knees to her old home had she believed he would have admitted her. From what has happened since, I know he loved her all the time, and that he was expecting a summons to come to her every moment of the day and night. What a little thing would have prevented all this; a word from you or me and it would have been done, but we have kept apart from the beginning until the end. We shall have to answer for it, I fear, and I shall not know what to say at the judgment."

I thought I knew what he would say: "I could not help it," but

338

what would my own answer be? Perhaps only what millions of other trembling men will say: "I did the best I could; I did not think."

In looking toward him to make reply, and assure him that he was right in his generous surmise, I became aware that some-one was standing just inside the door which led into the other room, and taking a quick glance I saw it was Mateel, dressed in a long white night-robe; that she waited rather than listened, and that she was much agitated. From the half-open door came the odor of a sick room, and in that one glance I saw that she was very pale, and very weak, and very ill.

Instinctively I moved in my chair, to get my face away from the door, instead of turning it, and betraying that I had seen her, and as I did this I heard her light step enter the room. I saw her father look up in wonder, and knew that her mother followed in a frightened way, and gently laid hands on her, entreating her to return, but she put them off, and came on toward me. I had only a side glance, but I could see that her eyes were riveted on me, and that she leaned forward in a supplicating way.

"Jo, my husband," she said timidly, and pausing to put her hands to her head, as her father had done, "why have you delayed coming so long?"

She fell on her knees when I did not reply, and looked at me with a pitiful face indicating that she would shortly burst out crying. I turned in my chair that she might see that I was not her husband, but her mind was troubled, and she did not realize it. Indeed, when I looked steadily into her eyes, she seemed to take it as an accusation from Jo of neglect and dishonor, and she staggered to her feet again, as if determined to tell her story. There was a look of mingled timidity, sorrow, and sickness in her face which comes to me yet when I am alone, and which I can never forget.

"I was afraid you might not understand that I always wanted you to come," she said, coming near to me, and gently stroking my hand, as if hoping to thus induce a fierce man to listen until she had concluded, "but I thought you would, and night and day since I have been away from home — such a long time it has been; oh, such a very long time — I have expected you every moment. Every noise I have thought your step, and when I found it was not, I listened and hoped again. You have never been out of my thoughts for a moment, but my prayers have been answered, for I was always praying for you to come. I wanted to tell you how truly I have always loved you, and how unhappy and ill I have been without you."

It was turning out as I had expected after the appearance of Mr. Shepherd at the grave, but how distressed I was to realize that the explanation came after Jo was dead, and Mateel hopelessly ill, I am not competent to write; I could say nothing then, as I can write nothing now, of the horror I felt when I knew that all this misery had been unnecessary. As Mateel stood before me she staggered in her weakness, and her mother hurried to her side, but again she put her off, and stood erect with an effort.

"I must tell you, to relieve my own mind, if for nothing else, that I have always been true to you, and that I only consented to receive Clinton Bragg in this house in the hope that you would rescue me. I was afraid it might be wrong, but I did not know what else to do. I hoped that when you heard that he was coming here, you would walk in like the brave man that you are, and demand to know what it meant; then you would give me opportunity to explain, and I hoped you would praise me for making us happy again."

I thought that her father and mother were surprised at this, for they looked curiously at each other, and Mr. Shepherd's hand went to his head again — I thought to upbraid it for not discovering the secret sooner.

"I am sorry it has offended you, Jo, but I could think of nothing else, and I desired to see you so much. I was always weak and helpless, and perhaps I did wrong, but I felt that I must do something. When still you did not come, I let it be said that I intended to marry him, but it was all for love of my husband; God is my witness and I appeal to Him! I had no more thought of marrying him than I had of forgetting you, but because you still delayed, I let the time be set, believing that you would not allow it to go on, and give me opportunity to explain. When the day arrived, I determined to let it go on, and if you did not rescue me from him before I passed our home on the way to town, I would take one fond look at the place where I was once so happy, and kill myself, so that I might be carried dead where I was refused admission alive. I was very firm in this purpose, and would have carried it out. See, I have the knife yet."

She took from her bosom a dirk knife of peculiar pattern, which Barker had given Jo and me when we were boys, and we had sharpened it so often that the blade was very thin and delicate. She tested its sharpness by passing her finger across its edge, and, holding it toward me, asked me to see how keen it was.

"When you sprang out from among the trees on that dreadful night (I had been expecting you to spring out just as you did every moment during the ride), my joy was so great that I fainted, and when I awoke it was with such a strange feeling in my head; but I will recover soon, and then we shall be happy once more. I can't remember when it happened; yesterday, maybe, but not long ago, and when I asked for you, mother said you had gone out, but would return presently if I waited patiently. After I had waited a long while I wanted to go to you, for I knew you loved me, and wanted me to come, but they said I must wait. I did whatever they told me, for they said I must or you would not come at all. But won't you speak to me now, since I have explained it all?"

She was again on her knees before me, and looking earnestly into my face; at first entreatingly, but suddenly I saw a change, and there was alarm in her pale face. She recognized me, I thought, and I steadily looked at her that she might realize her mistake.

Hurriedly rising to her feet, she walked to the other side of the room, and stood beside her mother, with an arm on her shoulder, still looking at me in alarm and fright.

"Oh, mother," she said hesitatingly, "maybe it is not Jo. What if he should be dead and never know! Wouldn't [1] that be terrible!"

She was so much exhausted now that she started wearily to

[1] Wouldn't: 1883 Oh, wouldn't

return to her bed, still looking at me as she went, apparently
better convinced than ever that I was not Jo, and her father and
mother tenderly supported her as she walked. They slowly passed
through the door and into her room, and I saw them gently lay
her down, where she asked again in a weak but excited voice if
it wouldn't be terrible if Jo were dead and would never know. I
looked again, and saw Mr. Shepherd and his wife kneeling at
the foot of the bed, convulsively sobbing, each one trying to comfort the other, and both of them trying to comfort Mateel. I noticed then that the minister and his wife were poorly dressed;
that the furniture of the rooms was threadbare and old, and it
came to my mind that they were very poor, and had been cruelly
neglected by those around them. All these circumstances affected
me so much that I stepped out at the front door to recover myself, and was surprised to find Agnes and Barker at the gate.

They explained that they had been oppressed with the same
fear that oppressed me, and could not resist the temptation to
drive over. I hurriedly told them that it was as I feared, and
gave them as many particulars as I could before we went into
the house. They were visibly affected, and as I pointed around
at the general evidences of decay, in whispering the fear that
during Mateel's illness, and while both were busy in caring for
her, they had suffered from poverty, I became aware that Barker
had been a friend to them during the time, sending them money
and such comforts as the country afforded, although they never
knew who befriended them. I cannot remember what it was he
did to convince me of this, but I was certain of it, and the opinion
was afterwards confirmed, for Agnes knew of it and told me.

It must have been an hour after midnight when we went into
the house, and though the minister and his wife were surprised to
see Barker and Agnes, they were pleased as well, and somehow
seemed to think that matters would get on better now, for they
were more cheerful than before, as though the neglect of their
friends had been very humiliating.

Mateel had fallen into a light sleep soon after lying down, but
she wakened in the course of an hour, and still talked of how
long, how patiently, she had waited for Jo, and how terrible it

would be if he were dead and could never know. At times she seemed to realize that he would never come, when she remained silent a long while, as if to think it all over, but she would soon forget this, and say that while she was patient, and would wait as long as she could, she hoped he would hurry, as she was growing weak so fast, and was so anxious to see him and explain it all.

We were all very quiet, occasionally walking carefully from one room to another as a relief after sitting a long time in one position, and it so happened that we were all standing around Mateel's bed when she asked: —

"Father, do you believe Jo is in heaven?"

The good man was startled by the question, not knowing how to reply, but, after thinking a moment, he answered, speaking with an effort: —

"It is my hope of the future that when I enter the beautiful gates I shall find Jo Erring waiting for me, where I can explain away all that has seemed mysterious here. As I believe in the mercy of God, I expect to meet him and enjoy his intelligence and friendship, both of which I have always esteemed. As I believe in my wife and child, as I believe in my religion, I believe in Jo Erring."

The invalid seemed much pleased with this assurance, and simply said: —

"I am glad he will know that I was not fickle or false; for I will explain it to him."

She closed her eyes then, and we all stepped softly out of the room to allow her to sleep, but when her mother went back a few moments later she found that the unhappy woman was dead.

XXXVI

CONCLUSION

IT has been ten years since we buried Mateel beside her husband in Fairview churchyard, and built monuments over their graves. I have been rid of my tiresome business so many years that I seem never to have been in it at all, and I can scarcely remember the time when Agnes was not my wife. Damon Barker lives with us in the stone house in Twin Mounds, which has been rebuilt and remodelled so often that it, too, enjoys a new condition, and I sometimes fear we do not think so much of Jo and Mateel as we ought, or of the Rev. John Westlock and the poor woman who died of a broken heart; for somehow we cannot help thinking of them all as having lived a long while ago, so many changes have taken place since they were among us. Many of the people who lived in Fairview and Twin Mounds when they did are dead; others have moved away, and so many strangers have arrived that it seems like a new country, and one in which those who occupy our graves never lived.

In looking through Jo Erring's room at the jail after his death, we found a will bequeathing his property to me, a certain amount to be paid yearly to Mateel, and the mill I have since leased to such advantage that it has been the source of a great deal of profit. If I have not mentioned it before, it may be interesting to know that my father's wild land, of which he owned a large quantity, has greatly increased in value, and I was thinking only a few days ago that I was worth considerable money, and that my income was ample to support me without work of any kind. In addition, Mrs. Deming died possessed of some property, which came into the possession of Agnes, and with Barker's money we are quite an aristocratic family.

Big Adam operates the mill on Bull River, under lease, and

I have understood that in a few years he will be in condition to buy it outright. I am sincerely glad of this, for he is a very worthy man, and has had a wife and children of his own these five or six years. It is said of Big Adam and his wife that they are the happiest couple in all that country, and I often go there to witness how contented and fortunate the good fellow is after his hard life. Not long ago I was sitting with him in the mill after dark, and when I told him how much satisfaction his happiness afforded me, he made the old reply of pulling an imaginary cork, and pouring out liquor in distinct gurgles. His bandit father was killed a few years ago in attempting to rob a railroad train, but Big Adam still occasionally tells that his father gave up his life in the early settlement of the West; in short, that he was killed by the Indians.

There has been little change in Mr. Biggs, or Smoky Hill, except that both have grown older, and improved a little. I drove over to that country not long ago in quest of a servant girl, remembering that Mr. Biggs had said that it produced good ones, and learned that two or three of his sons were very idle and bad, and made their mother and their neighbors a great deal of trouble. Mr. Biggs himself is a great deal in town, as he has opened a kind of office there for the sale of land, although I suspect that it is no more than an excuse to keep away from home. I hear from him frequently with reference to the management of children, for there have been several occasions to mention the subject; but for all that it is notorious that he has not the slightest control of his own. I have heard that his oldest son beat him on one of his visits to the farm, for he is much larger than his father, and of a very ugly disposition, in spite of the circumstance that he wore braid on his clothes until he was seven or eight years old.

I have never yet seen Mrs. Biggs, for her husband appealed to me a good many years ago never to visit his house if I respected him, as it did not correctly represent him. Agnes goes out occasionally to quell an insurrection among the children, who have the greatest respect for her, and she tells me that I may hope to see Mrs. Biggs soon, as she cannot possibly live much longer, and that we shall be expected to attend the funeral.

I think at least a half dozen of Theodore Meek's boys have married, and settled around him on the Fairview prairie, and their children are as much at home in the old house as in the new ones. When I was last there I could scarcely get into the house for them, and my impression was that the boys had married well, for they were all very prosperous and very contented. Their nearest neighbors were the Winter boys, who have developed into honorable and worthy citizens. Their father has been in heaven some years, and they seem to be very proud of the reputation he left in Fairview, and take good care of their mother, who manages their house, as they have never married.

The Rev. John Westlock has never been heard of since the stormy night when I saw him turn a corner in a Twin Mounds street and disappear; and if he is alive this night I do not know it, no more than I know he is dead. I have published advertisements in a great many widely circulated newspapers, asking him to let me know of his whereabouts, and soliciting information of an old and broken man of his description; I have made several journeys in answer to these advertisements, but the men I found were not at all like him, and I have come to believe that he is dead; but if he is not, and this should meet his eye, I trust that his stubborn heart will relent, and that he will consent to finish his days in peace under my roof.

Rev. Goode Shepherd and his wife returned to their old home in the East a few months after the death of their child, and twice since they have journeyed to Fairview to visit her grave. Their devotion to her memory is very touching, and it has always been a comfort to me to know that the minister still believes that Jo has been forgiven, and that the blessed Saviour blotted out with a tear the record of his desperate crime at the ford.

I hope the place where Jo and Mateel are buried is very pretty, for I have spent a great deal of time in attempts to make it quietly attractive, and my heart has always been in the work. While everything else has changed, Fairview church is just the same, and every night when the wind blows furiously, I imagine that the great bell is tolling a muffled requiem for their unfortunate history from the rickety tower; every bright day I think that the

346

birds are singing softly over their graves, and in their quiet corner of the yard, close by the path leading toward the old house where they first met, there is a willow that weeps for them in summer, and tenderly covers their graves with its leaves in winter. I think it was planted by Theodore Meek, in whose family there was always so much love and content; and I am sure that whenever the good man visits his own dead, he sends a message upward for Jo Erring and Mateel.

THE END

THE JOHN HARVARD LIBRARY

The intent of
Waldron Phoenix Belknap, Jr.,
as expressed in an early will, was for
Harvard College to use the income from a
permanent trust fund he set up, for "editing and
publishing rare, inaccessible, or hitherto unpublished
source material of interest in connection with the
history, literature, art (including minor and useful
art), commerce, customs, and manners or way of
life of the Colonial and Federal Periods of the United
States . . . In all cases the emphasis shall be on the
presentation of the basic material." A later testament
broadened this statement, but Mr. Belknap's inter-
ests remained constant until his death.

In linking the name of the first benefactor of
Harvard College with the purpose of this later,
generous-minded believer in American culture the
John Harvard Library seeks to emphasize the impor-
tance of Mr. Belknap's purpose. The John Harvard
Library of the Belknap Press of Harvard University
Press exists to make books and documents
about the American past more readily
available to scholars and the
general reader.